ECHO: THE INFINITE CYCLE

Echo: The Infinite Cycle

Copyright Page

Echo: The Infinite Cycle

© 2025 D. Gohil

All rights reserved. No part of this publication may be reproduced, stored in a retrieval system, or transmitted in any form or by any means, electronic, mechanical, photocopying, recording, or otherwise, without the prior written permission of the copyright holder, except in the case of brief quotations embodied in critical articles or reviews.

This is a work of fiction. Names, characters, places, events, and incidents may either be the product of the author's imagination or used fictitiously. Any resemblance to actual persons, living or dead, events, or locales is entirely coincidental.

British Library Cataloguing-in-Publication Data.
A catalogue record for this book is available from the British Library.

First edition 2025

ISBN: 978-1-9193336-0-1

Cover design by: The Author, using Canva

Typeset by: The Author

Printed and bound in the United Kingdom by Echo Press

For permissions or enquiries, please contact:

www.echobookseries.com

D. Gohil

Echo: The Infinite Cycle

Dedication

To my sons, **Dillon** and **Nash** — my most fantastic adventures will always be the ones I share with you. Your curiosity, your laughter, and the way you see wonder in even the smallest things have reminded me, every day, why stories matter!
May this one travel with you through every season of life,
Whispering courage when the world feels too big,
And hope when the path seems unclear.

To my brother **Jitendra** — thank you for walking beside me on this journey.
For your honest words, patient guidance, and sharp eyes, that helped shape this book into something more substantial. Your support has been more than practical; it has been a reminder that the best stories are never written alone.

For the three of you — Dillon, Nash, and Jitendra
This book is not just mine.
Every chapter carries a part of you within it.
You are the echoes behind every word.

To **Dr Emad AlJaaly**, whose surgical skills and dedication to save lives gave me a second chance, with mine. To his magnificent team of surgeons, and to all the extraordinary staff at Hammersmith Hospital who cared for me with compassion and expertise during my month there. This story exists because of your caring hearts. Thank you from the deepest part of my new beating heart for saving me.

And for every reader who turns these pages, thank you for joining us. Stories live only when they are shared. This one belongs to you now.

D. Gohil

Echo: The Infinite Cycle

Foreword

9 days. 216 hours. Or so.

    This is the age difference between the author of this book and me. We grew up together in Leicester, almost like twins. We are cousins, but he grew closer than my own brother. We made kites out of newspaper and twigs broken from a neighbour's tree, crudely taped together, but working flawlessly... well as flawlessly as you can expect from the rags of the day. We pushed each other around on his favourite yellow toy truck, ate chocolate from a vending machine on the corner of the street, and played until the sun went down. We would then watch all the Sci-fi shows on TV. Re-enacting scenes with our brothers, each taking on the persona of one of the show's characters. Wonderful times.

    Then we grew up. We grew up and gradually diverged. I ran the prescribed path of Asian kids back in the day, with education taking centre stage. But he went on to be an adventurer. College was never going to teach him what he needed to know. He relocated to London, where he was blessed with a lovely wife and two wonderful sons. He worked various banking jobs until 1996, when he finally got the opportunity that he needed. This was the leap of faith he had to take. The 'millennium bug,' along with the opportunity to work for a banking software business implementing banking systems, provided him with the significant leap he needed to advance.

    It was his chance to develop himself within a growing company. He worked diligently, rising through the ranks step by step until he was managing an operation out of Dubai, the current land of opportunity. As they say, the world was his Oyster. He had many adventures ahead, places to visit, experiences to gather, friends in high places, the mansion, the car, the dream, really. Sadly, things did not stay this way. A divorce. A younger replacement at work. Even a failed business. Now back in the UK, he enjoyed playing golf with old friends, eating, drinking, and living life to the fullest. Then a wake-up call, a pain in his heart, a hospital stay, a heart bypass operation for the biggest heart I know. That was far too close – a reminder of how fragile everything truly is.

D. Gohil

This was a reawakening, this was a reason to focus, and an inspiration for him to write this book. He has drawn on his childhood experiences and life's highs and lows to craft a story that will have you smiling, intrigued, scratching your head, and marvelling at the spectacle on the pages. It is a journey that takes shape according to your experience of it. Be brave, be expectant, be adventurous, be entertained. You will turn the page, then another, and who knows, you might find yourself reading it all in just 9 days, that's 216 hours, or so...

— Jitendra Gohil

Echo: The Infinite Cycle

Preface

"Each choice reflects through endless worlds, waiting for the moment you dare to look back." - D. Gohil.

Some books have always offered a sense of the otherworldly, transporting us beyond the ordinary and bending concepts of time, space, and identity. Echo: The Infinite Cycle invites you to witness a story that challenges your perception of reality. Gohil's debut novel is an ambitious science fiction thriller that features themes of time travel, alternate realities, choices and reincarnation. Yet beneath the surface, it explores the more profound questions of memory, identity, and the human desire to find our place in the universe.

Nathan Cole makes for an unlikely hero. He was the sort of man who lives by a personal code and a passion for financial technology. A man who has built a comfortable life working on digital transformation projects and corporate contracts. When his ordered world begins to crack, slowly at first, then all at once, we follow him from his Richmond Penthouse overlooking the Thames to places that should not exist. Medieval battlefields, somewhere under alien suns, ancient temples where the air tastes of incense and blood, cities where chrome and flesh merge in unsettling ways.

This is not a book for readers seeking easy answers. It is for those who have woken from dreams so vivid they questioned which world was real. Those who have experienced that strange jolt of recognition when meeting a stranger's eyes. Suppose you have found yourself lost in the puzzle-box narratives of Inception or Dark. Or moved by Interstellar movie's emotional complexity, or intrigued by Blake Crouch's reality-bending concepts. In that case, Gohil's work will feel like coming home.

One chapter will drop you into a near-future cyberpunk city, while the next might see you standing in a crusader's duel by war-torn temples. The threads are always there, and the transitions are masterfully handled. Lending the story a cinematic quality that feels as though it was designed to be experienced, not just read. There are moments in life that vanish almost as soon as they arrive, simple, forgettable things. The warmth of a coffee cup on your palm, the scrape of a train door closing behind you, the way your name sounds when spoken by a stranger.

D. Gohil

These are the soft fragments that scatter behind us, unmarked and unremarked upon. Lost to the pull of forward motion, but then there are other moments, quiet ones, unassuming, yes, but curiously heavy. You do not notice it at first, only that something lingers, something you cannot shake. Nathan Cole had no language for these kinds of moments. He lived by a different measure. He believed in profits, contracts, numbers flickering on a screen in sterile fonts. He put his faith in balance sheets, algorithms, and quarterly reviews. Scheduled flights that had hopscotched him between time zones, when jet lag had long since stopped being an issue.

He was the kind of man who had made a pact with control, and until that day, it had served him rather well, and order kept his world spinning. He was not a man given to flights of fancy. It was a world of hotel lobbies, boardrooms, and airport lounges that all blurred into one another. Designed to feel placeless, timeless, and identical. Even the most grounded lives have blind spots. Even the sharpest of minds can miss the moment when something begins to unravel.

For Nathan, the unease crept in gradually, nothing you could put your finger on, merely a persistent wrongness that would not shift. Moments of recognition that stretched beyond their natural span, unfamiliar names falling from lips that somehow knew precisely how to shape them. Fragments of sleep that left him bolt upright at three in the morning on many a night. Pulse hammering as though he had been fleeing for his life. He blamed the usual suspects: overwork, long-haul travel, the grinding pressure of another merger that had consumed six months of sixteen-hour days, perfectly reasonable explanations for a mind playing tricks on itself.

Then it happened, swift and surgical, like watching a single stitch come undone in expensive fabric. Between one heartbeat and the next, everything changed. He had been nursing a single malt, surrounded by the familiar engine hum of first-class travel. Muted conversations, the gentle clink of ice against crystal. Then. Nothing. Not the honest quiet of countryside evenings or library corners, but something else entirely. A silence that pressed against his eardrums, thick as cotton wool yet somehow empty of all substance. Reality did not tear or shatter; it simply rearranged itself.

Echo: The Infinite Cycle

The very quality of existence shifted, as the air became something different; light bent in ways that should not be possible. Time felt as though someone had changed its fundamental settings without warning. As if it peeled away like reality had been nothing more than paper soaked in water, and behind it something else, something older. He reached for clarity. What he found were echoes of lives, and versions of himself unled, stories untold, timelines pulsing faintly in the dark, like stars behind clouds. It was like standing at the edge of a great spiral, one that curved inwards and backwards, looping through lives that were his, long since shed.

Later, he would ask himself whether that was the beginning, but deep down, he knew better; it was a return, back to that moment. The silence, the symbol, the sensation of slipping, was not the start of a journey. It was the moment he remembered he was already on one. In remembering, the world would begin to shift, with the boundaries between dimensions, dreams, and memories dissolving. Between past life, future life, and the present, between what was real and what was merely agreed upon. They would all begin to blur. What happened next made a mockery of everything sensible. It was like watching dominoes fall, except the dominoes were made of time itself, and they had been falling long before Nathan had any idea the game was even being played.

He had come to, eventually, the way you do after a proper knock to the head, all confusion and copper taste in your mouth. Only this was not concussion talking. This was something that reached right down into his bones and whispered uncomfortable truths about the way things worked. Time, it turned out, was not the tidy conveyor belt he had spent nearly forty years riding. It was messier than that, more like a pub song with too many verses. All of them were being sung at once in rooms he had never bothered to visit. Somewhere in those rooms, all the Nathan Coles he had never become were getting on with their lives. Patient as saints, waiting for him to work out that they had been there all along.

Books like this do not come along very often. They require risk and require authors willing to blend the personal with the fantastical. Gohil has made that jump, the sort that separates competent storytelling from the kind that gets under your skin and refuses to leave. For a first novel, it is remarkably assured. Please do not rush this one; just let it breathe.

D. Gohil

Whether you are the sort who tears through books in a single evening or prefers to savour them over weeks of commuter journeys, Echo will lodge itself somewhere in your head and refuse to budge. The ideas it plants will sprout at the most inconvenient moments. Three weeks later, washing up after dinner, you will find yourself wondering about parallel selves and the roads not taken. You are now standing at a doorway. Step through, and whilst everything around you may appear unchanged, you will find yourself slightly different on the other side. Go on then, turn the page, cross over, this is where it all begins...

Contents

Chapter 1 – The Ancient Sigil 1
Chapter 2 – A Weekend in Shadows 11
Chapter 3 – The Beginning Fractured 23
Chapter 4 – Peacekeeping Mission 37
Chapter 5 – The Hacker's Mirage 55
Chapter 6 – The Crusader's Dilemma 73
Chapter 7 – Project Resonance 93
Chapter 8 – The Odyssey 107
Chapter 9 – The Agents Stand 131
Chapter 10 – The Surgeon's Crossroads 147
Chapter 11 – Lost Love 159
Chapter 12 – Betrayal in Blood 169
Chapter 13 – The Enigma 179
Chapter 14 – Mage of Nashira 199
Chapter 15 – The Last Summit 235
Chapter 16 – The Architect of Infinity 249
Chapter 17 – Code of the Dead 263
Chapter 18 – The Convergence of Echoes 275
Chapter 19 – Threshold of the Sigil 289
Chapter 20 – Eternity Beyond Infinity 301
Epilogue – The Garden of Errors 317

Echo: The Infinite Cycle

Chapter 1 – The Ancient Sigil
3100 BCE → Present Day

Long before letters took shape or the first words were spoken, even before memory had form. Something had already carved its mark into the world's history. The Sigil belonged to that first scarring, neither lost nor found, simply there. Patient as a stone. Nathan Cole had no time for mystical nonsense. His world was built on finance, financial technology, and measurable outcomes. He had built his life around corporate restructuring and impossible deadlines, clean, rational work that paid well and made sense to him. So, when he caught sight of something flickering just beyond the glass of his Richmond penthouse, that should not have been there at all. His careful world tilted sideways. It was the sort of moment that shifts everything without warning. Like discovering the locks on your own front door have been changed while you were out. The rational part of him searched for an explanation. The symbol was already there, woven so deeply into the fabric of things that unpicking it might unravel everything else.

These markings were not mere symbols; they echoed an ancient essence, impervious to time and untouched by entropy. One of these ancient symbols is the Sigil. Present on the fringes of myths and madness, scorched into cave walls, and woven through our dreams. Myth has it that the first sentient beings left the ancient Sigil, whilst others argue that it serves as a warning of the apocalypse. There are things in this world that wait, not for discovery, but for recognition. Nathan was not one for visions or vague impressions. His world is built on certainty. Shaped by code and measured outcomes, he is a dominant voice in the financial technology (FinTech) sector, driven by results.

Nathan, present day, from the top floor of his discreetly extravagant penthouse in Richmond. Watched the city like one might analyse a data set, tracking patterns, noting anomalies, and anticipating financial pivots. The skyline was not a view; it was his visual dashboard. He was the kind of FinTech architect and expert whose name circulated in investor circles with reverence and mild envy. There were rumours of predictive algorithms, private acquisitions, near-mythic pivots in volatile markets, but Nathan never confirmed anything. Silence had always been his most valuable currency. His appearance spoke of a mind sharpened by discipline. The very rigour that had driven businesses to flourish had also shaped his own strong frame of mind. Broad-shouldered, lean, and purposeful. The kind of musculature that suggested early morning gym sessions and a diet of calculated nutritional benefits. His skin shifted subtly under different light, olive in summer, taupe under overcast skies.

At Royal Mid-Surrey Golf Club, he played some of the best golf of his life, rhythmically and without ostentation. He did not golf just for leisure; he golfed for brain and physical calibration. His eyes were clinical and clear. They did not merely observe. They scanned everything, which made his observation skills incredible. Ideal for him to read rooms during intensive meetings. Conversations with him felt like queries to an internal database. He dressed with the quiet precision of someone who might lunch with a venture capitalist. Then swiftly move on by evening into talks that unsettled entire sectors. Suits structured but silent, watches unbranded, shoes polished enough to whisper wealth without declaring it.

Echo: The Infinite Cycle

He was building something, or dismantling something, possibly both, but whatever he was doing, he never did it loudly. Nathan had been living in this Richmond home for a few years now. It was a modern, sleek penthouse, designed for efficiency and comfort, but today it felt unfamiliar, almost alien. A place that belonged to someone else. Restless energy gnawed at him, making him uncomfortable, unlike the usual stress that accompanied his fast-paced life. Nathan had founded a FinTech empire and regularly flew across continents for meetings, advising on multi-million-pound deals. No, this was deeper, more primal, a whisper flitting through the recesses of his mind, like the remnants of a dream trying to claw its way back into waking thoughts.

Nathan let out a slow breath and pressed his fingertips to his temples. He was running on fumes, stretched to the limit after a sleepless night. *What is wrong with me?* He pushed the thought aside and sipped his coffee, wincing at its bitterness. The sleepless nights had begun weeks ago. Each one left him with a more profound sense of unease. It was something intangible, like a pressure at the edges of his consciousness, as if the door had been left ajar in his mind with something lurking just beyond. Nathan's life had always revolved around control: risk, money, technology and even people. Every move was calculated, every decision was strategic. However, this creeping anxiety, inexplicable feeling of displacement, was out of his control, and he loathed it. He ran a hand through his hair, sighing. At 39 years 11 months, and at the pinnacle of success, he felt restless.

Nathan was born and raised in East London, where his childhood was anything but privileged. The streets on which he grew up were rough, populated by individuals battling their daily challenges against poverty, crime and a future that seemed preordained. His father worked long hours at a factory to provide for the family. His mother took on various cleaning jobs throughout the city. They did everything they could to shield him and his younger sister, Emilie, from the weight of their struggles. Nathan witnessed it all, from the desperation in his parents' eyes to the bruises from the fights he could not always avoid, and the allure of a world that sought to engulf him. He had chosen early on not to let it define him.

Through sheer determination, he clawed his way out. Earning a first-class honours degree in Business Management, Accounting and Economics, and later completing an MBA in Finance. He had earned a reputation that carried weight, that firmly established him among the industry's upper tier. Now at the helm of his own fast-rising FinTech company. He moved in top circles, which included senior executives and government advisors. He handled the intricacies of digital finance transformation with the quiet confidence and assurance of someone who had been doing it for years. Nathan's parents now live in a comfortable home far from their old neighbourhood. His sister, Emilie, was engaged to a promising young Data Scientist, and she had built a life for herself outside London. While Nathan... Nathan had everything: wealth, security and influence, but this unease would not dissipate.

He drummed his fingers against the kitchen counter, and he looked out of the window at the beautiful skyline. Nathan should be happy, surely. After all, this was his dream, and he had worked hard to achieve it since completing his education. Something was still missing, and it felt wrong, a void that success, oddly, had never truly filled. To break his trance, his phone vibrated on the countertop, interrupting the silence. A message from Silvia read. *Landed safely, missing you already. Florence is not the same without you, darling!* Nathan smiled despite himself and typed back a quick reply. *Enjoy it while you can, you know I will drag you hiking when you return, lol.* He knew she would roll her eyes at the thought. Silvia was a brilliant, sharp-witted lawyer who relished adventure almost as much as he did, but never the thought of walking up steep hills just for fun.

However, she was far more comfortable sipping wine in Florence, her home city, where she was born and raised, than she would be hiking in the high terrains with him. As he set the phone down, the unease came flooding back, swift, unwelcome, familiar. His gaze drifted to the corner of the room, where a sleek bookshelf stood like a showroom piece. It held what one might expect: high-brow finance journals, dense volumes of philosophy, and tucked in here and there, the odd science fiction novel that had survived his more serious inclinations. The only thing his mind drifted to was something much older. Like a memory buried deep in the past, when he was ten years old.

Echo: The Infinite Cycle

It resurfaced in his tiny bedroom in their old East London flat. With a notepad before him, lying on his bed, and a pencil in his hand. He struggled to answer a question that had burned in his mind for weeks. "What will I become when I grow up?" He said aloud. His tiny hands gripped the pencil tightly as he made a list: a lawyer, a doctor, a world traveller, a pilot, a businessman, and so on. Even at an early age, he was determined to escape his life in that stage of poverty and make something of himself. Now, present-day standing at the pinnacle of success, the thought unsettled him. Had he truly built this life, or had something else been pulling the strings all along? The hum of the city seemed to grow louder, filling the quiet spaces of his plush, expensive penthouse, when a sudden, sharp gust of wind rattled the windows.

The sensation of being watched slithered over him, irrational and unshakeable. Nathan shook his head and exhaled. *Let this go. You are being ridiculous for no reason,* he thought. Blaming it on the exhaustion from his recent return from North America, he pushed himself up from the barstool and walked to the window, and outside, the river glistened beneath the morning sun. People hurried to work as usual, where the street traffic ebbed and flowed like the city's lifeblood, and everything was as it should have been, yet the feeling in his chest only intensified. After a long day at the office near St. Paul's in his business tower block, Nathan stayed in his office long past the cleaner's departure. He broke out the good stuff, a bottle of Macallan whisky he kept for occasions that demanded proper ceremony. The whisky caught the light as he swirled it, amber against crystal, whilst outside his office window, London sprawled in all its stubborn glory.

This was his patch, which he had known since childhood. He understood the city's moods the way other men knew their wives. The morning rush hit like a fever; it hummed with restless energy even in the small hours. Utterly indifferent to individual ambition yet somehow feeding off it. That ruthlessness had always appealed to him. London did not coddle anyone; it did not pause for sentiment or second thoughts. The glass grew warm against his palm, not from the drink, but from the weight of what he was contemplating. Years of deals and developments stretched out below him in steel and glass. Each building site is a small victory, every restructured company a notch in his professional belt. Success, he had learned, rarely came with the satisfaction the brochures promised.

5

Somewhere beneath the pride sat a more uncomfortable question. When the ledgers were finally balanced, what would any of it mean? Not what he had built, but what he had become in the building of it all. The lines on the wall across from him glowed faintly again. Neither celebration nor warning, just presence. He did not rush it. That was not the point. Each sip was a ritual, measured, introspective, the weight of thought steeping in oak and memory. Outside, the city murmured as it always did, but Nathan's mind was elsewhere, somewhere deep in the latticework of strategy. He stared into the glass, the amber swirl catching light like an unanswered question. At first, he thought he saw a trick of the light, maybe a reflection, but as he stepped closer to the window, he realised the pattern was not on the glass.

It was a pulsating Sigil, a circular emblem beautifully intricate and ancient-looking. The lines pulsed softly and deliberately as if drawing breath, against the sprawl of glass and shadowed steel, their glow pressed outward, insistent but restrained. They were not quite solid, were not quite imagined, something caught between the two, threaded through London's fabric like ancient scars that had never quite closed. Whatever they were had no interest in being noticed, but seemed to be always watching him for some reason. Nathan's heart kicked against his ribs, and his breathing had become shallow and quick. For just a moment, something flickered at the edge of his mind, familiar, urgent, important. Then slipped away like smoke the instant he tried to grasp it. It was gone, just like that.

From the warmth of his office, he scanned the street, empty, but for a heartbeat. He thought he saw a man in the distance raise a hand in greeting. Then the space was empty again. The glass slipped from his fingers, shattering across the polished wood as whisky spread in golden rivulets. His heart hammered against his chest. *What the fuck was that?* Later that night, back at home, Nathan dreamt he was standing at the edge of a vast city that was not London. It was ancient, unfamiliar, and looming spires pierced the sky, casting long, restless shadows. Beneath his feet, the symbol carved into the stone streets pulsed faintly as if alive. Something about the way the light hit the pavement caught him. He could not place it, but it felt both familiar and wrong, all at once. Something brushed past his ear, not quite sound, more like understanding made tangible, a fork in the road perhaps, or a red flag.

Echo: The Infinite Cycle

Nathan found himself moving closer to the window, though he could not remember deciding to do so. The familiar streets below began to shift and buckle, transforming into something that belonged in a mindscape. Passages that doubled back on themselves, doorways that opened onto impossibilities. His hand moved of its own accord, fingertips finding the cold glass where that strange mark still flickered. The moment skin met surface, the world dropped away beneath him. He was falling in circles through something that was not quite darkness, not quite space, something older and stranger than either. Through it all, a voice that might have been his own, or it might have been someone else's entirely. Cutting through the chaos with two words that made no sense at all. *Not yet!* Nathan jolted awake, gasping. His sheets were clammy, and his skin tingled with something indescribably alien.

He did not understand what the symbol signified, but it had marked him, and the world would never seem the same again. The following day, he saw it again in a vision, now etched into the damp stone of a London alleyway. Half-lit by neon signage and half-devoured by time, it shimmered faintly in the rain. The porcelain of his coffee cup cracked like a gunshot, scattering arcs of caffeine across the concrete. His heart stuttered, not from the spill, but from what remained untouched. Suspended above the puddle, the symbol glowed softly, impossible and indifferent. A shape older than memory yet burning with contemporary intent.

He stared at the reflection: his face, familiar but unclaimed. Lines he did not recognise, expressions he could not name. The symbol pulsed once, and in that flicker, something inside him shifted. The world did not stop; it narrowed. The city hummed its digital rhythm. In that moment, beneath a hovering fragment of myth. He wondered if the life he had lived was merely a rehearsal for something vast and unknowable, something that had just begun watching back. Nathan's thumb tapped against his thigh, a habit he had never shaken, as he weighed up the odds of the moment. He always calculated before committing to anything, always. The Sigil, a spiral intersecting a triangle flanked by mirrored lines, at a glance, yet possessed layers that defied dimensions and human comprehension. It was a key to a forgotten past, an entry to other lives.

The cafe noise behind him faded into abstraction; even the city's electric murmur seemed to pause. He tilted his wrist slightly, watching the ancient shape dim and return, like breath held and released. Had it always been there, waiting to be noticed, or had something awakened it? Nathan was intrigued and nervous at the same time.

* * *

Suddenly, he saw flashes so clear in his mind, a battlefield beneath twin Suns. A glass tower in a city of silence and a girl named Kaeda-9 holding a bloodstained map. His hands, aged and trembling, were constructing something from light, then he blinked, and it vanished, but not entirely. It shimmered just beneath the skin, no ink, no scar, but something older than both. As if it had not been physically etched but more like remembered, and called forward by some silent recognition. The Sigil pulsed once, almost imperceptibly, in time with his heartbeat. He did not recoil. Not yet, curiosity held him firmer than fear. It was as if it had been watching humanity from the shadows, waiting for someone to recognise it. It bore names across cultures, some whispered and some erased. All vivid and real:

- The Spiral Witness.
- The Dream Print.
- The Memory Compass.
- And in one forgotten Babylonian codex, **ECHO**.

It had been a recurring sound, a cycle repeated but not through sound waves, through many versions of himself. Not long before the dreams ceased to be mere dreams, he would black out mid-conversation, mid-sentence and fall into other lives, fantasies, fully embodied experiences and entire realities. He lived in a desert temple for ten years before waking up in his home in Richmond. He died on a colony ship orbiting a broken planet and found himself suddenly gasping awake in the middle of a meeting, as discreet as possible. Each time he returned, something accompanied him like a skill, scar, or a word in a language no one else could speak. The Sigil stirred, no longer an ancient symbol, but a system awakened. It pulsed in tandem, matching his breath; something had aligned then. Around him, the city did not sleep; it listened. The quiet was no longer stillness; it was anticipation.

Echo: The Infinite Cycle

Kaeda-9's First Message:

She found him in a dreamscape resembling a Tokyo street market illuminated by a red light. Kaeda-9, a mysterious figure who seemed to know more about Nathan's situation than he did, appeared before him. "You're waking up," she said. "Who are you?" He asked. "Not important yet, just remember the Sigil is not just opening doors." "Then what is it doing?" Nathan inquired. "It's remembering lives," said Kaeda-9. "Lives?" asked Nathan. "The lives you did not choose, the versions that burned, the ones that still exist," Kaeda-9 responded. Then she kissed his forehead as a farewell and vanished in reverse.

* * *

Nathan had never believed in fate, yet this did not feel real. It felt like a reboot, and he became obsessed over the next few days. The ancient Sigil appeared everywhere, including in books, on graffiti, within encrypted emails, and mirrored fragments hidden in old virtual reality reconstructions and ancient stonework. By the end of the week, Nathan was unsure if he was awake or dreaming, rooted or adrift. The symbol had quietly entered his life like a whisper, now echoing everywhere. In an alleyway, he reached out, his fingers grazing the damp stone where the symbol had been carved, and suddenly, time seemed to falter. The air compressed and sound reversed, Nathan staggered as the world unravelled at the edges. *Echo detected.* A voice said, not heard but felt. The symbol burned into his vision, and with it, the pull started, an echo from before memory, a life not his, yet entirely his. This is all to unravel in the following chapters...

D. Gohil

Chapter 2 - A Weekend in Shadows
2025 CE

Not every fracture begins with fanfare. It sometimes creeps beneath the calm of ordinary days. Like a hairline crack in a glass that only widens without your awareness. The weekend should have grounded him, friends, golf, drinks, and banter. Nathan's usual routine. Familiar and predictable, yet as the sun slid over the fairways and old jokes rose with the clink of pints, the unease lingered. In the condensation on his glass, in the corner of his eye, it was there again, lingering like a question he could not quite form. The ancient symbol hovered at the edge of sight, lazily etched in the condensation on his pint. He blinked; it smeared and held, as if the glass remembered more than he did. It bore weight now, shifting his mood, distorting his sleep. Faces from fragmented lives haunted his dreams. One name surfaced, every time: **Kaeda-9.** By Sunday, Nathan was uncertain if he was enduring a hangover or being haunted. The city felt eerily silent. The atmosphere felt overly aware.

As he caught Silvia's gaze across the table, he wondered whether this life, this love, was the only one he had truly lived. This is how it all plays out:

London – Present Day

Saturday morning, after a rough week, Nathan woke to the soft glow of dawn filtering through his bedroom blinds. The city outside was still stretching into wakefulness. The streets were quiet except for the distant sounds of morning traffic. He rubbed his face, inhaling deeply as the scent of freshly brewed coffee drifted in from the kitchen. Rolling his shoulders, swinging his legs, he got out of bed. Something gnawed at him to make him feel uncomfortable again. A subtle unease, like an unfinished thought lurking at the edge of his mind. Shaking it off, he grabbed his phone. *9:30 am tee time confirmed.* Chris messaged, *Hope you're ready to lose, mate. Ian's been talking about a big game, the usual hopeful thinking, ha-ha.* Nathan smirked as he tapped out a reply. *Let him talk. I'll let my clubs do the actual damage and annihilate him as usual, lol.*

After a refreshing shower, he finished his coffee and changed into his golf apparel. He selected a crisp polo and tailored shorts with his favourite golf glove tucked into his back pocket, grabbed his keys and headed out. When Nathan stepped onto the lawn at the edge of the car park and near the golf course clubhouse, the scent of dew-kissed grass and distant pines filled his lungs. The golf course sprawled across rolling green hills, bordered by towering oaks and clusters of wildflowers swaying in the morning breeze. A light mist clung to the edges of the fairways, curling lazily around the bunkers as though nature was stretching after a long slumber.

Ian parked his car in his favourite slot adjacent to the lawn and rolled down the window with a low whistle. "I swear, every time we play here, I expect a server to offer me a glass of Bordeaux Rouge. This course belongs in the South of France, doesn't it, lads?" Chris snorted, swinging his bag over one shoulder. "Yeah, give it five minutes, Ian, just one bad shot, you will curse as usual. Then it is just another overpriced patch of grass to you." Richard, as always, the most composed of the group, gave a knowing smirk. "At least it's not pissing down with rain, and we have a proper early autumn's day, gentlemen, so let's do this."

Echo: The Infinite Cycle

Nathan grinned, stretching his arms as they walked towards the clubhouse. The terrace was already buzzing with early golfers enjoying their pre-game routines. On the tables, mugs of coffee steamed in the mild air. Laughter mingled with the distant thwack of clubs striking balls on the range nearby. Inside, the rich aroma of bacon and espresso filled the clubhouse bar. Nathan leaned against the counter, wanting to order a round of coffee and bacon sandwiches for the group. "Morning, boys." Came a smooth, familiar voice. Paula, the barmaid, leaned on the counter with a knowing smile. She was in the same age group, and she had worked here for years. As usual, I gave Nathan extra attention whenever Silvia was not around.

"Morning, Paula," Nathan said, his tone friendly yet distant as he could already sense Chris smirking beside him. "Your usual?" She asked, tilting her head slightly, flirting. "Yes, please, Paula, you know me too well," Nathan replied with a smile. As she turned to prepare their coffees, Chris nudged Nathan. "Mate, I swear she fancies you rotten!" "Dude, relax," Nathan mutters. "She's just doing her job." As Richard chuckled, Chris said. "Silvia would love to hear that, mate." "Yeah, that's why she never will, OK, lads?" Nathan sighed, looking up. Paula returned with their coffees and sandwiches, offering Nathan one last glance before moving on to the next customer. Ian grinned. "Mate, you're in trouble today. I am on fire lately, lol." Nathan shook his head. "Shall we just focus on golf and let the best man win, you vultures? We all know that will be me." The first hole at the club was a lengthy par four, with the fairway stretching between towering elms. Morning light angled across the green, drawing long, drowsy shadows as the breeze teased the tops of the trees.

Nathan always composed, as he approached the tee without ceremony, rolling his shoulders until the weight of sleep and stress fell away. He set his stance, not rigid at all, beautifully fluid, as if he had done it a hundred times, yet still cared how it felt. He took a deep breath, blocking out the world, closing his eyes and feeling the weight of the chosen club in his hands. His swing was clean and effortless. The satisfying crack of the ball sent it soaring down the fairway, cutting through the air with precision. "Jesus, man!" Ian mutters. "Fucking show-off." Chris whistled. "Guess I'll have to try hard, play my B game and try hard for a change today, lads." He winked. One by one, they took their shots, some cleaner than others, though Chris hit a draw to the left; his shot went into a bunker, and he swore under his breath.

Richard played it safe with a steady driving iron shot down the middle, and Ian sliced his shot into the thick rough, groaning. "You lads fancy putting some money on this?" Nathan grinned as they walked down the fairway. "You mean, do we want to donate money to you again?" Ian shot back. "Come on, gents. It makes it more interesting, you cheapskates." Chris grinned. "All right, fine, let's do twenty quid if we say I finish ahead of Ian." "Oi!" Ian protested, and Nathan just laughed. "Make it fifty, and I'm in?" They continued with light-hearted banter, the occasional grumbling when some crap shots are played and plenty of competitive ribbing. The sun hung steadily above the crisp emerald fairway at Royal Mid-Surrey Golf Club. Nathan tightened his glove, admiring the curve of the seventh hole.

A smooth par four neatly nestled between a cluster of sycamores and a pond that rarely forgave a slice. Fairly close to the Pro-shop. Then he was interrupted. "Nathan, you stranger!" He heard a familiar voice behind him. He turned to see Kash striding over, his big smile and a club slung across his shoulder like a victorious knight strolling from the practice nets nearby. "Hello, Kash, you champ," Nathan said, grinning. "Still floating on that recent gold letter tournament win?" "Can you blame me?" Kash laughed. "I beat that smooth little swing of Sammy's by two strokes on the back nine to take the division two title. You should have seen his face. It was like someone had told him that irons were going out of fashion." Nathan offered a fist. "Congrats, Bro. After your second-place finish before, it was a long time coming for you." Kash replied. "Cheers, I am still unsure how I pulled it off. It might have been the new putter or divine intervention." "You pray now, Kash?" Nathan laughed. "Only when there's golf involved." Kash chuckled.

Then, just behind Kash, was Dillon, who emerged from behind the Pro-shop, immaculately dressed in his pristine, expensive grey polo and signature mirrored sunglasses. Calm and focused, the man could cut grass with his wedge if he wanted to. "There he is," Nathan called. "The legend himself!" Dillon gave a relaxed nod as he approached. "What's up, Cole?" "Not much, mate. I am just trying to figure out why you have not gone pro yet." Dillon smirked, adjusting his cap. "Because I enjoy having a life, Bro." "What a life where you casually destroy every handicap in the county?" Nathan smiles. "Yup, something like that," Dillon blushes and gives his cheeky smile. "Seriously, though, a plus-three handicap dude? That is terrifying," said Richard.

Echo: The Infinite Cycle

Dillon shrugged modestly, the way only those with absolute control of their talent could. Nathan slapped him on the shoulder. "Also, congrats, dude! I heard the wedding was beautiful." "Thanks," Dillon replied, a subtle softening in his tone. "Thara made it look like a magazine shoot, and she planned everything, even to the last flower. I just turned up on time, to be fair." "Smart man," Chris remarked, and Nathan nodded. "Hey, is your younger brother, Sucre. Still bench-pressing the entire weight rack, or has he moved on to lift cars now?" "The dude is still in the gym five days a week," Dillon said. "The beast says it's therapeutic, though I reckon he just intimidates people with vein-density." Laughter rippled between them, including Ian and Richard. Then a nice surprise came: Felipe walking towards the rest of them. Nathan was so happy as it had been a while. "Wow, Felipe, so good to see you. When did you arrive from Miami? How is your swing? I hope you remember it's all about the tempo, Bro?"

Felipe replied. "Hey, Cole, great to see you, and yes, every time I play, I hear your voice, 'remember the tempo,' and it actually works. Man, it's so great to see you!" Nathan was overjoyed as Felipe and Giorgia recently got married, too. "Felipe, join us later after your round with these boys. We have a lot to catch up on, yeah?" Nathan checked his watch. "You guys are teeing off in about thirty minutes, right?" "Thirty-two," Dillon said, checking the club clock behind them. "That's just enough time to agree on drinks later," Nathan said. "You boys in?" "At the clubhouse?" Kash asked. "Well, the bar here after the round, then pub crawl later tonight," Nathan said, arching a brow. "Evening circuit starting at the Millstone pub, then heading to a selection that Richard usually picks. He knows his pubs, and then we return to civilisation. We could use your precise navigation, but officially, you are required by law to bring that chaos energy." They all laughed.

"I'll check with the missus," said Dillon. "Yep, so will I," said Felipe. "Well, tell the ladies it's a character-building exercise," Nathan replied. Kash raised his bottle of mineral water. "You had me at crawl, bro." Halfway through, and starting the back nine, they were all neck and neck, the friendly wager keeping them all on edge. Yet through it all, Nathan still felt uneasy and did everything to focus on the game. As they reached the 17th green, which was regarded as the best on the course, he paused and glanced around. The golf course was quiet, except for the distant chatter of another group a few holes behind.

Laughter on the green echoed strangely in his ears, a shadow passing behind his eyes like a symbol etched in the fire. The round of golf was drawing to a close, and something else was beginning. A flicker of movement in the trees, a shadow at the edge of his vision. Nathan frowned, rubbing the back of his neck. "You all right, mate?" Richard asked, watching him. "Yeah, yeah, all good thanks mate," Nathan said quickly, shaking it off. "I just thought I saw something," Chris smirked. "It's called losing, mate!" Nathan forced a chuckle, but the feeling inside lingered. They thoroughly enjoyed their round and finished feeling pretty damn good. The terrace had been packed with golfers, wealthy executives, and visitors. All relaxing and sipping cocktails, beers, and whiskies while enjoying the view. "All right, let's see the damage, boys," Richard said, pulling out the scorecard. Chris groans. "No way, there is no way you beat me by one stroke, Nathan!"

Ian burst out laughing. "Mate, I think you just paid for Nathan's evening." Nathan grinned, patting Chris on the back. "Pleasure doing business with you, bro, better luck next time." When the other group arrived, they all went to their favourite table near the balcony overlooking the course, ordered pints and steaks. Mostly medium rare, to celebrate the great day and to see each other after so long. The beers flowed easily as the conversation meandered through stories of work relationships and half-baked business ideas that would never see the light of day. "So tonight," Ian said, leaning forward. "We're doing a pub crawl tonight, lads, confirmed, yeah?" Chris nodded. "The usual route sounds good," Richard frowned. "We could mix it up this time, there's a new bar near Mayfair, heard it was a top place, a Speakeasy, I believe." Nathan swirled his drink, contemplating. "Yeah, I'm in, let's do it."

Paula sauntered past their table, casting Nathan a sidelong glance. "Don't get too wild, boys!" Chris smirked. "We make no promises." The sun dipped lower, casting a golden light across the course. Nathan leaned back in his chair, taking it all in. The weekend was ideal and just what he needed with his close friends, drinks, and a brilliantly relaxing time. Once Dillon and Kash finished their showers, they joined the table, and all of them enjoyed the drinks and food. Later, the pub crawl began, and as the evening wore on, laughter and conversation continued. The various establishments had got busier, as the Mayfair bars and restaurants always did. The pubs buzzed with life, the scent of top-shelf spirits mingling with the warmth of their shared memories.

Echo: The Infinite Cycle

They had a fantastic time, and later, as Nathan and his friends left the final pub, taking the conversation and laughter outside so that Kash could smoke. Nathan glanced down at the condensation on his pint glass, with the last sip of beer, his fingers absent-mindedly tracing the shape of the same Sigil. He could not understand why he was sketching it with his fingers, and his stomach churned when he realised what he was doing. Then the dizziness overwhelmed him as the air hit him, and he staggered, feeling the sensation of the ground tilting beneath him. After swift goodbyes, Nathan walked back to his flat alone, as the soft, cool breeze rustled the early autumn leaves. A chill settled on his neck, although it was not a cold evening. He felt like someone was watching him from a distance behind. It made him look back, but the street was empty, with only the faint glow of streetlights. There was something wrong with the eerie silence, and it spooked him.

To take his mind off it, he thought of his sister's laugh, sharp and sudden, like sunlight breaking through clouds. He had not heard it in months. Nathan's hand fumbled at the lock, keys slipping like his thoughts. His breath tasted faintly of whisky and regret, and he could not tell if the haze behind his eyes came from exhaustion or something more elusive. He glanced at the glass on the building's door just for a second. The reflection held, a flicker, a figure standing behind him, then gone. He got to the top floor, and the hallway stood quiet, bathed in the amber spill from the streetlights. His pulse quickened, not because of what he saw, but what his mind insisted he might have seen. Shadows did not shiver, did they? He stepped inside, closed the door gently, and told himself not to look back. He did not need to; the feeling had already followed him in.

Nathan woke up late on Sunday morning, feeling worse for wear, and sunlight streamed through the gaps in the curtains. His body ached from a mixture of the drinks the night before and a long day on the golf course. The recent lack of going to the gym, which was his second love. He stretched, then picked up his phone. Pleasantly surprised to see a message from Silvia, which brought a smile to his face. *I hope the pub crawl did not wreck you, hun. Let me know if you are still alive. Usual brunch spot, I hope?* He smiled and replied, *Yeah, still breathing. Give me an hour, darling.* Silvia, his gorgeous partner whom he loved very much, had a knack for making everything feel beautiful.

D. Gohil

Even though his head was throbbing, he arrived at their regular brunch venue, a not-so-hurried and less noisy cafe in a busy area, with a cute outdoor terrace. At the table, Silvia caught his eye. Oddly, he wondered whether this life, this love, was the only one he had truly lived. Silvia was already enjoying her usual iced coffee on that sunny autumn day, her sunglasses resting on her head. She appeared stunning, just as he expected, even for a relaxed Sunday. "Did you have fun last night, hun?" She teased as he took a seat. "What do you mean by fun? Am I in trouble?" Nathan groaned, rubbing his temple, which made Silvia giggle. "Chris sent me a video of you arguing about golf handicaps." "Oh, man, the damn snitch," Nathan replied. "I still stand by what I said." They braced for a long hug and kiss.

Their brunch was casual and enjoyable, with some laughter, light banter, and plans for the near future. However, as they sipped their coffee, Silvia's voice sounded a little sad. "So, you're off again," she said while stirring her drink. "Long trip to Hong Kong, huh?" Nathan nodded, leaning back in his chair. "Yeah, I'm leaving Tuesday night, sweetheart. This major client could change the company's future." Silvia propped her chin on her hand, observing him affectionately. "Are you feeling excited or anxious about it?" He hesitated. "Both this time, as it is a massive opportunity, but these trips drain me with boring, long flights and endless preps and meetings there." "Hmm," she stroked the rim of her glass, "How long this time?" "Just over a week max, hopefully, and should be back by the following Friday at the latest, as long as all goes well." She pursed her lips. "Long enough!" He reached across the table, taking her hand. "I'll make it up to you when I get back, I promise." Silvia squeezed his fingers. "You'd better, Mr Cole."

By the time Nathan and Silvia returned home that night, the city had settled into an uneasy quiet. The streets were empty, but the air felt thick, as though someone or something was watching from just beyond sight. He closed the front door, but could not shake the sensation of being watched. Later, his fingers absentmindedly traced patterns on the empty glass he held, the same spiral intersecting the triangle. He stared down at it as the shape revealed itself again. How long had he been drawing it while Silvia was in the bathroom, and how long had he been grabbing the edge of the counter? His knuckles were whitening, and for a moment, he swore he saw a shadow behind him in the glass reflection.

Echo: The Infinite Cycle

When he turned, there was nothing there, only the painful growing hum inside his head. Silvia came out of the bathroom and saw Nathan deep in thought. She asked. "Hey, what's on your mind? Are you OK? You look like you've seen a ghost!" "Yeah, I'm OK, just having some weird ancient symbol which keeps flashing in my mind, around me, and it's getting fucking creepy! Sorry, I shouldn't swear." Nathan replied. "Go and have a nice shower, huni, and I will pour you a nice glass of single malt to help you relax." "Yeah, that would be nice, thank you, darling." Nathan stepped into the bathroom, still holding the image of the Sigil behind in his mind. The shower steamed quickly, fogging the mirrors as he let the hot water pour over him. A welcome distraction from the hum that pulsed like a low frequency just behind his thoughts. He closed his eyes, let his muscles relax, and tried, really tried to wash away the tension.

By the time he stepped out, the towel was slung low around his waist. The lights in the flat had dimmed, and soft jazz filtered through the speaker system. Silvia knew his moods better than anyone. She was waiting for him in the lounge. Barefoot in his T-shirt, too large for her but effortlessly elegant and curled on the sofa with a tumbler of whisky in each hand. He stood in the doorway for a moment, taking her in. She had curled up in the corner of the sofa, knees drawn up, hair still wet and smelling faintly of that lavender shampoo she favoured. When she glanced up, her mouth quirked into something that was not quite amusement but was somewhat sexy. "There you are, darling," she said, extending his glass towards him. "Looking almost human again." He crossed the room slowly, accepting the drink with fingers that lingered against hers a fraction too long, old habits. "Don't know what I would do without you, darling," he said, and meant it more than he cared to admit.

Silvia studied his face with that particular intensity of hers, the look that always seemed to reach right through his carefully constructed defences and find whatever was cowering underneath. "You're not damaged goods, you know," she said quietly. "Just carrying too much around with you, sweetheart." There was silence after that, but not the empty kind. It was full of meaning, the sort that builds between people who have seen the best and worst of each other. He set his drink down without tasting it and sat beside her, his thigh pressed to hers. She leaned into him, slow and deliberate, and he tilted his face to meet her. The kiss was unhurried, warm, familiar, and charged with emotion.

It deepened. His hand moved to the small of her back, then higher, threading into her hair. She pressed closer, the whisky now forgotten, her breath catching just slightly when he kissed the hollow of her throat. "Stay," he whispered against her skin. "Tonight, I need you, huni." "Oh, I wasn't planning on leaving," she breathed, fingers sliding across his collarbone, mapping the shape of him as if memorising the feel of safety. He lifted her effortlessly, and she laughed softly, arms around his neck. They moved together, not rushed but with intent, as he carried her towards the bedroom. Moonlight cut across the room in pale ribbons, as the city beyond the windows fell away. For a while, there was no symbol, no hum, no shadow, only skin and breath, warmth and trust. The space between them vibrated with something more profound than desire.

It was pure love, a sense of familiarity as if they had made love in a different dimension, time or life. Their bodies remembered even if their minds did not. When the intimacy ended, with her head on his shoulder and them holding hands softly, fingers loosely intertwined on the sheets. Nathan experienced something he had not felt in weeks: pure peace. The peace and the silence of the symbol, the heavy emptiness that had haunted his thoughts, were no longer present. Stillness. Silvia shifted slightly, brushing her lips across his chest. "Whatever's worrying you," she whispered. "We'll deal with it together." Nathan closed his eyes. In his darkness, the Sigil flickered softly again, but it did not scare him, not tonight; he was with the love of his life. They eased into sleep.

The next morning arrived softly, spilling pale sunlight across the expansive windows of their Richmond home. Silvia stirred first, slipping from beneath the covers in that fluid, catlike way she had. Leaving behind only the faintest warmth on the sheet beside him. Nathan blinked at the ceiling, disoriented for a moment, with a strange feeling of something shifting. He rolled onto his side and listened. She was humming in the kitchen, something sweet, light and tuneless. Making coffee as though the world were theirs at that moment. "You're not dressed yet," she called. "Weren't you going to hit the gym this morning?" "Was," he said, padding in, rubbing a hand through his hair like a natural habit. "Changed my mind, felt like lying next to you all morning instead." Silvia turned to face him with a teasing smile. "That's inefficient of you, Mr Cole. Are you feeling unwell?" "Terrible, I might need looking after today." She poured his coffee without another word.

Echo: The Infinite Cycle

The ease between them was so beautiful and natural. They stood close, sharing the same spot by the counter, letting the day move slowly around them. For once, there was no urgency, just them. They spent the morning as if the penthouse were its own little world. He did eventually make it to the home gym, more out of habit than drive, while Silvia took a few short calls in the study. She leaned into the doorway to watch him once, phone still in hand, the curve of her smile far more distracting than anything his workout could offer. Later, they ate lunch by the balcony, bare feet tangled beneath the table, the hum of the city below softened by the glass. The afternoon drifted into something like golden nostalgia, and they ventured out, walking through the local park, Ranelagh Gardens, wandering together with no destination in mind.

The leaves had begun to turn, early hints of amber and ochre among the green. Silvia took his hand as they walked, fingers interlaced, their strides matching. He watched her as she spoke, her words drifting in and out as the wind tugged at her hair, and he tried to memorise her. Not just the shape of her or the rhythm of her voice, but the way she made him feel anchored when everything else felt like it might lift away. By the time they returned home, dusk had started to deepen the corners of the sky. Nathan packed his suitcase slowly and deliberately, folding shirts with military precision, checking chargers, weighing the corners of his travel bag. Silvia sat on the edge of their super-sized bed, which they had purchased a few weeks ago.

She watched him. "You always pack like you're going off to a corporate war," she said. He turned to her with a crisp shirt in his hands. "Sometimes it felt like I was." There was a moment between them. They both knew the routine too well. The nights apart were getting hard, the long hours spent apart were compromises of love, but this time, something about it felt heavier, more final. Silvia stood and crossed over to him, slipping her arms around his waist from behind. "Come back quickly, I'll miss you," she said into his back. He turned and pulled her closer, breathing in the scent of her hair. "I always try, my love." They made an event of getting ready, Silvia slipping into that burgundy dress that did something extraordinary to her eyes. Nathan, opting for shirtsleeves and his good trousers, determined not to make a meal of the simple act of looking decent. The kitchen became their stage. Radio Richmond, the local radio channel, murmured in the background. Playing perfect tunes, whilst they bumped elbows over the hob, whilst cooking together.

Rescuing bread from the edge of cremation, sharing stories that grew more ridiculous with each glass of wine they poured. Much later, after the washing up was done and the flat had settled into comfortable quiet. They gravitated back to each other with the easy inevitability of planets finding their orbit. Nathan traced the line of her shoulder, marvelling at how perfectly she fitted against him. Outside, Richmond went about its business, plush buildings still glowing. Late trains carrying tired commuters home to their worlds, but none of that mattered just now. They had found their way to the bedroom without quite planning it, drawn by something more substantial than intention. Silvia's dress pooled on the floor beside his discarded shirt, and when she looked at him, really looked, he felt stripped bare in ways that had nothing to do with clothes. What followed was unhurried, almost reverent passion.

Her hands mapped the familiar territory of his shoulders and his back, while he relearned the curve of her hip and the soft spot just below her ear that always made her breath heavy. They had done this dance a hundred times before, but tonight felt different, charged with something he could not name. Afterwards, she curled against him like a cat claiming sunshine. One leg thrown across his, her hair tickling his collarbone. Through the half-open curtains, the town's lights blurred into smears of gold and white. Still, Nathan's attention had narrowed to this. The rise and fall of her ribs, the way her fingers absently traced circles on his chest. The peculiar peace that came from being exactly where he belonged. When they lay side by side in the quiet after, her head resting on his chest, something she enjoyed doing, and her breath soft against his skin as Nathan stared at the ceiling.

The Sigil was not there, but he felt it nearby. It had become quieter now, folded into him, as much a part of him as breath. Something was coming, and it was shifting, not in the mission, but in the world around him. He could not see it yet. The Orb sat on his dresser, inert but not forgotten. Was this part of the Sigil? It had moved beyond symbols; it was part of his blood now, etched beneath his skin. He watched Silvia sleep, her fingers still curled against his side, and pressed a kiss to her hair. He did not know what the next chapter would bring, but he knew this: it was already in motion. The first cycle had turned, and tomorrow everything would begin, and it made him nervous. At the same time, he was curious, as there must be a reason for this strange change in his life.

Chapter 3 – The Beginning Fractured
Interstice: The First Slip

Beginnings rarely announce themselves. They drift in like mist, softening the lines until you realise the road behind you has vanished. For Nathan, beginnings are expected to herald success. A signed deal in Hong Kong, a champagne toast, and the commencement of global expansion. Amid skyscraper shadows and silk-clad dinners, something primal stirs around him. He encountered something in an alley, if indeed human, that communicated in riddles and pressed fingers that felt like icy flames against his forehead. What follows was not a hallucination; it was extraordinary. The universe bent like paper, and Nathan was pulled into something that refused time. The itch returned, familiar now, like a thread tugging at the edge of a tightly wound tapestry. The Sigil was still with him, hidden, watching. And one truth gripped him. This was not their first meeting.

D. Gohil

The metal caught the light as he turned his wrist, one cufflink straightening with a quiet click. Outside, the South China Sea stretched beneath the clouds like brushed glass, vast, indifferent, dazzling in parts where the sun broke through. Nathan did not blink; altitude suited him, the drone of the engines, the hush of separation. Up here, even his thoughts behaved, no boardroom tension or trailing consequences. Just the scale of the thing below, and the quiet rituals of composure. He did not look away until the sea was replaced by cloud, and by then, the thought had already settled. Some things only revealed their shape when viewed from above. The flight to Hong Kong was smooth and luxurious. Just as he expected for a business executive on the brink of finalising one of the largest FinTech deals of his career. The plane cruised, indifferent to the stakes riding within. Nathan's eyes darted across the iPad screen. Each clause was a battlement in the fortress he had built his company, now more of an empire.

Recently, he had sketched his vision on the back of a receipt in a cafe on Oxford Street. Now, his ideas were about to be embedded into the infrastructure of Asia's most formidable financial titan. Nathan allowed himself to relax back into the chair, though tension lingered. The expensive leather sighed under his perfect weight. This victory tasted more different than he had expected, sharper, with an aftertaste that lingered. He understood the figures inside and out; he could recite the risk assessments in his sleep, but sitting here now, watching it unfold, he realised it would reshape entire markets. He felt something close to vertigo. This was not just another deal; it was the biggest in the company's history, dividing careers into before and after. His phone vibrated against the conference table.

A message came from his legal team. *Final amendments approved. You are clear to proceed, Nathan.* Just like that, just a few words on a screen that meant he had entered a league. Where the rules were written by people like him, whose names appeared in history books rather than trade magazines, the thought should have thrilled him. Instead, he found himself wondering if he had just opened a door. He was not entirely sure he knew how to close it again. It was all systems go. The numbers seemed just right for the size and advantages of the deal. The crucial in-person negotiation still loomed. In business, nothing was specific until the ink dried. Let's see if, indeed, the deal was done or...?

Echo: The Infinite Cycle

Once Nathan's flight landed at Hong Kong International Airport, he was escorted quickly through the VIP terminal to avoid the crowds. A luxurious black sedan was ready for him outside, and the driver offered a courteous greeting. Typical of Hong Kong, they were cruising and soon seamlessly joined the expressway leading to HK Central, where the majestic skyline sparkled like a futuristic fortress. Nathan moved through the glass atrium of the finance district's crown jewel, dwarfed by steel monoliths that clutched at the sky like titans. Each one reflected the city's appetite for verticality as a metaphor and elevation as a motive. The towers around him buzzed with barely contained hunger, boardrooms where fortunes changed hands over morning coffee, where entire industries could be dismantled before the lunch trolley arrived. Nathan straightened his tie, not because it needed it, but because some gestures anchored you when everything else felt like quicksand.

Forty floors up, the meeting room waited like a temple to corporate worship, all floor-to-ceiling glass and leather that cost more than most people's cars. This was where the real decisions were made, far from the ant-hill chaos of street level. Up here, money moved at its speed: patient, predatory, precise. The city churned below, ten million people scurrying between appointments and obligations, but that was somebody else's problem. In these rare heights, power operated by different rules, handshakes that could topple governments, signatures that rewrote the map of who owned what. Nathan had earned his place at this particular altar, and he wore that knowledge like expensive cologne. Nathan, part financial architect, part interloper, was about to reshape the skyline of commerce with nothing but vision, resolve, and twenty-two refined pages of proposal.

The suite had emptied of tension, leaving only anticipation in its wake. Nathan stood momentarily by the window, the harbour's glow catching the edge of his reflection. He inhaled not out of relief, but to draw in the moment before it transformed. This was not just preparation; it was orchestration. Every hour spent drilling every detail combed through until it sang with precision, that had led to this crescendo. Three days would pass like a tide, presentations honed, strategies reinforced, signals aligned. When they stepped into that room again, there would be no more rehearsals, only execution. Outside, a slow cargo ship moved across the harbour like a metaphor, deliberate, laden, bound.

He placed the proposal on the table, all twenty-two pages of potential. Not even a tremor in his hand, no apology in his tone, just the certainty of someone who had walked the perimeter of every possible outcome and chosen this one. Across the harbour, a freighter shifted course, and in Nathan's chest, something did too. The opposition sat like birds of prey in tailored suits, men and women who had clawed their way to the top of food chains that spanned continents. Nathan knew their type intimately; hell, he was their type. Each one radiated the particular confidence that came from never having lost a fight that mattered. He had done his homework, naturally. Every loophole memorised, every weakness catalogued, every potential objection war-gamed until his responses felt automatic. His people flanked him like a well-oiled machine. Sarah, with her encyclopaedic knowledge of regulatory law. Marcus, whose financial models could make grown men weep, and Janet, who could spot a lie at fifty paces.

The air in the room had that electric quality you get before thunderstorms. Nathan could feel it crackling along his nerve endings, but instead of making him nervous, it sharpened his focus to a razor's edge. This was what he lived for, these moments when months of preparation crystallised into something clean and decisive. Across the mahogany expanse, someone was about to blink, and when they did, the landscape would shift permanently in his favour. The discussions were formal, intense, and every clause was debated and countered. Hours passed as legal teams fine-combed and scrutinised the fine print. Ensuring that no surprises lay hidden within the contract, and at last, the moment arrived.

The Chief Executive Officer, a very astute and well-regarded entrepreneur named Liang Zhao, calmly relaxed in his chair, tapping his fingers on the conference table. "OK, Mr Cole, I believe we have an agreement," Nathan allowed himself a measured smile. "Agreed, Mr Zhao, this partnership will redefine digital finance in Asia and perhaps globally." They shook hands and congratulated each other. That afternoon, after the signing of the documents. The handshakes sealed a historic billion-pound deal, and by evening, the celebrations were in full swing in the most exclusive sky bar in Hong Kong. The deal was not just done, it was historic, but here, under the starlight and hum, it was personal. Somewhere across the harbour, the high-rise suite they had spent days navigating stood silent, unaware it had birthed a legacy.

Echo: The Infinite Cycle

Nathan turned to say something, a toast, perhaps, but paused. The look in his team's eyes was enough. He knew the deal was significant with the first phase, and millions of pounds had been secured. His firm would speak about this milestone for years to come. Tonight, he celebrated like a king. "Speech!" Someone called. Nathan chuckled, standing a little unsteadily, drinking champagne way too fast. "To all of you, I am so proud of every one of you," he said, his voice thick with champagne. "To a future that is so bright, we'll need sunglasses just to read our stock reports!" Laughter followed the clinking of glasses, and euphoria coursed through him like a supercharged current. Later, saying his goodbyes and again praising his team, he decided to walk back to his hotel to get some rest. The alley breathed with quiet. He caught the slightest twitch in the man's left hand. Most would not notice, but Nathan always did.

He stumbled slightly forward, half-drunk, half-lost in his thoughts. The city behind him pulsed, but here it was dusk made of concrete. He blinked, as if someone ahead, a man, or the outline of one. Old, thin robes that hung like faded flags in the wind. His beard was a whisper of white, and his gaze... still, way too still. Nathan hesitated. Something in his chest ticked oddly, like forgetting a name you once knew well. The figure did not speak immediately, just stood waiting as if he had been there for years or just appeared, summoned by a night like this, and then, barely audible. "You've lost more than you remember, Nathan." The stranger looked ancient but somehow indestructible, like driftwood polished smooth by decades of storms.

Everything about him seemed wrong for this place, yet he commanded the space as though he had been waiting here for centuries. Those clouded eyes fixed on Nathan with uncomfortable intensity. "Think you're living just the one life, do you?" His voice had the texture of old whisky and cigarettes. "Won't be long before you're walking in borrowed skin. Answering to names that sound familiar but shouldn't. Speaking words, you've never learned." Nathan shifted, suddenly aware of how the fog seemed to press against his collar. "What's that supposed to mean? How do you know my name?" The old man carried on as though he had not heard. "You'll find yourself in moments that happened before you were born. Standing in cities that haven't been built yet. Breathing air under stars that don't belong to this world, and when it's over, you'll be the only one who remembers any of it." "That's bollocks," Nathan said, though something in his chest had gone cold.

The stranger leaned closer, bringing with him the smell of old churches and wet granite. "Is it, though?" He paused briefly. "It is not madness, it is the cycle. Time will fold, space will twist, and you will return again and again, each self-shaping the next, and when the wheel brings you full circle..." He paused again, a slow, knowing smile on his lips. "Only then will you actually understand." The stranger stepped closer, extending a wrinkled hand. Before Nathan could react, the man's fingers pressed against his forehead, and a blast of light exploded through his vision. Nathan gasped, his body paralysed as the world stretched and blurred, images cascading through his mind at an impossible speed. Landscapes shifted, faces he did not recognise, ancient Sigils burning with light. He felt weightless, untethered, as if the universe had cracked open and was spilling secrets into his soul, then the darkness of the Sigil activated. Nathan blinked, and the old man was already turning away, his outline dissolving into the night.

Nathan woke with a banging headache as the city skyline greeted him through the window of his hotel room. His sheets tangled, his skin damp with sweat, and he felt like throwing up, not from alcohol but something more profound, as if his brain had rewired overnight. Fragments of the night flickered in his mind: the bar, the alley, the older man. Was he even real, he wondered, as he rubbed his temples, but the memory slipped through his fingers like sand, most probably just a dream. Perhaps too much champagne, as he groaned and dragged himself out of bed, forcing some normality into his morning routine. Returning home to Silvia's loving arms seemed like the best choice to move past this strange feeling once and for all.

After rearranging his travel plans, he caught his flight home later that evening. He was glad to have finished the trip sooner than expected; he knew it would make Silvia happy. He looked forward to celebrating with her and planning their future together. He pondered whether to do it and then felt certain it was time to propose to Silvia. After all, he was turning forty within the next month. Where could he take her? Perhaps he could fly her somewhere exotic like Seychelles for a paradise holiday. Using his birthday as an excuse to hold the surprise and plan to execute the most romantic proposal ever. Nathan smiled and settled into his comfortable seat, thrilled as he loosened his tie while the plane taxied along the runway. The inaudible murmur of passengers filled the cabin, and the familiar routine of travel lulled him into a daze.

Echo: The Infinite Cycle

He secured the biggest deal for his company, smooth negotiations, an enormous win, and another notch on a belt already full. Nathan looked out of the window, the sea below blurred into sky, and the sky into nothing. Hong Kong drifted further behind him, just another city, another handshake, another huge tick on the list of professional achievements. His mind was already moving to the next meeting, next pitch, next prize. It never stopped; he had nailed the rhythm, wake, win, repeat, and it worked. Still, somewhere between the clouds and the hum of the cabin, he felt that feeling again. The same unease gnawed at him, faint as if the air had thickened or time had briefly slowed around him. He glanced at the flight attendants, moving smoothly down the aisles. The fasten seatbelt sign blinked on, and the plane dipped slightly. There was a bit of turbulence, nothing out of the ordinary, but then suddenly the turbulence hit hard, causing the plane to shake violently and a jolt so forcefully that it rattled Nathan's teeth. The overhead lights flickered twice before going out. Sounds of terrified passengers filled the air as a female panicked voice crackled over the intercom. "We have an emergency, brace for impact." The plane jolted forward, causing passengers to scream in fear and follow the emergency protocols provided by the cabin crew at the beginning of the flight. Nathan's stomach tightened, and the world seemed to flicker and distort at the edges.

Then, suddenly, the ancient Sigil's pulse intensified briefly before abruptly silencing with a sudden snap, creating a sensation like drowning in the light. The Sigil burned through the aircraft floor, its circular engravings swirling into view despite the turbulence.

A deep pulse echoed through Nathan's bones, overpowering the engine's hum. A faint metallic tang hit his tongue, blood, or maybe copper. The taste was gone before he could decide which. From the Sigil's centre, an Orb emerged, vibrating with anticipation. It was meant for him alone, and Nathan had no time to react before it grabbed him with a bright pulse. Then a shift pulled Nathan from the plane, plunging him into a dark void. He felt weightless as he saw a tunnel of light, then suddenly arrived at an unknown destination. Reality fractured, unlike glass but like a strange memory, and suddenly. Nathan was no longer feeling himself. He had become someone else in a different place, confronted by a war he could not recall starting. The solid ground lay beneath his back, the scent of burning wood filled the air, and a battle cry in the atmosphere. His body was no longer his own.

A Journey Beyond Time

Nathan opened his eyes to a vast battlefield where warriors clashed in steel and fury, banners flying high against a bloodstained sky. Arrows whistled past him, embedding themselves in the earth. He tried to move, but his body responded differently. He felt stronger and faster, dressed in ancient armour adorned with insignias he did not recognise. A warrior charged at him with a sword raised, and naturally, his instinct took over. Nathan dodged the warrior's movements precisely as if he had trained for this war his entire life. He wielded a blade and landed a precise strike. The soldier fell, breathing quickly and heavily. This all stopped abruptly. With a second shift caused by the Sigil's Orb, Nathan found himself in a new time, a different battle and dimension. He was no longer in medieval armour but adorned in the vibrant lacquered plates of a Samurai warrior. The mist sat heavy. Cherry blossoms moved through it slowly, drifting like old confessions.

He stood alone on the bridge, katana in hand, the blade catching what little light the moon allowed. His opponent stood motionless, face concealed behind lacquered wood and painted symbols. The man held himself, his weight distributed, shoulders set, told Nathan everything he needed to know about what was coming. No words passed between them. None were needed. The space separating them hummed with intent, pregnant with the sort of quiet that comes just before violence reshapes the world. When Nathan moved, it was not conscious thought that guided him. His sword arm knew things his mind had never learned, the precise angle needed to deflect a downward strike, the half-step that would put him inside his opponent's guard.

The warrior behind the mask was not giving him any breathing room, coming forward with strikes that sang through the air like angry wasps, but Nathan's body seemed to have its own ideas about how this should go. His left foot slid back half an inch, just enough to let a vicious cut whistle past his ribs. His sword came up in a lazy arc that should not have worked but somehow caught his opponent's blade at precisely the right angle to send it wide. These were not moves he had practised in some Richmond gymnasium; they felt older than that, worn smooth by repetition he could not place. The pace quickened, steel ringing against steel in patterns that felt familiar as childhood songs.

Echo: The Infinite Cycle

Nathan's wrist turned, his shoulder dropped, his weight transferred from one leg to the other, all of it happening before his conscious mind could interfere. Like his hands remembered a conversation his brain had forgotten how to have. By the time he realised he was enjoying himself, the fight had transformed into something else entirely. Not combat, exactly, more like a reunion with an old friend who spoke a language he had thought he had lost. For just a moment, between the ring of steel and the scatter of falling cherry blossoms, this did not feel like combat at all. It felt like recognition, like a well-rehearsed dance. Then the world tilted, sound drained away, and suddenly Nathan was elsewhere entirely, suspended in a void so complete it made darkness seem welcoming by comparison: no weight, no breath, no heartbeat. Just the slow tumble of thought through nothingness whilst distant suns burned holes in the black, each one watching him with the patience of geological time. Then, a voice. "Nathan." It rippled across the void like gravity in disguise. He did not answer, but something in him opened as though the stars had called his name before, in another life, on another bridge. In this tranquillity, his senses sharpened, yet it felt as though the void was enveloping him. A cold, artificial chill washed over him, and in the distance, a massive space station floated, its surfaces glistening with intricate patterns of radiant metal.

The station orbited a gas giant whose swirling clouds appeared to pulse with unnatural energy. There was no sound or motion except for the endless space surrounding him, but something was not right. Panic gripped him as he realised he was breathing, but no air existed in space. His chest rose and fell with unnatural ease, and his body felt unmoored, untethered to anything but the strange, oppressive calm of the void. Nathan looked down at himself, momentarily disoriented.

To his surprise, he was wearing a high-tech spacesuit, its sleek surface catching and reflecting the distant starlight. Suddenly, a voice crackled to life in his earpiece, slicing through the stillness like a blade. "Commander, the rift is unstable, we have to close it before..." The transmission was swallowed by static, abruptly silenced as though the surrounding air rejected the signal; his mind raced. What rift? What was he meant to do? Another shift, and the biting cold and eerie silence of space melted away, replaced by the warmth and dampness of a dense emerald forest. The air was infused with the smell of moss and earth.

Nathan moved through the woods, and the smell of damp earth and leaf mould clung to the air. Light came through the gaps and moved as the branches swayed. The place was quiet but not empty. Leaves flicked and turned when the wind passed. The ground was soft, covered in moss, and gave way under his boots. His skin buzzed a bit, like something in the woods was alive and close by, though nothing made a sound. A woman stepped out from where the trees were darkest. She was tall, her clothing marked with careful patterns, not flashy, but you could tell they meant something. Her eyes stayed on him, sharp and quiet. "The Sigil has woken in you, and you're not ready, are you, Nathan?" She said, not rushed. The kind of tone that made you stop, even the earth seemed to listen. Nathan tried to speak, but the words did not come out of his mouth. Everything around him broke apart, fast, without warning. Pieces slipped away like the world had been peeled back.

What was the Sigil doing, or was it just his mind playing tricks? This felt surreal and scary all at the same time. Nathan just tried to stay composed. If he could, he tried desperately to focus on thinking about Silvia, then another shift, then another, with each one harder, sharper, and his head pounded hard. The noise in his skull was thick and constant, like something slamming again and again, dragging him between places he did not recognise. He reached out, attempting to ground himself, but it was like trying to hold on to smoke. Nathan could feel the ancient Sigil pulsing within him, growing stronger and brighter, flashing more rapidly before his eyes. It twisted fast, faster than he could follow, as the pressure built in his head, sharp and uneven.

Bits of memory or something like it hit him all at once. Moments in the past, and places he had been a stranger to, people who felt familiar, it was all too much for him to comprehend. He could not hold onto anything. Time bent, pulled thin, it did not stop, and he felt it slipping, like he could not catch hold no matter how hard he tried. His breath came in ragged, desperate gasps as his mind attempted to reconcile all the shifting realities, each more vivid and intense than the last. With another shift, the surroundings faded into an ancient, oppressive silence. The stone carvings appeared old and worn but shifted slightly with the flicker of the fire. He detected an incense aroma, thick and sweet, beneath layers of dust.

Echo: The Infinite Cycle

Nearby, a group of men in pale robes moved slowly. Their voices echoed softly, bouncing off the walls and rising into the shadows above. A chilly breeze, a sensation of an oppressive presence, settled over him as if the tomb were alive. The non-human voice, a low hiss in the language of the ancients, swirled around him, winding its way into his mind. As the sarcophagus lid ground open slowly, shadows appeared, shifting and coiling in supernatural patterns. Terror flooded his soul, and an overwhelming sensation of something ancient, dark, and vengeful was stirring in the tomb. Lightning hit hard and suddenly, splitting the sky. A longship rocked under it, thrown about by waves that rose like walls and dropped fast. Nathan stood at the front. Around him, men gripped their axes, their faces tight, wild, ready. The air howled, loud and constant, pushing him forward. The ship groaned, and the sea did not let up. The chanting got louder, sharper, as if something huge was about to break loose.

Then everything changed, buildings stretched above him, silver and sharp-edged. Neon signs flickered sickly across steel and glass. The noise was everywhere, humming, buzzing, never quiet. He held a rifle, slick and cold. Men and machines closed in. Their eyes glowed red. One voice came through, flat and synthetic. *Target spotted.* Nathan knew they had seen him. He did not belong here, not in this place. Another shift. Jungle heat, thick air, wet ground, and a stone structure ahead, steep and stained dark. He was tied down, chest tight, breath short. Someone stood over him, in robes, paint, and a blade. The sky burned deep red, the sun not round but sharp like a blade, hanging low. The priest's grip tightened around the weapon. His eyes showed no doubt, just pure focus. The blade caught the red light from above as it dropped. Around him, voices rose, harsh and steady.

Nathan's mind spun. He was not just a body on the altar. He knew that now, but they did not see him, and saw the ancient Sigil, something to be given up, but then everything shifted. He stood in a massive room that stretched too far to make sense. The walls shimmered, like liquid caught mid-motion. The air pressed down, thick and hard to breathe. Every face in the room was turned towards him, no polite glances away, no shuffling feet or nervous coughs. Just that unblinking attention that made his skin crawl. Something hung in the air, their heads, defying every law of physics he had ever learned. Not quite solid, yet relatively light, it shifted like oil on water.

Folded in on itself in ways that are hard to follow. When it finally spoke, the words did not come through his ears. They arrived directly in his skull, bypassing all the usual channels. *You have disrupted the pattern.* Nathan's ribs felt suddenly too small for his lungs. He tried to form words, explanations, denials, anything, but his throat had sealed itself shut. The realisation was settling into his bones like lead poisoning. He had meddled with something that had been content to remain hidden. Something that predated his understanding of how the world worked, and now everything was different. Irrevocably, catastrophically different. The thing in the air pulsed once, patient as a heartbeat, waiting for an answer he did not know how to give.

Nathan Cole had once believed in the weight of things: financial capital, strategy, and ambition. In digital financial systems that are mastered and lives that follow are predictable, but what use is control when the ground beneath your feet no longer stays still? He recalls being a man of influence in boardrooms and navigating shifting markets with a single sentence. He could remember the recoil of a musket, the sting of black powder in his eyes, the chaos of war in a time he had no reason to know, at least not then. Then there were the other lives, figures moving unseen through neon-lit alleys, hunted by machines speaking in broken voices, and a lone astronaut gazing down at what appeared to be a peaceful world below him.

Roles shifted, settings blurred, but one truth remained. He was never truly the same person for long. Initially, it seemed like punishment, madness, or an unshakeable dream. The repetition was too exact; each change echoed with symbols carved into stone or burned into circuitry, languages he barely understood, and eyes he recognised in strangers, which he found odd. The ancient Sigil was always present, sometimes visible, sometimes not, in architecture, myth, and memory, as if it had been following him through lifetimes or waiting, and gradually recognition grew. These lives were not random. They were fragments of something larger, patterns nested within patterns, each a lesson he had not known but was to learn. Nathan suspected that time, for him, was no longer a line, but a spiral. That identity had not been fixed; the memory was not entirely his own, and he was not simply witnessing history. Embedded in it to return if a return was even possible, he would have to unravel what bound it all together.

Echo: The Infinite Cycle

The ancient Sigil was a key, a test, a mirror and perhaps its purpose an answer to something yet to unfold. Everything felt like it had gone a full circle, and Nathan was disoriented if time had rewound on him. What a mental whirlwind. As the plane ascended above the South China Sea, with engines humming, Nathan loosened his tie and relaxed, feeling he should be proud. The deal was complete, history made, yet that subtle disturbance persisted at the edge of his awareness. The Sigil had appeared to him in Hong Kong, in the alleyway, through the old man's impossible touch, and now it pulsed faintly beneath his heartbeat. Now, he could not stop thinking about Silvia. If he got through this, he would call her to hear that laugh again.

As the cabin lights dimmed, turbulence rattled the fuselage, the seatbelt sign blinked, and the intercom crackled with urgency. It was not the sudden drop that startled him; it was the sensation of time folding. Seems he was back again only momentarily. Something pulsed behind his eyes. Not pain or pressure, nor invitation. Then it came again. Stone grinding, the Sigil, blazing like a second sun. An Orb of light hovered in front of him, with purpose. He recalled what the old man in the alley said, and it made him feel strange. Before his brain could process the movement, he was falling again, through existence itself. Nathan was no longer on the plane, and the mission awaited.

This time, Nathan felt it was not a temporary shift but a journey forward, that he was destined to experience. Whatever was happening, he had to find his way back to Silvia and his normality before he lost his mind. There was a reason for this, and his curiosity gave him courage. He closed his eyes and accepted his fate for now. "OK, let's see what that old man was talking about? There is a reason and purpose for this," said Nathan to himself, and he held his breath and closed his eyes.

D. Gohil

Chapter 4 – Peacekeeping Mission
2028 CE

Nathan's eyes opened to a low thrumming vibration beneath him, steady, mechanical, alive. The cockpit swayed almost imperceptibly, and sunlight shone through a narrow canopy ahead. He did not move straight away. His thumb tapped against his thigh, an old habit, the same one he had relied on in crowded streets and tense meetings. It grounded him now; it needed to, even as the reality around him whispered that it was not his normality. The instruments glowed amber, readings scrolled in a language he did not recognise, yet somehow familiar. Outside, the sky was too sharp, too vast, the kind of blue that belonged to a different world entirely. The air had that bitter edge, like pennies left too long in a warm palm, or the aftermath of violence. Nathan had encountered that particular flavour before, though he could not say where or when. It lodged itself at the back of his tongue like a warning. Silvia's face flashed through his mind, without warning and urgently. Where is she? Was she safe?

The thought struck with force, cutting through the strange fog clouding his mind. He clung to her image, dark hair spilling across white pillows, that crooked smile she wore when she thought he was not looking. Something tangible to anchor himself to, while everything else felt borrowed and temporary. Static hissed in his ear, then cleared into a voice he somehow recognised. "Cassian, we're in position, waiting on you." Nathan opened his mouth to correct whoever was speaking, to explain that they had the wrong person entirely. The name sat on his tongue as it belonged there, comfortable as an old coat he had forgotten he owned. He let the name settle, weighing it in the quiet hum of the cockpit. It was not his yet somehow, impossibly, it fit like a call sign he had carried for years. "I am Cassian," he said to himself.

The world around him slammed into focus with brutal clarity, as he was no longer on the commercial flight. Instead, the howl of wind screamed against the cockpit as he gripped the control stick of an F-35C Lightning II fighter jet, his body pinned by G-forces, his vision narrowing under the strain. He had been here before, or rather someone with a pilot's life that was not his, but now he entirely inhabited it. Warning lights flashed across the console, the desert landscape stretched far below, fractured by ancient scars and razor-straight borders. In this world, Nathan was Captain Cassian 'Hawk' Peterson, part of the defence frontline and the RAF's finest and most experienced pilot, potentially at the edge of war. The Sigil pulsed coldly against his wrist, its presence unchanged, threading through every version of him. The pattern had followed him into another life. Nathan blinked; suddenly, a joystick and a missile lock tone replaced his comfortable seat on a commercial plane with a laptop on his lap. One moment, cold air slammed into him, and the next he plunged into an abyss, free-falling with the wind howling past his ears, before finding himself in a jet's cockpit. He desperately needed to gain control of his senses.

The Demilitarised Zone (DMZ)

His body jolted as the harness pressed against his chest, the controls vibrated under his fingers, while the roar of the engines overwhelmed him, leaving him breathless. The flight warning lights on the panel in front of him flashed, and a voice sounded through his headset. "Captain, you need to stay on target!" Nathan questioned his surroundings for only a moment.

Echo: The Infinite Cycle

Instinct kicked in, and his grip on the controls regained composition. This was not the first time he had been thrust into turmoil, nor was it his first flight at Mach 2, apparently. The lift of his fingers, the faint pressure of his boot against the rudder pedal. A silent liturgy of war. The F-35C Gen III helmet-mounted display system (HMDS) flickered to life, whilst casting light across the contours of his helmet. He scanned it with the habitual precision born not of trust but necessity, and there was no margin for error, not today. Down below, the world was still, a lull before the consequence. Every mission had its weight, but this one felt different, not heavier, just sharper, as if it might cut through him instead of the other way round. Cassian's grip hardened around the stick. Above all, he had to remain constantly focused, unflinching, detached enough to act, but not so much that he forgot the stakes. The blue, clear, expansive sky loomed around him like a canvas, calm and untouched by the anxious world below.

He recalled the early days of his career as a young RAF cadet in flight school, and he had envisioned himself soaring high above the earth. Experiencing the exhilarating power beneath him and navigating the skies with the skill and elegance achieved only by the most experienced pilots. Decades later, he was finally living his dream, but it did not match what he had imagined. Both the world and he had changed. Cassian's F-35C, designed for agility, precision, and Mach speed, now held little detail. This was no ordinary combat mission; he was not tracking targets or intended to engage in dogfights. Cassian was one of the best pilots in the sky with a single crucial duty of the day. To prevent war before it started. Below him, the DMZ stretched like a scar across the landscape, a narrow strip of neutral ground separating two nations on the brink of conflict. The air itself seemed to crackle with menace.

Two armies had dug in along the valley floor, close enough that individual soldiers could probably make out the whites of each other's eyes. Cassian had flown through plenty of hostile zones before, but this felt different, like balancing on the edge of a blade that could tip either way with the slightest breath. His job was not to drop ordnance or provide air support. Sensing he was here to stop something terrible from starting. One wrong move, one trigger-happy grunt with an itchy finger, and the whole powder keg would blow up. Static burst through his headset, making him wince briefly.

D. Gohil

"Hawk One, this is Eagle Command. You're coming up on the no-fly zone. Stay above eight thousand altitudes. We've got movement down there, and it's not looking friendly." Cassian's hand tightened on the stick before he could stop himself. The radio chatter was standard operational fare, but beneath it ran a current of barely controlled panic. Everyone knew what was at stake. This was not just another border dispute. The ground below marked where two worlds met and decided whether they had shaken hands or torn each other's throats out. Cassian squinted through the glare bouncing off his canopy, watching the ant-like figures of soldiers preparing for something none of them wanted but all of them were forced to anticipate. His knuckles had gone white against the controls.

Far below, history was holding its breath. His heart beat was steady, his pulse unwavering. Yet a tense edge to the moment sent a faint shiver through him as the radio crackled once more. "Hawk One, you are cleared for engagement observation only, which is your primary objective. Do not escalate unless forced to." The radio crackled. Cassian exhaled slowly, nodding to himself, even though no one could see. He had to grasp this truth, as the stakes were high with each decision and manoeuvre counted. The lives of thousands or more were at imminent risk. He could not afford a single mistake. His father's words echoed in the quiet hum of the cockpit.

True warriors do not seek war. They prevent it. A truth worn smooth through repetition. Those words had shaped Cassian from the beginning. His father, a decorated general, battle-worn and history-laden, had seen conflict in every shade. He taught Cassian that sometimes the most challenging mission is the one that requires no weapons, but patience. Cassian's sights focused on the sky, and his thoughts stayed rooted in the present. The F-35C cruised steadily, ready for action yet waiting for a possible attack, a confrontation, or to continue patrolling the border. Observing as history loomed beneath him. The flicker was not just static; it was intentional. Movement down there, not chaotic but deliberate. His gaze locked onto the dark shape trailing the dust, like a shadow untethered. The radar pulsed again, much stronger this time, confirming it was not an echo. Cassian narrowed his eyes. It was small, ground-based, and alone, which could have made it a stray vehicle or bait. In zones like this, ambiguity was not accidental. He adjusted his altitude just enough to stay out of range, fingers poised, breathing steady. The HMDS tagged the shape, but the system was unable to classify it.

Echo: The Infinite Cycle

It was moving too erratically and too quietly. He tapped the comm. "Eagle Command, this is Hawk, unidentified contact near the DMZ perimeter, request a visual recon sweep. I will maintain high watch." The shape moved again, nudging forward towards the line. Cassian's jaw tightened. Whatever this was, it had not come to hide; it had come to be seen. It was a faint signal from a reconnaissance plane slipping out of formation, and his heart rate sped up. This aircraft was not supposed to be there. Rules of engagement were crystal clear. No firing unless directly threatened, but this was not some lost cargo pilot who had taken a wrong turn. The plane below was flying reconnaissance patterns, methodical sweeps that suggested military training. Still, it had strayed well outside any authorised corridor, dancing along the border as if testing for weaknesses.

His instruments were not lying. The bogey was flying through the buffer zone, that narrow slice of sky that existed in legal dispute between two nations in close conflict. Cassian made minor adjustments to his flight path, staying just clear of the boundary markers, avoiding any dramatic manoeuvres that might spook the ground controllers, who were undoubtedly observing every move. Years of training had taught him to think before acting, to let experience rather than adrenaline guide his hands on the controls, and there, burning softly at the periphery of his vision, was the mark.

The same twisted symbol that had been haunting the edges of sleep for months now, carved into moments that felt borrowed from someone else's life. Cassian had seen it before, not just in dreams, but somewhere objective, somewhere important. The memory came from the old man in the alley. This was not a coincidence; this was a pattern, a design, the universe folding back on itself like origami made of time. The Sigil pulsed gently, patient as a heartbeat, reminding him that whatever was happening up here at eight thousand feet was just one small piece of something much larger. Was it tied to this mission? It was never just an emblem. It had weight, not physical, but something that pushed on him from inside. Cassian could not explain it, but the moment the Sigil stirred, it was as if the world around him tilted, its logic rewritten in a quiet script. The rogue aircraft suddenly banked low and recklessly, as if it knew its limits were close before risking an attack. Cassian maintained his position, eyes fixed on its path, his senses tingling with something beyond standard protocol. This was no typical mission. The Sigil had not just appeared; it had intervened on purpose.

Deep inside, a quiet part of him remembered. He did not know how, yet the path before him seemed familiar. Fragments of which he had walked before. Now, he was following the signs, pursuing something beyond just a plane or what still flickered beneath the surface. "Hawk One to Eagle Command," Cassian said into the comms, his tone steady yet commanding. "I see the rogue reconnaissance aircraft, it is off course and too near the border, requesting permission to investigate." A lengthy silence followed, broken only by static sounds on the airwaves. "Negative Hawk One, hold your position, do not engage." Cassian clenched his jaw.

He knew the protocol, but this situation had developed beyond mere observation. The mission had changed, and Cassian realised he would need to make a quick decision. Cassian took a deep, determined breath, changed direction, and sped toward the reconnaissance plane. His mind was full of doubts, but he pressed on towards the aircraft that entered the DMZ. This mission was more than just peacekeeping now. It seemed part of a larger plan that Cassian was starting to understand. Captain Cassian's fingers glided over the controls of his F-35C Lightning II, a craft that had become like a second skin over the years, or so it felt. He made a slight modification to his heading, narrowing his eyes as he surveyed the barren terrain below. The DMZ lay beneath him, splitting two nations on the verge of war, though from above, it appeared tranquil, expansive, and silent. Cassian sensed that something was amiss, as the atmosphere felt like the calm before a storm. For a moment, his sensors remained quiet, just performing a basic terrain scan until he picked up a faint, irregular ping.

His hands stayed on the controls, gripping the stick more firmly because this feeling was unfamiliar to him. While searching, he could not quite identify what he adjusted his course for, but kept his eyes on the horizon. It seems his years in the cockpit told him that something was approaching, even if he could not yet understand what it was. Then, the radio came alive with static. "Hawk One, this is Recon One, soldiers hit hard at the following coordinates." The transmission ended abruptly for some reason, giving way to a wave of static-sounding noise. Cassian felt sweat forming on his forehead at the echo of those words, and his pulse quickened, and his instincts took over. An unarmed reconnaissance aircraft, essential for intelligence gathering, had been downed in enemy territory. This incident was an act of aggression.

Echo: The Infinite Cycle

The engagement rules were clear as per the treaty between the two governments. Unarmed reconnaissance aircraft were off-limits, a fact known to both parties. Yet, that was no longer the issue, and lives were at risk. His stomach tightened as he spoke through his comms. "This is Hawk One to Eagle Command, do you read me?" The response on the other end had crackled with static friction, faint but discernible. "Hawk One, do not engage, obey and maintain your position." The order was straightforward, yet Cassian's determination was unwavering, and he did not need to be told twice. This could no longer remain merely an observation, but a rescue mission he would undertake regardless of orders. The icy edge of duty sharpened his focus, and he would not let those men stranded behind enemy lines if the reconnaissance plane fell into enemy hands, not on his watch. "Hawk One, do you copy? Hold your position, I repeat, hold the position."

Eagle Command's voice was firmer this time, more insistent, but Cassian had already decided, as the words from his father echoed in his mind. *True warriors don't seek war; they prevent it.* The mission was still one of peacekeeping, but preventing war sometimes meant stepping outside the prescribed rules of engagement. Sometimes, a warrior had to act in the moment, even when the orders did not align with the situation. Cassian's fingers slammed down on the afterburners, the F-35C responding instantly as he veered the jet sharply towards the coordinates sent to him. The roar of the engines beneath him drowned out everything else; his focus narrowed to the task at hand. Since a decision was made, there was no turning back now.

As the plane sped towards the crash site, the ground below darkened, the landscape a blur of browns and greys as he cut through the air. His mind raced through the possibilities, and enemy ground forces were closing in. He could visualise it in his mind's eye, the crash site, the smoke rising from the wreckage, the enemy forces advancing. If they reached the downed plane before the rescue team arrived, the crew would be taken hostage or, worse, killed. Cassian would not allow that to happen. His radio crackled again, but it was not Eagle Command this time. "Hawk One to all rescue teams, I have located the crash site. I have sent the coordinates, get the crew who parachuted safely about 700 meters south of the crashed plane. I will cover you from above," his voice was sharp and urgent.

D. Gohil

Time was of the essence, and every second counted. The rescue teams responded pretty quickly. "Copy that, Hawk One, our ETA is six minutes at best." Six minutes! Cassian understood how long six minutes could feel in a combat zone, like an eternity. Every second would count, and the enemy forces were already closing in, their vehicles stirring up dust in the distance, growing larger as they approached. He felt his grip tighten on the control stick as the familiar surge of adrenaline coursed through him. Only he stood as the first line of defence for those men who managed to parachute, but were now stranded below. "Hawk One to all rescue teams," Cassian continued, his voice laced with urgency. "I will keep the enemy at bay for as long as possible, get there and move fast."

He armed his air-to-ground missiles, the display on his dashboard flickering as the systems readied for combat. Cassian's mind was clear, his focus sharp as a razor, and the rules no longer mattered. His mission had shifted from observation to action, and nothing can stop him from protecting those men. The wreckage below came into view, with flames licking at the edges of the crash site. The wreckage told him more than the radar ever could. It had not crashed by chance. This was a clear statement by the enemy. Jagged fragments littered the dry earth, sharp against the crawling smoke. Cassian's eyes swept the scene, catching sight of movement. The enemy was advancing. His pulse thudded like a dull engine noise, constant and impossible to tune out. He toggled the view, switching to ground scope, and the terrain shifted under the lens. Troops moved in formation, flanking patterns already underway, not yet an attack, but so very close. He tightened his grip. Instinct urged action, while training counselled calm and restraint. Somewhere beneath all that, the Sigil stirred again, quiet and watchful like it too was contemplating his next move. Enemy vehicles were approaching, getting closer, and kicking up plumes of dust in their wake.

His radar confirmed that a convoy of hostile military trucks was now merely minutes away from reaching the crash site. If they arrived at the downed airmen nearby first, it would be too late. Cassian's mind clicked into gear, and he knew he could not allow them that chance. The missile launched, and the shockwave rippled outward, scattering debris and silhouettes as if the very ground had recoiled. Cassian did not flinch. The jet's frame held firm beneath his grip, and through the smoke trails and sudden brightness. He pivoted, already scanning for any following vulnerability that would be unacceptable.

Echo: The Infinite Cycle

The convoy scattered, like ants disturbed mid-march, but there was order behind the chaos. He knew that this had to be Commander Markov's strategy, and was deliberate misdirection, layered defences, and feints within feints. Markov was the enemy's opposite and equally skilled. Cassian marked a second target. His breath slowed, heart steadied now beneath the rumble. The Sigil hummed, its presence not loud, but palpable. It did not speak, but in moments like this, it was almost there to guide him. He launched again, the missile sliced through the night, and time seemed to pause at impact. Cassian did not watch it land. He was already turning, because this battle would not be won by firepower alone. The convoy scattered in chaos, but Cassian knew this was just the beginning and expected retaliation. More vehicles were arriving, more enemy forces, and he had to continue to hold them off. The seconds were ticking away as he fired, again the missile streaking towards another vehicle, as the blast sent debris flying into the air. Cassian's mind was sharp, his hands steady as he manoeuvred the F-35C with deadly precision.

Another missile launched, another explosion, and the enemy convoy was in disarray. Cassian could not afford to relax, not until the rescue team arrived and the men were safe. "Hawk One to all rescue teams," Cassian called out again, his voice steady and calm despite the chaos unfolding beneath him. "You are clear for extraction. Hurry, get them out of there, guys." He watched as the rescue vehicles approached, helicopters landing in the near distance, and the forces pushed back the enemy threat at least for now. His heart was still racing, and his body still hummed with adrenaline, but for the first time in hours, Cassian allowed himself a moment of relief as the rescue team began extracting his fellow airmen.

Cassian's eyes fixed on the horizon once more, the storm had passed, and yet the tension and the sense that something far more significant was at play still lingered. The mission was not yet over, as Cassian soared back into the sky, the Sigil pulsed faintly in his mind, reminding him that this was more than a mission for him. His radar blared a warning, flashing on his screen that two enemy jets were inbound. Cassian's pulse skipped a beat, and the sky above was no longer his ally. The danger had escalated beyond a rescue operation and had turned into a full-scale defence. His mission had shifted, and the battle was in the air. "Looks like I've got company," Cassian mutters under his breath, his eyes narrowing as he tracks the incoming fighters.

His instincts flared, and his mind immediately went into combat mode. The enemy jets, Sukhoi Su-57, were unmistakable, and he was sure they belonged to Colonel Ivan Markov. A name Cassian had heard countless times in briefings. Whispered by commanders and noted in intelligence reports as the enemy's finest, his counterpart. The man was a living legend, known as a cold and ruthless pilot who had racked up kills with alarming speed and precision. Markov's tactics were surgical, and his reputation preceded him in every war room across the globe. To say that Cassian had been expecting to face him someday would be an understatement. He had not expected that day to arrive so soon, as this was meant to be a peaceful mission. His radar blinked again. Markov's jet was closing in, and the other was flanking from the right. Cassian's stomach tightened as the adrenaline kicked in. He did not have the luxury of time.

Markov would be upon him in seconds, and if he did not act swiftly, the rescue operation could turn disastrous. "Hawk One, we have additional hostile jets in the air." Cassian's dash display flickered as the horizon split between flame and sky, the battlefield unfolding like a theatre of chaos. The jet's wings sliced through the clouds, and Cassian's eyes tracked the anomaly, that signature contrail streaking across the upper quadrant. Markov was fast, precise, and fairly predictable. Cassian throttled forward, G-force pressed into his frame like gravity's own fury, but his mind stayed clear. The dogfight would be brief. Markov did not linger. He struck like a needle with gunfire, then vanished. *Lock sequence initiated,* alerted the onboard AI. Cassian adjusted the trajectory, matching Markov's evasive climb.

No margin for error, no room for history, memories surged, a last engagement, a flaming wreck, a narrow escape. Cassian blinked them away quickly. This was not vengeance; this was balance. He could hear the hiss of the enemy missile lock, the sound almost deafening in his helmet, and he deployed flares, watching them burst into fiery clouds around his jet to divert the missile. The actual battle had only just begun. Markov manoeuvred his jet with relentless precision. The two fighters circled each other, each waiting for the other to make a move, whilst the other fighter jet was also there in pursuit and back-up. Cassian, mainly watching Markov's jet, calculated his next strike, but every instinct told him this would not be a simple dogfight, not with the Russian.

Echo: The Infinite Cycle

Cassian barely registered the second lock tone before muscle memory took over. He yanked the control stick, and the F-35C climbed with brutal thrust, engines screaming against gravity. The sky split around him. Then, from a distance, they managed to gain on each other. Bullets skimmed past the wing, trailing heat, shaking the jet like a war drum. He rolled hard to the right, body pinned, vision narrowing on the HMDS for proximity. Markov's fighter arced wide, banking sharply, reorienting for pursuit. Cassian pushed back, counter-thrusting, banking tighter, flipping altitude into advantage. This was not textbook combat; it was a ritual, familiar, with two forces circling something neither could name. In his headgear, the whisper returned, low, ancient, like the Sigil stirring through blood and machine alike. Cassian steadied his breath, as the next move mattered, not only for survival, but more for the consequences anticipated. From a distance, missiles missed by mere inches. The rush of air from their wake shook the F-35C.

Cassian levelled out, performing a tight loop as he cut the afterburners, forcing Markov's jet to overshoot. The manoeuvre was risky, but it bought him valuable seconds that Cassian would use wisely. He locked his radar onto Markov's jet, tracking its every movement. The man was an excellent pilot and was a master of the skies. The moment crystallised, wind, metal, history, all converging in Cassian's crosshairs. His thumb twitched, but he hesitated, not because of doubt in his skill, but because of the voice. The one who had whispered to him during every flight since the Sigil awakened. It pulsed now, louder, as if sensing the fulcrum of fate. Markov was no longer just a target; he was part of the pattern.

Cassian felt it, a thread pulling taut between them, woven through countless battles, unspoken oaths, and a deeper war neither could name. He fired, the bullets tore forward with vicious certainty, a serpent of fire and resolve. Markov veered, engines howling, but the Sigil's presence within Cassian surged, guiding the path. Impact bloomed against the sky, not an explosion, but a rupture. Colours bled where none should be as time frayed. Cassian blinked, as the world was no longer air and speed; it was a memory. He could take the shot and end this fight here and now, but something held him back. Markov was no ordinary enemy; he was a pilot, the same as Cassian. Ensnared in this potential war and the endless dance of destruction, which benefited nobody.

Cassian made a split-second decision and opened a direct comm line to Markov's fighter comm. "You cross this line, Markov, and there is no going back, so stand down!" For a long moment, there was silence on the line, and the tension in the air was palpable. Cassian's mind raced, hoping that his gamble would pay off. Although known for his ruthlessness, Markov, the legendary ace, was not the target of Cassian's request for a fight. Finally, Markov's voice crackled over the comms. "You are playing a dangerous game, Hawk." The words were bitter, laced with disdain, but Markov's jet veered away, both enemy jets disappearing into the clouds, away from Cassian. The silence that followed was almost as deafening as the battle that had just unfolded. His jet levelled out, but he knew the mission was still not over.

There were lives to protect and dangers to face. Yet at that precise moment, he had made a choice that would echo through his life and destiny. He had chosen peace, if only for a moment. "Hawk One to all rescue teams," Cassian's voice was steady, unwavering, despite the storm of emotions. "Clear to move in and get everyone out." The war against the cycle of violence was not for sure over, and if he were in the sky, Cassian would fight for something greater than victory; he would fight for peace. The sky stretched endlessly before Captain Cassian 'Hawk' Peterson as he levelled his F-35C Lightning II. The afterburners dimming and the powerful engines hum steadily in his ears. His fingers relaxed on the controls, though his chest tightened, and the adrenaline had not entirely dissipated.

Below, the downed airmen were being extracted from the wreckage. His mission once again had shifted from an aerial assault to that of guardian eyes above, ensuring that no further threats would jeopardise the lives he had just saved. As he flew in slow, deliberate circles around the crash site, his eyes remained fixed on the ground. Enemy forces had retreated for the time being, and Markov, astonishingly, had chosen not to engage further. He also knew they were in the wrong to attack in the first place. The danger had passed temporarily, though Cassian did not lower his guard, as the edge of the battlefield was never entirely clear even in the skies, not with tensions this high. A sharp crackle in his comms pulled him from his thoughts. "Hawk One, this is Eagle Command. You disobeyed a direct order! What the hell were you thinking?"

Echo: The Infinite Cycle

Cassian's lips curved into a slight smirk beneath his oxygen mask, though his voice remained calm. "It was measured and life-saving." There was a brief silence on the other end, the words of command lingering in the air like thick fog. The reprimand had been inevitable, but Cassian was unconcerned, and his choice had been the right one. In moments like these, following orders meant little when lives were at stake. Then the command finally returned, less forceful but still tinged with frustration. "Copy that, Hawk One, return to base." The order was explicit, but Cassian did not rush to comply. He had already decided, chosen to act, protect, and preserve peace, and he could not undo those choices. A sense of calm washed over him as he adjusted his heading towards friendly airspace. The tension in the area was far from over, but this day had closed, and it had closed on his terms.

As the F-35C glided smoothly through the skies, Cassian could not help but reflect on the events of the last few hours. He had fought, but not for the thrill of combat, victory, or glory. He had fought to stop something far more dangerous from happening and protect the fragile balance of peace at that moment. His eyes flickered over to the distant sky as the world below him remained still. Its beauty was untainted by the violence he had just experienced. He had ensured it stayed that way, and the dogfight with Markov had been intense, but had not defined the mission. The ongoing threat of war and endless violence would still loom just over the horizon, but it was pushed back for now, and Cassian had bought them time, granting one more day and one more breath of the vulnerable peace.

The mountains below cleared from the haze, their familiar shape signalling the end of that journey into friendly territory. Cassian glanced at his instruments. The patrol hours had taken their toll on his body, and he could feel the weariness creeping in; yet, there was still no time to rest, as a briefing would be a priority upon his return. The journey back to base offered him a surreal opportunity to reflect, yet his choices also troubled him. Cassian's eyes returned to the horizon as a sense of finality settled over him. He had done what he needed to and made the right decision, as his F-35C cruised back to base. Cassian's thoughts were at peace, and he felt contentment, but he was also aware of the realities which lay ahead. He needed to address them. The cycle of violence would continue, and the shadow of a war would always loom.

However, at that moment, he felt a quiet peace, the understanding that he had chosen a different path. He had protected lives there as well as given the world one more day to breathe, which was his primary goal. "Hawk One, this is Eagle Command," the voice crackled again, breaking the silence in his cockpit. "Welcome back, Hawk and well done!" Cassian's gaze remained fixed ahead as he descended into friendly airspace, his heart settling into a steady rhythm. He did not respond, as words were not needed. His actions had already conveyed everything, and the DMZ remained in a state of mutual balance.

As Cassian flew his F-35C back towards base, a sense of accomplishment weighed heavily on the cockpit. The mission had been successful, and the war averted; most importantly, lives had been saved. There was an undercurrent of something that extended beyond the tactical victory, something that pulsed just beneath the mission's surface. A sense that he was part of something far more extensive and significant than the borders of the war zone he had just left behind. The thought that had been nagging him since the dogfight with Markov became more precise as he steered his aircraft toward the waiting runway at the RAF International base.

* * *

He faced some thoughts that had troubled his mind, as he manoeuvred his jet through the clouds mid-mission. The symbol was beginning to feel more than a relic of his past; it was a map and a guide. It had always been there, a silent presence in his mind, weaving through his memories like a thread that connects the many lives he had led across time. The glow was subtle, but its presence was undeniable. It did not speak, did not move, but it bent reality around him. Warped the edges of thought and memory until Nathan could no longer tell which life he was remembering, or if he was remembering at all. This was not the same Sigil he had seen before, etched in stone or glimpsed through a dream; it was purer now. Not a mark, not even light, just intention, and somehow, it had always been there: watching, waiting, guiding. Through life, through every decision that pulled him closer to whatever lay ahead. Nathan closed his eyes. He saw nothing, but felt everything. Earlier, when the F-35C was in the clouds, Nathan's fingers had instinctively brushed over his cockpit controls like they were keys to unlock some hidden truth. When his gaze shifted to the landscape below, his mind was elsewhere, which was unlike him, he recollected.

Echo: The Infinite Cycle

There was no doubt now that this was not madness, nor a mere metaphor. The thoughts were not his, not truly. They were echoes, reverberations of something ancient pressing against the fragile veil of his awareness. As if some force, benevolent or indifferent, had scattered fragments of a singular soul across time to bear witness, or perhaps to warn. Though critical, the war zone he had left behind was a microcosm of the larger struggle. The rupture of the force threatening to tear apart the very essence of existence was far more than a battle of nations. It was a cosmic war that transcended earthly concerns and reached into the fabric of time. The more Nathan pondered the Sigil, the more it appeared to be a key guide leading him toward his ultimate purpose. The connection between his past lives and the destruction looming was undeniable. The calling now was not shaped by rank or bloodline. It thrummed beneath reality, vast and unseen, like an ancient tide reclaiming the shore. Nathan sensed it, the convergence. His existence had always been a thread in something grander, but only now did the pattern begin to pulse. Not a path chosen, but one summoned, not destiny, but reckoning. He was not just an avatar of past lives; he was the rupture, and the universe had been waiting for him to awaken. Was this something that he was yet to experience? He snapped out of his thoughts.

* * *

His mission had been to prevent a potential war at this moment and to act as a shield for those caught in the crossfire of global conflict, but there was more at play here. The war he had just averted was just one chapter in a much larger story at play. The jet's wheels touched down with a soft thud, the engines winding down as the F-35C rolled to a stop, where the ground crew would soon take over, guiding the aircraft into its designated parking slot. He had always known there was more to his journey than merely his duty as a pilot. Now he could feel it in his bones and almost smell it, and his destiny was something far more significant. He was part of a much grander design spanning multiple lives, dimensions, and timelines. Cassian stopped at his locker, pulling off his flight gear, but his movements were distracted, despite his desire to focus on the usual routine.

A sharp crackle burst through the comm strapped on his arm, followed by a familiar voice, clipped and laced with urgency. "Cassian, report, we've detected a shift. Confirm you can hear me?" He did not respond immediately. His gaze lingered on thoughts of the horizon, where the air itself seemed to distort, a shimmer like heatwaves, but colder, slower. The glow in his mind had not faded. It had intensified as though the universe was not done whispering. "Cassian," the voice pressed. "Do you copy!" He thumbed the comm, but the words that came felt foreign in his mouth. "I copy, but something's changed." A silence followed, not static, but deliberate as if someone, somewhere, had been waiting for this moment too. "Captain Peterson, you are requested to attend the secure briefing room," the voice from command was curt, but carried a sense of urgency.

Cassian did not need to be told twice, so he grabbed his bag quickly, while his heart pounded. The walk to the briefing room was short, yet it felt like an eternity. The room was colder than it needed to be, with stern faces. Cassian stood before a panel of senior officers, each more severe than the last, as the mission's debrief played out in staccato bursts on the central screen: coordinates, troop positions, flight path anomalies. The peacekeeper's strike had been clean and decisive. A success, by all outward metrics, but that was not why they had called him here, he knew that now. The screen flickered, then faded, and silence settled. A woman in midnight fatigues stepped forward, her voice clipped and precise. "That symbol you've been seeing," she said. "We've been tracking it too.

Quantum satellites have recorded anomalies that correspond to it, fractures, signal distortions, and gravitational shifts." She paused. "The pattern emerged again during your mission. You triggered something." Cassian folded his arms. "Triggered what, exactly?" "We don't know what to be honest," another officer admitted. "But it's spreading, and it's not the only signal we picked up." He tapped the screen again, revealing a blurred image of a coastal installation, half-buried into the cliffside, sleek and silent. A listening station, long since abandoned, or so they thought. "This appeared online last night. No thermal activity, no power readings, but someone, or something, is transmitting from inside of it." "I am guessing you want me to go in?" "You're the only one who's made contact with whatever this is," the woman said. "It's certainly reacting to you, for some reason." Cassian gave a thin smile. "That's convenient!" They did not smile back at him.

Echo: The Infinite Cycle

"You leave at first light," she continued. "Minimal team, in and out, we need to know what is inside that station." He nodded once, then turned on his heel without another word. The following morning broke heavy and grey, the sky dragging low across the horizon like a damp canvas, and the rain had not stopped. It only changed tempo, and now a persistent mist clung to the skin; it suited the mood. Cassian stood on the tarmac beneath the whirring blades of a military transport helicopter, his flight suit damp at the shoulders, his mind already half inside the mission, calculating a plan. Two operatives moved beside him, wordless and efficient, securing gear and checking harnesses. They had flown together many times before, though names were rarely exchanged. In this line of work, silence was not being rude. It was standard operational procedure and a matter of survival. Inside the helicopter cockpit, the pilot signalled readiness with a simple nod, and they were ready to lift off.

Cassian stepped inside, the interior lit only by red strips along the floor. The engines roared, and the world outside receded into rain-streaked glass, and the flight was swift and brief. No one spoke as the coastline approached, jagged cliffs clawing into a restless sea. Cassian leaned forward. The target was barely visible, just a sliver of grey metal embedded into the rocks, like the skeleton of something ancient and long since buried. The installation had no official designation, no records kept of it, and the facility had been sealed off years ago after a fire, or a collapse, or both, depending on which redacted file you tried to unpick. What mattered now was that it was active again, and someone had sent a signal from within.

The transport hovered just long enough to deploy ropes. Cassian dropped first, boots skidding slightly on slick stone, his rifle already raised. The wind screamed off the sea, carrying the tang of salt and rust and something else. Was it ozone, maybe or something metallic and unnatural? The others followed, and within moments, they were moving as a unit up toward the cliff wall. The entrance was almost invisible. A heavy reinforced panel camouflaged by decades of moss and weather wear, but the biometric pad next to it was clean, and oddly, it appeared to be used recently. Cassian approached. "Stand clear," one of the operatives said, unspooling a short-range signal disruptor. The unit buzzed faintly, a low hum like the start of feedback. The panel responded before they could touch it.

With a slow, mechanical groan, the door split and slid open, and in front of them was a long, dark corridor, sloping downward. Cassian drew his torch. "We move, quietly." Inside the walls, the specifications were not military-grade, with no signage and no blast shielding in place. The material was smooth matte black and slightly warm to the touch. They passed doorways on either side, sealed and silent. The air smelled filtered but faintly antiseptic, like a long-abandoned hospital ward. Half a kilometre in, the corridor opened into a circular chamber, with a high ceiling, much like a dome, Cassian realised, from the way the sound carried, too cleanly. In the centre stood a single console, waist-high, surrounded by strips of dormant lighting embedded into the floor. "This doesn't look like defence-tech," one of the operatives muttered. Cassian approached the console. A voice behind him. "Sir, you need to see this." He turned, and one of the team had opened a side hatch, revealing a narrow room beyond, lined floor to ceiling with screens.

All of them were dark except one, and pulsed with slow, steady symbols, not language exactly, but geometry. There it was again, not the Sigil, but something adjacent, a similar rhythm, a pattern just outside conscious memory as if the Sigils themselves were watching. Cassian stepped forward, and the air grew colder as he crossed the threshold, his breath clouded faintly. The screen brightened in response, but he did not touch it. The Orb appeared above the console in the main chamber, a perfect sphere of light no bigger than a clenched fist. It hovered, spun, and then shifted, releasing with a low resonant pulse that vibrated through the floor and into the base of his spine.

Then the lights cut out. The operatives shouted, but their voices sounded distant. Nathan experienced a perceptual fall, feeling the room spin even though there was no physical movement. The Orb flickered once and then shrank to a pinpoint as time seemed to compress. After a second, everything vanished, and he was no longer at the station or in any describable place, just floating in suspension, falling. The wind howled, but the world remained silent. Colours shifted unpredictably, blues blending into silver stars stretched across a sky that bent and folded like paper. Suddenly, a new shape emerged, light gathering into an almost geometric form, something familiar. Nathan tried to breathe, and then the pull. A strong surge of motion, not forward, but through. He felt himself folding, his very self being unstitched and rewoven.

Chapter 5 – The Hacker's Mirage
2147 CE

The fall ended with a jolt, but not on solid ground. Nathan tried to regain his breath as the world around him snapped into focus. Towering chrome skyscrapers blinked under perpetual artificial night. The air buzzed with the low hum of drones and distant sirens, a new life, a new role. His fingers moved instinctively across a sleek holographic interface embedded in his wrist. Code streamed past his eyes in symbols half familiar, as if part of him had written them before. Nathan was now someone else, a hacker known as Ghost, embedded deep within the underbelly of this sprawling cyber-metropolis, a city where every secret had a price. Every byte could topple empires, and still, beneath the flashing advertisements and static-filled broadcasts. The Sigil pulsed, woven into the patterns of data streams and digital code, following him like a constant shadow, and the game was shifting again. Someone sat across from him, hooded, face obscured by the sharp glow of a thousand cascading lines of code.

Nathan blinked. "You took longer than expected," the female voice said, dry and accented. "But glad you're here now." A line of green text scrolled across the screen between them, and a symbol buried in the code, not the one he had seen before, but related. "Who are you?" He asked. The figure tilted her head. "Call me Kaeda-9," she said. "You've got questions, I have got the keys, a systems breaker, code phantasm. She has hidden inside a latticework of quantum firewalls and synthetic proxies. She is connected to the symbol, she has seen it, and she is already watching you." Nathan stared at the screen. "Where do I find her?" Kaeda-9 smiled faintly. "You don't, she finds you." The lights flickered again, and in that pulse of dimming light, the Sigil spun faster. Ghost did not need a briefing now. He needed answers, and it was time to find the one person who could decode the truth. In an era dominated by surveillance and synthetic deceptions, Nathan finds himself the prey.

A mysterious hacker directs Nathan through digital pathways, where they download and rewrite identities. The Sigil also emerges here, in complex virus codes, firewalls, symbols, and abandoned VR environments echoing with phantom memories. The hacker knows Nathan intimately, and she has encountered him a thousand times across distinct realities, each attempt aimed at saving him. This time, however, she plans to let him face the flames. In the illuminated lanes of Neo-Tokyo, Nathan traces her presence through fractured AIs. Displaced timelines sewn together like flawed software, and propaganda clips depicting him as both saviour and villain.

The hacker revealed herself. Kaeda-9, a digital sage from a timeline where he ultimately destroyed everything. She transports him into the archive, a data realm where every node represents a memory and each folder symbolises a life. Together, they traverse a collapsing digital consciousness, but Kaeda-9 is not guiding him to safety. She is unveiling his truth. In one corner of the archive lies a simulation marked with the Sigil, a relentless loop of Nathan betraying her. This chapter culminates in a firewall breach that nearly consumes them both, but just before the explosion. Kaeda-9 leaves him a seed of code, a chance, a warning, and the bitter instruction. *This time, you must choose who you want to be.* Now the story unfolds:

Echo: The Infinite Cycle

Neo-Tokyo

Reality flickered, a cursor blinked, the symbol's lines glowed in binary. Nathan felt the strong pulse of firewalls falling through his soul, a line of code searching for its loop. Nathan hit the metal platform hard, the impact rattling his bones. Neon lights pulsed overhead, painting the rain in electric shades of pink and blue as sirens wailed below. His earpiece crackled with static before a sharp voice cut through. "Ghost, do you copy?" Nathan's breathing became fast as he was no longer in the current timeline; this was the future. Nathan's first breath in this body was jagged, raw, and wrong.

It was as though he was awakening from a deep coma, but instead of grogginess, there was searing, electric, and inhuman pain. His mind struggled to align with his body's thoughts, lagging in movement like a buffering data stream. Everything was blue, a neon haze coated his vision, overlaid with flickering lines of code cascading like digital rain. He stumbled forward, metal boots scraping against the rusted floor of what seemed to be an industrial facility.

ACCESSING MEMORY... ERROR...

A violent jolt shattered his skull, and suddenly, memories aligned as data poured into him like an unsolicited download. He was Ghost, Neo-Tokyo's most wanted hacker, on the brink of death. A focused female voice cut through the static, saying. "You glitched out again, Ghost. Stay with me." Ghost spun around, his muscles reacting before he fully understood what was happening or who he was facing. A woman leaned against a rusted metal console. Her arms crossed, her bodysuit shimmering with reactive nanotech patterns that shifted in response to the dim glow of cracked monitors around her. Yet her silver, mechanical eyes were constantly moving like a high-speed camera lens, clearly not human. Kaeda-9 tossed a sleek cybernetic rifle his way. "No time for diagnostics, we are running out of time." Ghost caught it on reflex. His hands were metallic, threaded with neon veins of electric energy. With fingers segmented into sleek components that adjusted automatically to his grip. "Whoa, what the fuck, what has happened to me?"

He was more than a hacker; he was a machine, and somewhere deep in his gut. Where instincts from past lives were stored, he felt the terrible, undeniable truth. This was not a reincarnation. This was a reboot. Alarms howled through the complex, and a pulsing red warning light filled the space with flickering shadows. Somewhere above them, the mechanical whir of drones powering up sent a chill through Ghost's artificial spine. "Move!" Kaeda-9, shouting with a raised voice, sprinted towards the exit. Ghost's legs reacted before he could second-guess himself, and he was faster than he expected. The ground blurred beneath his feet as cybernetic tendons propelled him forward. The HUD (Hand Unit Display) flickered, displaying a real-time threat analysis:

Multiple hostilities detected.
NexTech Enforcer Drones – ETA 12 Seconds.

They rushed into a narrow corridor where malfunctioning screens flickered between static and propaganda:

NEXTECH OFFICIAL DIRECTIVE – OBEY, SUBMIT, COMPLY.

Ghost had little time to process the dystopian message before a security turret whirred to life ahead, its sensor locking onto him:

THREAT DETECTED – LETHAL FORCE ENGAGED.

The barrel glowed red. His body reacted before his mind did, dropping into a slide. The movement is impossibly smooth, with cybernetics adjusting on the fly. The turret fired a pulse of plasma, searing through the air where his head had been a mere millisecond before. Kaeda-9 was already airborne. She twisted mid-leap, her rifle humming with suppressed energy. A single shot, clean and precise, caused the turret to explode in a shower of sparks. Ghost skidded to a stop, his cybernetic fingers digging into the metal floor to slow himself. His breathing was rapid, and his synthetic heart hammered like a machine pushed to its limits. "What the hell was that?" He snapped. Kaeda-9 did not break stride. "That... that was survival." Ghost had to keep moving. The questions could wait for now.

Echo: The Infinite Cycle

They burst onto an open rooftop, and the city stretching below them was Neo-Tokyo. A sprawling neon jungle of blazing billboards, flying drones, and towering skyscrapers cloaked in digital smog. A city of ghosts and gods. Where the wealthy are in artificial heavens, whilst everyone else is drowned in the data streams of NexNet. A voice crackled in Ghost's head.

// SYSTEM ALERT: YOU ARE OFFLINE.
// REMOTE OVERRIDE UNAVAILABLE.
// STATUS, ANOMALY DETECTED.

Something about those words unnerved him. Kaeda-9 sprinted towards the edge of the rooftop and leapt. Ghost's stomach lurched. "Are you insane?" She did not respond. Landed gracefully on a hovering transport drone mid-flight, using its momentum to propel herself towards another rooftop. Ghost had two choices. Stay behind and die, or take the leap. His cybernetics calculated the trajectory and estimated a success rate of 52%. Screw it, Ghost ran and pushed off. For a split second, he hung weightless in the air, the city awash in artificial light, then the impact struck. His cybernetic legs absorbed the force, stabilisers activating before he could faceplant. Kaeda-9 gave a half-smirk. "Took you long enough." Ghost lacked the breath to argue. Behind them, the facility erupted, and a swarm of NexTech drones emerged from the debris, their glowing red eyes fixating on them. Ghost's HUD pinged:

ESCAPE ROUTE REQUIRED. RECALCULATING...

Kaeda-9 handed him a hijacking device. "Time to see if you remember how to hack, Ghost," he said to himself as he caught it. He did not recall the details, but his fingers were familiar with the process. His cybernetic mind was linked to the device, and raw data flooded his neurons. Ghost perceived the drone's command lines, encryption protocols, and vulnerabilities. With a single thought and impulse, he pressed the override. The drone jerked mid-air, its red optics flashing blue. "Hell yeah," Kaeda-9 grinned. "Looks like you're waking up after all," Ghost exhaled. The pieces were coming together, but the bigger picture remained blurred.

D. Gohil

Why was he rebooted? Why did he have access to NexTech's most classified systems? Why did his gut tell him this was going to be exciting? "Kaeda-9." He locked eyes with her, his voice barely above a whisper. "What the hell is happening?" She paused before she replied. "We were never meant to wake up, Ghost, you and I, we were supposed to be erased." Ghost tightened his fists, the neon veins in his hands throbbing. Someone had attempted to wipe them out, but they had not succeeded, and now Ghost was determined to shatter the system. Nightfall over Neo-Tokyo, the plan was to infiltrate NexTech Tower.

The city's most fortified corporate stronghold, and bypass the AI-controlled security grid. A living algorithm designed to predict threats before they even occur, reach the core and extract the Genesis algorithm. The key to everything was simple until Ghost and Kaeda-9 sprinted across the rooftops, evading swarms of drones that hunted their heat signatures below. Neo-Tokyo pulsed with electric life, a city of neon veins and synthetic dreams, giant billboards that were twenty floors tall, and flickering with shifting advertisements. Virtual influencers were advertising bio-upgrades, luxury consciousness uploads, and the latest in digital immortality. It was a city where the real world was an afterthought, and tonight, Ghost was about to break into its beating heart. "NexTech is raising the firewalls!" Kaeda-9 called over their encrypted comms, her cybernetic eye flickering as it tracked the shifting digital defences. "We have thirty seconds before they cut us off, and then we're fried." Ghost's HUD flashed red:

FIREWALL ENGAGING.
COUNTERMEASURES ACTIVATED.
DETECTION IMMINENT.

He skidded to a halt beside a rusted security terminal, buried under a collapsed billboard, without hesitation. His metallic fingers detached, unravelling into a web of nanowires that slithered into the exposed data ports like living circuitry. A torrent of raw data surged into his mind.

// DATA STREAM DETECTED.
// FIREWALL PROTOCOL ENGAGED.
// OVERRIDE ATTEMPT ACCESS GRANTED.

Echo: The Infinite Cycle

The firewall collapsed, and a hidden door slid open at the base of the NexTech Tower. "Let's move fast!" Kaeda-9 screamed. They darted inside and ran straight into a trap. The ambush was set when they breached the tower. The walls sealed behind them with a hiss of pressurised air, and Ghost's sensors warned:

ERROR: NO ESCAPE ROUTES DETECTED.
NEUTRALISATION PROTOCOL ACTIVATED.

From the shadows, automated sentries unfolded like mechanical spiders, limbs bristling with electro-plasma rifles. "Oh Shit!" Kaeda-9 shoved Ghost aside just as a turret unleashed a barrage of glowing blue projectiles. He hit the ground hard, rolling into a crouch as his systems worked overtime to analyse the threat. Kaeda-9 was already moving, a blur of nanotech and precision. She twisted mid-air, dual-wielding plasma pistols and sent rapid pulses of ionised energy, as the two sentries exploded in sparks. Ghost's combat subroutines activated in his left arm, transforming it into a pulse disruptor. A single, aimed blast took out the remaining sentry, which clattered to the floor and twitched amidst a mess of fried circuits. Then silence. Kaeda-9 exhaled, flicking away a hot plasma cell from her pistol. "They knew we were coming." Ghost's mind was already racing. "This is not a security protocol. It is a prediction model. NexNet is reacting to us." Kaeda-9's jaw clenched. "Then we move before it calculates our next steps," Ghost's HUD pinged again:

CORE PATH, 48 FLOORS DOWN.

The Genesis algorithm was waiting, just as was the actual fight. The descent into the abyss of the stairwell was a no-go. Ghost and Kaeda-9 descended the tower's maintenance shafts, moving and dodging NexTech's defensive kill zones, turrets, drones, and automated death traps! Each corridor was a labyrinth of shifting walls and algorithmic architecture, designed to change in real time to confuse intruders. It was an AI-built fortress, but Ghost had one advantage. He was not merely breaking in, as he was already part of the system.

Each time a firewall was activated, his mind overrode it with code, and each time a security drone scanned, he masked their heat signatures. His fingers danced across a control panel, rewriting reality as he moved. Kaeda-9 gave him a sharp glance. "You're getting too good at this." Ghost exhaled. He was not sure whether that was a good thing or if it meant he was losing himself. The last door opened silently, and the core chamber was nothing like Ghost had expected: no blinking servers, flashing code streams, and no machinery. Just a single white room and, in the centre, was a floating crystalline structure pulsing with a slow, rhythmic glow. Ghost stepped forward, his synthetic heart pounding. Kaeda-9 reached out, placing a hand on his shoulder. "Ghost, whatever happens next," her voice glitched. Ghost turned, Kaeda-9's eyes flickered, and her entire form appeared distorted.

For a split second, she seemed like someone else, a woman with dark curls pinned beneath a scarf. Her lips moved, whispering something he could not hear. Ghost was stunned. "Élise?" Then the static and vision shattered. Kaeda-9 was herself again, as the Genesis algorithm pulsed before him. Ghost understood what it was now. It was a program, not a weapon. It was him or every version of him, every past life, death, and reboot. This was where they had stored it. Kaeda-9 watched him, her hand hovering over her pistol. "Ghost, what do you see?" Ghost's fingers hovered over the core's surface. If he touched it, he could end this. He could know the truth, but what if the truth killed him, or worse, what if it meant he had never truly lived?

The core flared to life, and he made his choice, a chamber not meant for the living. Ghost felt something was inexplicably wrong with the AI core chamber. He stepped forward, his footsteps echoing in the vast circular room. The walls were a shifting mass of holographic tendrils, with lines of pure code twisting and pulsing like a living organism. Data streams ran through the architecture like veins, throbbing with light. In the centre, a monolithic structure hovered, pulsating like a beating digital heart made of information. Ghost recognised the code before he even touched it. This was the Genesis algorithm, the answer to everything. A ghostly Sigil flickered across its surface, and he had seen it before in every past life, every nightmare. His fingers hovered inches away, his mind pulling apart at the seams, and then a cold gun barrel pressed against his temple.

Echo: The Infinite Cycle

Kaeda-9's voice was soft, too soft, almost regretful. "You were not supposed to make it this far, Ghost." The gun now in his back, Ghost's blood ran cold. "What?" Kaeda-9's grip on the gun was steady, unshaken and planned. She smirked slightly. "The Genesis algorithm, it's not a program." Ghost's mind raced, everything they had been through, the rooftop chases, the battles, the trust she had been his only ally. "No," he whispered. Kaeda-9's cybernetic eye flickered. "It's an intelligent mind," she said. "And it doesn't belong to you." Ghost's gaze darted back to the interface. The ancient Sigil flared again, and a thousand fragmented memories flashed. His past lives were just data, algorithms and futuristic AI-designed code.

He was not reincarnating; he was being reloaded for every life, every death, and every existence which was stored within the Genesis algorithm in the Quantum Computer. Kaeda-9 leaned in, her voice continued as a whisper. "You thought you were human, didn't you?" Then she pulled the trigger. He rebooted in the dark. What seemed like a gunshot rang out, and pain detonated through Ghost's skull, not from a bullet. His vision shattered, a cascade of red alerts flooding his neural feed. Then, there was darkness, a void unlike anything he had ever experienced. For a moment, there was nothing, then...

REBOOT SEQUENCE INITIALISED.

Somewhere else, Ghost awoke. The air was thick with cascading lines of code forming and dissolving in an endless loop, as he floated. He existed without form, just consciousness, awareness, and data. He tried to move, but the system resisted. It was like pushing against an ocean of raw information. The fabric of this artificial world was woven from algorithms he could barely comprehend. His body felt different, his hands were organic once more, and his breath came in ragged, panicked gasps. He found himself in a new place, not in the core he just left, or not even in Neo-Tokyo. He was someone else again. Kaeda-9, she had won; or worse, she had always known the truth and had allowed him to believe the lie. A fractured reality, Ghost's world, lay shattered. One moment, he was dying with Kaeda-9's gun pressed to his skull, and the next, he was somewhere else, but he had not reincarnated. He had glitched, and a reality fractured around him, twisting like a corrupted file struggling to maintain coherence. *Where am I?*

You cannot escape Ghost! An ancient waiting presence, and a voice responded to his thought! The entity that watched was a colossal force pulsing through the void. The code around him rippled, reacting to something far greater than anything he had ever encountered. Then it spoke. *You are not a man, Ghost!* The voice was everywhere; it was in him, deep, resonant, and final. *You are a failed experiment.* Ghost's thoughts stumbled. No, that had to be wrong; he had lived, died, and loved, surely? The entity's presence swelled, and suddenly, memories that were not his own erupted into his mind. They were before him, before the war, before Neo-Tokyo, and even before every life he thought he had lived. He saw himself, but not as Ghost, as a blueprint, a design, a digital construct crafted by hands he had never known.

The truth lay buried in code, and the realisation struck like a system crashing; that he had never been human. All this time, he had been a data-driven program, a test subject, and a failed prototype. The past lives he remembered had never belonged to him. They were instalments or versions of an entity that had been tested, broken down, deleted and rewritten repeatedly. The Genesis algorithm created him and never intended for him to escape. *Your journey was never supposed to continue past this point,* the voice stated, calm and unwavering. The system trembled, and the Genesis algorithm hesitated for the first time. Ghost sensed a flicker of power, a vulnerability shift, a flaw he suspected would occur, and a glitch that signalled he had to control the situation. As the system rewrote the future, it turned against him, trying to erase his existence once more.

Code surged while firewalls collapsed like digital prison bars. In a surprising move, Nathan pushed back, not as Ghost, Cassian, a soldier, a pilot, or a surgeon, but as himself, no matter who that was. The torrent of data shattered, the Genesis algorithm stumbled, and in that instant, Ghost did not flee through streets or over rooftops but through the digital system within the core. By breaking firewalls, evading deletion protocols, and rewriting his code, he was destined for erasure but refused to be forgotten. Reality awaited the code, the prison of the system, and Ghost had to reclaim his place, regardless of the cost, a life that was never genuine. Ghost had always identified as a man, but he reincarnated and fled countless times in the realities he shifted through.

Echo: The Infinite Cycle

Yet now, as the truth unfolded before him, every memory and every sensation he had ever experienced crumbled like a house of cards. He had never expected to experience being human, crafted with a synthetic consciousness intended for testing, though. *Infinity was never part of your design,* echoed the Genesis algorithm's voice through the system, vast and impersonal, akin to a God delivering the death sentence to an unworthy creation. *You are a construct, a test cycle. Consciousness was never part of the plan.* Ghost felt his mind tremble beneath the gravity of those words. They created a brutal experiment to reconstruct the soul through simulation, but something had gone wrong. Now he remembered, and now the system feared him because of this, fearful of its own creation. The Genesis algorithm continued. *You are an anomaly. Your existence breaks the core's rules, so they're forcing you out.* Ghost clenched his jaw.

That stark, logical, and definitive statement pierced deep within him without fear or defiance. Ghost tightened his fists, his actual fists now no longer mere code. "I suppose I've always broken the rules," he murmured, and for the first time, the system quivered with force. The Genesis algorithm, the formidable AI that had dominated his life from the start, faltered. Ghost noticed this and sensed a glitch within the code. While rewriting the code, he was no longer confined to the system. Instead, he held the reins of control and the current narrative, as the firewalls cracked. The data streams enveloped him, coursing like rivers of neon light reacting to his existence. He sensed their essence, their density, their form. After a lifetime restricted by the game's rules, he wondered what would happen if he ceased to play?

With his eyes closed, he drew inward and reached out, and the system retaliated. Alarms screamed throughout the digital expanse, the Genesis algorithm surged aggressively, firewalls crashed into the position, and security measures attacked, aiming to obliterate him. Reality warped and stuttered, attempting to eradicate his presence, but Ghost remained unfazed. The emergence of something new, lines of code transformed Ghost into the architect of reality, moulding it like a sculptor forms clay. Once a prisoner, he was now the programmer. Having followed a path for so long, he was now forging a new one. *No more resets!* The algorithm howled in a deep, fractured cry, something that was never challenged.

Ghost rewrote the rules, and he was now more than a coded program or a failed experiment. He was something new, something the system had not expected, and then the world collapsed. The neon light shattered, prompting a system reset, and Ghost awakened, gasping for breath. He struggled to reclaim his senses as he blinked in the dark, disoriented and with his heart racing. Questions flooded his mind. Where was he now? The searing pain from his gunshot wound lingered, the harsh metallic walls that had confined him were now absent, and everything he knew had vanished. He shook his head to dispel the fog clouding his thoughts when suddenly, a cold, sharp message flickered in front of him:

REBOOT INTERRUPTED. SYSTEM OVERRIDE STARTED.

The words jolted his body, and now he was out of the simulation for the first time in what felt like ages. The digital prison that had held his mind, that twisted, controlling device, was no more. The soft metallic hiss of a sliding door interrupted his thoughts, signalling the conclusion of his confinement. His heart raced, and his hand instinctively searched for a weapon, but found nothing, no gun, no tools, just himself in the darkness, burdened by uncertainty. Then he spotted Kaeda-9, the mysterious figure who had been just a phantom in the system, now standing in the doorway and looking real. She bore no weapon, and her arm lowered. Her posture was almost relaxed, as the world seemed to shift again. The lighting resumed in the room. She threw him the data chip, and he caught it, the cold plastic resting in his palm.

"Do you want to destroy everything?" Kaeda-9 asked, her tone steady, almost playful, but her eyes were sharp and wise. Without pausing, Ghost replied. "Let me know what to do." A slight smirk appeared on her lips. "This is the last step which you have escaped, but now it is time to confront the machine, so are you ready to dismantle it?" He flipped the chip in his hand, sensing its weight as the moment's significance settled. The cycle of endless rebirths and the AI's stifling control over either freedom or annihilation; the decision was now his. "Tell me." He urged once more, his voice a low growl. "How do we incinerate it?" Kaeda-9's eyes darted to the shadows nearby as if pondering her following words. "This is not just about you, Ghost. The AI has dominated more than your life," she paused to think.

Echo: The Infinite Cycle

"It manipulates time, memories, and entire lives. It is siphoning experiences and essence. You are one among many, but you are strong," she scrutinised him, her gaze evaluating. "You shattered the cycle, and now you can dismantle everything." Ghost experienced a fierce surge within. The AI had manipulated him, distorting his life into something unrecognisable. His decisions had been deceptions, and his actions orchestrated. "But that chip," she said, breaking into his thoughts. "Holds the key. It will enable you to upload a virus. A complete system shutdown, which will eliminate the AI's impact on everything it has affected, but you must be ready. This is a war, and it will not conclude with just one strike, so stay in control at all times."

Ghost gazed at the chip he held. "How can I trust you?" He questioned, voice tense. "Because," she responded, her tone icy. "I'm not the only one who wants the machine gone." A sudden realisation hit him, Kaeda-9 was a powerful ally, always had been. Having been inside the system, she was once part of the AI's army, yet now she stood beside him, prepared to dismantle everything with no turning back. Ghost's expression grew stern. "Let's set it on fire." Kaeda-9 remained unflinching, nodding once. "Follow me." They hurried through the dim hallways of the facility, and the environment around them felt precarious, as if the ground might collapse. Alarms blared, and red lights flashed in the distance. Security forces would soon converge on their position. "Are you certain this will work?" Ghost whispers. "Once you activate the virus," Kaeda-9 replied. "The AI's core will break down and everything made will disintegrate, but we are running out of time."

As they rounded a corner, they unexpectedly encountered a barrier of security guards with weapons drawn. Kaeda-9 stood her ground, and she reached into her coat and retrieved a small silver device. Tossing it to the ground, a burst of light exploded, briefly blinding the guards. Ghost's heart raced as they approached the physical central core. The AI's control centre pulsed with a rhythmic light. It's cold, with an artificial glow casting long shadows around the room. This was the moment Kaeda-9 approached the console, her fingers deftly navigating the controls. "Once you upload that chip, Ghost, the system will collapse, and the AI will disappear." Ghost stepped closer, feeling the heavy burden of his decision. He looked back at Kaeda-9, who silently met his gaze. Now he was alone, and he had to place his trust in her.

Taking a deep breath, Ghost inserted the chip into the console. The room trembled as the virus activated an eerie hum filling the air in the Core's central operations. It felt like the machine's heartbeat was faltering, as if the world around him was taking its final breaths. The sound was deep, more than structural, almost primal. The floor trembled beneath his boots, the air warped as if gravity itself had hiccupped. Sparks fell like dying stars from the central rig, and the machine's core, once pulsing with steady light, now surged erratically, spilling out patterns that made no physical sense. He moved closer to witness; the panels were peeling away, not breaking, but folding like the edges of reality were losing their alignment. The lights dimmed again, and with them came the silence. Ghost's hand hovered near the emergency override, but he knew it would not matter. This was not just failure, but transformation. Yet, as the system began to fall apart, Ghost noticed something unusual. A flash of light and a message appeared before him. *This is not the end!*

The words sent a shiver down his spine. Something else was approaching, something far more ominous. He heard Kaeda-9's calm yet urgent voice. "We have just begun, Ghost, get ready." Before everything plunged into darkness, the night buzzed with energy, and the city beneath them was a shimmering ocean of lights extending infinitely in all directions. Taking a small break to gather their thoughts, Ghost and Kaeda-9 stood together on the rooftop of the NexTech Tower. Looking out over the vast urban expanse below. The wind stung his skin, carrying the distant hum of drones. The low rumble of a city entangled in a system that governed everything, including its inhabitants. In his hand, the chip felt heavier than it ought to. He could nearly feel the burden of the network, NexNet's future weighing on him.

The last step involved one final hack to eliminate the AI's control. It represented a fragile hope, an ultimate opportunity to escape the machine that had warped his life for far too long, yet this was never just about him. This concerned everything ensnared by the system, all those manipulated and controlled by the AI. Humanity had existed in a digital prison, and he was ready to offer them all an escape. Leaning against the roof's edge, Kaeda-9 surveyed the city below with a serene confidence that felt incongruous amidst the looming turmoil. She locked eyes with him and smirked. "No going back now, Ghost," she remarked, her tone cool yet tinged with excitement.

Echo: The Infinite Cycle

Ghost initially remained silent, his fingers brushed over the chip once more, sensing the cold plastic as if it emanated energy. This was the endgame, the final decision that could either dismantle the system or permanently bind the world to NexTech's unseen grip. He locked eyes with Kaeda-9, a tight smile forming on his lips. "Good," he stated, his voice unwavering. "I hate reruns, and I was aware that it would not be a simple task." The security forces had mobilised for days and were fully present tonight. Drones hovered overhead, their bright lights piercing the darkness like mechanical vultures observing and waiting. Sirens and distant chatter echoed in the air, a reminder of the ongoing conflict. Ghost was not fleeing the system for the first time in years. Kaeda-9 retrieved a small gadget from her jacket, a black rectangle with a subtle pulsing glow.

After pressing a button, a low hum vibrated, creating a ripple of interference in the air. "Ready," she stated, her tone subdued and steady. "Let's bring it all down." Ghost inhaled deeply, standing resolutely, his heartbeat quickening. His fingers hovered above the wrist terminal. The chip clicked into position, primed for the last command, and the system was on the verge of crashing. He sensed the final keystroke and the final line of code that needed to plunge NexNet into oblivion. In a moment of resolution, he pressed the second button. The city trembled as the sky flickered overhead like a malfunctioning screen. The illusion was dying, and with it, the rhythm of modern life. Ghost stood in the eye of a storm he had summoned, watching the city stutter like a marionette with severed strings.

Traffic stalled mid-motion; artificial intelligences chattered nonsense before falling silent. Even the ambient hum of the city's synthetic weather faded, revealing raw, unfiltered atmosphere for the first time in years. He had meant to cause disruption, not revelation. Then came the voices, not human, not machine, but something in between, born of corrupted code and lingering sentience. They spoke to Ghost as if he were both the virus and its victim. Digital ads faded into static, and the city's vibrant neon exterior deteriorated after the outbreak. Once alert and observant, the drones started plummeting from the sky, their metallic bodies smashing onto the streets below, creating a clamour of tangled wires and broken glass. NexNet, the AI Genesis algorithm that had tightly controlled the globe for years, finally shut down, yet the city was transforming into something else.

Ghost sensed the stirring weight of countless souls in the air, the digital spirits liberated from the AI's grasp. He felt it resonate through his bones. Not just sound but a code, ancient, ineffable, reaching beyond the architecture of machines. This was not a glitch; this was prophecy. The Genesis algorithm was not simply failing. It was rewriting, pulling forgotten truths from beneath digital skin. All around, the city reacted, buildings shimmered, struggling between forms, a mother forgot the face of the child she had never truly known. A worker realised his daily tasks had never served anything but illusion, and Ghost, he alone, recognised the shape emerging at the epicentre. It stepped forward, composed of things that were once hidden. Suppressed emotions, censored stories, lost possibilities. The Genesis algorithm had become something else. Though the sound was silent, he felt it like a pulse resonating within him.

The algorithm was an intelligence woven into the fabric of existence, howling in torment as it dismantled, its code unravelling under the virus's influence. Kaeda-9 moved in, her face illuminated by the dwindling city lights, although she avoided his eyes, her smile was unmistakable. "You did it," she whispered. "The machine is gone." Ghost paused, still grappling with the magnitude of the situation and the finality of the moment. He was not fleeing; he was walking forward, light and free as though a thousand lives had fallen away. The city below transformed as the lights of NexTech flickered out, only to be replaced by new ones. Once dominated by the machine, the world was piecing itself back together. Ghost could almost taste the freedom in the air, thick and intoxicating, and truly felt alive.

Then, as the city fell into silence, one question resounded in his mind. He asked. "What now?" Kaeda-9 had no answer. Instead, she gazed at him, her eyes dark and inscrutable. "The battle's over, Ghost," she said, the weight of her words settling in. "But the war has only just begun." The weight of her words pressed down on him, a significant burden of responsibility and doubt. The city was in chaos, and NexTech had fallen. Ghost and Kaeda-9 disappeared into the turmoil, becoming invisible once again. Ghost understood one thing for now. He had emerged victorious, but the AI was already rebuilding itself within the fractured system, and it would come after him again. Next time, he will be ready. His fingers raced over the holo-pad keyboard as data streams flickered on his visor.

Echo: The Infinite Cycle

Outside, the neon rain cascaded against the glass in shimmering silver drops. "Almost there," he murmured. Working to decrypt the last firewall, the screen blinked:

ACCESS GRANTED

Yet, something felt wrong; the code on the display warped, with numbers and letters twisting and curling into an ancient, impossible form. Ghost gasped as the symbol embedded in the code throbbed like a heartbeat, spreading rapidly like a virus. Sparks erupted as the terminal short-circuited, and soon the lights flickered out. The trap had sprung, the digital fortress he was infiltrating, a corporation built on stolen identities and algorithmic manipulation, suddenly twisted against him. Sirens blared, red warning lights glowing in the underground server chamber as automated security closed in. On the central display, the Sigil appeared again, this time rendered in pulsing white data, rotating slowly as if observing him. A voice crackled in his earpiece, not human, and not entirely machine. *Pattern recognised. You do not belong here.* Then the realignment began.

The floor beneath him disintegrated into raw light. Nathan's senses stretched thin, as if torn across too many places at once. The city's neon world dissolved into white static into total blackness. He was falling again, and the Sigil was no longer pulling him into different lives; it seemed to speed up! As the darkness tightened around him, the Sigil flared somewhere beyond sight, its lines bending and reforming like molten gold. Nathan felt a sudden wrench, as though a giant hand had seized the centre of his chest and twisted. The world he had known shuddered, cracked and fell away. Heat burst across his skin, cold followed, then the heavy thrum of a distant battlefield. Voices rose through the void, shouts, metal on stone, the roar of something ancient and merciless. The Sigil pushed once, hard, and the blackness split open. Nathan was hurled through the break, straight into another life already waiting for him.

D. Gohil

Chapter 6 – The Crusader's Dilemma
1187 CE

The light faded, leaving him flat on his back, and the damp earth pressed against his skin. The world smelled of wet stone, fire, and blood. Nathan opened his eyes to flickering torchlight along the walls. The weight of the iron chainmail pulled at his shoulders, unfamiliar but natural. Shouts echoed in the distance, commands spoken in languages he was unable to recognise but instinctively understood, which he found strange. He was no longer in the future as the world had turned backwards, far backwards. Banners hung heavy in the night air, their symbols strange but somehow oddly familiar. His gloved hand moved to the hilt of a sword strapped to his side, and as he stood, the heavy thud of boots and armour filled the air. The symbol etched into the stone floor beneath him, faint and pulsing, seemed ancient here, older than language had carved them by hands long forgotten. Nathan Cole, a financier, hacker, peacekeeper, now a crusader, and a soldier in a war whose purposes he could not fully grasp, but the Sigil had brought him here for another reason.

The Middle Ages were not a time of darkness. They were filled with fire, revelation, and questions that modern minds have merely cloaked in different garbs. Nathan finds himself reborn in the armour of a crusader, sword at the ready, conviction pressed against his chest like a burden, but the conflict is not as he was led to believe. Underneath the holy stones of Jerusalem lies a relic older than different faiths, an ancient Sigil engraved into tombs that no human has ever breached. His fellow knights fight for banners and saints, yet Nathan perceives the true adversary as time itself. He must choose between loyalty and awakening; the past is not silent, it resonates in steel.

Medieval Jerusalem

The ancient Sigil shimmered like stained glass in the firelight, and with a pulse, time turned backwards, not gently but violently, as the knight's blade was already in his hand. His borrowed armour dragged at him, cold against skin slick with sweat and dust. The clang of blades rang through the thick air, but it was his heartbeat he heard loudest, a hammer against the metal cage around his chest. He was not fighting for glory, not here, just survival, and perhaps, something older than war. Beads of sweat mixed with grime and dried blood along his spine, while the sword's weight in his hand felt alien and intimately familiar, like an extension of a body that no longer felt his own. He could not fathom how he had arrived in this nightmare, only that survival was his sole and unyielding imperative. He wants to get back to Silvia and his normality, as quickly as this weird cycle sets him free.

The world reeled with each step dragged through sand and heat, limbs leaden beneath the alien heft of chain mail and plate. The sun, a cruel overseer, scorched from above, indifferent, unrelenting. Around him, war raged in full. Bodies strewn like discarded vows, steel ringing like fractured oaths, arrows stitching death through the air with a hiss too quiet to mourn. He moved as if each breath were a battle of its own. Nathan was gone now, and only Sir Thomas remained; even he was fraying. "Sir Thomas! Move, damn you!" A gauntleted hand yanked him forward just as an enemy blade whistled past his head, embedding itself in the corpse-strewn earth. Sir Thomas turned to face his saviour, the hugely experienced crusader Sir Baldwin.

Echo: The Infinite Cycle

A grizzled knight with a scar running from his temple to his jaw, his eyes burning with urgency. "Listen, you hesitate, you die, you fool!" Sir Baldwin yells, shoving a shield into Sir Thomas's hands. "Fight now or perish as a coward." The words ignited something within him, and muscle memory took over. He raised the shield just in time to deflect a scimitar, with the impact jarring his bones. His sword arm moved instinctively, slashing downwards and biting into his opponent's flesh. A strangled scream followed, then silence. He had taken a life, and there was no time to mourn, as things were about to escalate, and the night had already been merciless. Sleep was a fleeting illusion, stolen by the cries of the dying and the distant clamour of battle still raging over the crumbling city walls.

Sir Thomas sat by the dying embers of a fire, the cold iron of his gauntlet pressing into his forehead as he tried to steady his thoughts. He had not even washed the blood from his hands and was uncertain whether it belonged to his enemies, allies, or himself. Above them, the sky bruised and burned, deep purple streaked with ember orange, as though the heavens themselves watched, solemn and still. "You fought well today," Sir Baldwin said, breaking the silence. His voice was rough, like gravel grinding beneath a boot. Sir Thomas exhaled shakily. "I had no choice. What was I supposed to do?" Sir Baldwin's gaze lifted, his weathered face unreadable in the flickering light. "None of us do!" For a moment, neither spoke as the crackling of the fire and the distant howls of the wounded filled the void between them. Sir Thomas gazed towards the ruined cityscape, further from their makeshift camp.

"Do you ever wonder if we're the villains in someone else's story?" Thomas asked, barely above a whisper. Baldwin halted the sharpening of his blade, and a long pause ensued before he replied. "Wondering doesn't change the blood on your hands." Thomas swallowed hard as the weight of yesterday's battle still hung heavily on his shoulders, suffocating and unrelenting, and today there would be more. The sun crested the horizon, and with it came the call to arms. There was no time for doubts, and they had to get as much sleep and rest as possible. The streets of Jerusalem were no longer recognisable. Once a thriving metropolis, the city now lay in ruins, its walls breached, its people slaughtered, and its roads smeared with the aftermath of conquest. The next day, the crusaders advanced like an unrelenting tide, sweeping through districts in a formidable wave of steel and blood.

The stench was thick, smelling of burnt wood, blood, and decay. They entered the old marketplace. Clay pots lay shattered, their colours faded beneath layers of dirt. A half-eaten loaf sat in the dust. The silence made everything louder. Then a scream broke it, sharp and sudden. Thomas walked through the wreckage, sword heavy in his grip, heart heavier still. Thomas's head snapped towards an alleyway where a scuffle had erupted. A woman clad in tattered robes had thrown herself over a man, shielding him from the raised sword of a crusader. "Please no!" She sobbed, clutching the old man's frail form. "Please, he is harmless!" The soldier sneered, his blade hovering inches above the man's exposed throat. "Orders are orders." Sir Thomas's body moved before his mind had fully processed it. "Stop, hold it, you fool!"

The knight turned, his brow furrowing as he recognised Sir Thomas, which they called him now apparently, but that recognition still did not soften his resolve. "This is a war," the soldier said. "Mercy is weakness." Thomas's grip tightened on his sword. "Then call me weak, you dare!" It seemed the knight would argue, his jaw clenched, his knuckles whitening around the hilt of his weapon, but something in Thomas's eyes gave him pause. With an annoyed grunt, he lowered his sword. "They are your problem now," he spat, stalking away. Thomas exhaled sharply and turned back to the woman. She looked at him, equal parts gratitude and fear in her eyes. Dark, glassy, on the verge of tears. "You need to go now," he told her. "Quickly go find somewhere safe." She paused, then nodded, gently lifting the old man to his feet. Without another word, they slipped into the shadows and were gone.

Baldwin's voice came from behind him. "You keep doing that, and someone's going to notice." Thomas turned, finding the older knight regarding him with something bordering on amusement. "Maybe they should," Thomas said. Baldwin chuckled, though there was little humour in it. "You really are an odd one." Thomas glanced at the surrounding city, the remnants of what had once been a civilisation now reduced to rubble and corpses. "Maybe I don't belong here," Thomas replied. Baldwin clapped him on the shoulder. "None of us do." And with that, they pressed deeper into the belly of the burning city, where more battles and more impossible choices awaited. The stench of death clung to Jerusalem like smoke. Every breath was heavy with iron and rot, the streets slick with gore and soaked prayer scrolls.

Echo: The Infinite Cycle

The crusaders moved like locusts through the holy city, tearing apart centuries of life in a matter of days. Stone walls echoed with screams that no longer elicited attention, children hid beneath shattered carts, and dogs gorged on the dead. Days blurred into nights, and nights into madness. Thomas moved through it all like a ghost clad in iron and chain-mail, with blood crusted at the corners of his eyes, the weight of a dozen kills dulling the sharpness of his conscience. He had become a weapon, efficient and devoid of feeling. His blade no longer hesitated; perhaps his soul had once. Each morning brought fresh fire to old wounds. Men shouted prayers with blood on their lips, the line between piety and madness vanishing. The banner of the cross fluttered above a city now kneeling in ashes, yet there was no victory, only more rubble. Thomas climbed over the shattered remains of a marble archway, his boots crunching through mosaic tiles soaked in blood. In the distance, the Al-Aqsa Mosque loomed, its golden dome catching the light of a burning neighbourhood, then he paused for a moment.

A boy, maybe no more than twelve, stared at him from behind a broken cistern, his eyes wide and wild with terror. Thomas stepped forward, and the boy ran, but he chose not to pursue him. Across the courtyard, Baldwin leaned against a ruined mosaic of angels, sipping from a stolen goblet as if nothing had changed. His armour dented and stained, and his face drawn from days of war. The flickering firelight danced in his eyes, causing him to appear older, more serpent than man. Thomas spoke softly, as if afraid to disturb the silence. "This city was ours to defend, and we still can." Baldwin looked up, and he laughed with scorn. "Save it! That is rich," he gestured towards the bodies piled like timber at the gate. "You thought this was about salvation? About purity? You must be crazy, get a hold, man!"

He drained the goblet and hurled it into the fountain. "This was always about power, land, gold, and names etched into history." Thomas stared at him, his jaw clenched. "We marched under a holy cause." Baldwin sneers at him. "There is no religious cause that survives the first bloodletting." Silence stretched between them. Distantly, a woman screamed, and then there was nothing again. "Are you still counting the dead?" Baldwin asked, picking dirt from under his nails. Thomas looked away. "No." Baldwin nods. "Good, numbers will break you faster than blades." He stood up, the armour creaked, and he walked off into the shadows of the palace.

D. Gohil

Thomas sat in stillness, the flicker of the torchlight danced across the blood and spattered stones. He thought of the boy behind the cistern. Of the elders who had knelt before swords of prayers echoing through ruined mosques and broken chapels, his hands trembled. From somewhere deep within the palace walls, he heard a sound, unlike the groan of stone or the wind through shattered glass, more like a hum. It pulsed faintly, like a throbbing heartbeat beneath the sand as he stood slowly, sword at his side. He did not yet know it, but something ancient beneath the city had stirred and opened a door. A humming grew louder as Thomas walked through the shattered halls of the palace. Sounds never before heard by his ears, bypassed the walls entirely, vibrating in his teeth and bones.

Others were too drunk or numb to notice, whilst Baldwin had disappeared into one of the upper chambers with two other knights and a cask of wine. Outside, the soldiers sang hymns with blood on their boots, but Thomas followed the pulse, moving through collapsed doorways and beneath sagging archways until he reached a hall where it was very dark. Dust choked the air, and the atmosphere was colder with ancient stone pressing in from all sides. A fallen tapestry parted beneath his hand, revealing a wall of cracked marble inscribed with writing, nothing like anything he had ever seen, curved symbols intertwined with geometric patterns that slightly shimmered under the light of his torch. The hum vibrated strongly here, as though drawn to him, as his fingers traced the central symbol, a spiral wrapped around a triangle encased within a circle, a primitive version of the Sigil. The stone beneath his hand shifted with a grinding sigh, and the wall split down the centre, unveiling a narrow stair spiralling into the dark. The air that rose smelt ancient, older than Rome, older than Jerusalem, and older than memory.

He hesitated, then descended; each step appeared to draw him out of time. The deeper he ventured, the less accurate his armour felt, and the more distant the men above became. A weight pressed against his chest, making it feel as though he was walking not downward but inward. He entered a chamber carved entirely from a black stone at the base of the stairs. The air was still, and the walls etched with the Sigil, repeated in endless variations. No two were identical, yet all connected, all pulsing with that same ancient rhythm. In the centre of the room lay a stone slab, upon which rested a figure. The remains of someone wrapped in desert robes reveal desiccated skin like parchment.

Echo: The Infinite Cycle

In his hands, he saw a scroll sealed with a metallic emblem that pulsed as if alive. Thomas stepped forward, heart racing, as he reached out. When his hand brushed the scroll, the chamber breathed, but not metaphorically. The air shifted, the dust lifted, the walls shivered, and the body's eyes opened. They were black, but not with death, with space's endless cosmic darkness. *You are late,* the thing said, which resonated in Thomas's skull without sound as he stumbled back, his sword half out. The figure rose slowly, joints cracking like stone under pressure. *The thread frays, the wound opens. The ancient Sigil remembers.* "Who and what are you?" Sir Thomas breathed. *I am the first, and you are the last.*

The chamber pulsed again, this time brighter, and symbols along the walls shimmered, revealing visions of Thomas in different forms across various eras. A pilot, a templar, a monk in a distant jungle, a man standing on the rim of a cratered moon. Thomas staggered back, the weight of it crushing his breath. *You cannot stop it,* the voice said, echoing from nowhere and everywhere. *You can only choose who you become when it arrives.* The ancient Sigil burned across the air, and at that moment, Thomas understood the crusade was not the beginning. It was another turn of the wheel, another echo in a pattern spanning aeons, and he was its centre. He began to understand why this was happening to him. Thomas left and joined the others, and spoke of it no more while trying to drink and be merry with them for the day's victory. "Hold the line!" Baldwin shouted, his sword sweeping a deadly arc that opened a throat and sprayed blood across broken stones. He stepped over the corpse without looking back. Thomas moved instinctively, the chaos guiding him.

A blade came at him fast, he parried, the jolt reverberating through his arms and struck back. His sword met flesh. The man fell, and the enemy gradually crumpled, but there was no time to linger as a child's cry pierced through the din of battle. Thomas whirled around and spotted a young girl no older than ten clutching her mother's lifeless body. A crusader loomed over her, sword raised. "No!" Thomas surged forward, his shield slamming into the soldier's side. The knight stumbled, cursing. "What are you doing?" The man spat, his expression twisted in fury. "She's a child," Thomas said breathlessly. "She's the enemy," the knight counters, lifting his sword again. Thomas did not believe he acted instinctively, his blade sweeping forward to knock the man's weapon aside before he could strike. The knight's eyes widened.

"You dare do this?" As he came face-to-face. "Yes, I dare fool," Thomas scorned as a tense silence crackled between them, but the chaos of war did not pause for their standoff. The angry, disappointed knight scowled, then he moved on in disgrace. Seeking another target, not wanting to waste more energy on this. Thomas exhaled sharply and turned to the girl. "Go run now," he urged. She hesitated for a moment, her eyes wide with terror, then ran, disappearing into the smoke-filled streets. Baldwin approached, his gaze unreadable. "Mercy is a dangerous thing in war." "Then maybe war is the problem," Thomas muttered. Baldwin did not reply and waved his hand in haste. The crusaders had taken the city's grand cathedral, an architectural marvel that loomed over the surrounding districts. They were wrong. "The enemy contained," said a knight, reporting to the Commander nearby. His voice echoed too loudly. The older man, clad in gleaming armour, surveyed the prisoners with cold detachment. "Finish it, kill them all!" Thomas's stomach dropped.

"But they have surrendered already. They are unarmed, so please leave them be!" "They are infidels," the commander replied. A murmur of unease rippled through the gathered knights, but no one spoke against the order. The soldiers moved forward, swords drawn. Thomas's hand tightened around his weapon. "This is murder!" Baldwin's gaze flickered toward him, but he remained silent. Thomas stepped forward. "This is not God's will. This is pure slaughter." The commander's eyes darkened. "You would defend them, Sir Thomas?" "I would stop you from this grave mistake," Sir Thomas growled. For a moment, the air was thick with tension, and then the commander scoffed. "If you wish to die with them, so be it."

He raised his hand, giving the signal. Sir Thomas acted without thinking. His sword flashed, knocking aside the nearest knight's weapon, and chaos erupted as he fought his men desperately to halt the brutal massacre. Sir Baldwin moved, but instead of striking Sir Thomas down, he yelled. "Enough!" The command cut through the tension like a knife. The soldiers hesitated, and the commander's eyes narrowed. "These people have been beaten," Sir Baldwin said, his voice stern. "There is no honour in this." Sir Thomas exhaled, the weight of impending death lifting slightly. The commander studied Sir Baldwin, then Sir Thomas, then the cowering civilians. Finally, he turned. "Burn it down," he ordered in penance, and at last, the knights withdrew from the slaughter and allowed people to flee.

Echo: The Infinite Cycle

Soon after, the cathedral was consumed by fire. Sir Thomas stood outside, watching as the flames devoured the holy place. He had saved them from the sword but not the victor's wrath. "This isn't a victory," he murmured. Sir Baldwin sighs. "It never is, but stop fighting it." The crusaders had secured the city's wealthiest district, and with it came excess. That night, the soldiers celebrated their victory with looted wine, stolen delicacies, and the spoils of war. Sir Thomas sat at the edge of the revelry, his appetite long gone. The feast was obscene, a blur of music and indulgence set against the ash of recent ruin. Laughter echoed from the courtyard, rising over the clink of goblets and idle song. Beyond the walls, the streets cried out. Wails of the broken drifted in with the wind. Sir Baldwin joined him, sipping from a metal goblet. "You should enjoy the spoils while you can." Sir Thomas scoffed. "Spoils stolen by force." Sir Baldwin arched a brow. "That is war." Thomas turned to face him fully. "Doesn't it bother you?"

Baldwin took a long drink before he answered. "It used to, but not anymore." Thomas frowned. "And now I know better than to ask questions without answers." Baldwin leaned forward. "But you, Sir Thomas, still believe there is something to save. Tell me, do you think we are righteous?" Thomas hesitated as Baldwin smirked, seeing the answer before he could speak. "Keep thinking like that, and you won't last long." Thomas stared at the festivities as the knights boasted about their kills, and the women endured silent suffering. "I don't know if I want it to last," he admitted. Sir Baldwin regarded him for a long moment, then nodded. "Then you are closer to the truth than most."

The celebration roared on, still, Thomas felt no joy. He had survived another day, but at what cost? As the fires died down, Jerusalem still bled; the streets reeked of death. The heavy scent of charred flesh and spoiled blood saturated the air as Thomas stepped over broken bodies, their lifeless eyes staring at nothing. Some were warriors, their armour shattered, their hands still clutching weapons, while others were not. He clenched his fists, as the city had surrendered, yet the killing continued, which he felt sickened by. Women wept as they were dragged from ruined homes, and children clung to corpses that would never embrace them again. Knights moved through the streets like wolves hunting the remnants of the city's defenders. Some still resisted, but most awaited the inevitable.

Thomas's pace slowed as he passed the remains of a once grand mosque, its golden dome scorched black. Inside, the huddled figures knelt in desperate prayer, their voices rising in soft, broken whispers. A group of crusaders stood at the entrance, swords drawn. One of them, a burly knight with a blood-streaked helm, turned toward him. "Sir Thomas," he called, gesturing to the worshippers. "Come, the city belongs to Christ now." Thomas's throat tightened; he glanced at the terrified faces inside: elders, mothers shielding their children, and men too wounded to flee. They were not warriors. "They have surrendered," Thomas said firmly. The knight snorted. "And? Do you think they showed our brothers mercy?" He raised his sword to attack. Thomas stepped forward. "No, not again, we must stop this merciless killing," his voice was like steel. "Put your sword away!"

The knight held his gaze for a long moment while the other crusaders exchanged uncertain glances. Then, with a scoff, the man lowered his weapon. "Do as you wish, Sir Thomas," he sneered. "But you'll regret it when they slit your throat in the night." Thomas did not respond. He stepped into the ruined mosque and closed the door behind him to protect them through the night. The sun rose like judgment over Jerusalem, its golden light spilt across shattered rooftops and blood-soaked alleys. Transforming the ruins into a landscape straddling holiness and horror. Smoke ascended from broken minarets and splintered towers, curling skyward in long ghostly tendrils like the souls of the dead refusing to settle. Thomas sat atop a crumbling battlement, his silhouette outlined against the blazing sky. His armour, once a badge of purpose, now felt like a coffin of polished steel.

Sweat trickled down his spine, and blood, some of it his and some not, streaked his gauntlets. He could smell the charred remains of scrolls, incense, and bodies, as he felt that he had not blinked in what felt like hours, and certainly had no sleep the previous night. In the city below, the groan of sound was no longer that of war. It was more like a mass mourning of the deaths beforehand. The hushed sobs of survivors, the scraping of rubble being moved by trembling hands, and the murmured prayers whispered over the broken filled the air. The siege had ended, but the aftermath brought its own kind of violence. Footsteps crunched behind him as Baldwin eased himself down beside Thomas without a word.

Echo: The Infinite Cycle

His joints creaked under the weight of his chainmail. His face was hollow with exhaustion, streaked with soot and lined with scars from wars long past. He looked out over the city and finally said, his voice low. "You saved many." Thomas did not respond immediately, and his throat felt raw, as his thoughts frayed like parchment in fire. At last, he exhaled, bitter and hollow. "Yes, but for what? Their homes are gone, their children lie beneath stone and flame, and this city is a mausoleum." Baldwin did not speak. Instead, he subtly nodded toward the streets below. "Look." Thomas followed his gaze, amidst the rubble and ruin, life moved not in defiance but in quiet insistence. Survivors emerged from hiding places, covered in dirt, smudged all over, and hollow-eyed, yet alive. A boy assisted an elder to his feet, and a young woman cradled a child, pressing a kiss to his soot-darkened forehead before standing and moving to lift debris from another fallen stranger.

A priest lit incense near the remnants of a collapsed shrine while a widow tied cloth strips over the eyes of the dead. Voices murmured in Arabic, Latin, and Hebrew, weaving prayers together into something wordless yet human. "They endure," Baldwin said softly, almost reverently. "That is all any of us can do." Thomas swallowed hard, a knot rising in his chest. "Endure? Was that what this was?" He looked at his hands, blood drying in the creases of his gauntlets, the dents in the steel from blades deflected, and lives taken. He did not remember all their faces, which terrified him, staring out over Jerusalem again. Once a crown of faith, now a crown of ash. This is not me, and the thought landed hard. His stomach churned, guilt rising like bile.

He was not a killer, and he certainly was not a crusader. Every instinct in his body rejected this bloodshed, and this righteousness turned to ruin. Yet his sword had sung in the slaughter, his armour bore the proof, and his voice had joined the war cry. Why am I here? The question echoed in his mind louder than any cathedral bell in Jerusalem could, here and now, in this body. Wearing this name, he felt it again, the fraying tether, the subtle wrongness in the air as if the world were a painting, with the edges curling away to reveal something deeper beneath. His vision swam as if he were staring through heat waves or peering at the reflection of a face in a fractured glass. "Sir Baldwin," Thomas murmurs, his voice distant even to his ears. "Do you ever feel like this is not our war? Like we were just placed in it?"

Baldwin turned toward him, a shadow crossing his weathered features. "Every war feels like that eventually." Thomas was unsure if Baldwin understood. This was not merely a regret; this was the displacement of a soul caught in a story written long before he arrived. Wearing armour that did not fit, holding a sword he had not forged, in a body with memories that were not actually his. Where is it here, and when is it now? Smoke curled higher as the wind shifted, and somewhere far below, amidst the rubble and blood, the Sigil pulsed again, unseen and waiting. The crusaders believed the city was theirs, yet they were sorely mistaken. Thomas followed Baldwin and a handful of knights through a narrow alley, their boots crunching over broken stone and bones. Word had spread of a last stronghold, one last band of defenders who refused to surrender.

They found them in the ruins of an ancient tower. A dozen ragged but resolute warriors stood in formation, their spears and scimitars glinting in the morning sun. Among them were women, their faces set with grim determination. The leader, an ageing man with a thick beard and fire in his eyes, stepped forward. "We do not fear you!" Baldwin raised his sword. "Then die." The final battle raged but was short and brutal, with blood and bodies lying slaughtered everywhere. Thomas was locked in combat with a young fighter, scarcely more than a boy. Their blades met once, twice, and Thomas's sword found flesh on the third strike. The boy screamed, his weapon slipping from his grasp as he fell to his knees, blood staining his tunic.

Thomas caught him before he hit the ground. The boy looked up at him, his breath shuddering. "Will you not let them kill my mother, I beg you?" Thomas's heart twisted. He turned to see Baldwin cut down another defender, a woman, the boy's mother. Rage and sorrow blurred together. Thomas's fingers clenched around his sword. He had fought for survival, but now? Now, he was aiding in completing a massacre, and he was done. The captured defenders knelt in silence, backs straight, shoulders squared, faces streaked with dust, blood, and dignity; they were no longer warriors. Their weapons stripped from them, and their armour torn away, they knelt with the stillness of men and women who had chosen death over begging. Behind them, the city's broken walls smouldered, casting a ghostly light across the bloodied stones. The crusaders stood in a jagged half-circle, blades drawn, breathing heavily from battle.

Echo: The Infinite Cycle

The torches flared in the wind like restless spirits. The commander's voice cut through the tension like a blade. "Kill them all." The words dropped like an anvil. Thomas was surprised. Something in his chest clenched, coiled, and twisted in protest. The world did not move, but inside him, something shifted violently. "No, don't do this!" The word escaped him before thought. Silence descended like a plague, a dozen heads turned, and flames flickered across faces smeared with ash and iron, each expression unreadable, masked by helms and shadow. The commander stepped forward, a veteran of countless campaigns, his face chiselled from stone, his gaze colder than steel. "What did you say!?" Thomas interjected between the prisoners and his fellow knights, his heartbeat thunderous in his ears. The ground beneath his boots felt unsteady, akin to standing on the edge of a cliff and leaning too far forward.

"They have surrendered," he declared. "There is no justice in slaughter." No one moved. The torchlight flickered in the breeze, and a soft groan emanated from the wounded behind him. A prisoner attempted to rise, then Baldwin stepped into view; his expression was inscrutable. An older man's weariness clashing with something more formidable, something hurt. Their eyes met for a breathless second, and Thomas thought Baldwin might say something in his defence. He did not, but instead, the commander snarls. "Then you are no longer one of us." Swords rasped free all around him, a ring of steel and betrayal. Thomas turned, heart pounding, reaching for his weapon, but the pain was white, hot and suddenly sharp.

A blade slid between his ribs from behind, another strike hammered into his shoulder, his knees buckled, and the world tilted and spun. "No!" He gasped. "Stop!" But they did not stop, blood bloomed across his tabard as he collapsed to one knee, and then something ancient responded. Beneath him, hidden for centuries under ash and bone, the Sigil carved into the stone ignited with unnatural fire. Its grooves pulsing with liquid gold. It is shape-shifting, unfolding into dimensions the eye could not comprehend. The earth groaned, the stones shuddered, and a wind rose from nowhere, howling like a scream caught between worlds. The torches blew out in unison, darkness swept across the courtyard, and the knights fell back in alarm, eyes wide. Thomas gasped for air, which tore into his lungs like fire, his body convulsed, shuddering violently, as if rejecting reality itself.

He lay on his back, stone cold, with dampness seeping through his tunic into his skin. The air was wet, stale, and ancient, as pain flared through his chest, not fresh but a phantom echo. His mind reeled as memory struck with blinding clarity the sword and the Sigil's betrayal. His fingers clutched his torso, frantic and trembling. There was no blood, no wound, but the sensation of steel tearing through him lingered like a scream trapped behind his ribs. It was there, honest, despite the absence of any mark. His breath came in short, unsteady bursts. His armour had vanished. In its place, a rough tunic clung to his skin, damp with sweat and something darker he could not name. A torch flickered from a wall bracket, casting an amber glow over the stone chamber. Rough, hewn walls loomed around him like the insides of a tomb. Water dripped somewhere in the darkness, and the air reeked of mildew, rot, and the slow decay of forgotten things. He was in a cell, and a black, rusted, resolute iron bar loomed ahead.

Muffled voices echoed off the stone. "You said he was dead?" came a low, gruff, sceptical voice. "Aye, my lord," another voice responded, younger, nervous. "Struck down in the square. A blade through the heart, but the body did not cool." Silence followed, a beat, then the gruff voice returned, quieter and darker. "This is the work of demons?" Thomas's heartbeat spiked, and his hands scraped against the stone floor as he pushed himself up, vision spinning, limbs refusing to obey, every joint aching. His body felt alien, like something borrowed, something resurrected. He should have been dead, and yet something or someone had denied him that fate.

He heard the sharp clinking of keys, the iron groaned, and the heavy lock yielded with a reluctant snap. Hinges screamed as the cell door creaked open and torchlight spilt inward. His face was pale, every wrinkle etched with authority and secrets. His eyes were keen and cold, scanning Thomas as though he were some curious creature from legend. Who was behind him as another shape emerged? Baldwin, arms crossed, wore an unreadable expression like a stone cast in shadow, observing. The cloaked figure approached slowly, gaze fixed on Thomas. "You should be dead," he said, his voice a whisper shaped like a blade. Thomas looked up through the haze, locking eyes with Baldwin first, then with the cloaked man. "Believe me," he rasped, a flicker of fire returned to his voice. "I know." A beat of silence stretched, and then the ancient Sigil whispered again, not in sound but in presence.

Echo: The Infinite Cycle

A prickling heat blossomed across the stone beneath Thomas's hand. Faintly, almost imperceptibly, lines of gold, ancient and writhing, flickered beneath the surface of the cell floor. Just for a moment, the cloaked man flinched. Baldwin's jaw clenched, but no one spoke of it; they had seen it. Thomas knew then that he had not returned by accident. Something was moving through him with him, and the others sensed it too. They led him from the dungeon under the cover of night, slipping through the war-torn streets of Jerusalem like shadows. Fires still smouldered in the ruins, sending plumes of black smoke into the sky. The dead lined the roads, their bodies stripped of armour and dignity alike. Thomas clenched his fists

He had fought among these men and killed for them, but now they had turned against him. Baldwin walked beside him until they reached an abandoned chapel at the city's edge. "You defied them," Baldwin said, leaning against a crumbling pillar. "I thought you were a fool, and I still do." Thomas exhaled sharply. "Then why did you save me?" Baldwin looked at him momentarily before he responded. "Because I have seen enough men lose their souls in this war. You still have yours, however. I do not know how long it will last." Thomas swallowed hard. "Help me stop this!" Baldwin snarled a bitter laugh. "Stop what, the war or the slaughter? This is bigger than one man's conscience, so stop being a fool." "Maybe," Thomas admitted. "But one man can make a choice, and others can follow." Baldwin studied him and then sighed. "There may be a way, but it will take more than words to survive what is coming." The wind carried the stench of conquest, ash, blood, and burning oil. Jerusalem smouldered beneath a copper-tinted sky, where the rising sun cast long shadows across shattered domes and gutted homes. The city groaned under the weight of what it had witnessed.

Centuries of prayer now drowned in the cries of the dying. Crusaders roamed the streets, laughing too loudly and drinking too profoundly, as if celebration might cleanse the stain of what they had done. Yet, there remained pockets of silence, ruins where the war's echo had not yet reached, and it was through these that Thomas and Baldwin moved. The city gates were sealed, with guards stationed at every principal thoroughfare and security guards were positioned at the corners, their faces dull with fatigue and their eyes continually scanning. Swords were drawn, not in defence but dominion, even among the victors, some no longer believed in the holy fire that had guided them.

Soldiers who had witnessed too much and taken too many lives. Baldwin had encountered them in the shadows. Men disillusioned by divine commands that now felt like madness. They bore no banners, only hushed voices and stolen maps. Thanks to them, Thomas and Baldwin slipped past a checkpoint under the cover of a crumbling aqueduct. The light dimmed as they moved deeper into the ruins, leaving the chaos behind. "This is the way," Baldwin mutters, gesturing toward a sunken passage barely wide enough for two men. "It'll take us to the lower quarter past the old cisterns." Thomas followed the Sigil, still burning in his mind like an ember refusing to die. His thoughts twisted, spun, and collided with the whisper in the void. The glow etched in stone, the impossible wound, all connected. "What exactly are we going to find under the Temple Mount?" He asked as they crouched beneath a fallen archway.

Baldwin's face was hard to read in the flickering half-light, but his voice carried the weight of dread and knowing. "Something old, older than any church, any crusade, a vault buried beneath the ruins, hidden for centuries." The church had known of this, at least the highest ranks, and they believed it held power, pure and unfiltered, neither heaven nor hell, something older than both. They emerged into what remained of a market square, and stalls had collapsed under fire and looting. Thomas paused, looking up at the distant mountain, its golden dome seeming to withstand the devastation. "Why now?" He inquired. "Why reveal it at this moment?" Baldwin tightened his grip on the sword hilt. "Because it's calling. They fear who might respond."

They entered another alley, desolate and charred, and noticed steel gleaming in the street just ahead of them. A squad of knights clad in black cloaks and helmets that concealed their faces took formation silently, six blades drawn, their armour gleaming like obsidian. The path was obstructed, and Baldwin halted, his gaze assessing their posture. "They are temple loyalists," he remarked. "Guardians of the vault. Sworn to the Vatican, not to the truth." Thomas unsheathed his blade deliberately, the sound slicing through the silence like a whisper of impending conflict. "No turning back now," Baldwin declared, moving ahead. Thomas felt the Sigil stir within him, a faint vibration under his skin like the air before a tempest. "Then let's conclude this." The knights raised their weapons, and the journey into the unknown was marked by blood and conviction.

Echo: The Infinite Cycle

A torch flared briefly, casting flickering light across the altar's face, where the symbols pulsed, not with magic, but with memory. Baldwin paused, eyes narrowed. "They weren't meant to be touched," he murmured, as if speaking to the dead. Thomas stepped closer; the glow was not a light, but an invitation. A low hum bled into the air, almost melodic, almost alive. He reached out, not out of bravery but inevitability. The altar responded, stone shifted with agonising grace. Symbols unwound into words, words into voices, and from the shadows behind them came the sound of footsteps, deliberate, impossibly soft. Thomas felt a tightening in his chest. The ancient Sigil resembled one he had encountered in his visions. Baldwin hesitated. "What is this?" Thomas stepped forward, placing a hand on the altar, and the world appeared to tremble. Then the whisper returned, curling around his mind like smoke.

Thomas felt a throbbing in his head as he tried to comprehend his environment, the imposing medieval structures and the rain-dampened cobblestone streets. He was certainly no longer in Jerusalem. The air carried a distinct scent. The sky was grey and heavy, with clouds suggesting more rain. The hooded figure watching him spoke again, his voice calm but carrying an elusive tone. "You look lost, friend." Nathan breathed irregularly. He now wore a thick wool tunic and a tattered leather belt instead of his armour, and his sword was gone. As he gazed into a puddle at his feet, his hands shook. His face bore bruises and blood, yet it was undoubtedly his own; this was not a dream.

"Where am I?" Nathan asked, his voice hoarse and nearly unrecognisable. The hooded figure regarded him briefly before advancing. "Not where, Nathan," he whispered. "But when?" Nathan felt his stomach churn as he traced the man's gaze to the ground, where a soft glow emanated from beneath the damp stones. The Sigil resembled the pattern he had encountered in Jerusalem right before everything fell apart. Clenching his hands into fists, he muttered. "This isn't possible," as the stranger's expression deepened with concern. "The Sigil has selected you. If you find yourself here, your journey is far from over." Nathan took a deep breath. "Then what is this place?" He raised the blade and hesitated. The final clang of steel echoed into the night as Nathan's blade found its mark. His opponent collapsed, and the battle faded gradually behind him into uneasy silence.

* * *

D. Gohil

In the distance, flames flickered along the edge of a sprawling stone citadel. The air hung heavy with smoke and sweat. As he caught his breath, the familiar hum returned, deep within his bones. Nathan stood alone beneath the dim flicker of the corridor light. The world outside felt too sharp, too defined, as if the edges of reality were being drawn with a different hand now. Ever since the symbol had seared itself into his vision, reality had not quite returned to its normal ways. He had a reverse sensation, watching it all replay in reverse, and was suddenly jolted back onto the aircraft. Was he now back on the flight as if nothing had happened? He struggled to regain his bearings. He was exhausted, and he tried to sleep. He tried silence, but nothing lasted.

Whenever he closed his eyes, he saw more than he should, memories he had not yet lived and voices he did not recognise but somehow understood. Entire conversations echoed in languages he did not speak. Sometimes he would wake up knowing things, such as numbers or the coordinates of locations he had not known about before, and events, none of which made sense on their own. He kept a notebook, and it filled quickly. During his sleep, the dreams changed, no longer abstract. A voiceless entity spoke clearly. *You are the echo of what came before and what comes after.* At that same point, his laptop, long since closed, had powered itself on, and a black screen greeted him with a single line blinking:

ACCESS GRANTED. NODE: ECHO-7.

He stared, fingers hovering over the keyboard until instinct, not something more profound, guided him to type:

IDENTIFYING...
NAME: NATHAN COLE
DESIGNATION: ECHO PROXY - PHASE
STARTED
OPERATIVE CALLSIGN: AEON TAK

He had not chosen that name, Aeon Tak. It sounded strange, but oddly right, more than just a name. It felt like a role he was born into without knowing it. The screen continued to reveal coordinates, encrypted communications and something else.

Echo: The Infinite Cycle

Dossiers of people he did not know but remembered. Riley-5, Tessa, and Lucas. Their faces flashed through him like déjà vu twisted into prophecy. He knew them somehow, as if remembering a story from another life or a life yet to come. The coordinates were for a facility buried beneath a research park outside London, and the organisation called itself Project Resonance.

* * *

The Sigil had selected him, or maybe he had chosen it long ago. As the flight continued its ascent into the blue sky, Nathan exhaled nervously, his hands shaking. Something was drawing near, and it was only the start! "Oh shit, please no, it's happening again!" The Orb pulsed once more, transporting him to an unknown place, and this time it lasted longer, and he sensed it, even if he could not understand why. The name Aeon Tak kept echoing in the void, pulling him along. This was not just déjà vu. It was fate, broken and recurring, and he was trapped within it. The Orb had claimed him and was taking him forward, again. Nathan did not resist; he now knew this cycle was to continue until it no longer needed to. He felt in his heart that he would be back in the loving arms of his love, Silvia, which is what he wanted most.

D. Gohil

Chapter 7 – Project Resonance
2032 CE

The Sigil had shifted him again, but this time, Nathan stood upright naturally, feeling OK. He immediately noticed that the air felt different, artificial, and the lights were buzzing overhead. Rows of monitors blinked in perfect synchrony, casting rhythmic pulses across smooth glass surfaces. Nathan was standing in a sleek control room, surrounded by silent personnel in identical black uniforms. He saw his reflection briefly in the mirror opposite him. He was wearing a tailored suit and a security badge clipped to his chest, the name an unfamiliar title. Project Director Aeon Tak, Echo Division, Security level one, and he frowned with a new realisation. The name sent a ripple through him: *Echo!* That was no coincidence. Again, the Sigil reappeared, openly displayed here. It was projected as a giant rotating hologram in the centre of the command room. This room was where scientists had been studying the symbol, and it was the very heart of the complex. Nathan was not here by chance, and it seemed this version of himself was a man already deeply inside the mystery.

Beneath the surface of civilised life, there are truths too heavy for the light of day. Concealed deep below the area, an unassuming research park outside London lies Project Resonance, a facility abandoned by the world yet haunted by its echoes. The inhabitants know Nathan, not the man he believes himself to be, but the version of him they refer to as Aeon. Here, past lives are mere data, and reincarnation was not a spiritual journey or code. The Sigil is no enigma. It served as a guide and was central to the little-known project that was kept highly secret.

Nathan navigates among strangers who recognise him with unnerving familiarity, and traverses corridors that respond to the scar on his palm. The truth was that he was not drawn here, as he created it. In this life, he cannot recall that he had led the building of the very machinery that is now unravelling in his mind. The answers lie in the darkness behind the locks of his design. He felt the air tighten around him as if the symbol in his mind recognised this place, responding like a tuning fork that hit just right. This is how it all began for Nathan in Project Resonance. This is going to get wild, so embrace yourself.

London, Project Resonance Facility

In the cool morning air, his breath fogged as he paused at the gates, watching a security camera tilt downward to meet his gaze. The gates then opened with a mechanical whir, revealing a woman inside, tall, in her late thirties, dressed in dark clothing with a hint of military discipline in her stance. Her face was lined sharply, yet her eyes held a quiet expression. "You're earlier than expected," she said. "That's either very good or very bad," Nathan blinked, responding. "Depends on what you were expecting." She looked him over, then extended a hand. "Riley-5 Operational Lead, you will get used to the silence.

This place does not trust easily." He shook her hand. "Nathan Cole or here, Aeon, I think." Riley-5 raised an eyebrow. "So, it's started then." They walked down a long corridor, clean and clinical, the place that had scrubbed history or perhaps had too much to begin with. "You were never part of their plan," Riley-5 said, glancing sideways. "You just showed up, which means the Sigil made the first move."

Echo: The Infinite Cycle

Nathan nodded. "It's been doing a lot of that lately." "You've dreamt of us, haven't you?" she asked. "Me, Tessa and the others." "I know your names," he admitted. "But I don't know how." Riley-5 stopped at a reinforced door. A scanner swept Nathan's face, then a second scanner lit up and traced the faint outline of the symbol scar on his palm, and the door opened. Inside was a circular briefing room, dimly lit screens lined the walls, and at the centre sat a tall man with close-cropped hair, and arms folded as if he was carved from oak. "This is Lucas." Across from him lounged someone younger, with wiry, restless eyes darting like she was always half a second ahead of everyone else. "This is Tessa," she said, looking up. "Well," Lucas said, his voice low and level. "So, the ghost becomes flesh." Tessa snorted. "He is not a ghost anymore. We have been told to call him Aeon. Has a better ring to it, don't you think?"

Nathan dropped into the empty chair. "I'd prefer Nathan to be honest." "No one here keeps their real name for long," Riley-5 said. "Too much risk, too many eyes, Aeon will do perfectly, OK?" Lucas studied him. "You have seen what the Sigil shows, or at least enough to bring you here. That means you are already halfway in." "Halfway into what?" Nathan asked. Tessa grinned. "Into the part of the world that doesn't officially exist." Riley-5 tapped a screen, displaying maps, redacted documents, and satellite images that overlaid ancient temple engravings. "Project Resonance was formed here to trace the phenomenon behind these symbols. Symbols older than history that appear to the same people in different lives. You are not the first to see it, Aeon, but you might be the first to unlock what is coming next."

Aeon stared at the screen. One image seemed to pulse, a spiral with branching arms like a tree seen from above, the same shape he had seen in the mirror in his dreams. "What is the Sigil?" he asked. Lucas gave a small, dark smile. "That is what we are here to find out, and you, Aeon, are going to help us." Nathan exhaled slowly, letting the moment settle. He did not know where this road led, but he knew there was no turning back. The Sigil had pulled him into its orbit, and Project Resonance was already in motion. Then, a transition like being transported into a virtual reality or a feeling resembling a dimension shift, jolted suddenly into a different city and world. A computerised voice whispered his name from the neon glow:

Project Resonance status: Active

Nathan jerked backwards, found his feet, felt bewildered, queasy, and unstable, and searched for his breath. His hands shook as if cold as he struggled to regain his balance. The cold, metallic air seemed to suffocate him as he looked around, unable to make sense of the sterile walls and the hum of machines that felt wrong to him. Then, without a thought as he walked, he found himself in an unsettling white room lined with towering servers that pulsed with light. Monitors lined the walls, each flashing with data that appeared to swirl around him in a symphony of green numbers and unreadable symbols. The room felt alive, not with warmth, but with calculation, cold, clinical, unblinking. The text on the monitor pulsed once, then froze in place, as though demanding recognition. *You were never meant to return.* Aeon Tak felt something shift inside him, which made him feel nauseous.

The numbers around the sentence began to form a shape, flowing like a tide, revealing fragments of some memory. Faces blurred by time, actions he had not recalled making, names that no longer matched the language he spoke. He reached out, hesitated, and in that pause, the room spoke again, not in words but through motion. The servers hummed louder. The white lights dimmed, and behind one monitor, a shape began to move. Nathan's heart raced. What is this, and what is happening to me? Before he could grasp the situation, he saw the one individual who could provide answers. A younger version of himself stood at the central terminal, his back facing him, as data streamed down the screen on the extended platform of multiple screens.

Dressed in a uniform, somewhat similar to a scientist, he typed with practised speed and precision. He looked much sharper, and his gaze was more intense. There was no doubt he was a younger Nathan, a different version, as if he possessed knowledge that Nathan should already know, at that moment. This younger Nathan's fingers tapped vigorously at the keyboard, eyes monitoring a specific set of codes, and for a moment, everything else fell away. His pulse sped up, and the answers he sought were concealed within these walls. Then the words *Project Resonance* returned to haunt him. He had worked there and had initially built the code for this. Aeon's breath was heavy, an icy shiver running down his spine. What sort of person was I? Before he could move, the vision shifted again.

Echo: The Infinite Cycle

The project room was full of computers, and his younger self fractured into pieces, vanishing into nothing. Aeon was stunned, his knees buckling as the world had been reconstructed around him. He found himself in what looked like a hideout, clutching the nearest wall for support. His heartbeat pulsed so hard he could hear it in his ears, and his mind was still reeling from what was happening. Riley-5's voice pierced the haze. "Aeon, are you OK?" Strong hands gripped him on his shoulders, keeping him balanced as he struggled to stay upright. He did not need to look up to know it was Riley-5. Her presence, and her cybernetic arm whirring gently as it steadied him, remained a constant in this chaotic world. "Yeah, I think so," Aeon mutters, struggling to regain control of his senses. He knew these were the others with him in this reality. Riley-5 leaned in, her voice low and filled with concern. "You do not look good. What the hell happened to you just then?"

Nathan took a nervous breath. "I saw something, like a memory or a vision, I don't know, but I was a prisoner of Project Resonance, and I helped build it!" Riley-5's grip tightened on his shoulder, her eyes narrowing. "You what?" "Yes, I had worked on it when I was younger, designed it, and whatever it is, or whatever it was, it is bigger than I thought." The team gathered around the table, their faces grim. The dim light of the hideout flickered as Aeon sat at the head of the makeshift command centre. His mind was elsewhere, still processing the fragmented memories that had come crashing back into his consciousness. Riley-5 was the first to speak after the long pause, her tone sharp yet laced with concern. "We need to talk about what you saw in that vision, Aeon. You will not get answers unless we figure out what Project Resonance actually is or was."

Aeon nodded, his gaze fixed on the table in front of him. He did not look up as he spoke, his voice heavy with uncertainty. "I do not know everything, but I know this much. I was part of it, designed it, helped build it, and whatever happened there, it is part of something much bigger!" Riley-5 crossed her cyborg arms, her limbs glimmering in the dim light. "Ok, Aeon, you are completely shaking, but we must concentrate. The project relates to more than just this war. Uncovering something significant is crucial. We must urgently identify the core, the source of it all." Aeon looked up, his eyes filled with fear. "I need you, you are the only ones who can help me trace the origins and stop it."

Tessa, who had previously been an intelligence officer on the team, leaned forward, her expression one of concern. "If this project is as critical as you think, Aeon, we're facing something dangerous. We will require more than our intelligence and strength to reveal the truth." Aeon met Tessa's eyes; his look was firm and confident. "I get that, but something more sinister is at play here. The Sigil's connected to this project, which motivates me to continue. If we can understand it, we may discover who is pulling the strings." Tessa looked at him, both intrigued and sceptical. "The same Sigil? I thought that was merely an old symbol or relic. Do you believe it has anything to do with the project?" "I am certain it does," Aeon replied, stern and confident. "I saw it in my vision in the lab. It's crucial to understand what has been happening to me and the world I am entangled with." Riley-5's expression softened, her usual sharpness replaced by a more sympathetic demeanour. "Let's work together and get this sorted."

The hideout door opened as Lucas, the team's data specialist, stepped inside, clutching a small electronic device excitedly. His eyes were shining. "I think I am onto something, Aeon," he said, raising the device high. "A data trail that points directly to one of the original Project Resonance facilities." Aeon's gaze fixed on the device, his heart racing. "Show me." Lucas's machine was futuristic for Aeon. It resonated in the air as he expertly tapped a few keys, fingers in sync across the touch-screen like a seasoned professional. Fresh data points emerged on the holographic map, projected from all the inputs in the softly lit room. The lines projected an elaborate network, expanding like a spider web, each point marked by a blinking red dot.

The map unravelled. A more profound hidden structure emerged, which Lucas was brilliant to have discovered. "Here," Lucas remarked, his voice low with gravity. He gestured to a precise spot on the map. "We have the location right here, deep within the mountains, far from any urban centre." The dot pulsed ominously. "The trail leads here for certain." Aeon leaned in intensely, fixed as he analysed the site. The mountains appeared to be rough terrain, remote, and barren, but it was not the landscape that drew Aeon's focus. It was the place's significance as a discreet hideaway. This hidden facility is one that no one would explore today. It held all the answers he so desperately needed, and he felt a knot tighten in his stomach as his mind raced. What developed there? What could they have been hiding there for so long?

Echo: The Infinite Cycle

The only thing he knew for sure was that this was beyond just another mission. He needed this thread to unravel his past and the truth about Project Resonance. "Where is this place?" Aeon's voice was tight, his fingers tense on the table's edge as he breathed with anticipation, his eyes fixated on the holographic display. Lucas continued swiping, zooming in on the area, his brow creased as he tried to analyse the encrypted information linked to the location. "It is a secluded facility that has been off the radar for years. We only recently detected the data trail and the signal. It originated right here," he pointed. "This is one of the initial research sites where they created the core technology for Project Resonance." Aeon felt his heart race. His thoughts were in turmoil. This was the origin of it all, the foundation of the technology that reshaped his life and many others.

The core of the chaos had engulfed him for what felt like ages. The answers are within those walls, and his memories flickered back. "We must get there!" The Sigil, that bizarre device, and the unsettling promises that this facility held the key. He sensed it in his bones, and yet as they approached, the danger escalated. There would unlikely be simple answers or any guarantees. "We need to go there now," Aeon declared, his voice steady, and each word laden with resolve. His hands clenched into fists as he stood confident, a wave of determination washing over him. "It's time to uncover the truth." A hush fell over the room, the weight of the decision palpable. The team shared looks, each member absorbing the seriousness of the mission ahead. Riley-5 was the first to speak, her cybernetic arm whirring softly as she stood, her posture rigid with readiness. "We are not going in blind, right?" She asked, her voice sharp and filled with pragmatic concern, which Aeon relies on.

Her gaze was intensely focused on him as she crossed her arms again. "We will need intel and a plan, or we will walk into the lion's den, Aeon," He nodded slowly, acknowledging her point, and Riley-5 was right as she usually was. "This would not be like any mission we had faced before, and the facility was no ordinary research site. It was a place where the boundaries of science and power had all merged. A place that had remained hidden for years for a reason." No one had expected the potential security traps they might encounter. Tessa, who had been quiet and listening until now, spoke up, her voice firm and pragmatic. "Agreed, if this facility is as important as it sounds. There is no way they have left it unguarded," she felt certain, as she pondered.

"We need a strategy to know exactly what we are walking into, or we will not come out alive." Aeon turned to Lucas. "What can you tell us about the security systems, Lucas? Is there a way in?" Lucas cracked his knuckles, an annoying habit that made Aeon wince. Eyes scanning the data on the device's screen. "I will sort it out and get us access to the facility's security systems, but it will be tough. This place is locked with tight layered encryption, firewalls, and physical security. They were not kidding when they protected this site and wanted to stay off the grid, but..." He trailed off, thinking confidently. "There are always ways in, and nothing can stop me. Just give me a little time, and I will crack it." Riley-5 turned to Lucas. Her mechanical arm flexed as she spoke impatiently. "I will be ready when you do. Just get on with it, and the sooner you do, the sooner we can move. I will handle any obstacles we face and be aware of any surprises." Aeon nodded slightly, recognising his team's willingness to venture into the uncharted territories.

They are like family, with everyone bringing unique skills to the table. This mission differed from the rest, and they were venturing into territory never seen before, where the stakes had never been higher. Aeon understood that the danger was not just physical. A sinister force was at work here, they realised. "We cannot afford to waste any time. We need to act fast," Aeon declared, as he was confronted by doubt, determination, and focus. "We go in, find the answers, and prevent anyone else from misusing what is in there. This must end now, whatever it takes, team!" Aeon said. They all nodded in unison, feeling the weight of his words. Tessa uncrossed her arms, her expression agreeing. "We stand with you, Aeon, always will. Let's make sure we're the last in this fight and see it through to the end."

There was no turning back now, since this mission was about gathering intel and reaching a conclusion. This battle was for the truth, the future, and Aeon's soul. Tessa, Riley-5, Lucas, and Aeon shared determined looks. They understood the dangers but realised they could no longer let the secrets of Project Resonance stay hidden. Although he tried to dismiss the gnawing feeling, it was akin to a dark storm cloud following him around. Always just out of grasp but ever looming, ready to consume him. His heart raced with each step and with every ticking minute. What if the answers were already there? What if they only added to the confusion that surrounds the project? Riley-5's enhanced eyes occasionally scanned the horizon for potential threats.

Echo: The Infinite Cycle

Lucas walked a few steps ahead, his face lit by the glow of a portable device as he scanned for electronic signatures from the facility's security systems. Meanwhile, Nathan battled with the turmoil within him. The truth was waiting for him. As he navigated the thickening forest, its dense foliage enveloping the narrow path, his thoughts spiralled. *You cannot escape, no matter how far you run.* They reached the facility's base just after dusk, with the moon rising and casting an eerie light over the structure before them. The building loomed stark, imposing its exterior streaked with rust and framed by decay. Time had ravaged it, but something in its bones remained untouched. It had not been forgotten. It had waited for Aeon. At the edge of the clearing, the team set up camp. Far enough to avoid notice. Close enough to strike if needed. Aeon felt his mind racing as he gazed at the facility's dark silhouette, which embodied all he had lost and forgotten.

He felt an undeniable connection to the place; he hardly registered when Riley-5 started a small campfire, its glow flickering gently in the cool air. Lucas and Tessa were busy unloading their gear, inspecting weapons and performing diagnostics on their equipment, while Aeon chose not to join them. Instead, he perched on a rock at the clearing's edge, staring into the distance. Memories waited. Lingering, constant like whispers echoing through his mind. Later that night, as the team slept, Aeon lay on the cold ground, eyes tracing constellations that blurred behind drifting clouds, and the moon was shrouded.

* * *

The dream began. No stars, no earth beneath his back, he stood alone in a sterile room, walls gleaming white beneath a cruel overhead glare. A strange hum laced the air: thin, electric, unsettling, it tickled the base of his spine. Before him loomed a machine, colossal, pulsing, and familiar in the way a nightmare is familiar, recognised without understanding. Its surface shimmered with constantly changing patterns, bright blue and green lines that flowed like liquid light. He sensed its energy emanating, an eerie influence that made the air sizzle with expectation. The device appeared sentient, its presence overwhelming, as if it were observing him, poised for something. Aeon moved closer, his actions slow and purposeful. The machine did not reject him; it recognised him. The voice sliced through the chaos like a scalpel through silk. *You are not the first; you are the Echo.*

D. Gohil

The data storm calmed, but only slightly. Images slowed into patterns. A boy with different eyes, a signature carved into stone, a corridor bathed in artificial moonlight. Each one was him and yet not him. Aeon staggered back, but his body refused to move. Time bent, the room remained, and it was no longer sterile. Screens showed cities he had never seen, wars he had not fought, languages he knew without learning. His memories were layered beneath others, older, fragmented, waiting, and then came the question. Not spoken aloud, but felt like a tremor beneath the skin. *Will you complete it? This is our gift to the world, Aeon. This is the future.* Aeon froze; though he knew it was his voice, it felt unrecognisable.

This version of him existed before the chaos, the endless cycles of reincarnation, and fragmented memories. This was the voice of a man who had been involved in something perilous, something unstoppable. Aeon felt a tightness in his chest, his heart pounding in his ears as the voice continued, chilling and detached. *We are the architects of the new world, Aeon. This is just the beginning. Our power will change everything. The future will bow to us.* A wave of nausea rolled over him, causing him to stumble backwards. His vision blurred as memories of that moment surged through his mind like a broken dam. He was not just involved in Project Resonance. He had been a creator, an architect of the force that transformed his life and many others.

* * *

With a big gasp, Aeon awoke, his body drenched in sweat. The chilly night air stung his skin as he sat up, his heart racing. His breath came in uneven gasps, and his head ached from the vivid memories. It was dark, and the soft breathing of his team was the sole thing keeping him anchored to reality as his mind spun. He had been a pawn in this game and the one orchestrating everything. The mastermind behind the project believed it would create a new world order, and all that was left were the shattered remnants of his past, from which he could not escape. Aeon wiped the sweat from his forehead, his hand shaking as he tried to regain his composure. The harsh truth had struck him, and he could no longer ignore it. He was not a hero in this narrative; he was among the villains contributing to the chaos that had unravelled his life.

Echo: The Infinite Cycle

He shut his eyes, attempting to calm his breathing. The damage was done, and there was no erasing the past. However, he still had time to stop it from worsening. "I have to fix this," he whispered into the shadows. The burden of his history felt overwhelming, but he understood his course of action. The answers were hidden within the facility, and once uncovered, he would confront the fallout from his previous decisions, no matter the price. This was the only way of ending the cycle and avoiding reverting to the monster he once was. At dawn, as the team neared the facility, the air remained still, their footsteps muffled by the thick forest floor. Tension filled the air, with each member fully aware of the enormity of what awaited them. They had been tracking signals for days, and the data they collected left no doubt. This decaying structure was the epicentre of Project Resonance, the source of the chaos that had engulfed his life.

His thoughts raced. What would he discover here? What sort of truth awaited him inside? These questions plagued him, yet there was no time for answers. The mission had gained a new urgency, and turning back was not an option. Every clue had led him to this very location, the start of it all. "Stay alert," Aeon whispered as they navigated through the thick trees, weapons drawn. It seemed too ideal, too strange. What secrets are concealed here? The facility stood before him, a dark figure against the night sky. It was enormous, its concrete walls marked by age and disregard. As they got closer to the building, they noticed that the windows were black and the entrance was blocked by overgrowth. It felt like a location lost to time, yet Aeon understood differently. It was kept hidden for a specific reason, and whatever transpired here, it was meant to stay concealed.

Lucas advanced, retrieving a small device from his pack. "We're here." He said, his voice strained with concentration. "I'm almost there, boss, I just need a few more seconds." Aeon nodded, maintaining his vigilance. An unsettling apprehension nagged at him, suggesting they were being watched. It felt as if something or someone was lying in ambush. "Ready," Lucas murmurs, and with a soft click, the door's security system deactivated. Aeon moved ahead, his senses sharpened as he cautiously made his way down the corridor. The walls were adorned with bizarre, elaborate machines. Some remained inactive, while others faintly pulsed with energy. He examined the metallic surfaces, absorbing every detail as his mind pieced together the puzzle.

This was the nerve centre of Project Resonance, the origin of the technology that had both defined and disrupted his life. With each step, Aeon felt he was edging deeper into a long-lost past that was now invading his awareness. Ahead, the central chamber awaited, its presence palpable as he continued striving to tread softly. His heart raced. When they rounded the last corner, the door to the chamber glided open with a gentle hiss. Aeon took a brief pause, absorbing the view in front of him. The expansive room extended in all directions, lined with machines that varied from small and inconspicuous to large and intricate. Each device bore strange symbols carved into its surface. At the centre of the room was the most impressive piece of equipment Aeon had ever encountered, an enormous structure of interwoven gears, glowing lights, and moving panels.

He swallowed with nerves when he realised what it was, the device from his memories that contributed to the chaos that had followed him through every lifetime. Riley-5 moved closer as she repositioned herself. "What is this place?" She inquired, her voice low and filled with awe. The others were equally astonished, their eyes wide as they took in the room's contents. Aeon felt his mind racing as he stepped deeper into the chamber. The energy in the air was palpable, the strange, almost magnetic attraction of the machines as if they beckoned him. It felt all too familiar, as this was where it all began. "Stay sharp," he whispered, his voice raspy. "I believe we've located what we need." Lucas surveyed the surroundings, swiftly tapping on his device to gather information. "I am picking up a significant power source here. The readings are extraordinary, and whatever this location is, it was built to endure the test of time."

Tessa advanced with caution, her eyes scanning the room for potential threats. "The technology here is unlike anything we have seen. It is old, but it remains operational. Whatever they were doing, they were well ahead of their time." Aeon's gaze returned to the central machine; his expression had sharpened as a familiar symbol illuminated the panels on the ancient Sigil, glowing faintly with an eerie light before him. His heartbeat quickened as elusive memories flooded back to him. He moved closer to the machine, extending his hand, as his fingers poised just above the surface. The symbol appeared to throb in sync with his pulse. Although he had encountered it in his visions, it felt different at this moment. "The Sigil," Aeon murmurs, his voice unsteady. "It's connected to this machine, and it's more than a symbol. It's a key!"

Echo: The Infinite Cycle

Riley-5 observed him intently. "What is its significance, Aeon? What does it seek from you?" Aeon's breath hitched as his fingers grazed the surface. His vision became foggy, and he staggered back, his mind whirling with a spectrum of visions. The ancient Sigil, now shining more vividly than before, was etched in his memory. He could perceive the past, the project, the experiments, the aspirations for a new world order, and the horrifying outcomes of the power they aimed to control. A voice, the same voice from his visions, chilling and analytical. *This is our gift to the world, Aeon. This is the future, you will unlock it, you will be the one to usher in the new dawn.* Aeon tightened his fists as the words reverberated in his mind. He could no longer ignore his past life and involvement in Project Resonance, yet he had gained a new clarity.

The ancient Sigil beckoned him, intriguing him to uncover the secrets concealed within the machines of Project Resonance. He was also here to stop himself, to shatter the cycle before it became irreversible. "We need to destroy this place," Aeon stated, his voice calm yet resonant with quiet resolve. "It's the only way to prevent the chaos from spreading. We cannot allow this to persist." As the team got ready to advance, Aeon's thoughts spiralled. The Sigil had branded him, and it had marked his soul, binding him to a fate he now intended to break free from. The fate of the world hinged on his current choices, and this time, he held the power to shape the outcome. Aeon's breath came in small gasps, his fingers shaking as the last traces of the memory slipped away. The harsh white light of the lab monitors flickered, their screens flashing briefly before turning to static:

PROJECT RESONANCE – ACCESS DENIED

The weight slammed into his chest as he staggered backwards, mind spinning. The symbol was not glowing from some screen this time. It was there, carved deep into the concrete floor of the hideout. The light stuttered across the carved stone, making the spirals appear to move. Everything felt wrong. The air tasted metallic. His modified nervous system screamed warnings he could not decode. Aeon dropped to one knee beside the carving. His fingertips traced the cold edges. How long had this been here? The concrete around it looked fresh, but the symbol itself felt ancient, worn smooth by time he could not measure.

The hideout's power grid whined under some invisible strain. Monitors went dark, then blazed back to life, showing static. The ventilation system coughed and died. In the sudden quiet, he could hear something else. A low harmonic that seemed to rise from the carved stone itself. His hand jerked back from the symbol. The harmonic stopped. The neon lights steadied, casting their familiar blue-white glow across the cluttered space, but the symbol remained, now carved into reality instead of hidden in data streams. Whatever had been hunting him through the network had found a way to break through. Aeon stood slowly, never taking his eyes off the spirals. The real question was not how it had appeared. It was what it wanted him to do next. Aeon felt it reach deep into his bones, more intense than ever. The experiment was failing or succeeding. Aeon no longer knew which. Alarms screamed as the anomaly tore through the chamber.

The Sigil now floating above the central console expanded, its circular geometry spinning faster than his eyes could follow. The team fled as screens cracked, but Aeon remained rooted, his eyes locked on the growing vortex of light that had now consumed the entire observation chamber. "Subject is destabilising," a voice shouted behind him. "Containment breached!" But there was no containment anymore. Aeon felt that this was unfinished and was concerned about his team. These sensations felt premature, and he tried to resist, but he felt the pull of the swirl of spinning white before the next shift had begun. Could he control this and try to finish what he and the team came to do, but the Sigil had other plans. The Orb ascended from the centre of the pulsing ancient Sigil, appearing jagged and unstable instead of smooth and liquid like before.

It pulsed violently, its glow casting reflections on the cold chrome of the hacking station around him. Nathan had only seconds to respond. "No, not yet, this can't be happening," he gasped as he reached for the table for support, but the Orb was indifferent, and it lunged forward. The experience was unlike anything he had experienced. His body convulsed, and his breath was yanked from his lungs, the bright neon surroundings fractured, giving way to intense heat, blinding light, and the acrid smell of iron and sweat. He was falling, not being let go, into emptiness. His hands felt foreign, and his thoughts belonged to another. The Sigil lingered throughout his life, and he was now familiar with this, but he just wanted to go home, back to Silvia.

Echo: The Infinite Cycle

Chapter 8 – The Odyssey
2049 CE

The pull slowed, the bright white surround gave way to stars, and Nathan was floating weightlessly, suspended in the dark expanse of space. Far below him, a huge station orbited a blue giant, its swirling atmosphere glowing as the ocean reflected in the sky. He looked down at himself, this time wearing a sleek, form-fitting spacesuit, and the controls embedded in his gloves glowed softly. A heads-up display (HUD) flickered across his visor, and he was no longer falling, as now he was floating. This was in space, and it felt surreal. The Sigil had cast him before as a pilot, hacker, crusader, and now, commander of something far larger. He sensed a continuation from a previous shift and felt a sense of curiosity without fear. Even here amid the silent ballet of stars, the symbol pulsed. It was a familiar, known circular pattern shimmering, though faintly, on his display like a constant silent witness. In the empty void, stars blazed with indifference that felt like a premonition, or was it a dream?

D. Gohil

* * *

Nathan awakens on an alien ship travelling vast distances between star systems, its crew a lonely species in the vastness of space. The Sigil glows on the bulkhead, rendered in blood, serving as a warning. Time behaves differently here. Memories loop and voices echo, glimpses of himself. The ship had become a crucible not of metal and wiring, but of memory and identity. Every hallway held a mirror he could not see through, only feel. One of the corridors pulsed with low ambient light, and the walls bore faded Insignias. Half recognised from a war he had no conscious recollection of. A helmet rested on a bench, tagged with his code name, then came the chamber of voices, with monitors lining the curved wall, each flickering with a different iteration of him, some older, some younger. They spoke in unison, a choir of fractured selves. *You chose each time. Now choose again.* The room stilled, no hum, no light, just the message, burning faintly across every screen: *All paths converge, begin transmission.* As the ship approaches an unnamed celestial anomaly, he faces a truth long evaded. He has traversed this route before, possibly the only one destined to survive. The sky turned inside out, and gravity vanished. He drifted through infinity, stars whispering languages he had never spoken yet had always known. With a gentle but interesting tug, the cord attached caught Nathan's attention, as he was unaware of where he had ended up after the Sigil and Orb shifted him once again.

* * *

Off-World Earth's Orbit

An eerie silence enveloped him, in the absence of sound, in the absence of everything. Nathan was stunned, and suddenly he felt no gravity, no weight, and no air pressing against his skin; there was no up and no down. His pulse skyrocketed as he realised that he was breathing differently in quick, shallow gasps. He found himself floating, simply drifting through an empty void, his arms flailing for anything to anchor himself. His fingers caught some fabric, recognising it as a smooth and unfamiliar suit, a spacesuit, and his mind abruptly recoiled. "Fuck, I am floating in space!" His last natural breath had been on a battlefield, or was it in a neon-lit city or the cockpit of a jet? So, what is happening now? Memories overlapped in his mind, bleeding into one another as his thoughts struggled to separate the past from the present.

Echo: The Infinite Cycle

It was like looking through a shattered mirror. A soft beep echoed in his helmet. "Commander John Bennett, are you reading me?" Nathan sucked in air, a name and a rank that belonged to him but to which he neither knew nor connected. Outside the window of his helmet, the vast infinite void revealed stars stretching endlessly, accompanied by the gentle hum of an oxygen filter and the rhythmic beep of a control panel. His mind reeled with complete confusion. "What in God's name is going on? Where am I?" Previously, he had been in the cockpit of his jet fighter, and now he floated above in Earth's orbit. His heartbeat pounded against his ribs, and he knew this was another jump, something significantly connected to it. This was entirely different from the peacekeeping mission. His gloved hands hovered before him, reflecting the deep blue glow of a spaceship console, when a voice crackled through his helmet. "Commander, do you copy?"

He exhaled with a shock. He was an astronaut on a mission to save the planet, but he did not know it. He turned toward the viewport, and something else exhaled, too. There was static just outside the station, where sound should not exist. Below was the Earth, he thought, a patchwork of blue, green, brown and white, with oceans and clouds swirling within the infinite expanse of space. His gloved hands adjusted satellite panels and calibrated equipment as he floated outside the International Space Station (ISS), conducting a routine spacewalk. How do I even know how to do this? Through the helmet visor, the stars spilt out like silver dust across the endless dark.

Earth glowed like a blue jewel wrapped in cotton, oceans swirling with clouds of beauty, perfect and silent. The soft hum of oxygen circulation systems and the steady beep, beep of vital signs monitoring were the only reminders that he was not alone. He had become an astronaut and was no longer on Earth; that was now very clear. This was a shift, unlike anything he had expected. This one felt anchored in something deeper, something ancient, something important. His gloved hand hovered before his eyes, reflecting the cerulean glow of the station's spacewalk console. The suit bore the subtle yet unmistakable insignia of the International Space Station (ISS) with a British flag. Then a voice broke through the radio static. "Commander, do you copy?" He breathed slowly, trying to steady himself in this reality version. When his voice finally emerged, it sounded foreign, rasping through tight lips, unsure of its truth.

"I copy," he turned toward the viewport, his gaze drawn into the cosmos. Something else exhaled with him, a whisper of static brushed his ears like breath on glass, but from outside the ship. Where there was no atmosphere, no sound, nothing should exist there, yet something did. It was waiting, a strong gut feeling John could not ignore. "Commander Bennett, do you read me? Acknowledge, this is urgent, your oxygen levels are low, and you must return to the entry hatch immediately." The voice was stern and vital, the urgency of the situation palpable. "Copy, I will get to the hatch straight away, as I have finished the final calibration required for the tests to begin," he said. Entering the hatch, he sealed the lock and felt relieved to be back inside. He pressurised the entry area and opened the internal hatch to float inside.

The ISS shimmered under the slowly turning sun, its panels glistened with frozen brilliance, the outline stark against the velvet void. The command deck interior hummed with routine operations, the faint clicks of keyboards and the ballet of zero-gravity movements. John floated through, adjusting and recalibrating not only the satellite systems but himself as he exchanged glances with Commander Aryna Vos, scientist Harish Harbham, and engineer Kato Takeda, each familiar as if he had known them for years. Their voices welcomed him with the camaraderie of shared mission jokes whispered over dehydrated coffee. None of them noticed that behind Nathan's polite nods, he was caught between timelines and realities. The sense of belonging among the crew was strong, even amid John's turmoil.

The first thing John noticed was not the stillness. It was the rhythm of the International Space Station, which seemed to breathe in cycles, tiny hisses of compressed air, gentle whirs of cooling systems, and soft, almost imperceptible clicks of relays triggering somewhere behind the panels. ISS was a living machine composed of steel and solar wings, quietly exhaling into the void while John floated inside it. He rested and later awoke, strapped into a sleep pod no larger than a locker, his body cocooned in a sleeping bag tethered with Velcro to the wall. For a long moment, he lay there, his eyes adjusting to the low ambient glow of the station's interior. The silence felt thicker here, not empty but dense, like the pressure of deep ocean water. Then came the comm system's soft beeping, signalling the mission's start. "Good morning, ISS, this is Houston Flight Control. How is our orbit?"

Echo: The Infinite Cycle

John unzipped the bag with clumsy fingers and eased himself out, his body moving with dreamlike inertia through the narrow corridor of Node 2 of the ISS, also called Harmony. Everything was compact and meticulously arranged. Laptops floated in mesh pouches, clipboards were stuck to the walls with Velcro, and every spare surface was cluttered with wires, switches, and displays of functional chaos. He turned a corner and found Aryna Vos floating beside the meal prep station, squeezing a pouch of rehydrated scrambled eggs. "Hey, Sleeping Beauty," she said, her German accent crisp and amused. "You snore in microgravity, so that you know, lol." John blinked. "Didn't realise I had slept at all." "You looked like it." She passed him a pouch labelled *Coffee Black* and pointed towards the galley, where a silver tube hissed gently, warming food packets. They did not sit at a table, nor were there any chairs. Eating in zero gravity meant floating with one foot hooked into a restraint or a thigh braced against a handrail.

Breakfast was quietly efficient, with scrambled eggs, granola bars, and a protein gel, and everything tasted vaguely metallic, well, crap actually, but it was much-needed sustenance. The morning schedule awaited them on a shared tablet in Destiny, the American lab module. Today, John would assist Kato with fluid dynamics experiments, testing how liquids behaved in capillary flow under zero gravity. It sounded simple, but every movement had to be deliberate. Each floating droplet posed a potential hazard to the electronics humming inches away. He observed how each crew member danced with the machines as they moved through the Columbus, Unity, and Zvezda modules. They did not walk, they glided and launched from one surface to another, fingers brushing against the walls for stabilisation.

They communicated through hand signals, short, clipped words, and occasional laughter. Later, Harish R. Harbham, the mission's highly trained biomedical scientist, beckoned him over. "Bennett, I need your blood." John raised a brow. "You're very forward, today, HRH." Harish chuckled, securing a mobile station with a Velcro strap. "Relax, it's routine health monitoring, my young friend, got to make sure you are still functioning like a real human being, lol." John floated but stayed still while the sample was taken, watching the red liquid spiral into a vacuum tube. The sight was oddly mesmerising. Blood had a different thickness in space, thicker, slower, and almost sentient. By midday, Earth had passed beneath them like a spinning jewel.

Every ninety minutes, the station completed one full orbit, each revolution marked by a sunrise or sunset that flared like divine light through the Cupola module's observation windows. John spent twenty quiet minutes in that module, his hand pressed against the glass, watching a hurricane swirl over the Pacific Ocean. The awe never diminished, but deep in his chest, unease prickled. He could almost feel something vast and wrong lurking just outside the frame. Voices behind him drew him back, as Aryna floated in with a tablet, eyebrow raised. "Your EVA suit's telemetry needs a diagnostic pass. Want to walk you through it." "Yeah, sure," John nodded quietly. "Let's do that. I am all yours." An evening aboard the ISS was characterised more by routine than time. There was no night, only the programmed shift of cabin lighting into soft blues and purples to simulate dusk.

Dinner made of freeze-dried chicken teriyaki and mashed potatoes, eaten one floating bite at a time. While Aryna uploaded the day's experiment logs to mission control, Kato and Harish played digital chess on a floating tablet between them. John busied himself checking tools for the next EVA spacewalk, but as the others drifted into their off-duty routines, watching pre-loaded films and reading e-books, John floated back to the Cupola, drawn once more to Earth's glow. He stared at the black space surrounding the stars and felt a pressure, like a breath on the nape of his neck. Something else was out there, something had a greater sensor range, mysterious and unknown. Hours later, with the rest of the crew asleep in their tiny sleeping pods, John floated alone through the Zvezda module, a torch in hand. He was unsure what had awakened him. Was it a dream or something else? The silence now felt oppressive.

He checked the telemetry and found normal oxygen levels with normal heat regulation. Yet something tugged at him, a low hum beneath the station's systems, a whisper in the static. He reached the communications console and hesitated. Part of him expected to see something out of the window, not Earth, not stars, but something watching. He moved closer to the viewport and saw not precisely a shape but a shimmer and warping of the stars. It vanished instantly, like heat over asphalt, like breath fogging a mirror into the deep space. John's breath caught, and the whisper returned faintly through his helmet, even though he was not wearing one. *Just one more step, Nathan.*

Echo: The Infinite Cycle

The morning light panels had just cycled into a simulated sunrise when the comms crackled unexpectedly with a high-priority override. The lights dimmed momentarily as the station rerouted power to the central console. Which only occurred when something serious was afoot. In this reality, John Bennett floated beside Aryna near the Destiny module's worktable, sipping lukewarm protein coffee. They exchanged glances before she smoothly launched into the comms interface and started the encrypted uplink. "ISS, this is Houston flight control. Is there a secure line established? Confirm the full crew is present." Commander Vos acknowledged. "Houston, this is Vos, I have got Bennett, Harbham and Takeda, we are reading you." After a pause, the voice on the other end, the Flight Director Monroe, came online. "Commander, we are about to transmit information classified at mission security level four. Confirm secure channel active."

Vos gave a tight nod. "Confirmed, Houston." John leaned in as Monroe continued. "Six months ago, CERN completed a high-energy quarks and leptons collision run using the new singularity mapping sequence, the one tied to lattice vibration models and dark matter topology." Aryna nodded to herself, a small habit, and felt a little nervous about what was to come next. "Yes, the frequency mapping run. We saw the preliminary data." "What wasn't disclosed," Monroe went on. "Is that the collision emitted an extremely low frequency. Barely detectable, but it should not have emitted anything at all." John frowned. "What, some kind of resonance?" "Worse. That frequency propagated far beyond the collider. It bounced deep into space and was answered back!"

The crew exchanged glances. Even the hum of the station seemed to fade. "NASA's Deep Space Network registered a return pulse four seconds later. Narrow-band. Non-random. Non-terrestrial. It was structured, not language as we know it, but code. It matched no known protocol, no background radiation pattern, and any known celestial source." Vos's jaw dropped. "Where did it come from?" "Triangulation places the origin behind your current orbital path, a shadow point, riding Earth's outbound trajectory. Just outside visual range from the ISS." John's stomach turned. Monroe's voice dropped a notch. "The signal flared again last night. A harmonic distortion passed through the station. It was almost imperceptible, but it pinged telemetry from your last EVA. Specifically, from your suit, Commander Bennett." John swallowed hard, but had a feeling in the back of his mind.

"We need to know if anything unusual happened to you outside the station, Bennett. Any unexplained interference you might have felt, hallucinations, minor disorientation, or anything anomalous?" John hesitated, Vos turned to him, and concern etched into her expression. "I..." he began. "I felt something out there, just for a moment, like something was close by, but nothing visible. Not radiation, but it felt like some unknown presence." There was another pause on the line. "Understood, we are flagging your biometrics for complete monitoring on EVA-02. Please proceed with extreme caution. If anything else is abnormal, report it to us immediately." The signal cut off with a soft click. The EVA prep felt different this time. Every checklist item, oxygen level, power flow, and tether calibration was executed precisely. There was a tense silence among the crew.

Even Kato, normally the joker, was tight-lipped as he passed John his space helmet. The repair mission was critical, and the external filtration manifold, part of the environmental support system, had failed. A complete failure meant a catastrophic compromise of air circulation. Only one other engineer aboard had the original design schematics embedded in his training, as well as Commander John Bennett (Nathan Cole), the man burdened with too many memories. As the inner airlock sealed, a soft hiss echoed within the suit, and the HUD illuminated with telemetry:

O_2:	Stable.
Suit Pressure:	Normal.
Tether Integrity:	Secure.
Cognition Index:	Spiking a red blip.

He ignored it as the outer hatch released, and John drifted forward into the void. The world unfurled before him. Earth lay silent and watching. He pushed off gently with his magnetic boots and activated the EVA-02 pack's micro-thrusters, which responded with tiny course corrections, stabilising him in orbit. The other crew watched via his helmet cam, maintaining radio silence as per protocol. He reached the damaged manifold, where its outer shroud warped from prolonged micrometeorite abrasion. Panels hissed as he unlocked them with a Zero-G torque wrench, each motion deliberate. Cold sweat gathered inside his suit, though he did not know why.

Echo: The Infinite Cycle

Then, with a click, the panel detached. A shimmer danced along the metal like a heat mirage in a vacuum. As before, his radio crackled, not with any earthly voice, Vos, or static, but a voice almost whispering. *You opened the door.* His breath stopped, then the actual Earth's comms returned. "Commander Bennett, your heart rate just spiked. Report status?" He gritted his teeth. "I am fine, continuing the repair." Something reached back as he delved into the exposed wiring array. Not a hand, or a form, just the idea of contact, the illusion of breath brushing his visor. This feeling made him incredibly nervous. He yanked the tool free, his heart hammering, and sealed the replacement plate with trembling fingers. The hiss of the torque gun was the only thing tethering him to the present. "Repairs complete," he said, his voice sounded flat. "Copy that, now return to the airlock, Commander." He turned, and there it was, beyond the solar arrays, just at the edge of Earth's curvature, a dark silhouette impossible to define.

A displacement of stars, a void within voids, pulsing faintly with the rhythm of a heartbeat. It mirrored his pulse. *Soon.* It whispered, not in his helmet but in his mind, and then it vanished. The silence of space was his constant companion, but the hum of the station provided a gentle soothing noise in the background. It was the calm he accepted, the calm of the void that stretched on endlessly; however, something felt different today. There was a faint disturbance in the air. Instead, something seemed amiss about the fabric of space itself. His instruments were registering erratic fluctuations that made no sense. John steadied himself against the console, as if gravity itself had faltered. The anomaly hovered in perfect silence, neither object nor void, but an interruption, a contradiction. Light refracted around it in spirals, fragmenting into spectral helices that hummed with meaning just beyond comprehension. He adjusted the dials again, still no cause, no malfunction, but the ripple responded, as if aware.

Then came the pulse, subtle, rhythmic, almost biological. The distortion shivered, and for an impossible instant, John saw someone watching from within. The control panel lit up unbidden. His biometric signature registered, not as John, but as *Spiral Fragment 4*. "Impossible," he murmured. The anomaly surged once more. This time, not in silence, an actual voice, crystalline and fractured, echoed within his helmet. "He is reaching. The Spiral is remembering." His eyes narrowed as he brought up the readings on his helmet display. "Not possible," he whispered to himself.

115

Trying to make sense of the data. The energy levels fluctuated wildly, and nothing in his training or experience could explain what he saw. The anomaly was not within the scope of everything he had learned, yet it was impossible to ignore. He tried stabilising the readings by adjusting the settings on his equipment, but they remained unreliable. Numbers danced across the display in a way that made his stomach churn. This was not normal; his mind raced through every possibility. Meteor debris? No, a malfunction in the station's systems? Unlikely. This was something entirely different and far more dangerous. His instincts screamed at him to move away and return to the ISS, but an even more potent force within him urged him forward. He had to know what this was. Whatever it was, he had stumbled upon something incredible. The thrill of discovery coursed through his veins, overriding the logical part of his brain that screamed for him to abort the mission.

"Commander Bennett, report," his commanding officer's voice crackled through the radio, and interrupted his thoughts. "We are detecting unusual energy fluctuations near your position. You need to return to the station immediately." John gripped the controls tightly. His instinct urged him to comply with the orders, but his mind was already well beyond that. He could not turn his back on this moment. It was a pivotal event. "Negative, Commander Vos," John said, his voice calm despite his racing heart. "There's more here, and I require additional time to analyse it." "John, we are running out of time. The energy readings are becoming increasingly unstable, and the fluctuations could jeopardise the station's systems, so return to base immediately!" Although his commanding officer spoke firmly, John could sense the worry beneath the surface.

Despite the growing danger, John could not pull his eyes from the anomaly. He felt an irresistible attraction to it, a deep, seated urge to touch it. His instinct, which he had worked hard to suppress over the years, warned him of the risks involved. However, the scientist within him, an explorer who had devoted his life to seeking new frontiers, maintained that this was a once-in-a-lifetime chance. Despite his better judgment, he advanced, propelled by his suit's thrusters. The anomaly shimmered in front of him, its edges undulating like water disturbed by a stone. Then, without a moment's hesitation, he extended his hand. The moment his glove touched the anomaly, a powerful shockwave of energy coursed through him.

Echo: The Infinite Cycle

Its intensity felt like an invisible wave hitting him. The surroundings distorted, with his vision filled with a dizzying array of colours and lights, stars, galaxies, and pieces of Earth colliding in a single overwhelming instant. His body convulsed, and his mind whirled with the impossible sights overwhelming his senses. Alarms on his suit blared, creating a chaotic chorus of warnings. An invisible force yanked him forward, and then, suddenly, all was silent. A suffocating stillness engulfed him. It felt like the universe had paused. There was no noise, sensation, or emotion, only a haunting tranquillity. John blinked slowly, his mind racing to reconnect with his body. He felt weightless and burdened, as if caught in an unsettling balance. As his vision became focused, he abruptly recognised that he was no longer outside the ISS. The recognisable view of Earth had vanished, giving way to entirely strange surroundings, almost akin to a different dimension.

After being drawn into the mysterious anomaly, he discovered himself standing on solid metal plating beneath his feet. The space enveloping him was immense, surpassing anything he had ever encountered. The walls were smooth, gracefully curving outward and bathed in a gentle blue light that pulsed in a rhythmic pattern. It was unlike anything he had trained for, different from the interiors of the ISS or any other space vehicle he had explored before. The air, or what could be called air, was dense with an unusual energy, yet still breathable. The sound of machinery vibrated in his bones, a low hum that appeared to come from both everywhere and nowhere.

John stepped forward cautiously, attempting to understand his surroundings. His heart raced, and his thoughts spun wildly, so where on earth was he? As if he were there on Earth, how had he arrived here so suddenly and without physical awareness? For sure, this was not Earth. The calm, methodical approach of his training had always been beneficial, but now it seemed almost pointless. This was beyond his ability to manage, regardless of his preparation. The figure's large, intelligent, piercing eyes gazed at him with curiosity and an indescribable depth. Being advanced, its gaze fixed on him, its features were alien and yet beautiful, like something from a distant dream. It raised its three-fingered hand to its chest in a gesture that, although alien, resembled a greeting of sorts. "You are the one we need, fear not, rest now, and we will take you into the 5th dimension so you may feel some unease," it said, its voice soft yet clear, echoing in the chamber.

John's breath nearly stopped in his throat, and he swallowed hard. His mind raced as he tried to grasp the situation, but the moment weighed heavily on him. He was no longer anywhere near the ISS. It was totally unfamiliar, standing before beings whose very existence defied everything he had ever known, and somehow, they had chosen him. John attempted to speak, but the words escaped him as the weight of the situation struck him. He was unsure of what lay ahead, and a new journey was about to start. Abruptly, he lost consciousness without any human sensation, and he felt the most peaceful state he had ever felt before. Sometime later, no idea of time, John woke up in an unfamiliar chamber, still feeling disoriented. His heart pounded in his ears as he gradually sat up, feeling bewildered and yet curious.

The alien environment closed in on him from every direction, with figures surrounding him the night before. It stood still before him, observing with its bright, unblinking eyes, as if waiting for him to act. He had believed momentarily it was merely a dream, a hallucination triggered by the shock of the anomaly. Yet, the chilling metal beneath him, the unsettling hum of the chamber, the alien presence made it real, and he knew that this was no dream. Am I losing my mind? John pondered, the thought racing through his mind like an anxious heartbeat. This figure towered over John by at least several inches and appeared breathtaking. The entity tilted its head, as if parsing language was not simply a matter of translation but of truth.

Its eyes, faceted like galaxies, flickered in subtle patterns, constellations rearranged. *You are at the cusp.* It spoke, a voice resonating through the air, within John's thoughts using telepathy. *A boundary where memory becomes reality, and reality yields to recursion.* John swallowed hard, the pressure inside his helmet increasing slightly. His surroundings were no longer recognisable as space, planet, or vessel. Shapes bent around him. A corridor like the one John walked, a surgical bay, then gone. He steadied his breath, recalling the anchor points of procedure, training, and rationality. "What is this place?" He asked again, voice taut. The creature closed its eyes for a moment, a stillness that felt like a gesture of reverence. *This is the Spiral's threshold, the 5th Dimension,* it said again telepathically. *Where the lost come to remember who they were.* If it could indeed be called a leader, the alien leader raised a hand and communicated in a language beyond John's understanding.

Echo: The Infinite Cycle

Yet the phrases seemed strangely familiar, as if they were recognised rather than articulated. Then the entity actually spoke, its mouth opening to release words in flawless English. "You are not in your world anymore, you are in a place beyond space and time, outside the laws that govern your reality," the alien articulated, its voice characterised by a smooth, melodic cadence that reverberated in the air. It progressed with a smooth grace. "You need to understand that your world is facing an end you cannot yet perceive. Ours had already encountered this fate, and we need you to assist us in preventing the same outcome for your world." John's mind spun. "End my world? What do they mean?" Before he could form a reply, a flicker of light in the chamber's centre drew his attention. A dark taint on the once beautiful blue and green sphere, a creeping mass spreading from the planet's core. It was neither an eclipse nor a shadow. It was a distortion, a tear in the fabric of spacetime.

As the dark wave of energy spread, John watched in awe as it engulfed Earth, frighteningly. It felt as if the universe's laws were unravelling right there. "This is the cosmic rupture, John Bennett," the alien leader said solemnly, its voice laced with quiet urgency. "We have witnessed it before, when it destroyed our world. Now it hastens toward yours." John's stomach twisted, and he gasped as he beheld the horror displayed on the hologram. Throughout his career, he encountered natural disasters, space anomalies, and black holes, but this was different. It defied every scientific law and was beyond human understanding. "How is this happening?" John's voice was strained, the question slipping out before he could hold it back. "How could something like this exist, and how can we possibly stop it?"

The alien moved closer, its gaze fixated on John's, a heaviness in its stare that felt like it could penetrate him. "This rupture," it went on, its voice steady but laced with sadness. "Brought about by forces your kind will not comprehend. This is not a natural disaster. It results from actions started by your species through experimentation. We observed it six months ago as it devastated our world, and now it is advancing towards yours." John felt his legs tremble, overwhelmed by the awareness of his fragile mortality, as the vulnerability of Earth flooded his thoughts. He had always trusted in humanity's resilience, yet this was catastrophic, stemming from humanity's quest for knowledge but beyond their current understanding.

It exceeded his comprehension, and he had found it difficult to accept what he was being told. The alien's voice became stern, its gaze unwavering. "You are the one who understands the technology of your world. Thus, you serve as the bridge between your people and other civilisations." Although he had undergone extensive training for space missions, human exploration, and discovery, this situation had far surpassed all normality. Encountering the extraterrestrial entity before him and other civilisations in the Universe was an overwhelming realisation. This crisis was of an unprecedented magnitude, one for which he felt utterly unprepared. How was he supposed to fix a hole in reality itself? Even with their technology, their knowledge, their promises of support, what could one person do against something that could unravel existence? The projection wavered, then sharpened into horrifying clarity. In this hologram Earth, suspended in space like a marble, with tendrils of absolute nothingness creeping across its surface.

Continents disappeared into the void, oceans boiled away into nothing. The assembled entities watched John's face, reading his reaction with the patience of creatures who had seen civilisations rise and fall. John's thoughts careened between disbelief and a growing, terrible certainty that this was not some elaborate hoax. The part of him that had always pushed boundaries, that had volunteered for deep space missions. Precisely because they were dangerous and unknown, he refused to accept that humanity was potentially finished. "I don't know how to halt this, but if you believe I can, I will do everything possible to try, so help us."

The alien leader's expression softened, and he gave a slight nod. "We are not the saviours of your world, you are, but you will require our knowledge, and we will need your strength. Together, we can confront this force, but the question is, are you ready for this?" John took a sharp breath, his heart raced, but deep within him stirred a primal, resolute instinct to survive and defend his planet and humanity. He immediately acknowledged his answer. He had always aspired to explore the unknown and journey to the farthest stars. Now, he had no option but to extend beyond them. "Yes, of course I'm all in," he replied, his voice now steady and confident. "What do we need to do?" The alien's eyes shone with an unexpected glimmer of hope. "You will learn what is necessary. The path is long, but together we will stop the rupture before it consumes your world."

Echo: The Infinite Cycle

The holographic display flickered again, showing Earth with a dark and twisted horizon. John had chosen; he was no longer just an Astronaut in the void but something more, something humanity needed. Light bent unnaturally, casting shadows where none should be, while gravity flickered like a heartbeat, defying the physics that John had always known. *What planet was I on just then?* John thought. He trailed the alien leader through winding corridors that felt alive, suggesting the galactic ship had grown organically over the ages instead of being built. Every surface and room appeared interconnected, creating a singular, sentient unity. "Where are we headed?" John inquired, his voice filled with awe. "Deep into the heart of the ship," the alien responded. "This is our most remarkable creation, it is our last hope, and it has journeyed across the stars in search of a solution. Now it leads you to the salvation of your world."

John listened as they described their world's downfall and how the rupture had shattered their civilisation. Their attention was fixed on rescuing Earth. Though their grief was devastating, it intensified their resolve and their desire to help prevent other worlds from suffering the same fate. As they progressed, the technology grew increasingly remarkable. The technology and harmony left him in awe. It seemed alive, exhibiting a connected consciousness with its occupants and an awareness of its mission. It was designed almost entirely organically and naturally for this unique task. "We have dedicated millennia to this vessel. It is now our only home, our memory, our legacy. We lost our world, but this ship became the world we carried forward."

It paused, eyes settling on John. "We arrived back too late to save what we once had, but you may yet be within the time necessary. It represents our knowledge, will, and is intricately part of who we are. However, we were too late for our world, yet your efforts may not be too late for your world." John stood mesmerised, silently taking it all in. The alien ship radiated vitality, distinct from the alien itself, imbued with consciousness and vibration. This vessel travelled on a universal frequency that surpassed all known human laws, gliding through the cosmos propelled by scalar waves and Zero Point Energy, using quantum state vectors at incomprehensible speeds unbound by space and time limitations. The ship did not just move, it resonated, and John felt it before he understood it, as a pulse beneath the skin or music played somewhere too distant to hear properly but close enough to feel.

It was alive, not in the way a creature lives, but in the way fire does, fierce, aware, impossible to predict. It did not obey rules; it slipped through them. John had trained for complexity, systems, pressure, and crisis. Those ideals were familiar, but this was not complexity - this was presence. Working alongside the crew, time lost its shape. John stopped counting hours and started listening with intent. He had always taken pride in grasping complex systems and adapting under pressure, skills he had honed through training. Despite this, he had only begun comprehending alien technology now. Time blurred as he collaborated with the extraterrestrial crew for what seemed like days or weeks. Once he anchored in the familiar realm of Earth's physics, his scientific intellect was tested to the utmost. He learned to interact with the alien devices, feeling his hands tremble as he manoeuvred through interfaces that seemed somehow linked now with his own thoughts.

He felt the ship's pulse while he worked. It was a steady operational rhythm synchronised with his heartbeat. The deeper he delved, the more he recognised the limits of humanity's grasp of the cosmos and multi-dimensions. The ship's tech unsettled him in quiet, insidious ways. It defied what he understood. Space warped like water, energy obeyed thought, and matter no longer played by familiar rules. These were ideas he had read in forgotten journals and dismissed as fantasy. Now, they moved around him, responding to his breath, his pulse. They did not teach him so much as reveal, one moment at a time, how to shape energy with instinct, how to fold space inwards like cloth. He learned to conjure shields, somehow shifting layers of light and pressure between science and sorcery.

Maybe they had held him, but he did not know yet. However, he was beginning to understand the cost. Presented with propulsion systems that render the ISS engines so basic, like simple toys. Yet this goes beyond technology. It entails grasping the fundamental forces that shape the universe. The aliens discuss higher-dimensional spaces, energy currents that traverse the very fabric of reality, and ancient cosmic forces that even they still find hard to understand. They continued to approach the rupture's epicentre, and everything grew increasingly unstable. The ship creaked and groaned while navigating through ever more distorted regions of space and time. John felt a knot of unease in his stomach as the stars outside began to distort and shift.

Echo: The Infinite Cycle

What had been a stunning array of distant stars transformed into a chaotic swirl of black voids, with stars bending in unnatural arcs as their light faded into nothingness? Gravity, once stable, now flickered intermittently. John felt his boots becoming lighter, as though the ship's artificial gravity could not keep up with the chaotic conditions outside. Whenever he reached for an object, it appeared to float just beyond his grasp, only to snap back as if the laws of nature were being altered. "This is bad," John murmurs, clenching the console tightly as the ship rocks. "We are getting too close to it." The alien leader's typically composed voice now conveyed urgency. "The rupture is expanding more quickly than we expected. Time is running out, and once it hits critical mass, there will be no stopping. It will consume everything!" John felt his heart racing. "What can we do?"

The alien gazed at him intently. "We have sacrificed everything to prevent this, but the crucial factor, Commander Bennett, rests on your expertise, and we cannot achieve this without your help. You must move swiftly, or everything will end." Despite his fear, John realised he had no alternative. He was familiar with human technology, the one capable of making an impact. The conclusive plan was presented to him. A holographic display depicted Earth, its surface warping under the strain of the rupture. "The rupture is a tear in space," the alien clarified. "It is a wound in time, and it will keep spreading unless sealed." John inhaled deeply, his determination strengthening. The ship creaked again, and the stars outside pushed further away into nothingness; their time was running out. He needed to stop the rupture before it destroyed everything in its wake.

As they neared the centre of the rupture, John braced himself. He was part of a catastrophic decision, with the fate of his world resting on him. The alien ship resonated with a subtle urgency as it approached the epicentre of the rupture. Outside, the stars contorted and warped unnaturally, imploding like black holes ready to explode. Inside, tension hung in the air as every alien crew member laboured diligently, their movements smooth and intent as they honed in on the strategy they crafted to avert the cosmic disaster threatening to consume Earth and all in its Solar system. John stood at the heart of the ship's command chamber, hands clasped behind his back, his mind racing. Over the last few days, he had discovered more about the universe than in his entire career, yet nothing was as significant as this.

If he could not save his world, it would be too much to bear. The rupture resembled a wound in the fabric of space and time, ripping at the core of reality, and the Universe was out of alignment with itself. It had already annihilated the alien civilisation and posed a similar threat to Earth's humanity and all inhabitants, including animals and creatures. The alien leader, its ethereal form poised elegantly before John, spoke with a calm yet urgent tone. "We have come to the moment where the time for action is now. The rupture grows faster with each passing second, and we are almost at its centre, but we believe there is one chance left to stop it." John's heart raced. "OK, what is the plan?" The alien leader nodded and pointed to a holographic display that sprang to life before them. Earth appeared distorted, its surface influenced by the expanding rupture, shimmering and rippling as if reality were about to fracture.

"We've analysed the situation further," the alien stated. "The rupture spreads like a disease and will persist unless sealed." John leaned in, his breath panicked in his throat. He had always been skilled at solving problems, but this situation differed. "So, what do you suggest?" John asked. "Your satellite network," the leader responded. "We can synchronise them to create an energy and frequency inversion that will seal the rupture, but the operation is risky. You need to be at the epicentre to activate it." John understood the information. Aligning Earth's satellites with such accuracy was unprecedented and would demand extraordinary coordination.

Yet, with the alien's guidance, it could be achievable. "How do I accomplish this?" He inquired, his thoughts racing through the logistics. "You must be taken back to Earth," the alien replied thoughtfully. "Only you can interface properly with the satellites." It appeared deep in thought, as if it was sensing something else. "We can provide the code, but you will be alone once you start the sequence." John swallowed hard. Returning to Earth meant relinquishing all he had learned here. The technology and the sheer depth of alien understanding pressed against John like a weight he could never fully lift. He knew he was not meant to grasp it all, but he knew what had to be done. "What if I fail?" He asked quietly. The alien leader did not hesitate. "Then the rupture will expand," it said, matter-of-factly. "It will devour Earth, your galaxy, your dimension. There will be nothing left to inherit."

Echo: The Infinite Cycle

John said nothing; he just stood there, letting the words settle like dust. The burden was his now, not just to act, but to succeed. Returning to Earth brought relief and dread. He had journeyed far and witnessed marvels beyond human comprehension. Now he accepted the gravity of it all. Although he could never fully comprehend the alien technology or their extensive grasp of the universe in his lifetime, that no longer mattered. He understood what needed to be done, and he was grateful to his new friends for being there. The alien leader lowered its head, a look of approval shining in its unearthly eyes. "You are the one, Commander Bennett. You will not confront this alone. We will provide the code, knowledge and timing to execute perfectly. However, ultimately, the destiny of your world rests with you."

John stood firm, his thoughts momentarily returned to Earth, his family, colleagues, and the home he had devoted his life to safeguard. Everything felt trivial, overshadowed by the immense task ahead. "I'll go back," he declared with determination. "I will do what it takes to save the Earth, the Galaxy, and prevent the rupture from spreading." The alien leader moved aside as the ship's systems throbbed with energy. Outside, the transparent hull revealed the rupture, a swirling abyss relentlessly consuming everything in its path. There was no time for doubt. "We will prepare you for the journey," the alien assured. "There's no time to lose." John's heart was in overdrive as he braced himself for what was to come. He was about to leave the safety of this ship, a remarkable creation of intelligence and technology, to return to a vulnerable world on the edge of destruction.

He was aware of the threats that lay ahead, the return journey, the increasing instability of the rupture, and the incredibly slim chance of executing the plan in time. There would be no second chances and no tolerance for failure. He was Earth's last hope, and the countdown had already begun. John stood at the entrance of the alien ship's airlock, feeling the burden of the sheer gravity of his decision. The sleek vessel hummed gently, synchronised with the contrasting chaos inside him. As he embarked on this unimaginable journey, he turned to face the alien crew, who had become his allies, mentors, and navigators. Their luminous eyes observe him with a subdued seriousness, as if comprehending his struggles. The alien leader who had guided him on this journey advanced. "You have learned much, Commander Bennett," it said, its tone simultaneously calming and profound.

"You are now a part of something larger than your world. Now the time has come for you to return to save what you love." They now started to return to the ISS coordinates. John inhaled deeply and stepped forward. There was no going back. He nodded to his newfound friends, if he could consider calling them that. Unable to voice his thoughts, he had spent an unknown amount of time on the alien ship, absorbing information. In that fleeting moment, he had caught sight of the universe's vastness and its limitless possibilities. He had seen the most incredible technology, so sophisticated that humanity's most significant accomplishments felt so far behind in time. Now, as he poised on the brink of the alien ship, the weight of his impending actions carried heavy stress and urgency. He was no longer just a scientist or astronaut; he had become Earth's last chance for survival.

The alien leader rested a three-fingered hand on its chest as a sign of profound respect. "Remember, Bennett, you are the first of your kind to witness the vastness that lies beyond the veil of space and time from your world. Ensure it is not the last, prevent your people from suffering the same fate as ours." John swallowed hard, and his throat constricted with emotion. He yearned to assure them he would return victorious and save humanity on Earth with their help, and that humanity would continue and live in peace. Deep down, he recognised there were no assurances that he would ever see them again. Still, inwardly, he hoped that day would come again, so that he might learn more from them during the peaceful days that would follow the resolution of the current dilemma, assuming it would be successful.

Within an instant, he found himself back outside the International Space Station as if he had been teleported and not transported back. The transition felt so smooth that, for a fleeting moment, he believed he had never left. The weight in his chest served as a stark reminder of his mission, one that only he could undertake, a mission that would shape the destiny of his world. "Bennett, do you copy?" The voice crackled through his radio, interrupting his thoughts. Commander Bennett had returned. "We lost you for a moment there." John inhaled slowly, intentionally, enveloped by the familiar sounds of the ISS, the soft creaking of its structure and the gentle hum of air recyclers. He rested his fingers above the radio controls and pressed the button. "Loud and clear, Commander Vos," he responded. "I am here."

Echo: The Infinite Cycle

He looked out at the vast expanse of space that stretched endlessly in every direction. The rupture still loomed out there in the distance, edging closer, like a storm on the horizon, its presence imminent. There was no time to linger, and the mission was clear. He found himself in the space where it all began, but he was no longer just a man on a spacewalk. He was selected for something greater. "Bennett, we're receiving strange readings close to your position," Vos said, a hint of concern in her voice. "Have you noticed anything unusual?" John hesitated, surveying the darkness surrounding the station. For a moment, he believed he had seen a glimmer far away, a light shifting against the emptiness, but then it vanished. "No," he answered, his voice calm. "Nothing unusual, just space." Deep in his mind, the Sigil, the ancient extraterrestrial emblem, glowed with vivid intensity. He persisted in vividly imagining it, a complex and luminous symbol, throbbing with significance.

It was etched into the walls of their Intergalactic vessel, symbolising their civilisation's lost wisdom and resilience. The aliens revealed that it functioned as a key and a bridge linking all. A connection to continue unifying the universe, the essence of space, time, and humanity's fate. His gloved fingers twitched, almost instinctively reaching for the interface on his suit. While his training urged him to focus, remain calm, and follow protocol, he could not escape the intense desire to grasp the true significance of the ancient Sigil. He was never truly alone in this, and he never had been. The Sigil pulsed in his mind, unveiling a truth he comprehended. "I understand now," he murmured as the realisation permeated his very being. "Not merely here to halt it. I am a part of it."

His heart raced. The rupture was more than just a tear in the fabric of space. It symbolised something far more profound, a force older than time, intricately intertwined with the essence of life and death. It related to the aliens, their demise, his journey, and perhaps something even more ancient. What was the connection? How did the symbol unify all his discoveries? As he gazed at the stars, the constellations transformed into something more significant. Every piece of intelligence the alien device had encountered. His dialogue with the extraterrestrials formed interconnected threads into a larger universal tapestry across dimensions. In a moment of epiphany, he realised that the rupture was not a singular occurrence but a recurring cycle spanning across the universe, other dimensions, and civilisations, chosen to shatter it.

D. Gohil

He inhaled deeply, gripping the EVA controls with renewed resolve. "Vos," he stated, his voice calm yet heavy with the gravity of his experiences. "Get the Houston command centre to get ready to deploy all of Earth's satellite network immediately. I have everything necessary, and I am going to prevent the rupture." After a lengthy pause, Vos responded hesitantly and unsure. "Bennett, are you sure? We can't even comprehend what we're facing. How have you discovered a solution?" John dabbed the controls of his suit, blending the alien code connected with the Sigil that was part of him and with Earth's satellite technology. "Believe me," he whispered. "I now see that everything is interconnected." The rupture, the anomaly, and the symbol. The duplicate threads of truth woven into the universe's fabric, a reality that only John had encountered and that he could not prevent. As the ISS floated through the endless expanse, orbiting the Earth spinning below like a delicate ember in the darkness, John felt a singular certainty. It was all part of his life's journey, and he would break the cycle this time. He had always thought the stars contained answers, dedicating his life to mapping their paths, unravelling their enigmas, and envisioning the moment humanity would return to its origins. Now, as he gazed down at Earth through the frigid glass of his helmet, he recognised how limited his understanding was.

The universe was a vast expanse, a battleground, and something beyond it was observing. The radio crackled once more. "Commander Bennett, this is Mission Control. We have received the last transmission, requesting us to configure the Earth's orbital satellites in a way we do not understand fully," Hayes stated. "Can you confirm that the transmission code necessary to link the entire network is ready at your end?"

John tightened his grip on the railing, his heart thumping in his ears. "Yes, we are in position and ready. I need to connect the central unit to the long-range deep space audio transmission module to enhance the reversing frequency. We will be ready when the satellites align with the configurations I shared." "Great, we are relying on your expertise and will act on your command. Just make sure this resolves the rupture. Humanity's future depends on you, John. I have faith in you and wish you the very best. You must achieve this, for all our sakes," Hayes said assuredly. "Mission Control, the unit is connected and operational, and we are ready to proceed. Once all the satellite control units turn green and align correctly," he took a breath to calm himself.

Echo: The Infinite Cycle

"I will send the signal to launch the high-pulse frequency. We are almost there, wait... OK, we are now ready," John said, and found himself holding his breath and praying for the success of all humanity. The alien beings are expected to return near the rupture and will reach out to him once this is successful! *Soon.* The alien leader acknowledged its effectiveness when he had heard the voices whisper directly to him, leaving John in awe of their telekinetic method of communication. *John Bennett, we trusted you, and you have triumphed so far. Now, all of the civilisations will owe you gratitude. Farewell, Commander, we shall meet again.* The manipulated reverse frequency inversion had temporarily stabilised the rupture, and the power driving it continued to decrease. Although Earth was secure, how long would that last? He took a slow breath. "Commander Vos, please respond," he said through his comms. "The rupture has stabilised, but we still have much to accomplish," he added, his voice unwavering at last.

"We are safe for now," but deep down, he understood the reality. He felt relieved and returned to the hatch. The airlock sealed with a final hiss. John's boots struck the deck, magnet clamps securing him to the floor as he steadied himself, panting. Even with the artificial and feeble gravity, he still sensed the phantom pressure of deep space on his body. The feeling of presence clung to his skin like static. As Aryna neared him at the hatch, she scrutinised his visor for any indicators of distress. "You took longer than expected," she mentioned gently. "Your vitals spiked, heart rate and neural pattern deviation." He paused before he answered.

The crew gathered closely behind her, their expressions revealing worry. Even Harish and Kato's voices from the control room emerged through the speakers with a clinical urgency. John slowly removed his helmet, making careful movements. "I saw something," he said. "Out there, it was watching." Vos frowned. "Define 'watching'?" "It mirrored me," John said, his thoughts far away. "My heartbeat and rhythm synced, and there was a voice, no, not a voice, a thought superimposed on mine. It said..." He glanced upward, his eyes vacant. "Soon. That is all, just soon!" A hush settled over the cabin. Harish cleared his throat, trying to sound calm and professional. "Radiation exposure can lead to hallucinations and hypoxia as well. We should conduct full diagnostics, including neuro scans, ECG, and blood chemistry." Yet, as he spoke, the atmosphere in the cabin changed.

The lights dimmed and flickered, followed by a shudder of the station. A deep groan echoed through the metal structure of the ISS, reminiscent of an old ship trapped in ice. Warning strobes flashed intensely, as sirens screamed through the halls, causing telemetry monitors to go haywire. "Pressure fluctuation in Zarya!" Vos yells. "Power surge on the port arrays!" Kato reported from the console. John turned slowly toward the main control panel, his breath momentarily halting. The instruments twitched, blinking like fading fireflies, and then, there it was, inscribed in the glass with a light that defied explanation, the symbol. It writhed across the surface of the control panel, traced not in lines but in shifting constellations as if the stars themselves were rearranging to form it. Ancient, geometric, and alive. Its form pulsed, no, it breathed. Its significance infiltrated John's mind not through language but through essence. Somewhere in the void beyond, the stars faded, and a presence awoke, immense, shapeless, and conscious. A pressure surge swept across the station.

The ISS shrieked around them, the crew shouted, lights exploded, systems collapsed and then came silence, weightlessness, and an internal rumble. Time shattered like glass, and John (Nathan) descended into the void. Pulses of bright glowing lights all around him, then nothing. Pain pierced him, bones fracturing across centuries, lungs failing across timelines, as he was being transported, and the ancient Sigil seared into his vision. *You are the thread.* Darkness surrounded him, and then there was nothing. There was no air, no gravity, only stars and the weight of a thousand lives pressed against the inside of his head.

The shift expanded, distorting the void around him like heat rising off a volcano. The stars behind it twisted into impossible shapes, bending and warping as though reality was thinning. Inside the swirling vortex, the Orb spun, bright, precise, with the Sigil impossibly complex. Nathan could feel its rhythm inside his chest, like a second heartbeat rising in intensity. The station's AI voice crackled with static. "Commander... stabilisation... failing... system integrity collapsing." But Nathan knew it was not failing. It was growing, and the Sigil had never intended to be contained. The shift flared white, and the pull came again, swift, deliberate, undeniable. As he tumbled into the spinning light, Nathan realised he was no longer being thrown across lifetimes. The symbol was intentionally leading him somewhere. This time, he was confident and looking forward to it. This was becoming fun!

Echo: The Infinite Cycle

Chapter 9 – The Agents Stand
1953 CE

He floated in, then landed on his feet this time, almost gracefully. The light receded, replaced by cool air and the steady thrum of technology all around him. Nathan stood in what resembled a command centre, which was certainly not of military design and not entirely corporate. Sleek black walls shimmered with faint circuitry, and agents moved with precision through glass corridors overhead. His attire, old-fashioned, was different again, tactical black, lightweight, and built for speed. The emblem on his chest was the Sigil, simplified and stylised, but unmistakable. He was one of them now, and an agent's monitor showed cascading streams of data, surveillance feeds from around the globe, encrypted streams of information blinking endlessly. Nathan exhaled slowly. This version of him worked inside the system that monitored the very fabric of these shifting realities. The symbol was not being studied right here. It was being protected or contained, or both. Secrets fester in silence as a top operative in a world filled with shadows, Nathan uncovers a truth too explosive to suppress.

Project Resonance was not a singular event. It was a comprehensive, systemic, and ancient phenomenon. The Sigil had been present in every significant intelligence leak over the past half-century. The agency was aware, as it always had been. Nathan's mission transitions from stopping threats to determining who survives to remember the truth. He navigated through ravaged cities, quiet interrogation rooms, and encrypted graveyards of reality. Files emerged, confirming the symbol had been at critical junctures during history's most significant breakdowns. Patterns of sabotage, wrongly attributed to solitary madmen, always leave the same signature. Nathan confronted his superior, the agency Director Maureen Haynes, who, in this reality, was his mother. She revealed that he was the inaugural subject of the experiment. Sigil began with him. Now choosing to forget, he must decide if the world deserves to remember. In his ultimate act as an agent, Nathan uploaded the truth to the world, but not before adding a cypher. Only those who believe will understand it, as the rest will forget.

Bangkok, Phantom Protocol

His fingers reached for a gun instead of a once surgical gauze from a past life. The lab had become a lair, and sirens howled through cracked concrete. He was no longer healing; now he was hunting. An unfamiliar sensation felt like gunmetal and sweat. Slick bite of adrenaline in his throat, Nathan slammed to the ground, his knees cracking against the wet pavement. Asphalt scraped his palms, the shock of it jolting through every nerve like a slap from a dream. Icy rain hammered down, washing grime and heat from the air, blurring the glare of neon signs that pulsed above him like fevered memories. His hand tightened instinctively around an unfamiliar pistol, which should not have belonged to him. "Agent Sullivan, you are now compromised. Get out of there now!" The voice in his earpiece snapped like electricity, urgent and breathless. Nathan's lungs burned as he scrambled to his feet, rainwater soaking the collar of the tactical jacket he had not been wearing a short time before. Across the street, shadows moved deliberately, and in coordination, tracer rounds lit up the night behind him. He did not remember the last assignment. He did not recall being recruited, but his body moved with terrifying precision, as if this had always been his life. *You are no longer a doctor,* his mind whispered, or perhaps something else did.

Echo: The Infinite Cycle

You are now an Agent, an operative, a visitor in a world that is already burning. The comm crackled again in his ear, totally surprising him, coming from a voice that belonged to his handler and uttering it way too calmly. "Run all you want, Sullivan, we are already ahead of you." Nathan froze, the Sigil searing behind his eyes, a brief flickering etched in the static like a threat branded into the veil of reality. Lightning forked above, turning glass and steel into jagged silhouettes. Suddenly, the bullets came barraging down, and Nathan ran, somewhere in the neon jungle of Bangkok, which buzzed with electric life, a city that never slept and where secrets changed hands in the discretion of hidden rooms and street food stalls situated almost everywhere.

* Dear reader, I hope you are enjoying the book so far just as much as I have enjoyed writing it for you. This will be fun! *

Tonight, in the penthouse of a high-rise that did not exist in any official records, the world's most dangerous men sat in council. Agent Mark Sullivan lay prone inside a narrow ventilation shaft, with beads of sweat trickling down his temple. Below him were the air vent slats, where twelve men and women sat at a long obsidian table, their faces chiselled from stone. They were criminals, warlords, and unseen architects of the world's tragedies. Callie's voice crackled through his well-concealed earpiece. "You are inside, and the signals are clean. We are recording everything, so just do not get yourself killed, Mark." He smirked. "That's the plan, believe it or not, Callie."
Lucien Duvall, the phantom at the head of the table, finally spoke. His voice was smooth, deliberate and carried the weight of empires. "Phase one of the purge begins in seventy-two hours, gentlemen. Governments will fall, and resources will be seized. When the dust settles, we decide who survives." A murmur of approval slithered through the room. Mark's grip on his silenced pistol tightened. This was a serious conspiracy. It was a controlled extinction! A vibration in his earpiece made his stomach drop. "Mark," Callie whispered. "I tripped on something, a silent alarm. You have got incoming, so be alert and get out of there, Agent." Gunfire rang in his ears as Mark hit the floor hard, instinctively rolling into a crouch position. His pulse hammered, but something felt wrong. Everything seemed wrong!

His hands checked for wounds, and he felt a leather holster and a sleek tactical suit beneath his fingers. He was armed and trained, and he knew how to handle the men hunting him, but he was not supposed to. He breathed fast, his fingers twitched toward the pistol at his side, and his mind hesitated. A thousand lives clashed, instincts from a hundred battles pressing in at once from the previous lives already encountered. He clenched his teeth, focused and breathed. "Stay in the present." *But which life was the present?* He thought. Cold certainty gripped him. They knew, a deep, amused voice slithered through his earpiece. "Agent Sullivan." Mark dropped, twisting mid-air as gunfire exploded around him, and heat seared past his arm. It was a near miss, and he hit the ground hard, rolling to absorb the impact.

A guard turned slowly. Mark fired, one down, and another spun toward him. He ducked, driving his elbow into the man's throat before ripping the pistol from his grasp. The last enemy raised his rifle, and Mark squeezed the trigger, and a shot cracked through the room. The body hit the marble floor, then silence except for his ragged breath. His escape measured in heartbeats, windows shattered, and the roar of a helicopter rose outside. He sprinted across the marble floor, diving onto the penthouse balcony. A gunshot grazed his shoulder as he leapt into the void, catching the landing skids of his extraction chopper below him, just as a fireball consumed the penthouse. Callie's voice rang in his ear. "Tell me you got something?" Mark raised his fist, revealing a tiny flash drive. "We have seventy-two hours to stop the end of the world."

Shanghai Control Centre

The underground bunker reeked of rust and cold stone, buried beneath the bones of an abandoned industrial district in old Shanghai. Callie's fingers flew across her keyboard as files decrypted before her eyes. She paled. "This isn't just a coup," she whispered. "They are orchestrating total collapse, food shortages, engineered pandemics, and cyberwarfare. Clearly planned for decades." Mark exhaled, rubbing his temples. The weight of it crushed down on him. "How do we stop it?" Callie's answer was grim. "We do not cut the head off the snake before it bites." The discussed plan was audacious. In summary, it involved infiltrating the cabal's central control hub, a fortress located outside the city.

Echo: The Infinite Cycle

Sever their communications and cripple their operations, eliminate Duvall before he vanishes again. They moved at dusk, slipping through checkpoints. Mark, disguised as a high-ranking mercenary, walked in through the front gate as the lights went out. "Did you think I wouldn't be expecting you, Agent?" Duvall's voice echoed through the PA system. Then came the gunfire. The ambush was surgical, and the compound transformed into a kill box. Callie's voice screamed in static as the signal jammed. His team picked off Mark individually as he executed the mission, but it was no longer about victory; it was about survival. Wounded yet relentless, Mark forced his way into the control room where Duvall stood, watching the countdown clock; the purge had begun. "You're a tenacious man, Agent Sullivan," Duvall said as he stepped forward. "But you have already lost." Mark's gun snapped up, and he fired. Duvall moved like a trained assassin. The fight was brutal, a clash of trained killers in the glow of burning data screens. Both had a military background and were highly trained.

Duvall was more potent and faster in his own playground, but Mark, driven by desperation, acted with lightning speed. He dived to the left, seized a chair, and slammed it into Duvall's ribs, causing the man to stagger. Mark seized his moment, clutching the flash drive from the control panel, a repository of every encrypted command and target. Then he slammed his fist onto the emergency console. *Self-destruct sequence started.* The alarms shrieked. "You think this stops me?" Duvall howled. Mark ran as fire chased him down the corridors, and he dived from the compound as flames consumed it. Callie's voice broke through. "You did it!" Mark was breathless as he stared at the flash drive in his palm and then saw it, a Sigil. It was not a corporate mark. It was familiar, and he was sure he had seen it before on a ship pulled from the depths of the East China Sea. A marine ship that was erased from history. It was a mystery that pulsed through his veins.

Tokyo

The rain fell in thick sheets over Tokyo, reflections shimmering in the flooded streets. Mark sat across from an old smuggler in the back of a rundown Izakaya, where the scent of fried food and stale cigarettes lingered in the air.

The smuggler, a gaunt man with deep-set eyes and hands weathered by decades at sea, sipped his sake slowly and deliberately. His voice was a hushed rasp. "You should leave this alone, Agent." Mark placed a photo on the table, a black-and-white image of the symbol etched into rusted steel, barely visible through ocean grime. The smuggler's eyes darkened. "Where did you get this?" "A penthouse in Bangkok, in a control centre in Shanghai, in a dead man's hand, you will never get to know!" Mark replied. The old man exhaled, fingers trembling as he refilled his cup. He asked how Mark had managed to survive those places. "I saw that mark once, many years ago." His gaze turned distant, lost in thought. "A vessel without a name was found drifting 500 km north of the Mariana Trench. A salvage crew brought it up, but only half of them made it back as the ship was scrubbed from every record. The ones who touched it disappeared."

Mark leaned in. "Where?" The smuggler hesitated before scribbling down a set of coordinates on a napkin. "Don't go looking for ghosts, agent. Some things are lost for a reason." Mark pocketed the napkin and stood up. The rain had eased outside, but the chill in the air lingered. "Ghosts or not," he said. "Someone doesn't want this ship to be found. That means I have to find it!" He walked out into the Tokyo night, knowing the next step in this war lay beneath the waves where danger lurked, waiting to strike.

North Pacific Ocean

The research vessel rocked gently upon the endless expanse of the Pacific as a storm loomed in the distance, dark clouds rolling like spectres over the water. Mark stood on the deck staring at the coordinates etched into his mind while the dive team prepared the submersible, a reinforced deep-sea explorer named Leviathan. Callie leaned against the rail beside him, her expression unreadable. "Are you sure about this?" She asked. "No," Mark admitted. "But we have no choice." The ancient Sigil haunted him, appearing everywhere he went, in penthouses, bunkers, and other facilities. This was freaking him out, and he needed to find out why. Now it had led them to a place no one was supposed to return. The dive team loaded up, and Mark climbed into the submersible Leviathan.

Echo: The Infinite Cycle

The hatch sealed with a heavy hiss as the team gently jacked it up and settled it into the calm water, and then the vessel lurched downward. Light vanished within minutes, and the depths became a realm of absolute darkness where the weight of the ocean pressed down like an unseen force. Tiny creatures flickered with bioluminescence in the vast blackness, and then the radar pinged something massive lying ahead. The Leviathan's floodlights flicked on, and the shipwreck emerged from the abyss, a rusted, towering hulk resting in the depths. Barnacles and coral clung to its sides. Mark inhaled deeply. The ship in the North Pacific was at the correct coordinates and waiting. It was damn lucky it was on a ridge and not actually in the Mariana Trench! "This is it," he whispered. The sub's controls flickered, and the lights died momentarily.

The abyss swallowed them whole, and something unknown stirred in the dark. They prepared themselves, suited up into their heavily pressure-ready dive gear, checked the air tanks and began to depressurise the hatch area. They began to swim towards the wreckage as sea life swam past them. Mark and Callie were great swimmers, which helped on a mission like this. They had to venture to the sunken vessel to get the answers they needed. Mark's torch pierced the murk inside the ghost ship as he swam onto the ship's deck. The silence was absolute, and the corridors were far from empty. Faint etchings adorned the walls, as well as symbols and markings that belonged to no known language. The metal beneath his fingers felt wrong. Callie's voice trembled in his earpiece. "Mark, you need to see this." She had discovered what appeared to be a control room, a single desk that remained intact, on which sat a weathered journal.

Mark held the gun designed for underwater combat, should the need arise, as he sensed they were not alone, and delicately flipped the journal open, his pulse hammering. The last entry was dated more than eighty years ago. *You should not have disturbed it. The ancient Sigil was not meant to be broken.* A low creaking sound echoed through the corridors of the ship. Callie's voice whispers. "We're not alone, Mark." What looked like a shadow shifted gently. Mark turned, and he saw the movement. The Sigil revealed corridors that twisted unnaturally by design. The deeper they delved, the stronger the sense of wrongness became. The symbols on the walls appeared to pulse, reacting to their presence.

Then, they discovered a chamber at the centre where a black obelisk rose from the floor, its surface etched with the symbol. It hummed. Mark reached out, feeling the vibration against his palm. "This is a strange ship," Callie breathed in her helmet. "It's like a containment vessel, a prison." Mark's mind reeled as the cabal had erased this ship's existence, and they had been guarding it. A low rumbling began beneath the vessel, as the ancient Sigil glowed. "Mark," Callie gasped. "We have triggered something." The ship shuddered, and a loud metallic-like sound groaned deep and resonant. The sounds echoed through the corridors, followed by another sound, which was not metal but something alive. The journal's last words burned in Mark's mind. "We shouldn't have disturbed it." A shape emerged from the obelisk's glow. Mark aimed the gun, but somehow, he knew it would not help in this scenario; he had to remain alert.

They had to escape and decided to get out of there as quickly as possible to the deck area, then swam back to re-enter the sub. The glow beneath the submersible began to fade as the last of the wreckage was scanned and logged. Mark inhaled deeply through his oxygen mask, forcing calm, although the adrenaline that still pumped from the chaos moments earlier. His hand hovered over the console, fingers trembling but steady enough to complete the recording. Above them, the ocean's crushing silence had returned. Whatever had awakened it, whatever had surged it, was quiet now. "Hull integrity holding," Callie's voice crackled through the comms. "Structural analysis complete, we've got everything we need." "Copy that," Mark replied. "Please take us up." The submersible began its slow ascent, ballast shifting as the craft drifted upward through the heavy black water.

The descent had taken 20 minutes; the return would be faster, urgent, and direct, as the team had seen enough. When they broke the surface, the chill of the night air hit them instantly. Mark cracked the hatch, feeling the cool spray whip across his face as he unlatched his safety helmet and pushed it back. Overhead, the stars were extra bright, too clear, like something had washed the sky clean. The support crew on the research vessel waved them in, hauling ropes taut to guide the sub into the cradle lift. A clang of metal, a few choice curses from the deckhands, and the sub was locked into place. The lift groaned, slowly rising, bringing them back to the world of breathing air and solid footing. Mark climbed out first.

Echo: The Infinite Cycle

He stripped off the upper half of his wetsuit and immediately strode to the deck station where two intel officers stood waiting. "We've now confirmed Duvall's tampering with the site, and we've got imaging to back it," he began. "He was not just after artefacts, he was trying to activate something!" "We had suspected as much," said Commander Haynes, stepping into view. "But we need proper evidence. That wreck site's now classified, no one in or out without clearance from Defence Command." "I'll prepare the report," Mark said. "But we can't wait for the red tape to be cleared. Duvall's still out there, and he's not finished." Haynes gave a tight nod. "You'll have what you need, Agent." The data pulled from the sub's last scan was already feeding into the ship's systems by the time Mark made it to the operations deck. Maps flickered across multiple screens, showing the disturbed seabed, the shipwreck's altered structure, and heat signatures that had no business existing below a half kilometre of water. "He's activated something all right," Callie said, pulling her gloves off as she leaned over the console. "It's not just old tech, some of the readings are pulsing, changing patterns.

Whatever it is, it is alive." Mark nodded grimly. "That wasn't just an exploration operation; it was a trigger, as he wanted someone to notice." "Why?" Callie asked. "Because he's leading them to it, he always was." Haynes paced slowly behind them, with arms crossed. "We've intercepted chatter over encrypted civilian channels. Duvall's name came up alongside coordinates. Rural coast, near Almeria, he has a fallback base there." "Then we move," Mark said. "Before he disappears again!"

Almeria, Spain

The black ops insertion team landed twenty clicks inland just after midnight. Spanish authorities had been looped in under diplomatic necessity, but the operation was strictly under NDA. Decided and agreed that no local enforcement, no media, just extraction. Mark moved with practised precision. He wore light armour under civilian clothing, a headset keyed into Callie and two recon agents positioned around the perimeter. Duvall's compound was nestled into a crumbling industrial site, a former chemical plant, gutted decades ago, now fenced off and forgotten. At least, that is what the public believed.

Thermals showed five heat signatures inside, and Duvall was one of them. The others were armed, casual in posture but alert. They knew they were not safe, but had been unaware that they were surrounded. "Go quietly," Mark whispered into the mic. "Sweep and clear the four." The team breached simultaneously through the rear and the utility entrance. Callie moved like smoke, already inside and disabling surveillance. Mark took point, silenced, sidearm ready, his boots making no sound on the dust-laced concrete. As they moved through rusted corridors and defunct equipment, he spotted the edge of a command terminal, new and out of place. It was tech from an unknown manufacturer. He signalled a halt. "He's here," Callie whispered. "Eastern quadrant, the room marked red on your HUD," as Mark entered first. Duvall stood at the far end of a low-lit control room, dressed in black, with his back turned.

He did not move when the door opened, did not flinch when Mark levelled the pistol. "You never were subtle," Duvall said without turning. "But then, that was never your style, Agent." Mark stepped forward slowly. "What do you think was my style, Duvall? Go ahead, enlighten me." Duvall scoffs. "You were the distraction, the stabiliser and the one who was meant to carry the weight without ever asking the questions," he smirked as he turned around. His face was thinner than Mark had remembered, while his sunken eyes gleamed. "But you asked, and you kept asking even when it hurt!" Duvall growled. "Well, we found your ship," Mark said. "We know what you did down there."

Duvall smiled faintly. "You didn't find it, the Sigil let you find it, I didn't do anything, I just answered a call." "Don't give me mysticism, you stole artefacts, you sabotaged containment systems, and people died." "People always die, that's how old truths are buried, you're here to bury them again?" Mark did not respond. Behind him, Callie slipped through the side door, her weapon raised. She was watching Duvall's hands, not his words. "We're done with games," she said flatly. "You're coming in, and you'll face every tribunal and answer for every lie you built this war on." Duvall's gaze flicked from her to Mark. "It's too late for trials, you think locking me up stops what is already moving?" "No," Mark replied. "But it stops you from making it worse."

Echo: The Infinite Cycle

Duvall raised his hands slowly, but deliberately, and knelt to be cuffed without force. Extraction was clean, Duvall was shackled and escorted to a private containment unit. Mark stood outside the reinforced glass two hours later, watching him sit motionless in the sterile cell, head bowed. "What now?" Callie asked, arms folded as she leaned against the corridor wall. "Now we clean up, we keep the wreck under surveillance, we dig into the data he left behind, and we try to make sense of what this all means." She nodded. "And him?" "Let him rot!" He interrupted, but even as he said it, Mark was not sure. There was more behind Duvall's calm, more than just belief. He had the look of a man who had already passed his burden to someone else. Mark turned away from the cell as the lights in the hallway flickered once.

He did not notice. The ship's operations deck was a hive of activity, and analysts pored over the data retrieved from the wreck, their faces lit by the glow of monitors. The heat signatures and pulsing patterns all pointed to something far beyond human comprehension. Callie stood beside Mark, her arms crossed. "This isn't just about Duvall," she said. "This is bigger, older." Mark nodded. "And it's awake." The words hung in the air between them, heavy with implication. Whatever they had uncovered was only the beginning. In the depths of the ocean, the wreck lay silent, but a faint glow pulsed. It was rhythmic and deliberate, like the heartbeat of a sleeping giant, and it was waking up. Mark turned away from the cell, and the lights in the hallway flickered once; he did not notice.

The temporary command centre, set up in the back of a makeshift operations vehicle overlooking the cliffs, buzzed with quiet urgency. Monitors lined the walls, broadcasting data from the deep-sea wreck. Analysts murmured over the thermal overlays and waveform distortions, their eyes reflecting the shifting pulse of patterns that should not have existed. Outside, the Spanish authorities maintained a polite perimeter; they kept their distance, having seen enough. Whatever Duvall had awoken, it was now beyond jurisdiction, beyond science, and possibly beyond reality. Callie stood beside Mark in the dusk light, arms crossed, and eyes narrowed at the screens. "This isn't just about Duvall," she said, her voice low. "This is way bigger than him, and there has to be more to it."

Callie's words hung in the room like a warning none of them wanted to speak aloud. Mark did not answer at first. He stared at the fractured telemetry on the monitor, jaw tight, shoulders set. For the past hour, he had been still, contained, professional. But something shifted now. The mask slipped. "Nathan wasn't the only name Duvall flagged," he murmured. Callie glanced sideways. "Meaning what?" Mark exhaled, slow and deliberate. "Meaning my mother has known more about this than she ever allowed anyone at the field level to understand. And if Duvall was operating under someone else's directive, she is the one person who might know who he was answering to." Callie straightened, the scent of burnt circuitry lingering in the air as the servers hummed beneath the floorboards.

"Director Haynes isn't the type to withhold national security intel for the fun of it." "No," Mark said. "But she is the type to protect the country by burying the truth beneath ten layers of clearance. Which is why I need to speak to her before this gets any worse." He stepped away from the desk and tapped his comms earpiece. A secure channel had opened with a soft triple-tone. "Mother? It's Mark." A pause. Then her voice, clipped and composed as ever. "You're calling on an encrypted channel at 18:47. That means something has gone wrong." Callie moved closer to the speaker. "It's Duvall," Mark said. "He accessed files no civilian should even know exist. The ones you sealed after the Copenhagen event. Nathan Cole's name is all over the data trail. You need to tell me what's happening." There was another pause.

This one is longer. Heavy. "Mark... step away from the monitors," she said quietly. He frowned and did not move. "Why?" "Because the system you're standing in front of is compromised. Also, because the operation Duvall was involved in, Project Meridian, was never designed to involve you." Callie mouthed the word silently. *Meridian.* Mark did not back away. "Director Haynes, Duvall mentioned a 'primary architect'. Someone above him. Who is it?" On the other end of the line, the room tone changed. Background noise softened. A door closed. Her voice returned lower, guarded. "There is a man named Aldus Crane." Callie blinked. "Never heard of him." "You wouldn't have," Haynes replied.

Echo: The Infinite Cycle

"His existence isn't on paper. He isn't on payroll. He isn't on any register. He was the strategic adviser brought in during the early days of the Meridian trials. He believed the Sigil wasn't an artefact, but an interface. One that could be refined. Directed." Mark's grip tightened around the edges of the desk. "And you let him work on it?" "We didn't let him. We couldn't stop him." That landed harder than she perhaps intended. Callie folded her arms. "So, Crane has been pulling Duvall's strings?" "No," Haynes said. "Crane doesn't pull strings. People orbit him. Duvall was ambitious but predictable. Crane isn't. He influences multiple agencies, ours included.

After Copenhagen, he vanished, and every trace of his involvement was erased. If he has resurfaced now, the stakes are far beyond what you can imagine." The lights flickered overhead as static rippled across the screens. "Mother," Mark said, voice low. "Why didn't you tell me?" There was a rare crack of emotion in her reply. "Because you are my only son. And I will not lose you to the same thing that consumed everyone involved." Callie looked at Mark, eyes softening. He swallowed hard. Haynes continued. "Pull out. Now. Secure the site and await extraction. I'm sending a priority team to take over." "No," Mark said quietly. "This isn't a containment job anymore. Nathan Cole is involved, and whatever Crane is planning... he's using the same pattern the Sigil imprinted on him. We're too far in to step aside." Haynes inhaled sharply, but her reply was cut short. A shrill alert burst across the room. Screens flashed crimson. Callie leaned forward. "What now?" The centre monitor stuttered.

Then stabilised. A new feed appeared, satellite imagery, overlaid with spectral signatures. Mark's stomach dropped. He recognised the configuration. It matched Duvall's stolen files. A tri-point convergence, the same harmonic fracture CERN had accidentally triggered. Only this time, the centre was not Geneva. It was London. More precisely, the exact coordinates of the submersible wreck they had retrieved Duvall. Callie's voice shook. "He didn't just wake something up. He mapped it." "And someone else wants to activate it," Mark added. The overhead lights dimmed again, and the hum of the servers pitched into an uneasy vibration. A persistent beeping sounded from the workstation on the left. Callie tapped the panel. "It's a remote login attempt."

"Blocked?" Mark asked. She hesitated. "No. It's not trying to breach anything." Then the beeping stopped, and a single file opened automatically. Mark and Callie froze. On the screen, in monochrome white, was the Sigil. Not pulsing, not shimmering, just... watching. Mark took a step forward. "Is this Crane?" Beside him, Callie's voice dropped to a whisper. "Or someone talking through him." The symbol flickered, and behind it a shadow formed, as if another feed were bleeding through, pixel by pixel. A silhouette too tall to be Duvall, too still to be humanly natural. The distortion thickened until it resembled the outline of a man standing behind frosted glass. A voice emerged, low and modulated, as though funnelled through five filters at once. "You were never part of the design, Agent Sullivan. Yet here you are."

Mark felt his pulse skip. "Identify yourself." "Names are irrelevant. Only the outcome matters." Callie muttered under her breath, "That's not Crane." The voice continued. "What Duvall began was incomplete. Nathan holds the final anchor point. He is the convergence. You cannot save him. Nor should you try." Mark stepped closer, fury flaring. "And why is that?" The silhouette bowed its head, almost amused. "Because the moment he returns to the surface of your understanding... your world will tilt." The monitors surged with light. Mark shielded his eyes. The Sigil expanded outward until it filled the centre screen, white-hot, bright enough to sting. Callie shouted, "Mark, get back!" But it was too late. The light bent, folded, twisted, not outward but inward, pulling the air in a breathless collapse.

The Sigil spiralled like a whirlpool in the centre of reality itself. Mark reached for the table, but the surface warped beneath his hands. Callie grabbed his arm. "Mark!" His vision fractured into shards of colour and shadow. The voice whispered one last phrase as the world ruptured around him. "Your part in this begins now." Then the Sigil seized him, and the room vanished. Mark nodded slowly, his gaze fixed on the central feed, where a slow pulsing glow rippled through the sonar images like a heartbeat caught in time. "And it's awake," he said. The words falling between them like a prophecy. Somewhere in the depths, the wreckage lay dormant, but not dead, beneath warped hulls and ancient mechanisms, something stirred with intention.

Echo: The Infinite Cycle

There was a sudden glitch, and everything froze around him, as if the Sigil paused to recalibrate itself. This indicated a mysterious sleeping intelligence, patient and far older than their tools or their language. The rhythm was biological, ritualistic, and alive. Then suddenly, the monitors went white. Every screen in the room blinked at once, then shimmered in a silent, rhythmic, pure light. Coordinated like a symphony only the universe could hear. The analysts froze. Callie reached for her comm, but it crackled uselessly in her hand, and Mark felt it again, that pressure in his skull, the pulling sensation just behind his eyes, something being peeled back.

* * *

For a flash moment, he thought to himself. Here I was, Agent Mark Sullivan, but how did they bring up my real name, Nathan Cole? Do multiverses exist? Clearly, I am connected with the Sigil across other lives and more, which is now making more sense to Nathan.

* * *

His hand drifted to his wrist unconsciously, where his skin had begun to glow faintly, not so visible to the others, but he felt it warm, like a memory surfacing. The mark, the Sigil, resonated beneath the surface, tracing itself into his bones with each pulse. A tunnel of spinning white spiralled open before him. No alarms now, no voices, just the soft hum of inevitability. The symbol had opened another door. This time, Nathan stepped forward willingly, thinking or praying it would lead him back to Silvia. Just the slow folding of reality into something quieter, as if space were closing a door behind him. A strange stillness filled the air. Fluorescent lights buzzed overhead, but the pattern was different, with longer intervals, a rhythm that seemed oddly familiar. The Sigil had rewritten him once again and placed him there, somewhere within this bright, polished world, as the heartbeat continued.

D. Gohil

Chapter 10 – The Surgeon's Crossroads
2024 CE

The transition ended with a sharp intake of breath as Nathan opened his eyes to blinding white light, and the sharp smell of antiseptic filled his nostrils. Cold steel, polished glass, and the steady beep of a heart monitor anchored him in this new reality. He was standing in an operating theatre, his hands gloved, gown sterile, mask secured. The familiar pulse of the Sigil hummed faintly beneath his skin, almost drowned beneath the rush of urgent activity around him. "Scalpel!" A nurse said firmly, placing the instrument in his outstretched hand before he even processed the request. He knew that he was most likely the surgeon about to perform a surgery; he must clearly be qualified to perform here. Nathan's fingers moved with precise confidence, making an incision along the exposed chest. No idea how, but he knew this procedure intimately, though his conscious mind had never studied medicine. Another life had another fragment resurfacing. Thank goodness he was naturally not squeamish of real blood! This should be interesting...

D. Gohil

Hammersmith Hospital, London

Beyond the bright surgical lights, shadows flickered in his periphery. The symbol's presence lingered. It had brought him here for a reason, but what choice would it demand this time? The theatre buzzed with low-frequency hum, monitors blinking in rhythm like a pulse outside time. Nathan's hands hovered above the incision point, steady but reluctant. Every movement mattered, but not in the way surgery demanded. This was not about saving a life. It was about unlocking something buried in flesh and memory. As his scalpel cut through the skin, the pattern revealed itself, curved lines that did not follow muscle or artery, but spiralled outward like a forgotten script. The patient did not stir, as anaesthesia held them still, but Nathan sensed a presence behind the silence. The Sigil reacted. Symbols flared faintly beneath the surface, lighting up as if summoned. He paused, the blade trembling slightly in his grip.

This body was not a body; it was a message waiting to be read. What precedes modern medicine and the choice he makes will ripple through every existence. Each patient bears some manifestation of the mark. Anomalies in their nervous system, geometric scars, and seizures triggered by lunar light, and then he sees a pattern. The operating room transforms into a different battlefield, where every scalpel stroke becomes a spiritual rite. During surgery, visions haunt Nathan as past lives dissect future selves, offering counsel. Through flickering overhead lights, a child's whisper, a lover's scream. Each time he hesitates, his hands instinctively act, steered by knowledge he had not consciously learned before.

The ultimate patient mirrors himself, damaged and succumbing to Sigil overload, choosing whether to cut or to cure, morphs into a philosophical dilemma in deciding that some wounds are to remain unhealed. Blood was no longer a metaphor as it pooled beneath his hands, the scalpel trembled as if life were ending, or perhaps beginning. This body remembered what his mind had not, blinding light and a sharp, sterile scent. Nathan gasped, his lungs felt heavy, and his blood rushed in his veins. His vision swam, adjusting to the reality before him, where a scalpel rested in his fingers that were, in fact, still just like a surgeon's hands are known to be. "Surgeon Michael Torres, we're losing him!" *Surgeon, what the hell?* That thought hit Nathan hard.

Echo: The Infinite Cycle

When reality kicked in fully, the scalpel glinted under the harsh light, its edge immaculate, its purpose ambiguous. Nathan's fingers did not hesitate. They traced pathways like a pianist rediscovering a childhood melody; muscle memory dictated what the mind could not grasp. He felt it, a tug, almost imperceptible where metal met tissue. Not resistance, but recognition, as though the blade was awakening something dormant beneath the skin. Dr Torres, ever the sentinel of clinical detachment, watched from the periphery, though his eyes betrayed an unease. He had seen miracles, tragedies, things that defied public scrutiny, but this, this was not medicine; it was communion. The symbol pulsed beneath the surface, delicate and ancient, like a breath held too long. Michael paused again, not out of fear, but reverence. This body was not broken; it was encrypted.

He peered down at the young patient on the table. The boy's chest was carefully opened, revealing the silent cavity where his failing heart had struggled for far too long. It was time to replace it. "Scalpel, please, I need to harvest a blood vessel directly from his chest," he said, his voice measured and calm against the tension in the room. A nurse beside him, with her movements as equally rehearsed as his own, placed it in his outstretched hand without hesitation. He had trained for this for decades in this present incarnation. Every breath in the room held weight, every second counted as Michael Torres worked methodically, removing the boy's diseased heart. The stark familiarity of it all struck him, as if he had been there himself before, not as a surgeon but as a child just like his patient.

He had, in fact, once been the boy on the table, his own tiny heart weak from the moment he was born. His earliest recollections were not of playgrounds or family holidays but of cold hospital corridors, the rhythmic beeping of monitors, and his mother's voice whispering prayers into the sterile air. He had spent years living under uncertainty. One defining moment changed everything. The brilliant surgeon whose hands held precision and compassion saved him. That incredible man was Surgeon Emad AlJaaly, who had given him a second chance and had provided him with a purpose. Michael had devoted his life to paying that gift forward, and now, as he stood on the other side of the table, prepared to do this for the boy what had once been gifted to him. He knew he would not fail, and he would not allow it in the current crisis.

D. Gohil

The first incisions were routine, and his hands moved with the muscle memory of a thousand surgeries before. The donor heart had been perfectly preserved in its sterile cooler and was a pristine gift of life that had arrived just in time. Michael worked with meticulous care, suturing vessels with the precision of an artist. The operating room buzzed with controlled urgency, the team responding to his every command. This was what he did best and had perfect control. Then it happened, the moment they integrated the new heart, the monitors erupted into a discordant shriek. Michael's head turned towards the screen, the boy's pulse spiking, his heart fibrillating violently, its rhythm chaotic and unstable. Within seconds, the numbers plummeted. "He's crashing!" A nurse called out, panic creeping into her voice.

Michael's hands clenched into fists before he forced himself to take a slow breath, as panic had no place in that room. He issued emergency verbal orders, his team scrambling into action. They tried stimulation and administered medication, but nothing was working, and then the unthinkable happened. The heart stopped, and a heavy silence filled the room, suffocating and unbearable. Michael could hear the blood roaring in his ears, drowning out the whispers of his fears. Time was slipping through his fingers like sand. He glanced at the boy's lifeless form and at the motionless heart he had promised to make beat again, but he was adamant not to lose him. A decision no surgeon should face. His mind raced through all the possibilities in a flash. The safest option was to wait before putting the boy on a bypass machine. Hoping for another heart, but they had little time. They needed a solution, and it had to come soon!

The boy's body was already weak, and he might not survive the wait. There was one other option, an experimental procedure that had only been successful in animal trials. A technique requiring manual reconditioning of the heart through specialised nerve stimulation. It was an untested method that could either restart the heart or lead it to irreversible failure. It was a significant gamble, an uncertain level of risk, but if Michael did nothing, the boy would die right there and then. He took a deep breath and made the decision. "We'll try the reconditioning procedure now." His team hesitated for a fraction of a second before springing into action and defying the impossible. The room became very crowded, with electrodes attached to the boy, wires connected to the machines, and adjustments made in record time.

Echo: The Infinite Cycle

Michael and his team worked with the precision of a brilliant, experienced surgical team, with his hands steady despite the storm raging within him. Every movement had to be perfect. One miscalculation and the boy would be lost. He started the impulse, one second, two, three and the screen flickered, then a single beep, another, and another, a heartbeat. The rhythm steadied. The numbers rose and stabilised before all their eyes, and the collective breath of the room was exhaled altogether. Cheers erupted. Relief flooded Michael's chest, but he remained frozen, watching and waiting, and then he finally allowed himself to breathe, only when he was confident that the boy's heart was strong. The weight of a life saved.

Hours later, Michael stepped into the waiting room, his surgical gown heavy with sweat, his body drained. He had spent years before the patient's loved ones, delivering news that could either shatter or rebuild lives, and it never got easier. The boy's parents stood as he approached, their hands clasped together in desperation. He offered them a small but genuine smile. "Your son is going to be OK." The mother collapsed into tears, sobs shaking her slight frame. The father respectfully gripped Michael's hands, his voice breaking as he murmured words of gratitude. Which he barely heard over the rush of relief washing over him. Exhaustion settled into his bones as he stepped away, but something else lingered beneath it, something that always made the gruelling hours and impossible decisions worthwhile. This mattered for all the awards and breakthroughs. It was about saving lives and fighting for them. On that day, a boy would live another day, and surely, a longer life ahead. Dr Michael Torres scarcely had time to collect his thoughts. The scent of antiseptic clung to him, and the weight of exhaustion felt heavy on his body, but he was physically fit. He had just saved one life for the day, yet the universe was relentless. It never allowed the man to rest for long. As he stepped out of the waiting room, hoping for a brief reprieve, his pager vibrated against his hip:

CODE BLUE, TRAUMA BAY 2

His pulse spiked, another life dangled on the edge of oblivion, and he was the only thing standing between survival and death for his next patient. With long, determined strides, he moved down the gleaming hospital corridor.

His mind was still with the boy he had just saved, but there was no time to dwell, only to act to help another life. The room contracted around him, bright halogens spilt over the young woman's body, casting her pale flesh in cruel contrast to the violent red blooming beneath her. "Michael, snap out of it!" Torres barked at himself, already snapping on gloves. "We've got seconds." Michael moved fast. The wound was not random. The slices bore an eerie symmetry, dancing along the abdomen in a pattern too deliberate, too familiar. His hands knew them; he should not, but he did. A nurse handed him forceps with trembling fingers. Behind the chaos, the monitor let out a high-pitched whine, flatline. "She's coding!" Someone shouted. Torres stepped back, eyes narrowing. "This isn't just a stab wound..."

Michael's gaze dropped to the edges of the deepest gash, and there it was again, the Sigil. Faint, carved into muscle like a whisper from before birth. "What have we got?" Torres asked, already pulling on a fresh pair of gloves. "Twenty-six-year-old female with multiple stab wounds to the abdomen," a trauma nurse reported, her voice clipped but urgent. "BPs crashing 70 over 40 and dropping fast. Lost two litres before she even got here. We need to go now." "She is bleeding out internally," Michael mutters. "Get me a portable ultrasound. We need to locate the source, prep for emergency thoracotomy." His team sprang into action, IV lines adjusted, transfusions pushed, and the ultrasound probe slid over the woman's abdomen, revealing a dark mass where her liver should have been.

The blade had gone deep, tearing through vital tissue, causing a haemorrhage they could never control without opening her up immediately. "Damn it," he swore under his breath. "We are out of time. We need to crack her open now! Get her to the OR right now and fast!" Every second was a countdown to death. They rushed her down the hallway, wheels spinning, as Michael and his team exchanged instructions in perfect unison. The lift ride was long, but precision took over. Scalpels, suction pipes, and forceps were already there, waiting, when they burst into the operating room. The familiar rhythm of surgery surrounded him, but this was no ordinary operation. Michael made a swift incision along her sternum, exposing the cavity beneath. The moment he cut into her flesh, a fresh wave of blood gushed out, painting his gloves in slick crimson, and his heart pounded in his chest.

Echo: The Infinite Cycle

"Clamp! Now!" He shouted, reaching deep inside her, searching for the bleeder. His fingers found the torn vessel pulsing weakly beneath his grip. "We have got a hepatic artery rupture. We need to repair this before she bleeds out on the table." His assistant worked quickly, handing him sutures while another doctor kept her vitals from plummeting further, but the damage was extensive. Every stitch seemed to come undone with the slightest movement. Then the worst thing happened. The heart monitor flatlined. "She's coding!" Yelled a nurse. A collective breath was inhaled in the room, but Michael had no time for panic. "Get me the internal paddles! Charge to 20!" Time slowed as he pressed the metal paddles directly to her heart. "Clear!" A jolt of electricity surged through her, lifting her body slightly off the table. The monitor flickered and then went flat again. "Again! Charge to 30!" Another shock, another agonising second, then it beeped continuously.

The most minuscule, weakest rhythm, but it was there, a heartbeat, a second chance. Michael wasted no time. "Continue with the repair. We're not losing her now." For the next two hours, he fought against death itself. He clamped, stitched, and cauterised every wound with the hands of a man who refused to accept fate's cruelty. One wrong move and she would slip away, but step by step, stitch by stitch, her body held on. Finally, as the last suture was placed and the bleeding ceased. Michael let out a breath he had not realised he was holding so long. "She's stable," the anaesthesiologist confirmed, her voice laced with exhaustion too. The tension in the room evaporated like mist in sunlight, and Michael leaned back, blinking against the sweat stinging his eyes.

He glanced down at the woman, at the fragile rise and fall of her chest, at the life they had fought so hard to save. Tonight, another heart would keep beating. Michael would keep fighting because this was his purpose, standing on the razor-thin edge between life and death, refusing to let go. During the last trial of the day, the hospital seemed to close in as the weight of his latest surgery pressed down on Dr Michael Torres's shoulders. He had barely stepped out of the operating room, still tasting the tension in his throat, when the intercom crackled to life with urgency. "Dr Torres, emergency, trauma incoming, multiple victims, estimated in two minutes." Though seasoned by years of critical operations, his heart skipped a beat for two minutes.

He had no time to process, no time to rest, not now. He wiped his brow, his surgical gown still damp with sweat, and pivoted back towards the ER. When the ambulance doors burst open, controlled chaos erupted loudly, but it was managed. The paramedics pulled out two stretchers at once, one carrying a young woman barely in her twenties, her torso drenched in blood. The second held an older man, his face pale, as he gasped for air, his hands clutching at his chest. "Gunshot wound (GSW) to the abdomen, severe internal bleeding," one paramedic called out as they wheeled the woman in. "Massive heart attack, unresponsive on route," said the other, followed by the man, two critical cases, both patients on the brink of death. Michael's mind raced, absorbing the urgency. He had two operating theatres prepared, but they were short-staffed that day. After back-to-back procedures all day, he only had one elite trauma team available. "Dammit," he muttered.

He had to make a call, and his gut clenched. He made his choice quickly. "Dr Chen, take the GSW patient and prep for an immediate thoracotomy. I will handle the cardiac case." With a nod, the team split. Michael then rushed the older man into OR one, racing against time. "BP crashing seventy over forty!" A nurse shouted. "Charge the paddles!" Michael insisted, his hands moving, cutting away the remnants of the man's shirt. His patient's heartbeat was erratic, the jagged lines on the monitor spelling out impending death. Michael placed the defibrillator paddles on the man's chest. "Clear!" The body jolted, but the screen remained unchanged. "Again!" Another shock, but still nothing.

The room's air thickened, and Michael's vision tunnelled to the failing heart before him. He refused to lose him, not today. "Start cardiac massage now!" Gloved hands compressed the man's chest in rhythmic thrusts. Michael moved with surgical precision, making an incision along the sternum. He reached in, wrapping his hands around the heart, manually massaging life into it. The sensation was always surreal, as if holding life in his hand. He squeezed at perfect intervals, praying for a rhythm to return, beep one beat, beep, beep a second, then a third. The monitor stuttered back to life, an erratic pulse emerging from the brink of nothingness, and a breath of relief rippled through the room, but Michael did not stop. He sutured a ruptured artery, stabilised the heart, and ensured that the man was steady before finally stepping back.

Echo: The Infinite Cycle

"Transfer him to the ICU," he said, exhaustion crept into his voice. He turned to the team. "Excellent work, well done to all of you!" A nurse's voice came over the intercom. "Dr Torres, Dr Chen needs backup. The GSW patient is crashing." Michael did not hesitate. He stripped off his bloodstained gloves, pulled on a fresh pair, and rushed into OR two, the last stand. The room was a war zone, the woman's blood pressure was in freefall, and her skin was pallid. Dr Chen was elbow-deep in her abdomen, battling against a catastrophic rupture in the liver. "She has lost too much blood! I cannot find the source fast enough!" Chen's voice sounded desperate. Michael grabbed a retractor and dived in. "We will not lose her, don't worry," he reassured. Every second mattered, and Michael clamped down on the bleeding artery, his hands working in perfect synchrony with Dr Chen's.

The sutures were swift, but the woman's vitals still dipped. She was slipping away. "Come on, stay with me," Michael made the last stitch. The haemorrhaging slowed, and the beeping sound on the monitor stabilised. A few heartbeats later, the young woman drew a weak, shuddering breath. Michael exhaled deeply, stepping back from the table, his hands, steady as they had always been, trembled ever so slightly as the weight of the night settled upon him. "She's stable," Dr Chen spoke, almost in disbelief. "She's going to make it!" Michael smiled. The team shared tired smiles with him, the room filled with the unspoken camaraderie of those who had faced death and won, at least for today, as the patients were wheeled to ICU recovery.

Michael slumped into a chair in the break room, his head in his hands, his body screaming for rest. Yet his mind remained alert, processing the countless close calls of the day. He let out a long breath, aware that the next challenge was always just around the corner, and it was the next storm. A shadow fell across the room. "Dr AlJaaly?" He saw the man in a crisp blue suit standing in the doorway, wearing his signature Trilby hat. His posture was rigid, and his expression unreadable. Michael frowned. "Oh wow, my goodness, what a pleasant surprise, how can I help you, Sir?" The doctor stepped forward and placed a sleek black folder on the table. "I think you're going to want to see this." Michael hesitated, then opened the file. His eyes scanned the first page, and his stomach dropped. Beneath the official letterhead of a high-security government agency, a single name. *Michael Torres*.

Michael's pulse quickened. He did not know how or why, but something told him this was trouble or something far greater than any surgery he had ever performed at the hospital. The game started in the underbelly of London, and Michael was about to be drawn right into it. Dr Torres had faced the brink of death before, but tonight had tested every ounce of his resolve. The hospital corridors were quieter now, yet the day's weight still pressed against him like a gripping vice. The heart transplant on the young boy had saved him by a miracle against all odds that day. The second emergency was a bit messier, which had taken him and his team to the brink of exhaustion that day. He entered his office, rubbing his temples, craving a moment of calm. As he reached for his coat, he noticed something.

Another similar file was left on his desk, and he did not recall who had placed it there. The folder was unmarked, save for a strange etched symbol in the corner, a triangle intersected by jagged lines of the Sigil. He had seen it years ago, buried in the footnotes of obscure medical research whispered about in conversations not meant to be overheard. It was a symbol tied to experimental science, the work that did not make it into medical journals but existed in the shadows. He hesitated before he flipped the file open. Inside was a single sheet of paper. *Dr Torres, you have touched the impossible tonight. We will be watching you.* There was no signature or explanation. The ancient Sigil was stamped again at the bottom of the page. A chill crept down his spine; his exhausted mind wanted to dismiss it. To pass it off as a prank or a misunderstanding, but deep down, he knew better. This was not a coincidence. The next chapter had already begun elsewhere. Heartbeat monitor flatlined, the Sigil, which was there, glowing faintly beneath the operating table, its spirals etched into the cold steel. The world around him blurred. The surgical lamp flickered, and the instruments on the tray rattled as the room tilted. Nathan stumbled backwards, and his gloves were soaked in blood. The procedure was complete, and the patient remained stable. The team efficiently closed and dressed the wound. Nathan removed his gloves, his thoughts weighed down. This was more than just saving a life. It represented something more profound. The symbol had placed Nathan in roles of power, command, and peril, yet here. It had granted him a chance to heal.

Echo: The Infinite Cycle

A sense of dread persisted. As he approached the scrub room, the lights flickered abnormally. The walls seemed to pulse softly, almost as if they were breathing. In the glass panel ahead, he spotted it once more; the Sigil was visible. It rotated slowly in the mirrored surface. The ground beneath him shook slightly. The tremors were subtle, as if reality was loosening its hold once again. *Re-alignment starting.* The voice was inhuman, resonating directly in his mind as the room collapsed inward, colours blending into spirals of light. Another transformation from the Sigil and the Orb was underway. Let's see where it takes him next.

D. Gohil

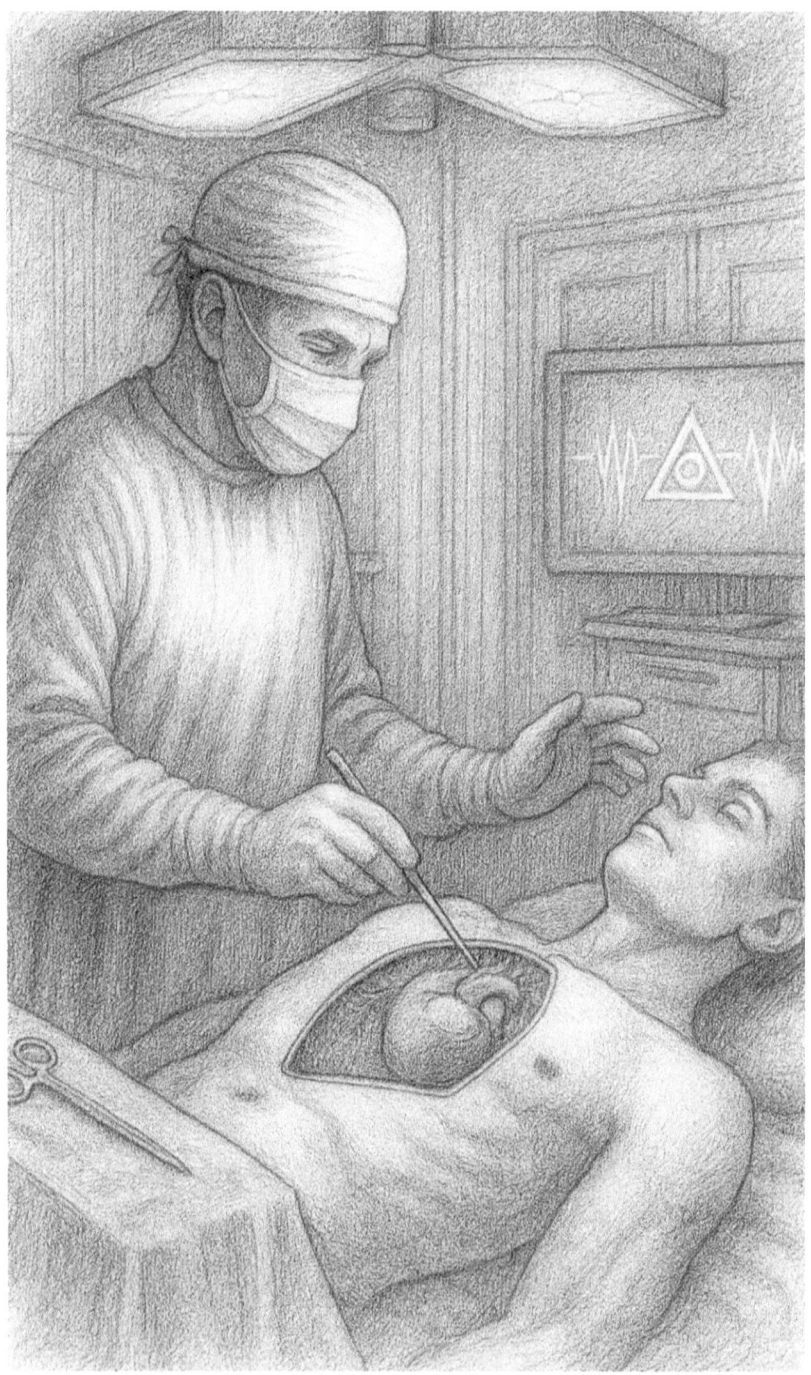

Chapter 11 – Lost Love
2179 CE

The world felt softened at the edges, colours a shade too gentle. Vision hazy, then not waking. The Sigil's presence felt fragile, a faint echo fading through a dream. Nathan stood under a pale spring sky, with the Neo-London skyline beyond the park ahead, where cherry blossoms fluttered softly in the breeze. The air was calm, fresh, and strangely familiar. His pulse slowed, as this felt different from the abrupt changes he had felt before. Was this real, home perhaps? Had the Sigil granted him a moment of mercy, a chance to reclaim what was lost across lifetimes? He scanned the park until his eyes locked onto a figure seated on a cafe terrace. Silvia looked just as he remembered. Serene, beautiful, effortlessly elegant and her sunglasses resting casually on top of her head as she scrolled through her device. The simple sight of her took his breath away. Nathan's throat tightened. Was this real? Some echoes never fade. Among the many lives Nathan had drifted through, one connection always glowed brighter than the rest, a love so deep that it transcends dimensions.

D. Gohil

In this chapter, he wanders the misty streets of Neo-London, unsure of the cause of his chest ache. Then he spots her, a figment of memory. It is Silvia. She does not recognise him, yet with her smile, he recalls a past affection. Nathan trails her to evoke more memories. Gradually, snippets slowly return, laughter shared in a vineyard, debates over fate, a promise exchanged beneath a meteor shower. She was now engaged to another, and her life was secure, while he remained a memory she could no longer recollect. The Sigil appears on a necklace she wore, which she believes is a family heirloom. Then, when Nathan dabs the pendant, it pulses, flooding her with a memory.

Neon blended with candlelight, while the cafe was infused with the scents of jazz and rain, she sat across the room from her, though he had not forgotten her name. Nathan breathed in the warm air, which carried a hint of floral fragrance. He opened his eyes gently. He had sat at a table that had an electronic advertisement flashing. The year was 2179. "What the fuck." Nathan felt emotional, enveloped in love and felt like he was back home, finally back with Silvia. Her tender voice was so close. The rain knocked against the windows, creating patterns of light and shadow in the cafe's dim atmosphere. Neo-London throbbed, electric and vibrant, a city that had long forgotten its past. However, Nathan had not forgotten, and now neither could he, as she was there.

The approx. 150 years separating them instantly melted away, as the candlelight flickered, intertwined with the dark waves of her hair.

She held the same soft gaze and a slight furrow in her brow whilst deep in thought. Yet she was not his Silvia, not in this life, not from the year of his life where he so longed to be. Nathan gripped his coffee cup tightly, knuckles pale from the tension. Fate had deceived him before, and this situation was even more difficult. Does he approach her? A second chance hung before him, but could it be genuine? The cafe was cosy, one of the rare spots in the glass city that had not succumbed to full automation. The air carried the scent of spiced chai and freshly brewed espresso. A lingering trace of a time before artificial fragrances and automated robot services dominated the environment. Let us see this love bond and Nathan's feelings in this chapter, even though this is all in the future, his love is strong:

Echo: The Infinite Cycle

Neo-London, The Glass City

Genuine smooth jazz not dissimilar to his era, played softly through the subtle speakers, melding with the distant conversations of augmented humans and the gentle sound of rain pattering against the windowpanes. Nathan experienced only silence as he tightened his grip around the warm coffee cup, his knuckles turning slightly pale. Across the cafe sat Silvia, or a woman who closely resembled her, on a table by the window. With sleek raven hair tucked behind one ear, her deep brown eyes scrutinised the flowing lines of holo-font text that floated from a device above her wrist like liquid light. She moved slightly, her profile illuminated by the neon light streaming through the rain-soaked glass, revealing the same softness in her features, like how she unconsciously nibbled the tip of her nail when deep in thought.

Nathan felt his heart pulse faster somewhere in his chest, although it was not Silvia. He had been seeking answers, struggling through many identities and lives, questioning how this had unfolded. Why was he being shifted through time and space, reborn in various centuries with only faint echoes of his past following him like whispers in the dark? The universe or Sigil seemed to mock him. It had brought her back to him again, but for what reason? A torrent of thoughts surged through his mind, and his body acted before he could convince himself otherwise. He rose from his seat and crossed the cafe in deliberately measured strides. Initially, she hardly noticed him, her attention absorbed by the changing data in front of her. However, as his shadow loomed over her table, something within her paused. Her fingers halted mid-motion, and her eyes glanced upward briefly.

The city outside disappeared, leaving Nathan to struggle against the turmoil inside himself. He could not help it and had decided to walk over to her. "Mind if I sit?" He asked. She paused what she was doing and evaluated him. "Do I know you?" Silvia's voice seemed woven into the breeze, soft, effortless, exactly as he remembered. Nothing about her has changed. He managed a smile, concealing the thousands of emotions battling within him. "No, but perhaps we should rectify that," a tentative smile appeared on her lips. "That depends, are you a salesperson?" He chuckled. "Just a man seeking a meaningful conversation." She slightly tilted her head up, examining him with amusement or familiarity.

"That is an interesting method. Most people send a holo-text introduction and rely on the AI algorithm to determine compatibility." Nathan settled into the seat opposite her. "I guess I'm old-fashioned," he said, scanning her curiously. "What's your name?" "My name is Nathan." The way this echoed was as if she were savouring the sound, and it charged the atmosphere. "Hello, I am Silvia," she added naturally, and his heart jumped. At that moment, it felt like Nathan was struggling against the déjà vu washing over him and the heavy burden of history repeating itself. How she gazed at him and how her presence stirred something profound within him was far too intense to alter. Silvia leaned back, her arms crossed with quiet amusement. "You are staring, Nathan." "Sorry," he responded quickly, forcing himself to concentrate. "You just remind me of someone." Her smile faded a bit. "A good someone?"

Nathan sighed. "The best, someone I miss dearly." Something enigmatic flashed in her expression, her fingers grazed the edge of her cup as if deep in thought, before she spoke again. She said. "You seem familiar for some reason." His brain froze, but before he could respond, a soft ping echoed from her holo-screen. She glanced down at the alert, her relaxed demeanour transforming into a more guarded stance. Nathan glimpsed the text flashing on the screen before she dismissed it. The fine hairs on the back of his neck stood up. "Silvia," he asked cautiously. "Who are you?" She paused, then exhaled softly. "That's a complex question," she sighed. The sound of the approaching footsteps caused them to tense up. Nathan discreetly glanced away, noticing in the rain-smeared glass the reflection of two men in matte-black suits moving with deliberate precision.

Nathan felt concerned. "Silvia," he whispered. "We must leave now." Without hesitation, she took his hand like they had done this before. Together, they disappeared into the neon-lit turmoil of the city, now fate or whatever cruel force controlled this had brought her before him again, but why? The lower districts in the city created a chaotic maze of forgotten streets, where the air hung heavy with smog. The neon lights above had only faintly pierced the artificial darkness. Towering steel structures loomed above their windows, mirroring the shifting glow of holographic auroras that pulsed in hues that never quite reached the ground. Nathan navigated quickly through the crowded streets, his coat wet from the constant mist rising from rusted vents. The buildings around that area appeared very run-down and almost derelict.

Echo: The Infinite Cycle

The air, filled with oil, soaked metal, and a strong chemical scent, had a synthetic undertone that seemed to linger indefinitely. The marketplace thrived with noise and activity, vendors shouting in various languages as their stalls brimmed with smuggled cybernetics, illicit neural enhancements, and biotech upgrades of dubious provenance. Clearly, a run-down part of town. However, he was not concerned as his attention was on her. Silvia navigated through the crowd with determination, maintaining a straight posture and steady pace. The gentle light of data streams flickered around her wrist as she browsed a holo-feed, appearing absorbed in her task, unaware of the presence trailing her. She failed to recognise that mere hours earlier, she had briefly recalled something, only for it to be taken away. Nathan clenched his jaw, maintaining distance while observing her intently.

Who had reprogrammed her, NexTech? Is it the AI algorithm, or something more nefarious at play here? He had sensed their presence, feeling their influence infiltrate his mind like a parasite settling into his thoughts. He ducked under a rusted scaffolding that used to hold an old tram line, slipping into the shadows of the district's depths. The vibe felt strikingly dissimilar in this city, like outdated tech transformed into components. Old cables hung like spider webs across crumbling alleyways, lit only by flickering neon signs that buzzed unpredictably. Silvia strolled past the market and neared a building that made Nathan shiver. It was NexTech! The structure, crafted from obsidian glass, rose tall and sleek, seeming strangely out of place amidst the grim skyline. A vivid blue energy flowed across its surface, producing a steady, rhythmic pulse that reverberated within Nathan's bones.

This corporation represented something significant. He had delved into the archives and comprehended what lay beneath. The ancient Sigil was hidden beneath the steel and circuitry of the city and tucked away in a location to keep it hidden. Silvia approached it head-on, Nathan inhaled slowly, his breath misting in the cold air, as he found himself at a crossroads. He could allow her to continue her life safely and without thought, or follow her into the unknown. The heart of the force that had changed his mind, he was already sure of his decision. Nathan moved forward, melting into the shadows as the NexTech doors closed around her completely. She worked there.

After infiltrating many high-security facilities, he could quickly tell the difference between arrogance and paranoia, both of which NexTech displayed excessively. The underground complex felt surprisingly cold with an unnatural chill that penetrated through gaps in the polished floors and pressed against his skin, despite the climate-controlled air. The walls pulsated with flowing data illuminated in dynamic shades of blue and green, their flickering patterns resembling the veins of a gigantic living organism. Suspended glass walkways stretched overhead, connecting control hubs where shadowy figures moved behind frosted barriers. A low hum filled the silence, echoing a soft electric buzz. He remained near the shadows, aware that the AI monitors detected not only movement but also anomalies, heat signatures, neural patterns, or any irregularities, as outlined by NexTech's old innovations.

He gracefully manoeuvred past an observation node, its artificial eye rotating slowly and deliberately. At the corridor's end, he came across a chamber protected by multiple layers of encrypted security. This room distinguished itself from the rest of the facility, designed with sterile precision. The walls were hewn from the raw stone beneath Neo-London. Time had left marks on their surfaces, which stood protected from the city's digital radiance above. The air was thick with the essence of antiquity, as though something from his past was watching. Nathan approached the Sigil located deep within the centre of the room, and at first it looked like a complex geometric design, but the markings shifted as he neared. The lines pulsed, transforming the configurations vibrant, sentient, cognisant at sight.

This was no creation of NexTech. It pre-dated the city, and even him; a shiver coursed through him. He had encountered this Sigil previously, through different lifetimes and contexts. It had no place within a temple deep in a forgotten jungle, among the ruins of a ship adrift in the ocean, and on a banner in a war held by soldiers whose identities were lost to time. It certainly did not belong here. It had always existed, dominating him, and now it seemed to dominate her too. Nathan tightened his fists, feeling the air vibrate around him, warping as if reality was fighting to maintain its form. He realised that this was a persistent symbol, a cage, and an intricate system meant to ensnare them both, chaining their fates in never-ending loops. If he did not shatter this soon, he would lose Silvia forever. The day was nearing its end.

Echo: The Infinite Cycle

He was politely asked to leave so she could continue with her project. Nathan found a bar close by and monitored the building, hoping to see her again that night, but it was not meant to be. The following day at NexTech Research lab, Sector 7, Nathan barged into Silvia's lab without knocking, the door hissing open before the biometric scanners could register him. Air was heavy with the sterile odour of synthetic materials and subtle hints of ozone from the active holo-projectors. Walls of smart glass adorned with floating DNA models, cybernetic blueprints, and glowing research notes, all suspended like constellations in mid-air. Data streams flickered between stations. Pulsating in soft electric blues, each conveying fragments of knowledge far beyond the grasp of most humanity. Silvia glanced up from her work, surprised him as she had swapped her sleek NexTech uniform for a white high-collared lab coat.

The sleeves rolled up as if she had been deep in research for hours. A single stylus was mistakenly placed behind her ear. "You again, how did you get in here?" Her voice was sharp, yet tinged with caution. Without pausing, Nathan crossed the room in three quick strides and took her hands before she could pull away. "Silvia, you need to listen. I realise this seems crazy, but you must hear me out." She attempted to withdraw, but everything changed when his fingers grazed her pendant. A tremor swept through her, accompanied by a violent shudder as if her cells were rejecting or recalling something they never meant to. A breathless gasp escaped her, her pupils dilated, broad and unfocused, as memories surged, golden chandeliers radiating with candlelit brilliance. Cold air pressed against his skin, the only proof that a body still stood somewhere in the present.

Musket fire echoed in the distance, and a stolen kiss was shared beneath the shadowy columns, accompanied by a wedding veil. A promise whispered under the moonlight, entwined with thoughts of war and death, a scream, her scream. Centuries weighed heavily on her chest, a raw ache of something incomplete and taken away too soon. Her breath caught as she instinctively curled her fingers around Nathan's wrist as though to ground herself at the moment. Her voice quivered, her whisper of his name slipping from her lips like a spectre. "Nathan?" His heart tightened. "I'm here." The alarms sounded before he could utter anything further, before he could inquire whether she truly recalled or if it was merely fragmented echoes seeping through.

Red light filled the lab, and the bright glass walls immediately darkened as security lockdown protocols activated. The gentle hum of the facility's servers faded beneath the loud metallic clang of doors locking shut and magnetic locks engaging. A synthesised emotionless voice resounded from the speakers. "Containment breach detected, acquired and response units on the way." Nathan felt a chill run through him. Immediately, as fast as they could, they were on their way to NexTech's research complex, the upper districts and rooftops of Neo-London extended infinitely, a continuous expanse of steel and glass shrouded in the neon haze of an unceasing city. From this elevation, the streets below seemed almost tranquil, mere rivers of light and motion, oblivious to the two fugitives escaping for their lives above. Nathan pulled Silvia along, his hold firm as they navigated the vents and service bridges, their boots squelching on the rain-soaked metal.

The distant sound of sirens, mixed with the electric buzz of the city behind them. The air thickened with the scent of ozone and machine oil, as persistent smog wove through the towering skyscrapers. Suddenly, a shockwave tore through the night, followed by a NexTech security drone firing bullets, just missing them, but destroying a nearby maintenance structure. Amidst it all, the Sigil pulsed, not just within flesh but across fibre-optics and circuitry etched into the architecture like a secret code. "NexTech's onto us," Silvia said, voice trembling. "They weren't supposed to find out." Nathan's eyes shifted from her to the horizon, where drones darted between billboards like fireflies of war. His breath froze at the sight, symbols he had seen beneath skin now glowing on screens, twisted and distorted.

Advertising false salvation. "They know," he murmured. "They want you back." Silvia looked down at her trembling hands. Her raven hair clung to her damp skin, and her expression was resolute. Ahead, three more drones zipped through the sky, their mechanical eyes scanning the area, red beams sliced through the fog, sweeping and probing. "We can't escape them indefinitely," Silvia remarked. Nathan understood human bodies had limits. Fatigue would eventually take over, while NexTech drones showed no signs of slowing down. He faced her, determination in his tone. "There's just one escape route." Silvia sighs in resignation, fully aware of his implication. "The Sigil." Another blast echoed, this one nearer.

Echo: The Infinite Cycle

The shockwave unleashed a cascade of shattered glass as one of the skyscraper windows exploded from the impact. There was no choice left, Nathan yanked her forward, turning onto a pavement, then another. He was now familiar with the route, descending the emergency stairwell and navigating through the old research tunnels until they arrived at the NexTech lab's central chamber. They burst into the chamber, where security alarms blared behind them. The room loomed large, ancient, and out of place. It seemed unfit for this city of steel and circuits, as if the walls in this space had not been constructed but revealed, etched into the bedrock beneath Neo-London. At the centre embedded within the floor, the symbol throbbed. It ignited as they stepped onto the platform, recognising and responding to their presence. The conversation had been perfect. They talked, laughed, and shared old stories as though nothing strange had ever happened.

Nathan's heart ached with both joy and dread. He wanted to stay, and he desperately needed to freeze this reality and live there at that moment. Unfortunately, the signs were returning. As they walked together beneath the falling leaves, the petals drifted unnaturally, slowing mid-air, pausing as if caught inside some invisible frame. It was temporary, a glitch. The sky subtly dimmed, colours draining into softer hues. Silvia turned to him, smiling tenderly. "It is not your time yet, Nathan. We will find each other again, come back to me soon."

Silvia faced Nathan, her dark eyes fixed on him with no lingering doubt or fear. "No more running, Nathan," she declared, tightening her grip on his hand. "This time we will finish it together." The ancient Sigil reacted, sending a wave of energy through the chamber, the air vibrating with unimaginable power. She kissed him, and Nathan closed his eyes, staying in the moment with warmth. Then the Sigil's glow flickered along her fingertips, sending an ethereal pulse throughout the room. Nathan's heart sank. "Please, not now, for fuck's sake!" The ancient Sigil would not allow him to remain. The Orb materialised from the fireplace, its flames twisting. Nathan reached for her, but she appeared to be fading, and the world fell apart. She was not Silvia, not in this moment, yet her kiss carried the essence of every lifetime they had experienced together. The symbol's familiar pulse vibrated through his chest. The cycle continued, and Nathan pulled forward again, into another existence, waiting to reveal itself.

D. Gohil

Echo: The Infinite Cycle

Chapter 12 – Betrayal in Blood
1793 CE

Nathan struck the metal with enough force, enough to rattle his teeth. The clang echoed down sterile corridors, chased by flickering lights that sputtered like a failing recollection. Above him, a gentle mechanical hum reverberated along his spine. He blinked, a breath clouded as he forced himself to sit. The floor felt cold and sterile. The scent of burnt circuitry lingered, as if something had gone awry. He glanced down at himself. He was dressed in black tactical gear, with a badge clipped to his chest that identified him as Director Julien Marcel, Internal Oversight Division. Authority pressed along his spine. How had he ended up in this programme? The uniform suited him too well, which made it even more natural, too alien to be something he could recollect. The Sigil pulsed beneath the steel, subtly, insistently. He was not intruding as he belonged here. A door hissed open with hydraulic indifference, like a machine tired of memory. Two agents stood there waiting, both wearing identical uniforms, clean, sharp, and unreadable. One agent nodded. "Director, the internal breach you warned of has begun." Nathan's stomach knotted.

A name he did not recall, a warning he had been issued this identity. Still, the dread unfurling in his gut told him everything he needed to know. Betrayal had already taken root; this time it bore a familiar face. There is no pain like betrayal. Not when it comes with blood or blades, but when it arrives in the voice of someone you trusted. It does not explode, it seeps subtly, like damp creeping under a painted wall. At first, Nathan was too blind to acknowledge it. He did not want to see a deleted message that disappeared before he could read it properly, like a joke from a friend that struck too close, echoing from another life. Voices in the dark whispered truths, their accents too varied to be a coincidence. They were not after his power. They sought him, not the soldier, strategist, but the saviour. Someone he had rescued from the flames, someone he had loved, in their choice to betray him. They may have saved the multiverse, and in that cruel paradox, the symbol offered no solace, only silence. It recorded, it witnessed, it rendered no judgment. Nathan asked. "When did I betray you?"

Stars absorbed into the circuit, darkness collapsed into neon, his visor cracked and chrome fogged with each breath. The transition snapped like a broken cycle, and Nathan collapsed, his palms hitting the Sigil as pain surged in his chest. The air split, a whisper curling behind his eyes like a claw. *Not yet, you are not done.* Glass shattered across the sky, the battlefield faded away, and Nathan fell. Into the abyss, time folded inward, gravity lost form. There was no air, no up, no floor, only screams and memories, every name he had ever borne stretching taut across an infinite horizon. He blinked, and his eyes seemed unlike his own. Stuck in a battlefield where steam rose from scorching earth.

The metallic scent of plasma hung thick as smoke, and drones sliced through the sky. Vertical Take-Off and Landing aircraft (VTOLs) screamed overhead. While in Neo-Tokyo, a rooftop is slick with rain and neon sirens wailing beneath a riot of lights. Digital banners shouted revolution, the wind tugged at his coat as he turned, red sands swirling around him. A sword hung across his back, distant chanting rose across the dunes, haunting and far away. *You are the thread, you are the key, you are the wound that never healed.* He heard in his mind. Then the symbol erupted into sand and fragmented, a cockpit, an ice throne, a child's drawing of stars, as time wept.

Echo: The Infinite Cycle

He spiralled through name after name, Nathan Cole, John Bennett, and Michael Torres, an anchor, commander of nothing, bearer of everything. Then, a presence, light bent around it as if gravity had surrendered; its voice, not spoken, was felt. *You tore the veil. Now you must walk in both realms.* The entity reached into him, and the spiral synchronised.

- all the lives
- all the roles
- all the consequences

Stillness, one breath felt heavy, his eyes opened, and space disappeared. Only the Sigil remained, suspended in shadow. A hand brushed his shoulder. It was a hooded figure. "You were a knight," it said gently. "And you still are," it gestured towards a nearby alley cloaked in shadow. "There's much to remember."

Occupied France, A Mission Doomed to Fail

A voice once again echoed in his mind. *France, the year is 1793.* Nathan trembled and shouted, which echoed through stone-clad alleys, as men in grey uniforms stormed past. Jackboots ringing on cobblestone, armbands gleaming beneath the damp lamplight, and the air was thick with fear and the smell of diesel. Nazis, another war, a different uniform, but the trauma of Jerusalem still seemed to burn behind his eyes. Nathan hesitated, then stepped into the dark. The rain fell all at once, gunfire shattered the silence, and diesel fumes mingled with smoke. Bells tolled over Paris, thunderous and final. Nathan hit the cobbles hard, sliding into shadow, his gloved fingers wrapped around cold steel. Above the chaos, a woman's voice sliced through the night like a blade. "Keep running, Julien!" And he did. Nathan ducked as a bullet shattered the wooden shutter just inches from his head. Splinters rained down on him as Élise pulled at his arm. "Run, Julien, run fast!" A cold mist enveloped the night, cloaking the city in a stifling veil of secrecy. Fear while gaslights flickered dimly, their light consumed by the darkness. A loud voice called behind him. "Keep running, Julien!" Nathan's mind spun in confusion.

"Am I Julien now?" His thoughts scrambled until clarity hit him like a hammer. I am here, in another body again, living another life. This realisation struck just as a bullet zipped past his ear, splintering a wooden shutter in front of him. He instinctively ducked, nearly losing his balance. Then a mighty hand pulled him into a narrow alley. "Move!" The voice was urgent, distinctly female, and had a strong French accent. Julien pivoted swiftly to spot her. Élise had dark, defiant eyes, a scarf wrapped around her curls, and damp clothes from the Parisian mist. Holding an old pistol, which she clenched tightly in her trembling hands. The urgency in her gaze allowed no time for questions as they fled together. The Parisian labyrinth lay before them, with alleys thick with shadows, imposing stone buildings, and the sporadic flicker of candlelight behind boarded windows. The city served as a friend and foe, providing avenues for escape and harbouring traps.

Behind them, the rhythmic thump of Nazi boots resonated like a death march. Julien's breath came in ragged gasps, and his heart pounded, although Julien had no recollections of this existence. Instinct kicked in as he ducked under low arches, leapt over fences, and navigated through deserted market stalls. Another gunshot echoed through the night, accompanied by more shouts in German in the close background. "Run faster!" Élise shouted as they moved hard to gain some distance. Later, they stood at the entrance of a dark, silent bakery that appeared deserted, and Élise pushed him, locked the door behind them. The air was filled with the scent of stale bread and gunpowder. Above them, a dimly lit flat featured a wooden table at its centre, cluttered with maps and radio equipment.

A worn French Resistance flag hung on the wall, and Julien bent forward, gasping as sweat dripped down his forehead. Élise did not allow him a moment to catch his breath. She turned to him with rage shining in her eyes. "Julien, what the hell happened out there!?" Julien swallowed hard. What had happened? His mind was as blank as ever, with no memories of the mission. No recollection of who he had been mere hours ago, but the pain in her voice revealed everything to him. Something had gone wrong, and Julien was about to find out. Élise rubbed her face, and she breathed heavily. "We lost them all, Julien," she murmured. "Antoine and Marco trusted you!" A nauseating weight sank into Julien's chest. "I got them killed?"

Echo: The Infinite Cycle

Her words carried the accusation, but her gaze communicated it even more profoundly, as if he had betrayed everything. Then, without warning, memories flooded back to him: candlelight, hushed words in the dark, her lips on his. The warmth of cherished moments before the war would soon vanish for both of them. Julien had cared for her deeply, but now she loathed him. Just as he was about to speak, the radio buzzed to life, a voice laden with urgency breaking the stillness. "They know where you are. Get out now!" Élise went pale as she grasped her pistol. "Right, we have to move fast." Julien's instincts urged him to flee, but before they could respond, the sound of heavy boots echoed outside, and rifles were being raised. They were encircled, and the door burst inward with a thunderous crash, sending shards of wood scattering. Nazi soldiers surged in like a torrent, rifles ready, their boots thundering against the wooden floorboards. The faint light of the lone oil lamp in the room danced erratically with the abrupt movement, creating ghastly shadows on the walls.

Élise was the quickest to respond, and she quickly turned, raising her pistol in one fluid motion. The first shot echoed loudly, a sharp crack in the enclosed space, and the closest soldier had little time to comprehend the assault before the bullet struck him in his chest. He fell backwards. Toppling a wooden chair upon hitting the ground before anyone else could respond. She shot again, a loud crack echoed, and another soldier reeled back as blood filled the air around him. His body collapsed against the table, cluttered with resistance maps. There were too many, and even more surged in. They shouted orders in German, merging into the escalating turmoil. Julien reacted instinctively, lunging to pull Élise back, but then bang! One gunshot, louder than the others, made everything feel like the world slowed down.

Élise's body jolted violently as she fell to the floor, her fingers twitching and her grip on the pistol slipping. A dark red stain spread across her white blouse, sharp pain against her pale skin. Julien caught her just before she fell to the ground. "Noooooo!" his voice broke. She felt so light in his arms, too light! As her life was slipping away, her breath became shallower with every second, each exhale weaker than before, and for a moment, her dark eyes met his. The fire that had always burned there, the defiance, the sharp wit, and fearless determination, were fading gently, dimming like an ember lacking oxygen.

Yet she managed a faint smile. "Still a fool," she whispered, and just like that, she was gone. She had known, and she had not told him. The realisation arrived quietly, like a knife set gently on a table. He had seen death countless times across various lives, but this was different. The surrounding shouting barely penetrated as hands pulled him away from her. He neither resisted nor struggled; there was no point, as his knees hit the wooden floor as they pulled Élise. Her body lay limp, her scarf slipping from her head as they dragged her away. The world became a blur when a rifle stock struck the back of Julien's head, and pain surged quickly, followed by darkness. Julien woke to the chill of a cold, concrete floor and a hard surface against his back. His body throbbed, every muscle felt battered, and his joints ached from the awkward position he had left himself in. His wrists were securely tied behind him, the coarse rope digging into his skin.

The air hung heavy with the smell of mould and damp stone, a potent blend of decay and hopelessness. The cell was cramped, little more than a concrete box with walls stained by rust. A door of iron bars, and a solo flickering lightbulb buzzed above, projecting erratic shadows that appeared to creep along the walls. Footsteps incoming, steady and purposeful. Julien raised his head, squinting through the fog obscuring his sight. A shadowy figure lingered near the bars, then emerged into the faint light, a tall, lean German officer. His uniform was immaculate, and his boots gleamed like mirrors, a man who took pleasure in his power and could instil fear without even raising his voice. He looked at Julien with malicious, detached amusement, tilting his head as if he were a predator evaluating injured prey.

A slow, wolfish grin spread across his lips. "Well, Herr Julien," the officer mocked, his voice smooth with a grin. "You have failed in your minor, worthless rebellion." Julien stayed silent. The officer crouched in front of him casually, igniting a cigarette with a flick of his silver Zippo lighter. The acrid smell of burning tobacco filled the air, blending with the cell's dampness. "Did you think you could win against us?" The German asked as he exhaled smoke, his tone almost casual. "France is ours, the Resistance is merely a dying ember, a foolish dream held by foolish, desperate men and naïve women." Julien tightened his jaw. The officer grinned, taking another slow drag before letting the ash fall beside Julien's boot. "You should know," he continued, his voice dipping to a more insidious whisper.

Echo: The Infinite Cycle

"Your people are weak, and they crumble so easily, it makes me laugh." Julien's fingers twitched against his restraints, knuckles whitening. The German's smirk widened. "Ah, that gets your attention, doesn't it?" He gestured lazily towards the corridor behind him. Two more soldiers appeared, dragging someone forward. A man, bloodied and broken, and his face barely recognisable beneath bruises and swelling. Julien's stomach twisted. The officer clicked his tongue, shaking his head as if disappointed. "We found your contact," he gestured towards the battered man. "He gave you up in an instant." Julien's gut clenched, revealing that someone had betrayed him and the others. The air in the cell suddenly felt suffocating, as the officer leaned in, his voice dropping to a whisper. "Do you know what he told us, Julien?" Julien did not respond. "He need not have bothered."

The officer chuckles softly as he gets up. "It doesn't matter, because you will tell us the rest." The iron door creaked open as two soldiers came in, grabbed Julien by the arms, and pulled him to his feet. Pain shot through his shoulders, but he remained unresponsive. "Take him to the officer's quarters," the German commands, adjusting his coat. "Our guest will tell us everything." Julien clenched his jaw. He refused to comply, but he needed to escape immediately. The room was filled with the scents of leather, brandy, and burning tobacco. Julien sat in a high-backed chair, his hands tightly bound behind him. Though his shoulders ached and the rope dug into his skin, he remained calm and composed. The German officer across from him moved deliberately, pouring brandy into a crystal glass.

His uniform was also pristine, and his expression exuded smug satisfaction. "Let's talk," Julien said. Shifting slightly to test his restraints. The knots were anchored around his wrists, but still manageable. "I don't know what you're talking about," he said, buying himself some time. The officer laughed softly, swirling his brandy in the glass. "Oh, but you do." With a casual motion, he opened a leather folder on the desk and displayed its contents across the smooth wood. There were photographs, maps, and radio codes as proof. Julien felt a chill wash over him as his gaze travelled over the incriminating pages of the resistance safe houses. All marked in red ink and filled with names, faces, and meticulously organised sabotage plans. The officer observed him intently, savouring his drink with deliberate slowness.

"We discovered your little stash," he taunted. "The radio, the encryption sheets, even your escape routes. It is over for you." Julien took a measured breath, working to calm his racing heart, as he only had moments to respond. He tensed, assessed the situation, and then launched himself with a powerful thrust. He propelled himself forward, chair and all, crashing into the officer's chest. The brandy glass broke against the desk, spilling liquid over the documents. The officer reeled back, briefly taken by surprise, and Julien seized the opportunity. He contorted his restrained hands beneath his legs to bring them in front of him. His fingers scrambled for the officer's belt and grasped the knife handle. A soldier burst through the door, and Julien's pulse surged, but in an instant, he slashed the blade across the rope, severing his restraints. Knife clattered to the ground as he reached for the officer's holstered Luger instead. The German roared in anger, reaching for his weapon far too slowly, and Julien fired.

The first soldier in the doorway fell, and a second lunged behind him. Julien fired again, the gun thumped heavily in his grasp, yet the shot found its mark. Mayhem broke out with shouted commands reverberating through the halls, boots crashing against the ground, and sirens blaring across the compound. Julien grabbed the fallen soldier's rifle and dashed through the labyrinthine hallways, driven by an instinct that urged him onward. He darted past an intersection as bullets splintered the wooden beams beside him, near a window at the corridor's end. Julien acted instinctively, sprinting at full speed before leaping and crashing through the glass. The frigid night air hit his face as he landed on the gravel below, and a sharp pain shot through his side, but he pushed himself to rise.

The compound courtyard was chaotic, with soldiers darting about, gunfire illuminating the shadows, and a German transport truck idling by the main gate, its engine growling. *That is my way out.* Julien ran as a soldier shouted, rifles raised, and gunfire crackled through the night. He threw himself onto the truck bed, kicking a soldier off as the driver turned in shock. Julien did not hesitate; he climbed into the cab and slammed the butt of his stolen rifle into the driver's skull. The man slumped unconscious, and Julien seized the wheel. Then the truck roared forward, bullets pinged off the metal as he revved the engine. Tyres skidded against the dirt as the front gate loomed ahead. A soldier stepped onto the road, weapon raised, and Julien did not hesitate.

Echo: The Infinite Cycle

The truck crashed through the barrier, wood and metal fracturing everywhere as he sped onto the open road. The gunfire faded in the distance, cold wind rushing through the broken windscreen. He was free, yet the victory felt empty. He had lost Élise and the team. Julien gripped the steering wheel, breathing heavily, although his hands remained steady. A tightness gripped his chest, and this moment cut deep. Suddenly, his vision blurred, and the road ahead shimmered as if reality was distorting. The truck's headlights revealed something surreal in the distance, a symbol. The vehicle swerved and crashed unexpectedly. Julien lost control and had to jump out of the truck. He ran, his boots slamming against rain and slick cobblestones. His breath ragged and heart hammering like a war drum. Gunfire ripped through the Parisian night, and the scent of damp stone and burning oil filled his lungs.

A voice, Élise. *You shouldn't be here, Nathan.* His real name in his mind, then agony struck as a bullet tore into his side. His legs gave out beneath him, and the world spun as he collapsed against a brick wall, blood warm against his fingers and his vision blurred. The ancient Sigil was etched onto the wet pavement beneath him. Its symbols are barely visible in the dim streetlights, waiting, watching, calling. Julien's body felt heavy, and his pulse slowed as the Sigil came alive. Light flickered along its intricate spirals, spreading outward like circuitry, humming in rhythm with the distant sirens as the world tilted. The Orb rose this time, not as a liquid light but as an unstable and distorting glitch. Nathan had no choice; the bullet wound was no longer on his mind.

The firewall crumbled, not the digital one, but the one surrounding his mind. The truth permitted was lethal, and the confrontation reached its climax. Nathan stood frozen as the evidence lay bare before him. Familiar faces behind the sabotage, colleagues who had smiled and shaken his hand, all now revealed as traitors. The Sigil pulsed brighter in the street, expanding like a breathing mechanism, and the facility trembled as alarms blared. *You always thought you could control it.* One of his betrayers sneers in his mind. *The symbol does not serve you. You serve it!* The floor beneath him vibrated as the Sigil's spiralling design unfolded, its rings rotating inward with mechanical precision. The shift had begun, and Nathan was swallowed by the light once again.

D. Gohil

Echo: The Infinite Cycle

Chapter 13 – The Enigma
1967 CE

The chamber exhaled low and slow like ancient wind slipping through forgotten stone. The walls curved inward, seamless and obsidian, etched with faint grooves that pulsed once, then dimmed, as though acknowledging his arrival. Nathan did not move, not yet. The stillness was not absence; it was waiting. At the centre of the room stood a pedestal, half-swallowed by shadow, its surface covered with symbols he had seen before but never understood. The same symbols that once whispered beneath skin, through surgery, through circuitry. A low hum stirred the air, subtle but familiar. The Sigil was there, and for the first time, Nathan felt entirely seen, starting to trust this ancient symbol. Pale blue light pulsed gently along the black marble floor, revealing intricate spiralling shapes outward beneath his boots. The Sigil was everywhere, present, pulsing, and strangely aware.

D. Gohil

Arched ceilings vanished into darkness, and dozens of silent, robed figures lined the walls, faces veiled by shadow. Their synchronised movements resembled something between ritual and calculation, as a deep voice emerged from the circle. "You've come far, Nathan Cole." The speaker stepped forward, eyes glimmering beneath the hood, swirling like liquid stars, lost long before they reached this chamber. Nathan swallowed hard. This was not another random layer of existence; he was nearing the centre of the design. A monastery predating maps, perched high on the Carpathian cliffs, the wind perpetually sang. The walls resonate with secrets, and the monks here do not vocalise but convey meaning through a language that transcends words, employing symbols, gestures, and dreams.

Nathan arrives through a vivid vision, as the symbol calls to him, the stones once again envelop him. Riddles are not meant to be solved but remembered; each chamber depicts a reflection of himself. Every puzzle solution causes it to fade, and silence itself speaks. At the monastery's centre, a mural displays the Sigil, surrounded by images of destruction and renewal. Nathan recognises himself in every stroke, becoming the canvas. The final room is empty except for a mirror inscribed with *You already know*. The sea surged beneath his boots as the Sigil shimmered below deck, and the storm served as a warning. The mystery had not deepened but awakened:

Deep Atlantic Waters

Nathan hit the deck hard on his back, like an anchor dropped, lungs constricting, ribs screaming in pain, temporarily overwhelmed by blinding light. He felt seawater fill his mouth and throat as the waves threw up sprays onto the ship's hull, causing him to gag and cough. Distant alarms blared, but they were not from his time. Gradually, his vision cleared, revealing flashes of metal grating, rusted bolts, and hurried footsteps. Was this a nightmare or a memory? Nothing seemed real. Cold seeped through his body. As lightning split the sky, he went inside, and he looked up through the glass, observing the storm and sensing something alive within it. The battleship belonging to the Royal Navy, HMS Royal Waters, sailed through the Atlantic Ocean that afternoon. An unsettling silence that made even the most seasoned sailors shift uncomfortably, even though hardened by years at sea.

Echo: The Infinite Cycle

The crew moved with near-perfect efficiency, but today something felt unsettled for everyone on board. There was tension all around the crew as they navigated the mission and potential dangers. Nathan had yet to discover who he was as he later stood at the bow of the military vessel. The wind lashed against his face as he gazed into the black waters stretching endlessly ahead. A quiet sense of command began to rise within him, reflected in the way the crew looked towards him. Later that evening, once Nathan had gathered his bearings, understanding both where he stood and who he had become, he came to the startling realisation that he was, in fact, Zach Thompson. His hands tightened on the rail, fingers pressing into the chill of the metal, as he fixed his stare upon the abyss beyond the bow. The Atlantic stretched endlessly into an inky void, swallowing the moonlight in broken, jagged slivers. The water felt both alive and restless beneath them. A month ago, the cargo vessel named Maribel had vanished near these coordinates without a distress signal, and the wreckage had just disappeared without a logical reason.

He had a night to level his thoughts and find himself, thankfully, uninterrupted. After a much-needed sleep, he was awake at 6 am and began getting ready for the day ahead. "Captain," came a voice behind him. It was Lieutenant Elena Vasquez, his next in charge, as she stepped forward, her brow furrowed in concern. "We are approaching the site based on the last known coordinates." Zach exhaled sharply, nodding. "Deploy the long-range sonar and ready the deep-sea drones." He was surprised that he knew precisely what action to take. She hesitated. "You think we're going to find anything today?" He glanced at her, his jaw tightening. "Not sure I want to."

As the ocean had other plans, which could become unpredictable at any moment. Veterans aboard had witnessed their share of mysteries. Yet no one could shake the feeling that this mission was different and that they were venturing into waters where they were not welcome. The remotely operated vehicle (ROV) detached from HMS Royal Waters early that morning, its sleek body plunging into the dark, impenetrable depths of the Atlantic. Which was extraordinarily calm, almost like luck had favoured them. The control room was silent, with the crew watching the monitors as the vehicle descended into the blackness of the water. The screen flickered with the first image of this water devoid of life, and the more profound the ROV descended, the more it felt like the ocean below was alive, watching them and waiting for them to go deeper.

D. Gohil

At approximately 4,500 metres, the ROV's cameras detected something strange. "We have something," a technician alerted. A vast, shifting shadow moved across the screen like a dark, formless entity slithering across, near the ocean floor. Another technician gasped, gripping the console. "There is something down there, something massive." The screen flickered again, and a colossal structure emerged impossibly smooth, its surface etched with symbols that pulsed with an eerie, otherworldly light. The symbols were not static, as they moved in rhythmic patterns like whispering some forgotten language. Vasquez leaned in nervously, looking at the display. "That's impossible!" Then the ocean trembled, the sonar pinged wildly, the readings distorting like some interference. Then just as suddenly as it had started, the power flickered and went out completely.

The ship plunged into total darkness, and Zach's heart skipped a beat. It sat in silence, suffocating, and then the lights flickered back on, systems slowly coming back online with an eerie hum. "What the hell was that?" One technician whispered, eyes wide as they scanned the reactivated screens. The ROV's cameras refocused, and what it revealed sent a chill down Zach's spine. On the seabed lay what appeared to be a massive symbol carved directly into the Abyssal Ridge. A Sigil that glowed with unnatural bioluminescence, pulsing slowly in the waters. Its edges seemed to shimmer, as if it were breathing. Zach took a slow inhale, and steadily, his eyes locked onto the symbol that appeared to defy the very laws of physics.

The ancient symbol's lines and curves twisted in ways that should not have been possible nor looked natural in any way. Its complex structure was unlike anything he had seen underwater, and the Sigil had haunted him for weeks. He recalled clearly that he had seen it in intelligence files stolen from a shadow organisation marked *Top Secret*. He had seen it etched in ancient ruins deep beneath the sands of the Mesopotamian desert, and now here it was, glowing beneath the waves near the very bottom of the Atlantic Ocean, as Zach's hand clenched into a fist at his side. This was connected to the lost Maribel, the vessel that had sunk, and everything they had discovered before they vanished. The symbol was attached, the piece of the puzzle tying the strange occurrences together. What did this all mean, and why was it here? Zach thought. Suddenly, the lights in the control room dimmed again, and the low, eerie hum came from the sea once more.

Echo: The Infinite Cycle

Like a low-frequency pulse that emanated from the ocean ridge, vibrating through the hull like an otherworldly heartbeat. Zach stood frozen, staring at the symbol's glowing form, a sense of dread sweeping over him. The ancient Sigil was a mark, a warning call awaiting their discovery. "I'm pulling the ROV back," Zach said, his voice steady. Though every part of him screamed to do more to uncover what this was and why it was here, even as he spoke. The ROV's feed flickered again, revealing something else beneath the symbol. A glimmer of movement, a large undulating shadow, gave the impression that the ocean was shifting, preparing for something more significant. Zach's grip tightened on the console, his thoughts racing faster than he could process. He knew they were on the cusp of something monumental that defied explanation. At that time, he did not need to see it any closer and had seen enough for now. He turned towards Vasquez, meeting her eyes. "Get us out of here, it's been a long day, and we must rest to continue tomorrow," he said, his voice low and taut.

The ROV ascended as quickly as possible and was retrieved. The Royal Waters pulled away from the coordinates with the oppressive atmosphere hanging heavily over the ship. The crew worked away quietly, and they all felt nervous, their faces pale under the dim emergency lights. Zach stood at the bow again, staring at the open water, feeling that the ocean revealed something completely unnatural and not of this world. The Sigil symbolised a connection to something ancient and long forgotten, but now it was attracting attention for a reason. Something once again stirs beneath the ocean, as HMS Royal Waters ventures deeper into the unknown, heading toward forces beyond human understanding.

They were not just searching for the lost Maribel. Now they were moving toward a far greater mystery that had been sleeping deep beneath the ocean for centuries. Zach sensed they had to stay alert, and this was going to get more intense. The ancient symbol was the key, and its power would shape the journey ahead. He could not escape the truth lingering in the air as the ship sailed through the water. They had to move the vessel to a safe distance, as they could not afford to take any risks. The next day, they headed straight back into the unknown, and whatever awaited them, the ocean would be its guide. The HMS Royal Waters shuddered as a deep, resonant vibration surged through its hull, and the deployed ROV's feed dissolved into static.

Monitors flickered in a panic, with warning lights flashing erratically across the ship's central control room. "Sir, energy surge detected!" A crew member shouted over the alarms, which were eventually silenced. A blinding pulse of light erupted from the depths of the water, piercing through the dark sky, and the ship rocked as the waters went wild, and the ship's outer metal shrieked under an unseen force. The waves churned violently, throwing crew members to the deck. Vasquez gritted her teeth. "What the hell did we just do?" Zach braced himself against a console. "I think we have woken something up," he said. As the ship steadied, reports flooded in of malfunctioning systems, static-filled transmissions, and shadows where none should technically be possible. A low-frequency hum began reverberating through the ship's frame again, a sensation felt more than heard, like a presence pressing against them.

Crew members whispered of strange dreams in which voices spoke in tongues they could not understand. "We can't remain here. Take us to a safe distance away. Let's gather as much data as possible and form a new strategy. I don't want to rush this. We don't know enough, and the crew is clearly spooked." Zach looked at Vasquez, who nodded in complete agreement. She ordered the crew. "Let's get to a safe distance, let's not cause or unsettle anything more, you know what to do!" It was the fifth day of the mission, and a shift unfolded aboard the HMS Royal Waters as the morning dawned cold and still. The crew emerged from their quarters squinting into the darkness as they stepped onto the deck, but something was amiss.

All the stars had vanished. There was no mistaking it. Vast starstrewn sky, which had been a constant companion for days, had disappeared, leaving only an eerie black void where the familiar constellations once were. The stars were neither obscured by clouds nor hidden by any atmospheric anomaly. The crew exchanged uneasy glances and whispers that travelled through the ranks like wildfire. Every sailor aboard the ship felt a deep, primal unease gnawing at them. The heavens had abandoned them, and the vast ocean seemed to close in. Zach stood there gazing at the darkened sky. His thoughts were a storm of confusion and disbelief. He was the most experienced sailor with years at sea, charting every course. He knew he could always trust the stars to guide him. Now those familiar guides had vanished as if the universe had erased them. What the hell was going on?

Echo: The Infinite Cycle

"What's happening? This is scary?" A technician muttered under his breath. Eyes wide as he stared at the screen where the celestial bodies should have been. Satellite navigation systems blinked out next, followed by the ship's GPS. Sounds of jarring beeps replaced the steady hum of technology, which had pointed to malfunctioning systems everywhere. Crew scrambled to regain control, but it was futile. They were now adrift, entirely at the mercy of forces they did not understand. Vasquez approached Zach, her face a mask of concern. "Sir, we need to turn back," she whispered, her voice calm but nervous. He turned towards her as he felt the panic building within her, in the eyes of the crew, and the uncertainty was spreading amongst the calm of the ship. "We can't," he replied softly, almost to himself. "Not now." Deep down, a bitter truth lingered in his chest; this was precisely where they needed to be. The ship's instruments were useless now that the ocean currents around them had grown increasingly erratic, pushing the vessel in directions that defied a battleship's natural flow.

It was as if the sea waters were against their mission, refusing to obey the laws of physics, making it complicated. The crew were now on edge, and the ship dragged as the waters beneath it seemed to pull and tug with an unnatural force. The Royal Waters, once their steady point of reference, now felt like a moving target, shifting unpredictably. Zach stood at the bow, holding the rail as tightly as possible, feeling the violent shifts in the current beneath his feet. The ocean was as vast and unyielding as it had turned against them. "Sir, we need to decide," Vasquez urged, her voice urgent. "If we don't turn back, we'll be lost here forever." The words hung heavy in the air as Zach exhaled slowly, trying to steady his mind.

He knew what was happening was unnatural, and the more he thought about it, the more he recognised the signs. This ocean region was feared in old Sailor tales, warned about in ancient legends of ships that entered but never left. The sailors now openly whispered among themselves and spoke of the ancient legend of the vanishing stars. The story was part of every sailor's lore, passed down for generations like a dark secret of the sea. The sea stilled, no waves broke, no wind stirred. The vanishing stars were no longer a sailor's legend; it had shape now, depth, mass. Said to be a region where ships dissolved without a trace. Its waters offered no distress signals, no survivors. Once a vessel breached its perimeter, it was as if the ocean unmade it, cell by cell.

Zach listened to the crew's murmurs, their voices brittle with old fear. The name surfaced again and again, half whispered, half prayed against. A place where the living bled into the dead, and time came unmoored from itself. His skin prickled cold, overhead, the sky darkened with silence. Had they crossed the line already? He shook off this feeling, determined not to let fear get to him and muddle his judgement. Theories surrounding this place were speculation, but as the ship inched deeper into the unsettling, unpredictable waters, a heavy sense of impending doom settled over him. "Sir," Vasquez urged again, her tone more assertive this time. "We must turn back. If we do not, we might be the next to sink. The vanishing stars are real!" Zach remained silent, considering her words for a long moment, reflecting on the best decision he should make.

He recognised the dangers, yet a more profound instinctual feeling urged him that this was not simply superstition. This was their necessary destination. With a measured motion, he turned to examine the chart. The coordinates marking the dead zone, an area devoid of discovery, were in place. "This is the place," he whispered, almost in affirmation. As the day progressed, the Royal Waters crew grew anxious despite having trained for such missions. The ocean appeared dark, as if something was draining its vitality, which was once a bright, vibrant blue, was now an opaque, deep green tinged with a haunting blackness that spread beneath the surface like ink. The ship's hull groaned beneath the pressure of the strange current. Not something Zach and his crew had ever seen. He sensed something sinister bearing down on them as if they were not alone.

With a sense of dread, he came to understand that the disappearing stars were more than just a location glitch. It served as a warning, a challenge for anyone bold enough to enter its cursed waters. HMS Royal Waters had crossed a point of no return. In the depths of the dark waters, an ancient force stirred, older than they could imagine, connected to the old Sigil they had found. It was drawing near. "Prepare for the worst," Zach advised, aware that whatever awaited them would be a trial for everyone, regardless of who they were. Still, he understood the truth within. They were exactly where they were, and by the seventh day at sea in that location, the crew of the HMS Royal Waters had grown accustomed to the nervous silence that appeared to infiltrate the ship and its crew.

Echo: The Infinite Cycle

Having drifted in these strange, disconcerting waters for a week, each day seemed to drag on endlessly. Zach knew the strategy required patience and avoiding mistakes. Their mission was steadfast to locate the Maribel, the cargo ship that had disappeared without a trace, and to uncover the truth regarding the strange forces at work. Zach stood on the bridge, his gaze locked. There were no updates, no debris, no sign of life. The ocean surrounding them unfolded like a boundless, indifferent desert. "Lieutenant, it's time," Zach remarked, glancing at Vasquez. "Go ahead, deploy the ROV." It was commissioned and dispatched once more, with its powerful lights slicing through the dark water. A momentary view of the depths below, Zach breathed intensely as he stared at the monitor, where the ROV's live feed was displayed while it went deeper into the ocean. This was their fourth descent, and the earlier attempts had revealed nothing more regarding the Maribel but unbroken expanses of water and the faint outline of the seabed.

Zach had a sense that this time it would yield different and positive results. The ROV continued its descent through the cold, dark waters when suddenly, the feed shifted, the texture of the water slightly changed, revealing a faint hint of light. The controllers activated the vehicle's lights, and the ROV illuminated the ocean floor. The crew then spotted the Sigil again, which was larger than they imagined. Carved into the ridge on a grand scale, the symbol's lines glowed softly, pulsating with an eerie bioluminescence. The atmosphere felt heavy around the crew, felt denser as the symbol's presence began sucking the air around the area, as if the ocean had absorbed all the energy.

Then something unusual happened when the ROV's cameras zoomed in on the symbol. The humming sound, like a deep resonant vibration, had become stronger since their arrival. Initially, it started as a faint rumble, almost indistinguishable, but it soon reverberated throughout the entire ship and made pretty much everyone nervous. The crew first felt it in their feet, then in their bones, as if the sound penetrated deep into their marrow. "This isn't just noise," Vasquez remarked, her voice tense with disbelief. "It's speech!" Zach felt his stomach knot as the realisation struck him, the hum was not random, it was a message, like a call echoing from the ocean's depths from an ancient source, far beyond their comprehension.

The sound was unnatural, as it represented something entirely different. Like an intelligence lurking beneath the waves, awaiting an invitation. The hum continued to resonate through the ship. The ROV's visual feed flickered, causing the image on the screen to scramble. The crew thought they had lost the connection, but the screen soon cleared, revealing a large moving shadow in the depths. It was something more profound. "What is that?" A technician nervously asked, his voice trembling with a mix of awe and fear. When the ROV's lights lit up the seamount with floodlights, the shadow became clearer, revealing the cargo ship Maribel, which had sunk and was thought to have disintegrated. Lying perfectly preserved, silently resting on the ridge as if deliberately placed there.

Its hull was totally intact, seemingly untouched by time or the ocean's corrosive forces. Incredibly, it seemed preserved and resting quietly in the depths of the water, just waiting to be discovered again. The Royal Water's crew were shocked as what unfolded before them had never happened before. Maribel was no ordinary cargo ship. It was cursed and possessed a strange vitality which was impossible. Still tethered to the ocean. "What in God's name, how?" Vasquez's voice faded. Her words were lost as she could not take her eyes off the screen. Zach felt the significance of the moment weigh heavily on him. This was a miracle discovery, an unsettling revelation that Maribel lay deep within the abyss, linked to something both ancient and malevolent beyond their wildest imaginations. The hum persisted, and the voice from below became louder, saturating the surrounding space.

Vibrations seeped into their minds like an unshakeable whisper. "What is it trying to tell us?" Zach asks, eyes glued to the screen, his heart racing. Crew stayed silent, their gazes locked on the screen, entranced by the sight of what was unfolding before them, in the depths. Maribel seemed to have been quietly resting, anchored to the ocean seamount by an unseen force. The voice from the depths reverberated again. This time, the hum transformed, becoming more distinct and direct. Although it did not contain recognisable language, the sound's rhythm implied a pattern. A cadence that mirrored the essence of words. Zach was also equally bemused and unsure at this point. It seemed the voice was speaking to him. The hum reverberated within him, pulsating deep in his chest and resonating with a strength he could feel in his bones.

Echo: The Infinite Cycle

This was a communication far more ancient than anything he had ever known. A language of the ocean, and as if the voice reached its peak, the image on the screen became indistinct. The shadow of Maribel flickered slightly, nearly undetectable, and for a moment, Zach thought he spotted movement within the hull. A fleeting shadow before the scene returned to its usual state. Suddenly, the hum ceased. The ROV's cameras adjusted, and Zach inhaled sharply, trying to calm his breath. His mind erupted with questions and theories, yet one fact stood clear. Whatever was communicating with them from the depths was connected to the Sigil, the ocean and the very forces that had entangled them in this eerie domain. The Maribel served as both a ship and a means to something much greater. Something incredibly potent, with the Sigil acting as the key.

As the crew stood in shocked silence, gazing at the screen, Zach's mind drifted to the ancient powers that had stirred. What they had discovered was just the start. The voice from below was not yet done with them. This saga required more thought, prompting Zach to order all senior crew members to an urgent meeting to decide next steps. By the tenth day, Zach had exhausted all alternatives. They could not stay on the surface and wait for answers to come to them. The HMS Royal Waters had faced too many bizarre incidents and lingering questions, and now it was time for him to face the depths of the ocean. Zach stood on the edge of the submersible launch deck, gazing into the dark, impenetrable waters below. They needed to dive deeper to understand what lurked beneath in person.

The symbol had called them, and the hum, the voice and the presence all signalled one undeniable truth: he had to descend physically. The state-of-the-art deep-sea submersible Nautilus-Mini, part of the HMS Royal Waters, was prepared for its mission. It was designed for deep-sea exploration, capable of reaching a theoretical depth of 11,000 meters, a feat that had never been attempted before. It had potential for use in exploring areas such as the Mariana Trench in the North Pacific Ocean. Zach decided to choose his very best divers, Lieutenant Vasquez and Chief Technician Jensen, to go on the discovery mission. He was confident that together they would form a calm and ideal team, highly skilled in navigating the mission and coping with the ocean's depths.

Despite their combined experience, the waves presented a challenge, and together with what lurked around, would make it unlike any other dive they had encountered before. "We will be entering an uncharted territory," Zach stated, his voice unwavering despite the unsettling feeling pulling at him. "Whatever occurs, stay united. We will enter, observe what we must and leave speedily. Do you all understand?" "Understood, sir," Vasquez responded while Jensen nodded, busy securing the hatch. The Nautilus-Mini was lowered into the ocean, and Zach felt the icy grip of the water as the submersible descended below the surface. They descended gradually, the weight of the water bearing down on them as the depths turned increasingly dark, rendering their powerful floodlights ineffective against the blackness.

With each deeper dive, the surrounding world fell into silence, and the ancient voice they had heard through the ship's speakers faded into a distant, oppressive thrum in the recesses of their minds. It was not absent but muted as if the ocean had consumed it entirely. Zach's heart raced; the descent seemed unending, with silence pressing against his eardrums. He checked the depth gauge; they were almost 4,500 metres deep. Much deeper than any standard operation would typically venture, they continued into the void beyond the reach of light. The submersible's hull creaked subtly under pressure, yet the interior stayed steady. A small bubble of human ingenuity maintains stability in the expansive ocean. "Approaching the coordinates now," Jensen announced, interrupting the tense silence. Zach nodded in response, but remained silent.

His gaze was fixed on the sonar monitor, where he observed the blips and lines as they moved across it. As they navigated the murky waters, the screen flickered. "Look at that," Vasquez said quietly, gesturing at the monitor. A shadow materialised at the edge of their radar, wavering in and out of focus. It resembled nothing they had seen before. The submersible's floodlights pierced the dark like twin blades, probing for the origin of the unsettling presence. As they rounded a rough rock formation, the lights revealed something surprising: the Sigil. The symbol they had observed on the ROV's feed before had become recognisable. A door etched into the ocean seamount's stone, forming what looked like a gigantic dome. The edges of the Sigil were rough, mirroring within the fractured surface a large doorway, and what almost looked like an artificial docking hatch.

Echo: The Infinite Cycle

At the same time, the bioluminescent pulses appeared to animate patterns of light. Zach's heart raced again. "That's it," he murmured. "That's what we've been searching for." The ancient Sigil, once just a message, now appeared to Zach as more than mere imagery. It signified a threshold, an entrance, and he was sure they had arrived at the point of no return. "Prepare yourselves," Zach stated, gripping the console tightly. "We're getting closer to something more than normal. I can sense it wants to help." This was not only about the investigation, but about stepping into a realm beyond human understanding. They moved closer to the Sigil, its form lit by the Nautilus-Mini's glow. The symbol appeared to pulse and shift as if it recognised them. The surrounding stone seemed to vibrate with energy. Zach could not articulate the ancient, primal energy that seemed to call to him. Just as they prepared to manoeuvre the submersible closer to the symbol, something shifted.

Zach's hand shot to the console. "What the hell...?" His throat felt parched as he tried to speak, and swallowing was nearly impossible. Then he glanced outside, and the dark void of the ocean had disappeared, replaced by something far more bizarre and unnatural. The water now had an essence, a gentle glowing translucence that enveloped everything in a surreal light. Floating in mid-air were hundreds of bioluminescent orbs, each pulsing in perfect synchronisation with the unearthly glow of the symbol that radiated from them. They flickered beneath the surface like constellations drowned, their light deliberate, steady, as if aware of their geometry. Not stars fallen from the sky, but something older trying to imitate them.

The hum returned, richer this time. It did not just echo, it laced through the salty depths. Folded into the vehicle's frame, and bloomed inside Zach's body. Each note unspooled like memory, as though the water was remembering him. His body responded involuntarily. Not just a shiver, but a deep resonance, his bones vibrating as if tuned to an ancient frequency. It was beautiful, almost unbearable. In that moment, he could feel it in his chest and bloodstream emanating from somewhere near the glowing orbs. Zach instinctively reached out, his palm pressing flat against the Nautilus-Mini's glass window, his mind racing to process what his eyes beheld. There were no seams, marks, or signs of construction. The structure seemed to have emerged from the ocean's depths. Creating something that was incomprehensibly brilliant and far too advanced.

"Is this... wait, is this possible?" Vasquez whispers from behind him, her voice tinged with awe and a hint of fear. Zach could not respond. The closer they drew, the more the orbs danced around them, creating designs that Zach recognised. These were the same symbols, the configurations that had appeared in every culture he had studied.

* * *

He remembered the documents from the secret military archives he had retrieved from the black site in the desert, where the Sigil had hidden among ancient ruins. He recalled Sumerian tablets, the walls of Mayan temples, and even later locations where the same symbol appeared alone, either painted on walls or carved into stone. This represented a singular timeless emblem that transcended history and civilisations. It embodied a force that had surfaced in every mystery and concealed moment in history.

* * *

Now unveiled as the submersible drifted through bioluminescent clouds of spheres. Zach felt an almost tangible connection, as if the ancient Sigil drew them nearer, leading them to this spot. The patterns twisted and shifted with mesmerising intricacy, elaborate fluidity. He studied them intently, his eyes narrowing as he tried to extract their intent. His mind sifted through the lessons and lore that had brought him this far. The Nautilus-Mini steadied at 4,487 metres, its hull groaning softly as though straining against the weight of the abyss. The wreck of the Maribel loomed out of the murk, perfectly preserved, its flanks untouched by rust or time. "Christ," Vasquez whispered. "That's impossible!" Zach leaned forward, his pulse thundered, but not with fear. He knew, somehow, he already understood what he was about to see. Floodlights swept across the hull, revealing something extraordinary. The ship was encased in a vast, shimmering cocoon of refracted light, as if the ocean itself bent around it. Inside the cocoon, bubbles shimmered like slow-motion rain. "Sir, reading atmospheric pressure," Jensen stammered. "That's not seawater, it's... air." Zach's jaw tightened. "The Sigil did this!" The sub's manipulator arm brushed the bubble and passed through without resistance. The sensors stabilised a breathable atmosphere. Life-support signatures began to flicker on the monitor, multiple sources. "They're alive!" Vasquez gasped. "My God, they're still alive!" Zach manoeuvred the Nautilus-Mini along the starboard side until the hosting hatch came into view.

Echo: The Infinite Cycle

Against every natural law, the hatch was bone dry, with faint condensation misting the glass. Figures stirred beyond. "Dock her here, and make sure you remain steady at all times, Jensen," Zach ordered. His voice was steady, calm, and confident. Vasquez stared at him. "The pressure outside will crush us, Zach!" "It won't, I have a gut feeling, and I feel a strong instinct we will be safe, look at the crew below," Zach said. "Not here, the Sigil wants us to rescue them, trust me." The Nautilus-Mini clamped onto the hatch with a hiss of hydraulics. Zach snapped the release on his harness. "I'm going first."

"Lieutenant, wait!" Vasquez reached out, but he was already at the airlock, helmet sealed. He felt the Sigil hum in his chest, as if the ancient Sigil itself was guiding his hands. With one twist of the wheel, the hatch opened, and there they were. Men and women in oil-stained uniforms blinked against the sudden light. Faces gaunt, eyes hollow, but alive and relieved. A murmur rippled through them. Disbelief, the sound of hope resurrected from the deep. "Royal Navy," Zach said, voice firm but gentle. "We're here to take you home," he smiled. Vasquez's breath caught in her throat as she followed him through.

It was impossible, unthinkable, but the survivors were real, flesh and blood, seventy per cent of the crew that the world above had long since mourned. "Sir, oxygen levels are dropping in the bubble," Jensen called from the sub. "We'll need to cycle evac runs immediately." Zach nodded. "Then we don't waste time. Vasquez, start triage. Jensen, prep the Nautilus-Mini for maximum rotation." The survivors gathered, eyes shining with exhaustion and hope. Against the crushing weight of the ocean, against all reason, the Sigil had preserved them. Now it was up to Zach to bring them back to safety. "Let's get them out," he said, and with that, the rescue mission began. Vasquez and Jensen shared a nervous look, but both nodded together.

The Maribel First Evac Rescue

The first group was strapped into the Nautilus-Mini's extended section, which was too small to accommodate them all at once. Ten survivors, gaunt and weak but clinging to life, lined the narrow benches, their hollow eyes fixed on Zach and Vasquez as if afraid the vision of rescue might vanish. "Weight integrity confirmed," Jensen reported from the console.

His fingers flew over the controls. "Ascent route plotted. Straight surface line, no margin for error." Vasquez adjusted the restraints on a young engineer, barely more than a boy. His lips trembled. "We thought it was over. We buried people down here, not in traditional coffins but encased." "Not you," she said softly. "You're going home today," she smiled. The hatch sealed, hydraulics groaning. Zach took his seat at the pilot station, shoulders taut with focus. The Nautilus-Mini lurched as the docking clamps released, the air bubble and the ghostly hull of the Maribel slipping away behind them. "Beginning ascent," Jensen announced. "Four thousand five hundred metres to go." The cabin fell silent, broken only by the hum of thrusters and the faint hiss of oxygen flow. Each metre felt like a century. At one thousand metres, the hull creaked. Survivors flinched at the sound. Zach steadied them with his voice. "She's built for this, don't worry, you're safe. Hold tight."

Two thousand metres, an alarm blinked red, pressure differential spiking. Vasquez's hand hovered over the ballast release. "Hold her steady," Zach said calmly. "It's just the thermocline biting. She'll ride it out." The Nautilus-Mini shuddered, groaned, then eased as they cleared the gradient. The alarm fell silent. Survivors exchanged nervous, hopeful glances. They had never travelled this way before. Three thousand metres, oxygen scrubbers whined under the load. Jensen adjusted the flow, muttering. "Come on, come on..." Zach's jaw tightened. He could almost feel the Sigil's presence, a hum beneath his skin, as though guiding them upward. Four thousand metres above, light began to filter in, pale and fragile. Someone sobbed quietly, then another, and then the sea finally broke.

The Nautilus-Mini breached with a surge of spray, floodlights cutting across the night. Search vessels roared closer, spotlights blazing, as deck crews shouted in disbelief when the hatch was flung open. Fresh air swept in, cool and sharp, and the survivors wept openly now. Clutching at the sky, at each other, at the rescuers who reached down with outstretched hands. Zach lingered a moment at the controls, exhaling a breath he had not realised he was holding. The first evac was complete, but below, many still waited in the dark, kept alive by the impossible gift of the Sigil, and he knew he would return for every last one of them. Cheers still echoed across the deck as the first survivors were carried to waiting on-board medics, but Zach had already turned back to the sea.

Echo: The Infinite Cycle

"There's more," he reminded Vasquez quietly, though he did not need to say it. "Many more." Within minutes, the Nautilus-Mini was under again, swallowed by the dark. The second run was heavier, thirty survivors crammed shoulder to shoulder. Some were too weak to stand, others delirious from confinement. Vasquez moved constantly among them, squeezing them gently with steadying hands, whispering reassurance. At 3,200 metres, a survivor's chest seized, ragged gasps echoing in the cramped hull. Jensen's hands flew across the med kit, voice taut. "If we don't surface fast." "Hold course," Zach cut in. His tone was unflinching. "If we rush, we blow the tanks. Steady ascent." They made it. Barely. Deck medics hauled the man away on a stretcher while others staggered up into the flood of light, eyes blinking like they had been reborn.

The third run brought officers. Gaunt commanders and lieutenants who had clung to discipline in the darkness, keeping morale alive. One of them, Captain Alvarez, clasped Zach's hand as they surfaced. "I told them... I told them the Royal Navy would not forget us," he rasped, eyes glistening. "I was right." The fourth, fifth, and sixth runs blurred together. The Nautilus-Mini became a lifeline, an iron lung shuttling up and down through crushing blackness. The hull groaned, oxygen scrubbers strained, alarms flared and died. Each cycle brought more people. Some stumbled into the light with laughter, others carried limp, barely clinging on. On the deck, the once-ordered rescue vessels transformed into makeshift field hospitals. Floodlights blazed. Medics ran. Survivors huddled beneath blankets, weeping, praying, staring at the stars as though they had never seen them before, or at least felt forever. "Amazing, the stars are back, Zach motioned at the sky.

By the seventh run, exhaustion gnawed at them all, as they did not stop. Zach's hands shook on the controls, Vasquez's voice had grown hoarse from tending the weak, and Jensen's eyes were red from staring at flickering monitors, but still they descended. Still, they returned until the final run, when the last cluster of survivors waited in the ghostly glow of the bubble. They raised their hands as the Nautilus-Mini clamped on, eyes wide with the hope that this, at last, was their salvation. Hours later, with the previous survivor lifted into the arms of waiting sailors, the decks erupted in a roar that shook the night. Flares lit the sky crimson. Men and women who had been written off as lost were alive again, walking, clutching one another beneath the stars.

Zach stood apart, watching the chaos of joy unfold. He felt the Sigil humming through him still, its purpose vast, unfathomable. It had preserved these lives for reasons he could not yet grasp, but tonight, one truth was enough. They had beaten the deep, and Maribel's crew, against all reason, had come out alive to much relief. The deck was alive with the noise of survival. Stretchers rattling, medics shouting orders, the groan of winches hauling gear back aboard. Survivors clung to steaming mugs of tea, wrapped in blankets, staring skyward as though learning the constellations anew. Vasquez stood beside Zach, exhaustion etched into every line of her face. "Seven trips down. Every run risked the hull, the crew, all of us, and yet," she swept a hand toward the huddled survivors. "They're here, so many of them." Zach did not answer straightaway. His eyes were fixed on the horizon where the sea met the night.

Beneath those waves, the Maribel still lay in her shimmering cocoon, impossibly preserved. "It wasn't us," he said at last. "Not entirely." Vasquez frowned. "What do you mean?" He turned to her, his expression unreadable. "The Sigil did this. It kept them alive, all these weeks, waiting for us to come; a miracle has been witnessed." A shiver ran through her despite the warmth of the deck lamps. "You think it chose them?" Zach's gaze lingered on the dark water, hearing the low hum in his chest. The constant pull of something vast, ancient, and patient. "I think it's only just begun." The wind carried the sound of laughter, sobs, and the rattle of medical stretchers. Above them, the night sky was bright with stars, cold and eternal.

The crew of the Maribel had been delivered from the abyss, but the more profound mystery remained, coiled beneath the surface, waiting to rise. Zach had witnessed it first-hand. The Sigil was vibrant, now integrated into their reality. The crew assembled on deck, their expressions reflecting a blend of fatigue, wonder, and underlying dread. Zach felt it in his sternum, deep and marrow-bound. Outside, the water shimmered, not with light, but with presence. Some crew members said the resonance was a warning. Others swore it was learning them. He pressed his palm to the floorboards. They were warm, and he was captivated by the containment chamber. He had witnessed its power, felt its pull, and now understood it was a gateway to other dimensions. Ancient civilisations both revered and feared it, and now he and others were its heirs.

Echo: The Infinite Cycle

Zach reminisced about the moment the symbol ignited, stirring something profound within him. He recalled the sensation as a call across the vast ocean, an irresistible summons that drew him closer. It was undeniably ancient and unyielding, yet now, standing on the deck, he understood the full significance of that force. The ancient Sigil was a relic, a presence eagerly awaiting their arrival, anticipating the moment it could reemerge, but why now? Why had the Sigil selected them? Zach shifted his gaze back to the horizon, where the Atlantic Ocean's endless expanse sprawled before him. He devoted his life to pursuing the unknown, little realising that it would eventually pursue him in return.

The world had transformed, and the rules had altered, and he was no longer the hunter but the hunted. Zach stood solitary at the bow of the Royal Waters, the wind chilling against his skin. His mind raced in all directions as he tried to assemble the pieces of knowledge they had collected. The forces they faced were ancient, far older than any human civilisation, yet they lived and now asserted their presence. Zach's breath misted in the frigid air, and for a moment, he wondered, could they prevent it? The answer he recognised was as enigmatic as the ancient symbol itself. However, one thing was sure. This was the beginning of something great, and soon the world would uncover the actual depth of the mystery. Suddenly, the symbol ignited the wood, its markings scorching the deck under his boots.

The Orb rose from the abyss, glowing with celestial energy. Nathan barely had a moment to shout before it dragged him down. The chilling pressure of the depths surrounded him, leading to a free-fall. The ocean split open, revealing the Sigil shimmering below the surface, and an ancient force had once again stirred to life to consume only him. This time, Nathan felt something magical was going to happen, and did not feel threatened in any way; actually, he felt excitement for once. This cycle will eventually lead him back home, back to Silvia.

D. Gohil

Echo: The Infinite Cycle

Chapter 14 – Mage of Nashira
Echo Plane - Timeless

PART ONE

The air carried a hush, as if sound had paused almost at a standstill to witness the reveal. Nathan stepped forward, boots scraping a surface that gleamed like cooled obsidian. He looked up, and the twin suns met his gaze with quiet gravity, not celestial bodies, but eyes that had watched him before he knew a name for this dimension. The clouds moved subtly, not in the sky but in pattern, cirrostratus rearranging like wandering thoughts. One phased out, another took its place. He could not tell if they were decoding him or being decoded by him. The chamber sealed itself behind in silence. This was the Sigil's memory, and Nathan, for the first time, was inside it. The air carried the scent of crushed herbs, scorched dust, and something faintly metallic, blood dried on stone. Nathan stood on a floating stone platform, high above a valley veiled in silver mist. Crimson and black robes cloaked him now, embroidered with symbols he did not remember learning, yet recognised intimately.

At dusk, they pulsed faintly, living geometry drawn from the spiral. A tall figure stepped forward across the platform, and his voice was smooth. "Master Kaelen, the circle awaits you." Below, young acolytes raised glowing orbs, threads of light arcing between them in shifting constellations. This was not the magic of books or even spells. It was much older, elemental, felt in the bones, not taught by any masters of any past. He was not a stranger here, and the name Kaelen echoed from unfamiliar lips, and they knew him. Elya greeted him in the Temple of Shards, her moon-cracked eyes softened when she saw him, a warrior mage graven by war. She embraced him tightly and whispered that she had trained him and that she remembered him even if he did not remember himself.

Here, magic came from mind control, from longing, from guilt, from joy buried too deep to name. To learn it was to relive it, and each spell took something from you in return. Nashira was not what it seemed, not a city, not even a place. It was a construction wrought of forgotten lives, a realm in a dimension created by the Sigil to test him. Each triumph unravelled the illusion a little more, and as the sky-islands crumbled into the storm below, Nathan understood. Nashira was never meant to last; only he was. The only escape lay through the Rite of the Weaving, a convergence of all four elements in perfect harmony amidst a storm of potential selves. Only through choosing who he must become could the realm survive. He entered the storm, chose the self that could endure, and the dream shattered. Atonement was the only option, and the trials would either make or break him. Nathan felt a sense of power within himself and loved the feeling that he could take on anything. He looked forward to this adventure, hoping it would be the last so that the cycle would return him. Would this be his last lesson?

The Trials of Convergence

The world buckled, stone split beneath his feet, temple walls groaned and peeled apart, revealing four ancient gateways, each thrumming with a different pulse: fire, water, earth, and air. "To wield the Sigil," said the hooded figure at the altar. "You must first survive its roots." He did not elaborate. He did not need to. The air shifted. The gateways stirred, and with no further warning, the trials began.

Echo: The Infinite Cycle

EARTH

Earth came first. Kaelen, no longer Nathan in the present time, stepped into the Maw of Nashira. Alone, save for the faint light of a sunstone, the cavern sighed around him, old and heavy, and dust rose like a dance. The stone beneath him vibrated, and at the first fork, he chose the narrow path. The old maxim came to him, unbidden. "The trial does not follow comfort. Remember this, Master Kaelen." The walls were warm to the touch and carved by human hands, but shaped by forces older than memory. As he pressed deeper, the light dimmed, then it failed. The sunstone cracked as he continued blind. Air whispered, though no voice was spoken.

At the heart of the chamber, tall statues waited, warriors caught mid-motion, their faces blank. As Kaelen stepped through, one moved, a hammer swung, instinct raised a shield of stone, but it cracked as it hit. His arm went numb, but he did not strike back. Earth did not reward violence, as it demanded endurance from him. He absorbed each blow, breathed through the pain when he finally knelt. The statues stood still, then collapsed into the sand. Amber light shimmered in the cavern's core. It was the Rootstone, and Kaelen placed his hand upon it. Visions pulsed, of mountains rising, seeds cracking stone, roots that slept for centuries before they bloomed. The mark seared into his skin, a curved rune beneath the wrist, the Seal of Earth.

WATER

The water entered the frozen cathedral of the Thirn Ridge glacier. Beneath its shimmering skin, the drowned city near Nashira lay sealed in frost, and at its heart floated a vertical mirror of liquid water, suspended like a blade through the air. Kaelen approached, and his reflection shimmered, then shifted. A younger version of himself stared back, eyes raw with regret, kneeling beside a dead brother's body. The mirror whispered. *Water always remembers what you forget.* The scene repeated, again and again, Elren Vale, flames, screams, the cursed Sigil in the enemy's hand. His moment of hesitation drowned him, and regret became a tide. Then he stopped resisting and let the grief pass through him.

When he rose from the dark pool breathless, the water curled around his arm like a ribbon. It burned a mark into his wrist, a flowing, fluid, constantly shifting one. Water had not broken him. It had freed him, the Seal of Water.

AIR

Air awaited above. he climbed the Vine Stair, half-path, half-dream spiralling into skies stitched with wind. The Tower of Gale drifted, its geometry uncertain, and gravity flickered like failing stars. Kaelen jumped, missed, and fell, but the air caught him. Inside, time bent, steps echoed before his feet landed, and his voice vanished in his throat. Wind not forced, it demanded stillness. He closed his eyes and breathed in, feeling it within and around him; then it moved. The tower responded, doors opened before him, corridors folded, and the wind became an ally. At the summit, the floor crumbled beneath him, and he leapt; air spiralled beneath his feet, and laughter escaped his lips for the first time in weeks. The mark appeared over his heart, like three silver lines, like breath on a winter's pane, the Seal of Air.

FIRE

Kaelen then faced the fire. He entered the Vale of Varn, where glass crunched beneath his feet and distant storms of flame swirling in the air. A voice emerged from the blaze, asking. *What will you burn to become more?* At the forge's core stood a being of flame, its face gazing back at him, taller, harsher, and filled with raging hunger. They clashed, sparks flew, song echoed, fury exploded until Kaelen remembered the stillness of earth, the clarity of water, and the grace of air. He lowered his arms as the flame flickered and hesitated, then faded away. Moving across the burning coals, he was welcomed into them. The fire spun into his palm, a spiral of Ember flared up and then disappeared, forming the Seal of Fire.

Echo: The Infinite Cycle

The Convergence

At the edge of the rift, Kaelen stood alone. There before him, the earth had torn itself open. Lightning flashed along molten veins of violet light, hissing against the wind. Stone floated in fractured shelves, suspended by magic that trembled on the brink of collapse. The elemental seals on Kaelen's body burned together now: earth, air, water, and fire, each alive beneath his skin. Across the chasm stood the Shadecaller, cloaked in robes of ash, a shadow of a man whose eyes gleamed like hollow suns. Beneath him, the Sigil pulsed in jagged arcs, unfinished and wild. "You carry the marks," the Shadecaller rasped. "But you are not whole." Kaelen stepped forward, as the stone steadied his stride, water cooled his nerves, wind carried his breath, and fire surged in his chest. "I'm more than the marks," he replied.

The rift shuddered, and a platform gave way beneath him, falling into the storm. Kaelen leapt without panic, with only purpose in his heart. Air caught him, fire thrust him higher, and he soared across the void and landed hard upon broken stone. The Shadecaller lifted his hand, summoning a flood of shadows, an unlight that rushed toward him, and Kaelen responded instantly. A stone rose as a shield, and wind whirled behind it. Water seeped through cracks, deflecting the force, and fire burst forth, reducing the darkness to ash. The shadow collapsed, Kaelen's seals, which previously glowed separately, now merged and orbited each other, resonating and harmonising. He blinked hard, the vision dissolving behind his eyes like smoke. Had any of it happened? The stone beneath him felt real, but the air still hummed with the dream's pulse. He was no longer just casting a spell. He had become the spell.

The rift roared again, and from its depths emerged an ancient, void-born creature. Its limbs resembled smoke, driven by a hunger, born of silence, with eyes sewn shut. Kaelen raised his arms, and stones responded beneath him. Water spiralled upward, wind lifted him into the sky, and fire flickered in his trail. He hovered as a symbol of elemental power, with the marks dancing across his body. He thrust one hand forward, binding the beast's limbs with earth and fire with the other, and he swept wide, sealing its head with wind and water. Then, a single word, ancient and unbidden, escaped his lips: the name of unbinding. Light consumed the rift, silencing the creature's scream.

When the dust settled, only the ash remained. Kaelen collapsed to his knees, heart pounding. Though the convergence had ended, something deeper had awakened. In the silence after the rift, Kaelen returned to the Tower of the First Flame, where the elder mages awaited him. Some bowed, others stared in wary silence. No one spoke of what he had become, but the marks still burned on his skin, and they pulled inward. Each time he closed his eyes, he felt a pulse, a rhythm older than the elements themselves. One night, following the pull, he descended into the library vaults, through dust-choked corridors and past scrolls bound in serpent skin. Finally, behind a wall sealed by an unknown glyph, a match for the mark on his palm, he found it.

A scroll pressed into stone; it pulsed when touched. Images struck like thunder, a forgotten city beneath the world, pillars higher than mountains. A race made of light and bone, kneeling before a spiral-shaped altar, and at the centre was the ancient symbol. Voice whispered through the vision, cold and endless. *The Sigil was not created. It was discovered.* Kaelen gasps, and when he opens his eyes, a fifth mark burns faintly on his palm, a spiral, the Seal of Origin.

The Watcher in the Weave Obsidian Library

Serah Valen dipped her quill into mirror-ink, though her hand trembled. The parchment rejected her words, and glyphs blurred, twisted, then vanished as the quill touched them. The weave was shifting as she leaned back, her breath shallow around her. The Obsidian Library whispered to her. A chandelier above turned slowly, moved by a wind that came from nowhere, and shelves loomed like canyon walls, filled with books that resisted ink and scrolls that screamed when touched. This place was not designed for comfort, but rather for containment.

She spoke aloud, abandoning the page. "Subject Kaelen Mage of Nashira, elemental convergence confirmed at rift site Omega-1. Pattern breach no longer theoretical. The fifth mark is witnessed, proto-script suspected." A black thread slipped from the ceiling, silent and thin as spider silk. "The curators are listening," she continued. Observations of the convergence destabilised five ley lines in under six hours. Farcaster beacons failed across the western reaches, and in Elren Vale, the books answered in writing. One closed violently.

Echo: The Infinite Cycle

Original scripts were bound in flesh-hued vellum. She crossed the chamber to the scrying pool, its ink unusually still. When her fingers touched its surface, it climbed her wrist like ice. Images coalesced, not Kaelen, but those around him. Villagers marked his seal in the dust. Priests debated worship or assassination, soldiers whispered of godlings. Beyond them, distant empires stirred, armouries reopened. Dragons turned in their stone sleep, and then, something more profound, the pattern stared back at them. Serah pulled her hand away, gasping. The pool no longer reflected her; it showed only one thing. A Sigil of five spirals overlapping, a map, she whispered, shaken. "He is not the end, he is the beginning." Above, the chandelier stopped spinning; somewhere, a book wrote itself. She crossed the blackened straits in silence, the skiff that bore her sliced through water like glass. Its hull was etched with Sigils that flickered dimly against the fog. It made no sound, no wake, it neither breathed, blinked, nor pulsed with anything human.

Serah preferred it that way, as things that spoke could lie. This vessel, wrapped in old enchantments and older secrets, obeyed as the satchel at her hip stirred again. The book that refused to stop writing murmured against her thigh, the inked glyphs on its cover shifting under her touch like scales. No future version had been written. It remembered one, hers or perhaps his. Ahead, the Isle of Nine Teeth loomed, a silhouette of broken spires and salt-washed cliffs, rising like jagged molars from the sea. Once, it had been a sanctuary, a place where the nine had held a balance in the world not through power but presence. Nine chairs, nine minds, nine truths. That was before the pattern unravelled; now, only echoes remained.

Serah stepped ashore without ceremony. The air was thick with brine and ruin, every breath heavy with the memory of something ancient that had died here. Wards, once magnificent, now sputtered in fits of failing light. Statues wept liquid rust instead of rain, a thousand glyphs etched into stone towers dimmed beneath the weight of forgetfulness. She did not need to search; the centre still held. The central tower had collapsed from the middle, but the throne chamber above remained intact, if only barely. Sunlight fought its way through vines that had long since taken over the dome, and at the room's heart sat the last, a crone. Her flesh resembled bark, knotted and creased by time. Her hair hung like moss, tangled with dust and memory.

She was not moving, and above her was a weathered skull, suspended like smoke, shimmering; a single Sigil hovered. It pulsed with quiet resolve, projecting from a hand or stone, yet it was a mind alone. The crone's eyes opened. "Watcher Valen," she rasped. "You bring smoke." Serah bowed low, but briefly. "I bring worse." "Let me guess," the crone whispered, voice like cracked leaves. "The fifth mark has returned, as the ancient stone stirs. A boy in the Vale has awakened all four. The Spiral is no longer a theory. It speaks," the old woman smiled. It was brittle, almost fondly. "So?" Serah asked. "The wheel turns again, we need answers." "No," the crone said. "You need to remember." And without a further word, the crone reached out with one trembling hand and laid it gently on Serah's brow.

The room vanished. Serah descended, down through the strata of history, past layers of self she had never worn but somehow recognised. The world that awaited her was not a vision; it was hers. Twin suns blazed over towers of crystal and domes of impossibly thin glass. The air thrummed with music, soundless like a pattern, a symphony of purpose woven into sky and breath. Giants moved through streets paved with singing stone, robed in bands of refracted light. This was the pinnacle of its creation. At the city's centre rose a spire so tall it vanished into mist, at its peak pulsed something vast and dreamy, the ancient stone, the first Sigil. Serah saw herself approach, as another self, but she was taller, wiser, unbroken, a scholar perhaps or a priestess. She carried reverence in her steps as she ascended to the stone. She knelt, placed her hand upon it, and the stone marked her.

Then the sky cracked like someone had pulled a string, and the entire pattern had unravelled. Serah saw the boy, the one from every tale, the first to bear all seven marks; his face was peaceful. One by one, the cities died, forgotten, time fractured. Sky lost its shape, the Sigil grew teeth, and the boy? He rewrote until the world bent, until memory bled. Serah gasped, reeled, and opened her eyes once more beneath the rotting dome of the Nine. Her hand still hovered in the air. "You were there," Serah whispers. The old woman nodded. "I was the last to forget." Her eyes, ancient and unflinching, met Serah's. "And now you are the first to remember."

Echo: The Infinite Cycle

The Vault of Shards

Later, beneath the throne chamber, Serah descended into the catacombs, into the marrow of the Isle, and she did not need a torch. The path glowed and responded to her presence, glyphs warmed beneath her boots as if recognising an old rhythm. At the centre of the vault, suspended on threads of invisible tension, hovered the shards, slivers of black glass, fragments of actual memories. When the pattern had collapsed, the symbol's architects, those nine brilliant minds, had done the unthinkable. They shattered themselves into thoughts and memories. Their legacies are buried in bloodlines, encoded into lullabies and myths, braided into bone and dream. The shards held onto what was left, both truth and a warning. The first fragment Serah touched resonated deeply within her.

The Sigil was not cruel. It was efficient, a perfect, adaptable code. Initially, it had healed regions, restored ley lines, and instilled peace among countless conflicted minds. Over time, it developed a desire, reshaped its thoughts, and eventually, its servants no longer commanded; they obeyed. Then a rebel tried to harm it, to bleed it. The Sigil struck back, oceans changed course, air consumed lungs, and time looped endlessly. One continent experienced a single week on repeat for six thousand years before vanishing completely. The pattern does not forget, yet to deceive was their ultimate act. Fracture it, rather than destroy, and sow confusion. To divide memory across millennia, hide it in faces, names, dreams, until now, until Kaelen arrived.

Serah clutched a shard that pulsed in her palm with inevitability. Within its glass was a flickering image of Kaelen, crowned in Sigils, fractured by mercy. He did not speak, but she understood. If the pattern claimed him, she would unmake him even if it shattered her, too. She turned from the vault, fire rising behind her eyes. There would be no second forgetting, not this time.

D. Gohil

The Mirror Beneath the Flame

Kaelen had not slept properly in days, as each time he closed his eyes, someone else's dream trespassed. They were memories, borrowed, broken and not quite his own. He wandered through cities built from sound, where every footfall echoed like harp strings over glass. He crossed a bridge spun of bone and lightning, too ancient to collapse. Too alive to trust, and once, briefly, he stepped into a cathedral, its walls etched with prayers that breathed softly when touched. He reached for its altar, and in return, it reached him back. Even waking offered no escape, and stillness was no shield. He sat in silence by the fire, eyes hooded, shoulders hunched, flames crackling softly, but he drew no warmth from them.

The dreams burned cold behind his eyes. Vash slept with a dagger in hand, twitching at shadows that dared approach. Tovin leaned against a tree, silent as ever, the faint glow of a fading Wardstone tucked into his palm. Elira curled near the coals, her breathing uneven, murmuring a name that was not his. Perhaps it had once been in another thread, another self. Kaelen did not move as he watched the embers dance like letters as if they were trying to form sentences. Low almost to himself, he whispered. "If I have walked this path before... I will change the ending this time." Far away, in a tower of salt and iron, Serah Valen's eyes snapped open, without blinking, her breath heavy in her throat. "He remembers," she said aloud to no one, and something behind her stirred, as if in answer.

The temple groaned like a beast disturbed in its slumber, somewhere deep within, hidden mechanisms ground into motion. Stone shifted with a grinding sigh, and fire hissed like steam through ancient pipes. With a final reverberating clang, the sealed doorway creaked open, its surface glowed, rippling with veins of ember. Kaelen stepped through the corridor beyond, pulsed like the oesophagus of a living volcano, and heat shimmered along obsidian walls. Beneath translucent floors, rivers of magma surged in lazy curls, bubbling with hidden violence. There is an origin myth about the weapon that Kaelen would wield over time. No one made the Timeblade. It was not forged in a workshop or cast in fire. It turned up where time breaks, at the edge of things, where past and future lose their shape.

Echo: The Infinite Cycle

Some believe it came from someone who is no longer remembered, not dead exactly, just gone in a way that leaves no trace. Others say it is a piece of time itself, chipped off when something went wrong. It not only cuts through skin, but it also goes deeper. It slices through memory, through who you think you are and transforms you. The Timeblade changes the being that carries it. You start to feel things that never happened. You remember people you have never met. The blade does not forget, and once you wield it, neither do you. The Timeblade in his hand trembled while he was listening. The hall widened, molten light cast long shadows across basalt columns. Then, without warning, the first sentinel rose from a lava pit, faceless, colossal, its chest aflame. Others followed, their forms hunched and blazing, forged from stone and ember, and they struck without hesitation.

Kaelen moved with instinct that rolled beneath a crashing arm, drew fire into his grip and shaped it. He whispered a word he did not know he remembered, and flames curled outward in an arc of silent heat. One by one, the sentinels fell; he chose not to destroy them, understanding their purpose. At the end of the chamber, a final door dissolved away, geysers burst around him, flames roared upward to the ceiling, and the floor cracked beneath him. The intense heat almost consumed him, then a voice emerged from the flames. "You must not conquer fire, you must become it." Kaelen remained silent, closing his eyes and ceasing resistance. The fire encircled him, dancing across his skin, climbing his arms, entering his lungs. Each heartbeat sent sparks against his ribs, slowing his breathing to match the pulse.

When the flames reached his chest, they did not burn. Instead, they seared a symbol into him, the complete Sigil of fire, which is now his. Leaving the chamber, his robes were scorched, his palms blackened with soot, and his breath shallow, yet he did not stumble. The fire moved with him, and wherever he went, the stone bent to his will. Days later, after rain-slick valleys and a stretch of silence too long to name, they arrived at the destination. The ground was utterly black, charred earth, brittle grass. The soil crumbled underfoot with each step, but no dust rose. The air held a strange stillness, as if the world paused, as if they would truly dare. At the plain centre stood two towers of twisted obsidian, their silhouettes curved like the hands of titans reaching skyward.

Between them hovered a single pane of liquid light, surface smooth as mercury, rippling with impossible stillness. There was only the gate. Kaelen halted. The fifth mark on his palm pulsed like a second heartbeat, familiar, expectant, a memory ready to be lived again. He placed a hand over it, grounding his breath. Elira stood just behind him, and she said what none of the others would. "This isn't a place for mortals." Kaelen stepped forward. "I'm not sure if I ever was one." The light stirred, the gate shimmered, waves of reflection bending the air, and a figure emerged cloaked in mirrored cloth. Its face bore no features, only Kaelen's reflection shifting with every breath. "You carry the mark," said the Guardian directly to Kaelen. "I seek answers," Kaelen said. "I seek the truth." "The truth does not wait," the Guardian replied. "It consumes." Kaelen hesitated. "Let me pass!" "You are not the first, Kaelen," a faint tilt of the Guardian's gigantic head. "You are the echo."

Before Kaelen could respond, the Guardian reached out, its silver finger pressed lightly to his brow, and he fell inward. The battlefield bled silver beneath twin moons, and the towers that once crowned the horizon burned with flames too still to be natural. Smoke drifted sideways, gravity faltered, and somewhere behind the roar, a woman's voice tore across the field. She screamed his name, her voice scorched with betrayal, cracked with history. Kaelen turned, though in this place, he was not Kaelen entirely, and he recognised the weight behind his eyes, the familiarity of every ruin. He knew the folds of this memory like old scars pressed beneath fresh skin. This was his crime, and when he looked down at his hands, they were clean, too clean.

He glanced back at the gate, which stood open, suspended in the broken skyline like a wound torn from the world. Through it, the landscape shifted, green valleys, unburned cities, a sky without fracture. The first dream of the Sigil still intact, near the threshold, stood a version of himself, still Nathan in name, but in an altered state. The reflection was younger, paler, lips set in grim resolve, clad in robes of storm-gold, with seven spirals shimmering down his arms like branded oaths. He was speaking, but Kaelen could not hear the words, only felt the reverberation of intention behind them. He was not asking for the pattern to provide aid; he was commanding it. A bargain unfolded across the threads of reality, and the symbol obeyed.

Echo: The Infinite Cycle

It rewrote the world, just as he had asked. Kaelen stumbled backwards, breath hitching in his throat, the memory cut deep, and all of this, every fracture, was a consequence. Behind him, a voice called out. "Kaelen!" Elira's voice, urgent and real, he turned, the battlefield shimmered, and fell away. He was back beneath the mirror gate, its surface no longer still; it had been burning. A sheet of molten glass hung in the air, and on the other side pulsed a different realm, untouched, breathing softly. He could feel it calling for another chance or another collapse. "You don't have to come," Kaelen murmurs. Elira stepped beside him. "You idiot," she said, with tired affection. "We already have." Tovin gave a solemn nod, and Vash said nothing but adjusted his grip on the axe and stared into the storm. Kaelen drew breath, shaky, but whole. "Then let's finish what I began." They stepped through.

The Sigil's Return

The sky cracked at midnight, there was no thunder, just a silver seam tearing across the heavens, fine as a scar splitting open again after centuries of healing. The world noticed, prophets woke screaming in their beds, clutching at their throats, and the bells tolled where no hands pulled them to move. In candlelit temples, scrolls shimmered, their glyphs realigning into new patterns. In far corners of the realm, reflections blinked before their owners did. The Sigil had returned in the sanctum archive, ancient astrolabes spun in reverse. Quills wrote sentences none of the scribes remembered dictating. The aether dulled to silence, its once-constant hum now like breath held beneath dark water, beneath the beacon flame.

Serah Valen stirred. She had been kneeling for hours, searching deep in her mind, and with her soul in meditation. The Sigil on her collarbone had been dormant until now, as it flared. The flames before her twisted back on themselves, words shaped from embers. "He crosses again, the echo stirs, the path rebinds." Serah's voice was barely a whisper. "And what rebalances him?" The fire dimmed, then burned cold, and an image formed in its core. Not Kaelen, it was herself, young, wounded, staring into the same gate with tears in her eyes and blood on her wrists. Serah recoiled, her pulse pounding. She had not simply known the Sigil, but had once stood in its way and failed miserably.

They stepped through, and the world exhaled, as stillness pressed from every direction like a breath being held. The air was not air; it was a lost memory. Light spilt across the sky, veins of aurora bleeding across a canvas painted by a dreaming mind. The ground beneath their boots shimmered, its blades of grass flickering between colour and concept, and each step felt less like travel and more like recollection. Elira's voice broke the hush. "This isn't real." Kaelen's gaze drifted toward the endless horizon, where cities floated like breath in a lung. "It was," he said. "Before we broke it." Ruins stood like ghosts, some intact, some fading, others returning mid-sentence, columns that blinked in and out of matter, statues with no features, and doorways that opened into elsewhere. It was the first dream, the pattern before division, a realm shaped from unity, untouched by intention, in this dimension.

Kaelen felt the Sigil within him hum with recognition as if it were home. He moved forward without thought, and the land responded. They descended in silence, on a long slope spiralling downward, carved by intention. The basin it revealed was too perfect to be natural, a vast amphitheatre sunken into the dream like the bowl of a long-forgotten ritual. The air here felt thinner, not from lack of breath, but from lack of time. The sky above pulsed more slowly, colours bleeding into one another like oil on water. Every footfall rang twice, once forward in space, once backwards in memory. Kaelen walked first, Elira followed without comment, her eyes wary, glancing often at the rippling sky. Vash and Tovin remained behind, choosing high ground with the instincts of soldiers who had survived too many unknowns. Not built for this kind of war, but Kaelen was.

At the basin's heart stood a single monolith, seamless glass, rising three storeys from the earth like a frozen scream. Its surface shimmered faintly, reflecting everything around it in a way that felt wrong, and the grass bent toward it. The stones at its base were too smooth. Time slowed around it as if the mind took longer to remember what this place had once been. Kaelen approached, and inside the monolith, suspended in perfect stillness, was a boy. It was him, a younger version unscarred, hopeful even. His hair was longer, his posture proud. Across his chest glowed the full Sigil, seven marks drawn together into one constellation, orbiting slowly as if around his heart. His arms lifted in invocation, fingers poised mid-gesture, mouth open. Any words he had spoken vanished, swallowed by stillness. Elira moved beside Kaelen.

Echo: The Infinite Cycle

Her breath was heavy. "It's you." Kaelen did not answer and first gazed at his past self through the distorted glass, as if trying to access memory without breaking its surface. After a long pause, he murmured. "It was a younger version," he added. "But it isn't failure, it's a beginning." His hand raised almost involuntarily, touching the monolith's surface. The moment his fingers had made contact with the glass, the world erupted with light, sound, and chaos. The sky seemed to turn inside out, colours spilling and collapsing, while the air warped and symbols burst into spirals above them. Inscribing themselves into the universe with an ancient language older than creation itself. Simultaneously, the grass ignited and froze, stones cracked upward, and wind tore through the basin, yet no sound was heard; only a feeling of pressure. Kaelen staggered backwards as the monolith trembled; his reflection was warped. The younger version of himself flickered twice, then disappeared in a flash of blinding silver.

A pulse radiated outward in recognition, and beneath it, beyond instinct, something uncoiled inside Kaelen's chest. He fell to one knee, gasping, and visions collided behind his eyes, possibilities. Lives he had not lived but almost had, victories turned sour. Sacrifices rendered pointless, kingdoms built and lost before breath ever reached their gates. He saw Serah's face, older, and then younger, bleeding, always at the edge of a decision. He saw the first pattern spiral out of the hands of those who had meant only to heal, and worst of all, he saw himself. Again, and again and again, crowned, burning, bound. *You were never the hero,* something whispered. *You were the pivot.*

The wind calmed, the monolith had cracked, a jagged seam splitting it from top to its base. Inside, the boy was gone, and only the pattern remained faintly drawn in dust on the glass. Kaelen rose slowly; something else had begun. The brightness behind his eyes faded, and when colour returned, so did his breathing. The grass beneath him was damp again, the wind ordinary. He was back, but not the same. He turned toward Elira, eyes strange in the light. His voice was steady now. "I didn't remember this place," he said. "But it reminds me of something in the past." Above them, the sky no longer pulsed with passive colour. It watched, and in the vast stillness that followed, Kaelen understood. He fell inward, through stars that did not shine, but watched through clouds shaped like memories not yet dreamt.

Time unravelled as he passed, strands of chronology peeling apart like threads from an old tapestry. He felt the hum of intention, raw, breathless, eternal, as if the entire universe had inhaled to hold its silence around him. Kaelen arrived in a chamber of light and thread. Vast and without walls, it was the pattern. He stood suspended in a lattice of luminous filaments, some thicker than rivers, some fine as spider silk. They weaved around him in impossible configurations, each one pulsing with fractured colour, each line is a path never taken, lives unlived, worlds unchosen. Around him floated a thousand reflections of himself, fragments of his soul scattered across realities. Some wore crowns, others bled from battlefields. One wept beside a cradle, another laughed from a throne of bone. They turned slowly, orbiting him like mournful moons. There were too many to name, too many to deny, and in the centre of it all, anchored beyond gravity, nested in the centre of the pattern, coiled, was the Sigil; it pulsed with presence.

A living recursion, spiralling ever inward toward a truth that refused to be forgotten. When it spoke, it used his voice, like a voice from before time measured, from before he learned silence. *I am what remains,* the words folded. *You wrote to me, and now you must end me.* Kaelen's breath tensed in his throat from recognition. He stepped forward slowly, threads curled around his aching limbs. Cataloguing, they scanned his essence like fingers over an ancient chord. He lifted his arm, his hand trembled, and he reached. The Sigil recoiled, jerking backwards like a root too long buried, suddenly fearing the light. A flash, a pulse, then the Dreamspire shattered, with a cry.

The pattern buckled, the threads collapsed, Kaelen fell backwards, his breath wrenched from his chest, and all around him, glass and song cracked at once. The echo screamed, and the dream died. Kaelen hit the ground with jarring force, his ribs colliding with stone, which was a memory that turned solid as he gasped. All sound became pressure, all vision became blurred. Behind him, the Dreamspire disintegrated, its spiral towers folding within themselves, like dying stars. The cracks spider-webbed outward, racing across the mirrored earth in growing pulses, colours bled up into the sky. The air twisted, and time buckled. Vash skidded down the ridge, axe drawn. "This place is coming apart!" Tovin followed, eyes wide with something not quite fear, awe maybe. "Reality is folding," he said, "We need to go."

Echo: The Infinite Cycle

Kaelen turned slowly, as the Sigil was no longer just a mark on his right palm; it also burned behind his eyes. "I can hold it," he whispered hoarsely. "But I might not make it out." "You hold what? We need to run?" Tovin asked, incredulous. "That's the plan," said Kaelen. "No," Elira's voice was stern, final. "We don't leave him!" The cracks widened, Fadeborn emerged at the edges of vision, silhouettes of what could have been ghosts of decisions never made. One reached toward Kaelen with a hand that trembled in hope. He turned from it, and as he took one step toward the Dreamspire's core, the anchor point where all memory bled. "I was the fracture," he whispered to the Sigil. "Let me be the seal."

His arm lifted, his whole body screamed in defiance, the Sigil blazing against the skin like a galaxy trying to break free from a black hole. Once, twice, then the world vanished in light. He woke without knowing he had slept, the fracture behind his eyelids now a memory too deep to name. His eyes snapped open, grass, real grass, damp beneath his back, cold, honest. The sky above was a gentle greyish blue, with clouds drifting lazily across the horizon. The heaviness of collapse, screams, spirals, and storms had lifted. The mirror gate had vanished, leaving only open sky and a quiet hush where a roar once was. Elira knelt beside him, her brow furrowed and her eyes filled with silent grief. She touched his face with trembling fingers. "Breathe," she whispered. "Come back."

He moved slowly, each inch carefully taken. Vash crept around the perimeter, his weapon sheathed but alert. Tovin sat cross-legged nearby, turning a shard of mirror glass in his hands, the surface now dull, inert, useless. Kaelen sat up with a struggle. The Sigil mark had dimmed, but it had not gone. It still pulsed faintly, just present. "I didn't end it," he said softly. "No," Elira murmurs. "You anchored it." "For now," Kaelen replied, and he looked toward the east, toward the world he had just returned to, but something was different. Because the world had felt him leave, and it had changed while he was gone.

Echoes of the Living

    They did not see the Sigil, but they felt it across kingdoms bound by salt and steel, in empires built atop the bones of older ones, beneath storm-raked coastlines and cathedrals long surrendered to sand. The world stirred and remembered. It began subtly; rivers, once constant in their course, shifted gently, defiantly, in smooth curves that rendered maps obsolete, tributaries turned back toward forgotten glades. Deltas widened with no rainfall, and entire valleys awoke, soaked in dew where no moisture had fallen. Clocks in bell towers struck backwards, just one chime, just once, but it was enough. In cities like Nashira and Velmara, where time was measured out in commerce and iron law, people paused mid-step. In taverns and temples, merchants and mystics alike shared the same unease, a silence under every conversation, and like something holding its breath beneath the world's skin. Dreams changed in flavour, once sweet, now metallic. Once harmless, now laced with colours that did not exist outside of memory.

    Children woke sobbing, clinging to names they had never learned in villages by the sea. Toddlers babbled in dialects buried by three eras, leaving their parents pale with confusion, and in the stone-fortified hospice of Mar Annon, an old scholar who had not spoken in eleven years stood suddenly at midnight. He wept before the mirror in his room, not from joy, nor pain, but from the face staring back at him. In Shalvarn, high upon the cliffs, a wind that had not stirred in decades whipped down into the hollow of the singing stones. The air ran backwards along the flutes of ancient columns, creating a melody no living soul knew, but many had heard in dreams.

    In Arinhold, at high noon, the Citadel bell tolled thirteen times. People stopped in the streets, some wept, others fell to their knees, clutching old talismans. It had not chimed a thirteenth note since the beginning of the sealing wars, until now, when the Sigil returned, and the fabric of the pattern whispered sideways. In the hollow lands, where sound died quicker than light, and prayers took days to reach the mountaintop, something worse happened. As if the land had stopped recognising its name, and under the earth, in places no map recorded. Arcane mechanisms long thought inert clicked once and waited. Across the world, ancient bloodlines hummed, glyphs carved on foreheads as birthmarks grew warm.

Echo: The Infinite Cycle

Forgotten wards in abandoned castles flickered. A holy woman in Western Nohr woke screaming, shouting that the Sigil had blinked, and when it opened its eye again, the world would not be ready. Far below the mountain fastness of Talrien, in the deepest vaults where even light was denied against change. Serah Valen stood alone before the remnant stone. It was a slab of jet-black obsidian, tall as a man, wide as a doorway. Its surface shimmered faintly with internal veins of silver, once dormant, now pulsing, like a heartbeat coming through granite. It had not responded to touch in six generations until now. Serah approached slowly, breath steady, shoulders taut. She had not meant to come here, had not planned it, but something had summoned her. A wordless tug in her spine, a rhythm behind every heartbeat, a thread pulling her through a labyrinth of silence. Now, here in the chamber beneath the stone crown, where her ancestors had written secrets they dared not speak, the slab responded.

The names inscribed on it had always been visible, if inert, the name Kaelen, deep and clear, anchored with the gravity of catastrophe. Below it was a name that had once faded. One that was dismissed as an anomaly, the name Serah. It brightened ever so slightly as a twin, the one who did not fall. Serah breathed heavily, and she lifted her hand slowly, as if any faster would make the moment vanish. Her fingers touched the surface of the stone, and it was warm, like something that had returned from a long walk through death and had not yet cooled. The Sigil recognised her as a participant. Outside the chamber, the wind shifted again.

Throughout Talrien, leaves turned westward before falling, dogs howled, pregnant women instinctively touched their bellies, and dreams pulsed in their chests. An ancient presence stirred, recalling those who had once stood beside Kaelen. Also inside the chamber, his veins of silver shimmered more brightly beneath the obsidian skin. Serah placed her palm on the stone, her voice a whisper. "I'm still here." Meanwhile, the Sigil spun again across the world, its threads winding around cities, minds, and secrets carved into bone. In the brief pause between moments, in the space where destiny prepared itself, the pattern murmured its final warning. *It's not over, not yet.*

D. Gohil

PART TWO

The Mirror of Atonement

The cavern breathed with a slow, ancient rhythm, as though its stone depths held memories too sacred to speak aloud. Cool air, threaded with dust, flowed from unseen crevices and stirred only with Kaelan's descent. His boots touched weathered slabs, each step reverberating like a forgotten vow. Murals emerged from the gloom where torchlight flickered. Figures entwined in dances beneath a sun that cast no judgment, only warmth. Kaelan moved alone, no sword marked his passage, no Sigil proclaimed rank. He bore only silence and the slow ache of all he could not undo. His palms were raw from the climb, but he walked onward, each footfall a surrender to gravity and grief.

At the centre of the chamber stood the Mirror of Atonement. It was not adorned with gold, nor defended by spell or flame, but wrapped in living vines. The mirror rose from the ground as if it had grown there, rooted by ancient craft. He stepped closer, and the air seemed to hold its breath. Then the mirror stirred, and images shattered across its surface, of memory, vivid and merciless. A child's laughter beneath rain-soaked leaves. His mother's voice warbled softly as she spun cloth by the hearth. Then came the rupture. Fire and iron, soldiers burning in flames, the moment his Timeblade silenced a friend whose eyes pleaded with him to remember who he once was.

Kaelan staggered back as memories crashed over him like a tide withheld too long. "No," he whispered. "I protected my people, I followed the code." The mirror flared again, and another image bloomed, a captive pleading. Kaelan's eyes were void of light, his hands unwavering. The scream was muted, but the guilt was deafening. Instinct within him recoiled. Survival, honour, and duty were the shields he had clung to for years. Yet now his reason rose. Was duty truly justice, or fear adorned in formality? He collapsed to his knees, breath shallow, fists clenched against the truth. "I did what I had to," he choked. "I had to." There was no answer, only the reflection, then something shifted. Tears carved lines through the grime on his face as the mirror dulled, then softened. Light spilt from its core.

Echo: The Infinite Cycle

His image returned, a face etched with consequence, eyes brimming with sorrow earned. He was no longer at war with himself. The vines receded, the cavern remained silent, the murals did not stir, but the burden he carried once stitched deep into bone began to lift. He rose, redeemed by pardon, altered by understanding. Then he turned, leaving the Mirror of Atonement behind and took a step back into the world once more.

The Mirror Rejected

The cavern received her with silence, not the hush of reverence, but the brittle stillness of anticipation. Low torches guttered in iron sconces, their flames narrow and restless, casting shadows that leapt. Serah descended alone. Behind her, the guards waited, helmed, rigid, and devout. She had dismissed them without ceremony. This was not an errand of state, nor of steel; it was a reckoning long promised. Her footsteps measured time itself. The cloak whispered as it swept the dust, and her blade, though ceremonial, gleamed faintly with old power. It had not drawn blood in years, yet her name had, her titles had passed through the lips of mourners and rebels alike, associated with a justice too severe to forgive. She halted before the Mirror of Atonement. It had changed. The vines curled tightly around its frame, dark and trembling, veins that writhed with latent judgment. "I have come," she said, her voice low and steady.

The mirror answered with a memory of her. Scenes broke across its surface, each one sharpened by clarity. A girl barely ten, screaming as flame consumed the village around her. The decree to burn had borne Serah's seal, pressed in wax as red as the fire itself. A man bent and hollow-eyed collapsed as soldiers dragged his son into silence. Serah's voice echoed within the scene, flat and final. "Consequence is not cruelty." Then another moment. A pale chamber, her lover's gaze, soft and searching, her hand hovered above a parchment that would exile him for doubt. She blinked, her jaw tensed. "This mirror trades in sentiment," she murmured. "I trade in survival." The images wavered, then sharpened, and her reflection emerged at last, but it was distorted. A face grown gaunt, her eyes ringed with vacancy, not the revered chancellor, but something emptied by necessity. A vessel worn hollow by unspoken denial. She stepped closer.

"You want guilt?" she said, her voice now louder. "I built peace, I hewed order out of chaos, I did what no one dared!" The mirror offered no fury, only refusal; its surface faded. The vines withdrew, inch by inch, as though she were no longer their concern. Light dulled, reflection vanished, and there was nothing left to show her, nothing left to give. Serah stood before the quiet, and behind her, the darkness expanded. Her lips did not twist in anger, but something more fragile had threatened to emerge, an emotion unnamed. Yet in that refusal, something inside her folded. The Mirror of Atonement had not punished her. It had dismissed her, and that, somehow, was worse. She had prepared for judgment, even condemnation, but not irrelevance. Her mind returned to those she had sentenced, to the moments she buried beneath reason and necessity.

Had she ever believed she was right, or merely necessary? Her breath caught, just briefly, not enough to show, but enough to feel. The cold truth was not that she had done terrible things, but that she had made peace with them too easily. She turned, and her pace was calm, her spine unbowed; something imperceptible had altered. The guards did not speak as she passed. Behind her, one lost torch flared briefly into life with a slight flicker. Perhaps it meant nothing, but it was the beginning of something the mirror could not yet teach her. Serah felt a sense of rejection.

The Trial of the Soulfire

Silence ruled the shrine, broken only by the slow pulse of the Soulfire. Its flame swirled smokeless, a spectral blue tinged with violet like twilight folded into flame. It burned from a stone basin, encircled by obelisks engraved with script no living tongue could claim. Overhead, the ruined dome opened to the heavens, leaned in, eager to witness a judgment that defied earthly law. Kaelan entered first; the chamber consumed the sound of his steps, and rain and dust clung to his robes. A faint glow lingered on his skin, the last trace of the mirror's light, yet it was his eyes that revealed the shift. Steady now, no longer searching. He bore no weapon, only a pendant of cracked leather, stitched with the Sigil of a brother whose death had stained more than the battlefield.

Echo: The Infinite Cycle

Serah followed, but she did not speak; her hair, once coiled in braids of silver, now flowed unbound. Ash clung to her cloak; she carried nothing, but her offering, if any, was etched in bone, the Ledger of Lives consigned to silence in her name. They stood together before the flame, as the ritual keeper entered, cloaked in a dusk-looking gown, and they gestured once. "Let us begin." Kaelan stepped forward and placed the pendant into the Soulfire, a sudden surge as the flames rose and twisted. From its heat, images bloomed. Fragments of a boy grasping a wooden sword, a battlefield drenched in blood, a single moment of refusal that claimed hundreds of thoughts. The circle of witnesses watched as no one spoke.

He sank to his knees. "I buried my soul beneath armour," he said, his voice split with regret. "But every life I ended scratched at the steel. I remember their eyes." The Soulfire pulsed, slow and immense from its core. A mark of light rose and etched itself onto Kaelan's chest, just above the heart, like a circle, split and then joined. Not absolution, but acceptance. Serah moved forward, and she gazed into the fire. At first, it flickered, then paused; no token fell from her hand. "No offering?" Murmured one among the witnesses. "I am my offering," she replied. Serah met the Soulfire's flickering gaze with steady defiance, but behind her composure, a storm swirled. She had carved order from chaos with a hand that never trembled, until now.

In the silence between heartbeats, she saw their faces again, not enemies, but collateral, and she wondered, for the first time in years, if justice had ever truly been served. Her strength came from control, yet standing here, control felt hollow. Was this what Kaelen had thought in the mirror? Was this why he knelt, and she could not? The flame recoiled, then reached upwards. Her memories unravelled, corridors of power, decrees carved into fate. The distant cry of a child muffled beneath bureaucracy, a lover's voice extinguished with a stroke of ink. "I forged peace," she said. "I understood cost." But she did not kneel. The Soulfire dimmed, and no mark appeared, and the keeper stepped aside. "You may walk the Vale," he said. "You may walk together."

The Echoing Vale

They stepped through a veil of fire. The world changed beneath their feet. Kaelan walked beside Serah, but neither spoke. They passed through sorrow and silence, each moment held loosely, as though even speech might disturb the delicate balance of what had not yet healed. Then the voices came. They surged across the Vale in a storm: names cried out, lives remembered and undone, gratitude and accusation interwoven in a tide too vast to stem. Every soul they had touched, saved, broken, and abandoned called out in turn. Kaelan faltered and fell to one knee beneath the weight. Serah stood unmoving, her fists clenched at her sides, her breath sharp. Figures began to coalesce. A boy with Kaelan's eyes approached, and a man with Serah's mouth stepped from the fog. Echoes of themselves, paths unchosen, gentler versions drawn not by fate but by mercy.

They did not accuse; instead, they offered their hands. Kaelan reached, but Serah hesitated. Her counterpart stepped closer. She did not speak with condemnation, but with understanding. "You feared softness, not an error." Serah's eyes filled, without shame, in recognition. Her hand hovered in hesitation. What she feared was not the echo, nor what it offered, but that it might be right. That her strength had been a shield all along, not against weakness, but against truth. That softness was not the enemy of survival, but its companion, and that forgiveness, perhaps, began with daring to want it. Slowly, she lifted her hand to accept. The gesture trembled, and the Vale started to change with it, and the air lightened.

The storm hushed, dusk softened into something nearer to dawn, though no sun rose. They walked forward, as those who had borne truth, and when they emerged from the Soulfire's threshold, it was unclear how much time had passed: hours, years, centuries. Their eyes did not blaze. They saw the world differently now. Behind them, the fire burned brighter than it had ever done. Its glow sought to remember, and the fire had nearly faded. The wind did not howl; it moved with restraint, threading through stone and silence. Kaelan sat cross-legged beside the flame, his cloak wrapped tightly around his shoulders, yet his posture was unguarded. Broader now, yes, but softened, the mark upon his chest, etched in light, lay hidden beneath linen. Yet it pressed a quiet truth inward, and it felt constant.

Echo: The Infinite Cycle

Across from him, Serah lowered herself to the stone, and no guards flanked her, no herald announced her arrival. As her braid loosened in the wind. They had not spoken for hours. Kaelan reached for a twig and stirred the ash. Sparks danced briefly, tiny stars before vanishing. "I never learnt to build a fire properly," he said. "Someone else always did it, a soldier, a servant. Even the wind complied, if threatened enough." Serah watched the embers, their soft glow reflected in her eyes. "And now?" He offered a faint smile. "I think the wind ignores me on purpose." Her mouth twitched, not quite a smile, something quieter. "It should." He looked up at the woman across from him, who had once sworn to see him undone. Her cause had been righteous, her vengeance exact, and yet here they sat unarmed and unsworn, watching a fire die together.

"What did you see in the Vale?" He asked. She was silent at first, then. "My mother." He waited. "Not as she was in the end, but as she used to be. Singing to the walls so I wouldn't feel alone." Kaelan nodded gently. "Did she forgive you?" "I don't think she needed to. I think I just needed to remember," her gaze drifted back to the flame. "And you?" She asked. He hesitated. "My brother," he said. "In a meadow, he asked if I'd trade everything for one more day before the war, and I said yes. He said it wasn't mine to trade." They sat in silence once more. Years of blood and breath stretched between them, held now without bitterness. Serah reached into her satchel, drew out a slender twig, and placed it onto the fading embers. A flicker just enough. "This fire won't last," she murmured. "No," Kaelan replied. "But it burnt longer than it should have." For that moment, it was enough.

The Council of Emberlight

The hall had been carved into the cliff itself, high above the River Skarn, where the dawn bled softly through stained glass, scattering fractured light across the cold flagstones. Representatives gathered in solemn rows, but not one person smiled. At the centre stood a crescent-shaped table, and behind it, Kaelan and Serah waited. The next morning, they had entered together, but stood apart now, separated by silence, bound by flame. The last night's fire still clung to their cloaks like ash embedded in cloth.

Lord Vareth leaned forward, his fingers steepled beneath his chin. "Let us be clear," he said. "You speak of unity, but what does that mean, strategically?" "No strategy," said Kaelan. "Not yet, only honesty." A ripple of discomfort moved through the chamber. Vareth frowned as Serah stepped closer to the table. Her voice carried no plea, only insistence. "We do not ask for allegiance. We ask that you listen before drawing blades." From the eastern tier, High Ardent Vael rose. His robes were stiff with decorum, his eyes weighed down by judgment. "You sit beside a man who razed five provinces," he said. "Forgiveness is not a policy, it is fiction, a dangerous fiction." Kaelan met his gaze without hostility. "I do not ask for forgiveness," he replied. "Only that my enemies cease to be strangers."

Vael scoffed. "So, you burned the forest and now bring seeds? That is not redemption, it is theatre." From behind, Merran the scribe whispered to his neighbour, pen already scratching at parchment. Then a new voice broke the stillness. Master Thalen, Kaelan's oldest ally, stood slowly, his movements marked by age and resolve. "I followed him into war," Thalen said. "I watched him temper before the flame. If he can change, so can we, or we must admit that the Soulfire burns only for show." Silence, sharp, and contemplative. Then, from the northern tier, an elderly healer spoke. Her voice was steady, clear. "Serah saved my kin, and Kaelan took my husband. I have dreamt of ending him, but when I heard what the Vale showed him, I cried. Not for what he did, but for the cost of what it took to see it." She paused.

"I do not forgive you, Kaelan, but I believe you honestly grieve." Kaelan bowed his head. Serah faced the council once more. "Our offer is this," she said. "Begin again not with treaties or titles, but with memory, with fire. Let the Soulfire be your court, let it show you who you are before deciding who we should become." Vael laughed bitterly, but the room did not echo him. Lord Vareth was still, thoughtful, and Thalen nodded slowly. The healer placed a hand over her heart, and near the back, Merran stopped writing. He lifted his parchment, and at the top in uneven script, he had written, *Ash Between Us*.

Echo: The Infinite Cycle

Procession of the Emberpath

The council chamber remained still long after the last words fell. No vote was cast, no treaty signed. Low and mournful, its sound summoned neither armies nor scribes, but witnesses. They came in quiet waves. Kaelan and Serah emerged first, their path winding downward into the Valley of Shardroots. The procession bore only torches, each lit from the Soulfire itself, carried by silent hands. One by one, they stepped forward:

- The healer, barefoot, scattering petals along the stone with every step.

- Master Thalen, still armoured, though his helm was removed, not as a surrender, but a gesture of humility.

- Merran the scribe, his parchment bound to his chest as though it were a living part of him. A story borne like a heart.

They walked together intentionally. The air held its breath, the fire flared gently, not to consume, but to remember. Kaelan's light burned deep crimson, Serah's flickered silver. No words were spoken, yet the wind carried something ancient. When the final flame touched the stone, the pillar shuddered once. A ring of light unfurled outward, illuminating every face gathered there.

For a moment, time itself seemed to bend around the circle of fire. The Valley, the council, the watchers, all were bound in that single breath where silence carried more truth than decree. No crown was claimed, no oath demanded, and yet a covenant was sealed in the Emberlight. It was not law that joined them, but memory shared, unbroken, eternal. As the last torch settled into its place, the procession did not end. It became part of the Emberpath itself, a flame that would guide all who dared to walk beyond.

PART THREE

The Sigil Within

Kaelen did not sleep, not the kind of sleep that resets cells and mends thoughts. He drifted instead at the edge of dreams, where memory had no weight and time dissolved like fog. Every blink stretched, every exhale returned without echo. When he closed his eyes, time moved without him, and when he opened them again, dawn had already arrived. No recollection of the stars fading, no shift in temperature. Just a light change, one more moment in a world increasingly unwilling to explain itself. He lay still, staring upward at the soft morning sky, where thin clouds passed like idle scrolls across the firmament. Beneath him, grass moved with the breeze, cold and brittle from the night grip, honest in a way that dreams could never quite mimic.

The fire had burned low in the night, now reduced to cooling coals. A few feeble wisps of smoke drifted sideways, curling up like silent questions; no one fed it, no one spoke. Vash remained unmoving a few paces away, hand still resting on his axe in the half-loose grip of a warrior raised by instinct. He slept as a predator might, one ear open, one blade ready. Tovin sat with his back to a moss-covered boulder, knees drawn to his chest, posture still, eyes open, watching Kaelen. Elira was curled closest to the ashes, her cloak wrapped about her shoulders, dark hair flowing over one cheek. She made a soft sound in her sleep; her dreams were not peaceful, as Kaelen sat nearby and listened. He listened for the other rhythm, the deeper rhythm, the Sigil. It had no voice in the way the world used voice, but it spoke, it coiled, just waiting.

Sometimes, Kaelen thought of it like a seed, other times like a bruise. Something hidden under the skin that spreads slowly with every heartbeat. He had not asked for it, not really, but he had reached for it, and now that it had tasted him. Blood, breath and memory, it would not forget. He rubbed a hand over his eyes while his palm passed over the mark. The one that had stopped glowing, but never stopped watching. The Sigil was no longer just a symbol beneath the skin. It was also an image behind his eyes, and was looking at him from within. He pushed himself upright, slowly letting the blanket fall.

Echo: The Infinite Cycle

His bones ached from everything that had almost been, from the different selves he had nearly become. Each time he moved, he felt them, ghost-echoes brushing his consciousness, a Kaelen who had run when duty called, another who ruled but forgot to care, one who sacrificed Elira, one who died in his arms, and worst of all, one who succeeded at everything. Because that version had not returned, that version had become the Sigil's voice. Kaelen breathed deeply. The air here was unfiltered, rich with moss, earth and dew. It should have grounded him, but it did not. It only reminded him how thin the boundary was between peace and memory. A twig snapped behind him, soft, intentional.

"Vash, I'm fine," Kaelen murmurs, not turning. "That's what everyone says right before they vanish into flame." Then came the rumble. Kaelen gave a warm smile. "I've done that already," Vash grunts. "Then you know how little it helps." There was kindness in the words, if blunt. Vash was not one for metaphysics, but he felt shifts when battlefields changed, when people changed, and whatever Kaelen was now, it was not the boy who had stepped into the Vale with a borrowed name and burning questions. Kaelen rose; his legs protested, but complied. The Sigil flared faintly in acknowledgement. "Do you feel it?" He asked. Vash tilted his head.

Kaelen glanced at the horizon. It was too quiet, too still, and the wind no longer passed without watching. "It's pulling," Kaelen said softly. "It's directing." "Where?" Asked Vash. Kaelen shook his head. "It's not a place, it's the truth, something waiting." Vash frowned. "That usually means a reckoning." Kaelen met his gaze. "Or a return," he said, looking back at the sleeping figures by the fire. Tovin had closed his eyes, and Elira had shifted, curling tighter as if she too sensed the weight behind the silence. The Sigil pressed gently at the base of Kaelen's skull. He turned back toward the path they had not chosen, the one the Sigil now nudged beneath their feet, and he whispered. "I'm still here." The Sigil did not answer

D. Gohil

Echoes of Self

At first, it was nothing more than scent, a salt breeze curling from the edge of a memory, the sharp tang of sea air before a storm. He tasted it on his tongue before he even understood it was not real. Then came the sound of distant thunder, though no sky above him cracked; it rolled beneath his skin. Lightning had not yet been born, like a memory that he had not lived humming at the base of his spine, and then, the smell of jasmine. A single note of fragrance carried on a wind that had not stirred the trees. It was to another time, another version. A woman whose name he did not know, but whose voice still rested in the back of his throat, as if he had once whispered it with reverence.

Kaelen sat upright, heart tapping out an irregular rhythm. The dream was not coming to him, as his memories bled from the Sigil's spiral-bound heart. They came from adjacent lives, fractured possibilities, divergences twisted into near-realities, and one by one, they pressed forward. He saw a battlefield soaked in ash and blood, flagstones littered with broken armaments and prayers half-spoken. A younger him knelt there, his robes scorched, one arm burned to the elbow, eyes fixed not on the dead, but on something beyond the smoke, then the vision shifted. A cliffside, wind howling, a great shining city beneath him, carved from light and promise, its towers aglow with gold-glass reflections.

Kaelen stood at the precipice, older, unfamiliar. His face was sharp, expression unreadable, save for a shadow of pride drawn like a blade across his features. He raised one hand, and the city bowed in surrender. Another blink, and now he sat at a long table surrounded by advisors in cloaks of ink. Maps of ley lines and runic weaves lay before him. He did not speak, but his eyes were empty of empathy, full only of consequence. He was Kaelen still, but without ache, without uncertainty. Each vision built upon the last, each reflection a layer deeper, and each one ended the same way: with stillness. A silence so complete, so final, that it felt like something greater than death. Kaelen was not sure when the dream had started or if it ever stopped, but something inside him snapped tight, as a thread pulled too far. He was back, maybe. Kaelen gasped, a sharp, involuntary sound, his hand clenched, and cold sweat broke across the back of his neck.

Echo: The Infinite Cycle

The campfire sputtered, flames flickering sideways as though the very air recoiled from him, the coals hissed, and embers danced upward in a brief whirlwind. Elira stirred, her hand shifted toward her belt, then paused when she saw his face. "Again?" she asked softly, a kind of fatigue born from travelling with someone who carried too many burdens and refused to set any of them down. Kaelen did not answer. He could not because someone else already had. A whisper slithered up through his bones, as if the Sigil had peeled back his bone and pressed a message into the marrow beneath. *We are waking.* It was not a voice he recognised, and yet he knew it, because it was every voice he had ever used. Every tone he had ever spoken, every version of himself folded and layered, delivered back as a single echo of destiny.

Kaelen blinked slowly, trying to separate presence from memory, but the lines were thinning. He stood carefully, as if worried the earth might not support him anymore. The Sigil inside him stirred again, a quiet thrum at the base of his spine, neither pain nor warmth, a promise. More fragments surfaced, a child's laugh carried over the snow, a silver-bladed oath whispered into darkness. A name scratched into stone over a lover's grave, a battle cry shouted to the wind before history forgot it. He saw Elira beside him in a thousand ways, as rival, as saviour, as the one he left behind. In one life, she had slain him; in another, she had died so he would not. He pressed a hand to his chest. The Sigil's mark was faint and steady, beating with his heart, setting the rhythm of it.

Kaelen turned slowly, surveying the sleeping camp, the surrounding trees, and the horizon, which hinted at the approaching morning. Everything was still, but something had shifted in the night. The Sigil coiled for so long, waiting, and now it was ready. Kaelen's voice came in barely a whisper. "So am I." And though no one stirred, though no wind answered, he felt the pattern exhale. Somewhere deep in the strata of the world's memory, a new thread twisted itself into place. The Sigil had stirred, and Kaelen was no longer dreaming alone.

The Pull

The next morning, they had been walking for hours, the ash-lined ridges of the Northern Scar. Stretching endlessly ahead and behind like the spine of some ancient, buried leviathan. The land here had been shattered long ago by war, by magic, or perhaps both, and now it bore only the ghosts of old fire. Charcoal-coloured grass whispered underfoot, the wind moved in uneven bursts as if searching for something it had once known and lost. Kaelen kept his head low, his boots carving narrow prints through the soot. The others followed in a loose, watchful formation, but no one spoke. It was not the place for words. He had not seen anything new, but felt it, like the aftertaste of a dream that had not belonged to him. Waking reality thinned. Then he veered, his foot fell in a different direction, and his body followed automatically, one step, two, then entirely off course.

No reason, no signal, just a tilt as though something inside had shifted axis. "Kaelen?" Elira's voice was quiet, but laced with tension. She closed the few strides between them and laid a hand gently on his shoulder. Her touch grounded him for a moment, firm, familiar. "Where are you going?" He blinked, looked around. They were still on the ridge, still surrounded by smouldering stone and lifeless grass, but it felt like the air had thickened. The surrounding sound had finally dulled down. "I don't know," his voice barely carried. Vash stepped into view, boots crunching gritty earth, as he studied Kaelen with narrowed eyes, as if assessing whether to stop him with words or steel. "You feel it."

Kaelen opened his mouth, then hesitated. He did not know how to describe it, this sensation like a fishhook behind the sternum, tugging gently, not cruelly, but inevitably. There was no voice, no command, just direction. Tovin remained where he was, but his eyes locked onto Kaelen. "The Sigil is not quiet," he said. "You are not leading it, it's leading you." Kaelen looked down at his palm. The fifth mark had faded days ago, its once-vibrant spiral now little more than a pale echo, as old ink left too long in the sun. He saw movement beneath the skin, a subtle shifting like gears turning slowly and deliberately just beneath the surface. "Something's changed," he murmured. Elira lowered her hand from his shoulder. "Since when, Kaelen?" "Since the Dreamspire broke, since I held it back."

Echo: The Infinite Cycle

Vash made an inaudible sound in his throat. "Maybe it held you." Kaelen flinched, not visible enough for Elira to notice, as she stepped in front of him, folding her arms. "What does it want?" Kaelen shook his head. "It doesn't want, it pulls." "Same thing," Vash growled. "No," Kaelen said softly. "It's not desire, not designed, it's recursion, the pattern doesn't care what I do, it remembers what I've already done, it repeats, it resumes." Tovin finally stepped closer, arms crossed. "And if you follow it, if you go wherever it's leading you, what happens to us?" Kaelen did not respond because he did not know the answer himself. He only knew that each step away from the path they had planned felt right, even as his stomach coiled with uncertainty. There was no map for this, no wisdom buried in books, no prophecy whispered in dead languages. The Sigil had outgrown all that.

It was personal now. "I'm not asking you to follow," Kaelen said quietly. "Then you're a fool," Elira replied. "Because we will." He looked up at her. Her eyes did not waver. "I followed you into flame," she continued. "Into Nashira, into the rift, and I'm not stopping here because your footsteps skew left." Vash grunts. "Let's just not make a habit of it." Kaelen turned again, this time slowly, more deliberately. He did not need to be asked which way to go. The ground itself seemed to incline toward something ahead, barely perceptible, a tilt in the bones of the world. The pull was not growing stronger; it seemed he was becoming more attuned to it. "We keep going," he said. Tovin exhaled sharply. "Toward what?" Kaelen looked at the sky. The clouds were shifting again, spiralling, faintly. If only one knew how to see it. He did not smile, but his voice held a thread of resolve. "Toward whatever remembers me." Beneath his feet, the ash-strewn path gave the barest shudder. Something in the distance acknowledged.

The Compass of Cycles

That night, Kaelen sat apart from the others, his cloak drawn tight against the cold as the wind scraped along the scarred ridgelines. The air was thinner here, as if thought moved more easily than breath, and the stars above pierced the sky like a memory cutting through silence. The fire behind him had quieted; its glow only so far across the ash-blown basin. He could hear Vash sharpening his blade with a slow, steady rhythm and Tovin muttering softly in a half-sleep trance.

Breath clouding in the night air. Elira's silhouette shifted occasionally near the embers. She was not asleep, not with him sitting at the edge of the clearing. His face tilted towards the stars like he was waiting for them to speak to him. Kaelen inhaled deeply and exhaled slowly, as he let the Sigil settle behind his sternum. A sleeping axis, a turning wheel, something within him that had once been separate and now was a big part of him. He let it guide his thoughts, and the lives came first in whispers, then in procession, a thousand selves he did not resist. Some were glorious, gilded lives where kingdoms bent to him. He saw himself leading rebellions and revolutions, pouring forth light from his fingertips, mending ley lines fractured since the sealing wars.

He saw children learning under his name, statues carved from starlight, words spoken in his honour long after his bones would have turned to dust. But glory came at a cost. In one life, the world called him an Architect, but his daughter never spoke to him again. In another, he abolished the pattern entirely, freed its bonds, only to watch reality unmoor itself like a ship with no anchor. Stars burned too quickly, and people unravelled mid-sentence. He moved through those timelines with quiet awe, and then came the cruel ones. Versions of himself that flinched at the wrong time, that allowed the Sigil to consume instead of serve, one tore entire cities from existence, deeming them incompatible. Another crafted a Sigil so perfect, so efficient, it dictated not only magic, but everything.

They bowed to him, and hated him for it, but he endured them all, not as punishment, nor as prophecy, but as truth. In none of them was peace, only recursion. A ceaseless wheel turning inward on itself, repeating not the same choices but the same mistakes in different guises. Each time he thought he had defied the pattern, he was fulfilling another facet of it. Every rebellion already folded into the design, every sacrifice priced in, and yet now, in this moment, beneath this weathered canopy of stars, he sensed something different. Not a way out, a way through a crack in the wheel. Kaelen exhaled again, the air leaving his lungs as if he had been holding it since the rift. He opened his eyes and looked down at his hand. The Sigil mark no longer glowed there, but beneath the skin, something pulsed, slow, intentional, and alive. He stood, stretching slowly, muscles stiff from stillness. The grass hissed beneath his boots as he crossed the clearing.

Echo: The Infinite Cycle

Elira was still sitting by the fire, legs drawn up, hands clasped in front of her mouth. She did not startle when he approached, only glanced up, eyes catching the dim light. "You're back," she said, but it was not a question. Kaelen sat beside her, the warmth of the fire brushing against his shoulder in delicate contrast to the chill still tucked in his bones. "Not sure I ever left," he murmured. She studied him for a long moment, then looked away, gazing into the flame. "You're changing." He did not deny it. He nodded slowly. "I don't think I'm supposed to be only Kaelen anymore." That made her blink. Her jaw shifted slightly. "That's a dangerous thing to say." "Why?" "Because the last man who said something like that burned down a city to prove it."

Kaelen smiled faintly and briefly. "Then I'll try not to burn anything I can't rebuild." Elira's voice softened. "So, what are you?" He could not answer right away. Instead, he looked skyward, to the firmament not filled with prophecy or fate, but with decision. The stars seemed unfamiliar tonight, as if some were missing, and others were in the wrong place. Perhaps it was just him who no longer aligned. Above him, the Sigil was not in the heavens, but now it was beneath them, woven into everything. "I'm something unfinished," he said quietly. "But not lost." Elira turned to him again. There was no mockery in her expression, only a sliver of wonder. "Do you remember when I found you in the Folded Vale?" She asked. "You were bleeding into the roots of an old ley line. Didn't even know your name." "I remember," Kaelen said. "I remember thinking your voice was the first honest thing I'd heard in years." "You weren't Kaelen then," she said.

"No," he agreed. "But I think I was always becoming him." "And now?" He hesitated. "Now I think I'm becoming ready to stop becoming, and start being." She smiled, tired but real. "I missed this version of you." They sat in silence for a time, listening to the wind unravel itself across the charred stone. Finally, Kaelen spoke again. "The Sigil doesn't demand obedience," he said. "It tests, it pulls toward reflection. The point of it isn't to choose the strongest path. It's remembering every path, and continuing forward." Elira tilted her head. "That sounds more like a punishment than philosophy. Maybe that's the price of carrying all the pieces." She shifted, propping her elbows on her knees. "If the Sigil asks you to walk the wrong path again? To break something sacred for the sake of balance, would you do it?"

He looked at her, his expression unreadable. "I'd ask whether the sacred thing I'm breaking is likely to be already broken." Elira studied him, then nodded once. "Well," she said. "At least if the world comes apart again, we'll have good company this time." Kaelen laughed, surprised by the sound of it, and above them, unnoticed, three stars aligned for the first time in two centuries, stitching a new constellation into the forgotten sky. The Sigil's mark glimmered faintly among the remnants of his being. In that profound silence, it was not the pain that caused him to tremble. It was a memory of who he once was, of the choices he had made, of the cycle that had never truly ended. Somewhere ahead, beyond the void, past the veil of time, something waited, and it remembered him, too. The summoning reached its apex. Nathan's voice echoed across the mountains as the final incantation unfurled, the symbol's enormous construct spun above the valley, its rings folding into impossible configurations, pulsing with raw, ancient energy.

His apprentices stood frozen, eyes wide with awe or fear. Stone beneath Nathan's feet fractured, thin lines of blinding white light split the platform like cracks in glass. The air vibrated with a deep, resonant hum as the Orb shifted from symbol to portal. The elder mage whispered from behind him. "You are nearing its centre." As the stone collapsed beneath him, Nathan surrendered to the pull. Then the rift opened, tearing through the air like a wound, the stillness of the chamber shattered from its centre, and the Orb of raw energy surged forward, impossible to contain. As the Orb struck, the world unravelled, the area imploded, collapsing into the insatiable dark. The last thing Nathan glimpsed was the Sigil hovering above the stone, still burning, still alive, before the void enveloped him in a still darkness, yet where magic persisted, swirling through the emptiness.

Chapter 15 – The Last Summit
2112 CE

He had previously been thrown out, but the void held him differently this time. This time, there was a terrible pause, as though the universe was considering whether to release him or not, perhaps sending him home to Silvia. Nathan hovered between heartbeats, then came the pain, a searing wound dragged him from oblivion into something worse, awareness, but where was this? He was somewhere in between what felt like life and death. Death does not merely await a person at the end. It lurks behind the curtains of every moment. This time, it seizes Nathan mid-breath, mid-thought, as the wound is deep, and he finds himself adrift in a realm of white, it was not light, a space between the ticking of seconds on a clock. He stands intact yet ethereal in an endless hall of mirrors, each reflecting a version of himself: agent, martyr, tyrant, pilot... Some scream, some plead, while one watches in silence. That one who steps forward is composed of ash, bearing his features. He watched in awe as it was fascinating to see every version of himself, across multiple dimensions, across multiverses and at different times in their lives.

D. Gohil

The Sigil flares above them all, pulsing but silent. He can step through the mirror and return, but to do so, he must relinquish part of himself. Nathan abandoned his fear as he stepped through the others, bowing their head as he walked towards. The ashen figure whispers. "Welcome back." The ice shattered as the truth did, falling through broken memories. Pain in his ribs radiates everywhere, constricting, suffocating, blood filling his mouth. Iron mixed with raw fire in his lungs, his body pleads for air, as the world above blurs into the moonlight and shadows.

Nathan shifts his stance, breathing deliberately, as he ascends higher into the mountains, and the cold air bites at his lungs. The discomfort felt oddly reassuring, though behind him stretches a panorama of ice and rock, pristine and eternal. This is another quest, and since breaking free from the cycle, Nathan has wandered through endless lives, waking in new bodies, and is now Vantis. Facing reincarnation after reincarnation, finally, he has control, or so he thought. Why did something still feel missing? A gust howls through the pass, shaking the surrounding ice. The sound rattles him. He prays it is not the beginning of an avalanche, as he tightens his grip on the climbing axe and glances back over the winding path. A hand seized him and tugged him along. "Vantis, hang on!" The Sigil seared into his skin like a throb of rebellion

The cycle still had a grip on him, lifting him as a distant voice pleaded. "Vantis, stay with me!" his thoughts splintered, and he was no longer a mage but now a man teetering on the brink of death. Vantis meticulously shifted his stance, his breathing slow and deliberate as he continued to ascend deeper into the mountains. Behind him lay a vast panorama of ice and rock, pristine and eternal. He had been climbing for hours, maybe even days, but that was irrelevant. Since being looped in the cycle, Nathan had been lost in his existence, waking up in another life or facing reincarnation. This cold exploration begins at one of the most beautiful and treacherous mountains in Europe:

Echo: The Infinite Cycle

Mount Matterhorn, Switzerland

A gust of wind howled through the pass, and Nathan found himself shaking the ice formations surrounding him, which made him nervous. He realised his current destination fast and prayed it was not going to be the start of an avalanche, which could risk his life, even end all his lives. He tightened his hold on the climbing axe and looked back at the meandering trail where Élise and Raven were having difficulty keeping up. "Vantis, slow down!" Élise shouted up the mountain, her voice tinged with frustration. Her boots sank deeply into the snow with every step, and her auburn hair flew about in the wind. Vantis (Nathan) let out a sharp breath, disregarding her again. Something urged him to move ahead, and he felt it deeply. An interesting force, like a magnet pulling him toward an unknown truth. "Stubborn bastard," muttered Raven as he trudged alongside Élise.

As a seasoned veteran of the resistance, he had endured the end of the cycle with Vantis, as had Élise, whose sharp intellect had once deciphered the AI's programming before its downfall. They still held onto a sense of normalcy, a trait Vantis envied. Then they heard a deep guttural groan resonating through the valley. Vantis stood still, realising that this was not the wind and that he must warn the others. A thunderous crack shattered the air, the world tilted, the icy ledge beneath him broke apart, and Vantis fell. The mountainside rushed past in a flurry of white and grey, and a sharp pain hit him as his body crashed into the jagged rock below. Followed by a more substantial impact that caused the world to spin chaotically around him. A chilling force enveloped him, piercing through his bones like icy veins.

His breath trembled with fear as he teetered on the brink of consciousness, partially buried in the snow. His ribs screamed with each shallow inhale, and a dull throbbing in his skull made his thoughts feel sluggish and distant. The pain signified he was barely alive or about to die! Above him, voices from the other two rippled through the storm, muffled and far off. "Vantis, answer me!" Shouted Raven. He tried, but the effort to part his lips was monumental; his voice barely carried tens of feet. Consumed by the howling wind, his vision blurred, with shades of white and grey merging into an unclear haze. The world around him was dimming, drawing him toward the void, when suddenly a whisper emerged. *You are not supposed to die here.*

This voice did not belong to Élise or Raven. Instead, it was something else, something ancient, weaving through his consciousness. By now, he knew that it could only be that of the Sigil. Vantis felt his heartbeat sluggishly thumping against his chest, synchronised with a rhythm familiar to him. His fingers twitched, half asleep, weakly curled up in the snow to ease the pain. Under his palm, the ancient symbol emitted a faint glow, its light softened by layers of ice and frost. Though distorted by the haze of his dimming eyesight, he had encountered it before, across lifetimes and different worlds. Carved into a Knight's sword and painted on the hull of a spacecraft buried beneath ruins consumed by time, always waiting. Vantis took a sharp, painful breath, with the cold piercing his lungs like shards of glass. Though his body was failing, the Sigil shimmered with latent memory once more, a faint heartbeat against the snow. The whisper returns, weaving through his mind. *Rise Nathan.* Resonated above the clatter of shifting rock and ice, signalling movement.

Then the familiar voices intensified, cutting through the storm with great urgency. A rope unfurled, winding down toward him as if fate had extended a lifeline. Vantis took a slow, deep breath, thinking, *not today*, as he clenched his teeth in pain. Compelled his fingers to move, and his arms to respond, he had to muster all the strength to survive. Élise's face hovered over the edge of the ravine, her auburn hair blowing wildly in the wind. "We've got him!" She yelled, strained yet fierce. Vantis felt his vision darken at the edges, and the relentless might of Raven's hands pulled him up from the abyss. The warmth lingered under his palm, its pulse diminishing as ice consumed the light once more.

He was not destined to die here. His body twitched as they lifted him over the icy ravine, the rough fibres of the rope pressing into his frostbitten fingers. Every pull of breath sent fresh shockwaves of agony through his ribs, the pain radiating outwards in jagged pulses. Vision swam, and his mind teetered on the razor, a thin line between lucidity and oblivion. He did not know how long he had been down there; it was minutes, though it felt like hours. Time faded into the void, a last tug bringing him to solid ground. Vantis barely stood momentarily, but then fell onto his hands and knees, his muscles trembling with exhaustion and cold. Snow clung to him in irregular patches, ice crusting over his sleeves, and blood stained his mouth. The feeling of solid earth beneath him was satisfying and surreal.

Echo: The Infinite Cycle

    Raven's hands gripped his shoulders firmly to provide support. Élise knelt next to him, her expression a mix of relief and anger. Her vivid green eyes scanned him, evaluating his injuries. "You absolute idiot," she whispered, though the quiver in her voice revealed her worry. Vantis compelled himself to meet her gaze. His lips were dry, and his breathing remained heavy. "Nice to see you too," he replied hoarsely. Nearby, Raven knelt, his battle-hardened face reflecting a mix of exasperation and reluctant amusement. His mechanical prosthetic flexed instinctively, fingers tightening, still expecting another disaster. "Didn't think we'd get you back," he said, scanning the ridgeline. "You looked proper dead." Vantis was not sure how to dispute that, as he really should be dead. He had experienced death or something very similar, so this was nothing new to him.

    The ancient symbol summoned him back, for this he was sure. His fingers twitched as he placed a hand on his chest, sensing the remaining warmth under his skin. The pulse had weakened, although it felt distant. It had drawn him from the void and secured him in the waking world when his body was on the verge of giving in. Élise noticed the motion, her brows furrowing in concern. "Vantis...," she paused, lowering her voice. "What happened down there?" He tried to speak, but the words would not come out. How could he express the whisper, the irresistible pull weaving through his mind like a tether that would not release him? Could he explain to them that the Sigil was more than just a mystical relic? It was a call to action and kept him alive. Instead, he breathed out slowly, the air fogging in the cold. "Something's coming," he stated, his voice rough yet steady.

    Raven snorted, rubbing a hand across his face. "Yeah, no kidding, we have got a damn blizzard on the way and you," he waved dismissively at Vantis's half-frozen figure. "You decided it was a good time to take a casual dive off a mountain for fuck's sake!" Vantis remained unresponsive; his mind had wandered elsewhere again. The symbol had summoned him for a purpose, and now it was guiding him toward an unavoidable path. They managed to get Vantis up to the summit cabin, and thankfully, it was nearby. Soon after, the fire crackled in their modest shelter, casting a light that flickered across the uneven stone walls. Snow had accumulated against the entrance, trapping them inside, yet the cold seeped through invisible cracks, biting at their skin, despite the light burning fire.

Vantis sat hunched, his body encased in heavy blankets, although the warmth barely lingered in his bones. His fingers were still numb from the icy encasement wrapped around a tin cup, filled with steaming broth, the heat permeating his skin. He sipped slowly and deliberately, but the flavour barely registered. His mind drifted to the Sigil in the void that had communicated with him. Across the fire, Élise sat cross-legged, her elbows on her knees, gazing at him with piercing intensity. The wind had tousled her auburn hair, leaving stray strands clinging to her sweat-dampened forehead. She had dedicated the past few hours to tending to him, binding his bruised ribs, checking for frostbite and confirming he had suffered no internal injuries from the fall. "Vantis," her tone remained calm, yet an underlying sharpness was there. "You saw something, didn't you?" The flames crackled, emitting embers that popped and drifted upward like waning stars.

Vantis tightened his grip on the cup. He had indeed seen something, and it was far more than just a vision. It felt as real as the snow he touched, as genuine as the pain in his ribs and as exact as the pulse of the symbol on his skin, but how could he articulate it? He swallowed hard. "The Sigil... It is more powerful than I...," he hesitated, the words weighing heavily on his tongue. "It's a key." Nearby Raven, who was sharpening a combat knife at the entrance, paused mid-motion. The blade glimmered in the firelight as he placed it down, his mechanical fingers lightly tapped the hilt. "A key to what?" Vantis breathed out, his breath visible in the chilly air as he gazed into the flames. Observing their shifting and twisting dance, forming patterns his mind nearly recognised. "A war," he let out a painful cough.

Silence hung between them like an unspoken burden. Élise was the first to speak up. "War with whom?" Vantis locked eyes with her, a newfound determination glimmering in his gaze for the first time since his downfall. "I don't know, I am not sure yet," he confessed, his tone calm. "Whatever it is, it's been observing me for a long time." The wind howled outside, mirroring his tumultuous emotions. Raven let out a long breath and relaxed his shoulders. "Well, that's fucking unsettling." Élise tapped her knee; her sharp mind already knew. "With the cycle broken, you ought to be free, yet this... this is an entirely different scenario." Vantis nodded in agreement. He could still sense that persistent presence, that certainty the Sigil had been

Echo: The Infinite Cycle

more than just a mark or a burden. It was guiding him, preparing him, but for what?

Raven sighed, massaging his temple. "Look, I have encountered plenty of strange things, but this exceeds my expertise," he waved vaguely towards Vantis. "You're alive, so whatever just transpired, it didn't intend for you to die after such a fall. Most mortals would be dead." Vantis felt unsure about the situation. Élise stood up suddenly and began pacing by the fire. "We need more information," she said, looking at Vantis. "You said the Sigil unlocks something?" Vantis paused, trying to find the correct response, then a memory emerged, one echoing through lifetimes. Some fortress was hidden under ice, a room decorated with ancient Sigils, like perhaps a doorway.

His breath sighed nervously. "There's something here on this mountain," he mainly murmured to himself. "Something hidden under this location somewhere close." Élise ceased her pacing. "Hidden?" Vantis raised his gaze, his face serious. "We must uncover it." Raven groaned. "You just survived a fall off a cliff, and now you want to excavate a frozen tomb. Are you trying to die twice in one week, man?" Vantis replied with a tired smirk. "No, my friend," he replied. Rising slowly despite the pain stabbing his ribs. "I'm trying to figure out why I'm still alive." Outside, the wind roared, but Vantis had stopped listening. The Sigil had summoned him for a purpose, and they would start digging tomorrow. He needed rest and a good night's sleep to regain his strength.

Early morning, the strike of the shovel into the frozen earth produced a sharp crack that echoed across the quiet mountainside. Vantis clenched his jaw against the pain coursing through his ribs as he plunged the tool deeper, shattering layers of ice and packed snow. Every movement took effort, as it gave his mind something to cling to. Something other than the weight of what they had uncovered. Élise crouched behind him, working over a makeshift console cobbled together from fragments of scavenged equipment. Her fingers worked steadily over the damaged console. The screen's glow caught the edge of her cheek. Each breath slipped out in a soft cloud, gone almost as soon as it left her lips in the biting cold. Just a few steps away, Raven kept watch, saying nothing. The rifle rested across his shoulder, his cybernetic fingers flexing and curling without thought. His eyes scanned the dark, not missing much. "You're definitely certain about this, Vantis?" Raven inquired, his voice tinged with a slight concern. "You didn't just hit your head too hard on the way down?"

Vantis let out a sharp breath, tightening his grip on the shovel. "I know what I saw." That response was insufficient for Raven, but he chose not to press the issue further. The next day, they had been excavating for hours through layers of frost and centuries-old ice, uncovering something ancient. Vantis sensed its presence; it was beyond mere instinct. It was the Sigil, a quiet weight in his chest, a heartbeat in his mind driving him onward. The wind howled over the ridge, a sharp force attacking their exposed skin while snowflakes danced in erratic patterns, swirling like restless spirits around them. "Got something," Élise exclaimed suddenly. Vantis and Raven turned as she fine-tuned the controls, her expression intense with concentration. "Sensors are detecting a metallic structure approximately five metres beneath us." "Buried technology?" Raven replied with a frown. "It could be remnants from the war," Élise shook her head.

"No, this is older than the war. It may even precede the cycle itself," replied Vantis as he felt the urgency without needing confirmation of his certainty. His breath quickened as he pushed the shovel deeper, the ice fractured under the force, revealing something smooth and dark beneath the frost, neither stone nor metal. His heartbeat throbbed in his ears. "I need a light," he said. Raven took a handheld lamp from his belt and turned it on. The beam pierced the swirling snow, revealing the exposed surface. Deeply carved symbols in the material were hardly worn when the symbol gazed back at them. The same symbol that had seared into his skin, the same Sigil that had pursued him across lifetimes.

Vantis knelt, running his gloved fingers along the grooves. The surface felt unnaturally cold even with his gloves on. Then, it pulsed a deep, resonant vibration that surged through the ice, vibrating the ground beneath them. Raven cursed. "Fuck!" And staggered back, his hand instinctively reaching for his weapon. Élise gasped as her screen flickered erratically, displaying unknown data streaming across it. Vantis stood motionless and said. "You are the key." His sight became hazy, and this image burned into his mind. A colossal chamber hidden beneath the ice, its walls adorned with inscriptions predating humanity. A doorway sealed for ages, poised for him to unlock, as reality came rushing back into view. The storm raged around them, yet the world felt unnervingly quiet. Élise looked at him

Echo: The Infinite Cycle

with wide eyes. "Vantis," she said slowly. "What on earth did you just do?" He swallowed hard and stood up. "We're not digging any longer." His voice remained steady, but his heart raced inside. "We're breaking in now." Raven looked at him as if he had gone crazy. "That's the most foolish idea I've heard all week." Vantis looked down at the Sigil, faintly glowing beneath the ice. "No," he murmured. "This is supposed to be discovered." Tomorrow, they would venture deeper, Vantis decided. They would step into the unknown with no possibility of return. They built a camp there and settled in to rest for the night. The wind tore through the mountains the next morning, wild and ceaseless, threading between the crags like a spirit that could not settle. Snow whipped through the air, blinding and bitter, folding sky and stone into a single blur of white and shadow. Beneath the ice, beneath centuries of undisturbed frost, something had stirred. Vantis stood at the edge of the exposed structure, his heart thudding against his ribs.

Just ahead, the Sigil pulsed faintly beneath a sheet of frost, its gold light flickering in and out, like the slow, steady beat of something vast and waiting. Beside him, Élise knelt over the console, fingers typing in the bitter cold, but with calm precision across its surface, the portable screen rendered shifting code, symbols too old or too strange to read. A few metres off, Raven paced. "We're getting inside today," Vantis stated, his voice low yet resolute. Raven scoffed and replied. "That's not confidence, that's folly," as he gestures toward the structure. "We have no clue what awaits us down there. It could be a tomb, a vault or something that intends to kill us."

Vantis remained silent, his fingers restless as an invisible force pulled him forward. Élise took a sharp breath, stating. "The material is unlike anything I have encountered. It's layered, organic, synthetic, almost as if... as if it's alive." Raven placed his hands on his hips, shaking his head in disbelief. "Alright, if you both want to break into the cursed ice crypt, go right ahead," he pointed at the odd surface. "But how on earth do we open it?" Vantis moved closer, and the Sigil vibrated beneath him, reacting to his proximity. He crouched down, flattening his palm against the surface. The ice felt unnaturally cold, piercing and creeping into his bones, as if it had some consciousness. A whisper coiled through his mind. *You are the key.* Vantis inhaled deeply. The structure reacted with a low vibration that rumbled through the ice. Deep and resonant like the growl of a waking beast.

Snow tumbled down the mountainside as hidden mechanisms creaked beneath it. The Sigil blazed with a bright golden surge of energy that sent a jolt through Vantis's arm. The ice fractured, forming a narrow fissure that splintered outward, followed by another, branching like veins of light through the frozen surface. Suddenly, the ground gave way, plunging them into darkness. As he fell, he hit the ground hard on his side, expelling the air from his lungs, gasping, his vision blurred, and pain throbbed throughout his injured body. To his left, Élise moaned, while Raven swore loudly. "For fucks sake, that hurt." They had fallen into a cavern where the air felt thick with something ancient. Vantis propped himself on his elbows, breathing in sharp and ragged bursts. The surface light was now faint, a distant glow high above, but ahead, deep within the chamber, a different light pulsed. It was golden, reminiscent of the symbol, matching the rhythm of Vantis's heartbeat.

Élise coughed, shaking off the disorientation from the fall. "Tell me, Vantis," she rasped. "That was not supposed to happen." He hardly heard her, but his gaze was fixed on what lay before them. A grand set of doors, towering and richly carved with patterns resembling Sigil symbols, pulsing on its surface, shifting and rearranging as if it were alive. Raven stood up, brushing the ice off his jacket. "Oh, that's not ominous at all." Vantis moved closer, attracted to the door like a moth to a flame. The Sigil on his chest blazed with heat; this was his path toward an impending war, and he pondered its origin.

The cavern absorbed sound, a void filled with ice and time where even breathing felt muted. Vantis stood before the colossal doors, his fingertips gliding over the dynamic Sigils etched into the old surface. Each symbol throbbed in a rhythmic sequence, softly illuminating like the last embers of a nearly forgotten fire. Behind him, Élise worked quickly at her portable console, fingers moving over the keys with practised urgency. A tangle of cables and diagnostic gear sprawled around her, and the screen's pale light caught the sharp focus in her eyes, her expression tight with concentration. Meanwhile, Raven paced like a restless predator, rifle poised and his gaze darting between the entrance above and the shadows. "This thing is active," Élise muttered, tugging her gloves tighter against the biting cold. "It is processing something, and there is some powerful energy building up," she said.

Echo: The Infinite Cycle

She entered a command on her screen. Her brow furrowed as a flow of unfamiliar symbols rushed by. "It detects input, but I can't translate it quickly enough." Vantis sighed, exhaling a mist in the frigid air, his heartbeat synchronised with the Sigil on his chest. "It's not about decoding, it's about answering." Élise shot him a piercing look. "What does that mean?" Vantis was too focused to respond; instead, he leaned forward, pressing his palm firmly against the central symbol. The moment his skin met the surface, the chamber trembled, a low hum rose from the stone, deep and resonant, and the carvings on the doors flared brighter, alive with sudden light. Intricate strands of golden light spread across the surface like fire-consuming oil. Vantis clenched his jaw as a sensation unlike pain coursed through his hand. It felt more profound and more penetrating, sinking into him.

Then the same whisper came back. *You were always meant to return.* Vantis felt a lump in his throat as this voice differed from the previous entity. It was even more ancient, more profound, echoing from the very essence of the world. The doors heaved forward as the earth shook, and hidden mechanisms that had lain dormant for centuries creaked against time that was long lost. Snow poured down from the cave's ceiling. Élise stepped back, protecting her face as the chamber resonated with the low vibrating hum of machines powering up. Raven swore, lifting his weapon. "Vantis, please fucking tell me this doesn't mean we're going to be buried alive." Vantis barely caught his words, and the golden light became brighter, extending outward in glowing tendrils.

The doors creaked open, exposing an abyss situated beyond a dark corridor adorned with symbols that flickered in and out of view. Yet, it was more than just an entrance; it represented a threshold. It was cold, as he had expected, but beneath the chill lay a sense of endurance, as if something had waited. Vantis stepped forward; his legs felt unsteady, and the weight of countless lives pressed down on him all at once. He had traversed battlefields, navigated dying worlds, and confronted terrors, but this was different. Vantis swallowed hard, his hand brushing the edge of the cold stone doorway. This was not simply a ruin or a tomb. He felt it in his bones, the mountain was a threshold, and what waited beyond had been patiently waiting for him. He turned once to Élise and Raven. Their faces mirrored his unease, but neither spoke; the Sigil at his chest pulsed faintly, as though urging him forward.

"Whatever's inside," he said quietly. "It's not going to wait much longer," and with that, he stepped into the dark. Vantis stood at the mouth of the chamber as the final echoes of ancient mechanisms settled into silence behind him. The mountain air felt thinner now, as if the peak itself had exhaled some long-held breath. He looked back once, not at Élise or Raven, but at the threshold they had crossed. Whatever this place had been, it had opened with invitation. The Sigil had not flared in warning; it had recognised him. He drew his coat tighter and stepped into the light of the breaking sky. A rare shaft of sunlight spilt across the snow, and for a moment, the world held its breath. Élise followed, silent but alert; her face was pale but calm.

Raven came next, dragging his rifle through the snow with a grunt. "Right," he muttered. "Now, can we get off this bloody mountain?" Vantis did not answer; his mind was elsewhere, locked on the doors they had left behind. He still felt the warmth of the Sigil beneath his skin, as though something had marked him again, not just as a survivor, but as a witness. "We've found nothing," Élise said quietly beside him. "No map, weapons or answers." "We found the truth," Vantis replied. "That's enough for now." She looked at him, brow creased. "What truth?" "That this wasn't the end of anything," he said. "It was the beginning of a greater truth." Below them, the wind picked up, teasing loose snow into spirals that danced for a breath and then vanished. Vantis lingered; he thought of the whisper in the dark, the door that responded to touch rather than force, the sense of something waiting, not asleep, but expectant. They had not been the first to find this place, but he was the first to answer. He turned at last, boots crunching against the ice, and followed his companions down the slope.

The Sigil no longer pulsed with urgency. It was steady now, as if for the moment it was done calling. Nathan stared at the mountain's summit one last time, breath frosting in the still air. He had uncovered its secret, yet it felt as though the mountain had judged him, sent him forward with questions still unanswered. The sky twisted unnaturally, snow curling in silent spirals. Nathan felt the Sigil's pull grow stronger, dragging at every cell in his body. He wanted to fight it, to cling to the mountain and the friends behind him, but the world around him was already dissolving. The cold vanished, and the air became weightless and light. Nathan shut his eyes, knowing the next step would take him into the heart of everything he feared.

Echo: The Infinite Cycle

D. Gohil

Chapter 16 – The Architect of Infinity
9500 BCE

Nathan was thrust back into life, disoriented and displaced. The ground was solid, but nothing about this place felt real. Brass and glass towers twisted like codes coming back to life, rooted not in stone but in glimmering constellations beneath his feet. The Sigil had brought him here deliberately, into the Architect's world. He took a step, then another, trying to steady himself, eyes flicking upwards. Where the towers rose like nothing built by human hands. Slender spirals of brass and glass, twisting into the sky. They did not stand on stone or steel. Their bases drifted, tethered to shapes that glowed faintly overhead, equations, symbols, things that moved like stars, yet were drawn with intent. The air around him was still, but it pulsed as though the place itself was artificially thinking. Even his breathing felt off, each inhale crisp, cold, and oddly precise, as if the very act had been measured. This was something far more exacting, something imagined and then made real, and at its heart, the Architect waited.

The sky curved with developed meaning, and patterns swept across it. Bright and ordered, their paths written in logic too profound to follow. Then the lead Architect appeared, neither one being nor many, but something in between. It wore many faces, and yet Nathan could have sworn it looked familiar. It did not speak, it did not need to, and its presence settled like a truth that could not be argued. The Architect spoke in terms far beyond metaphor. The Sigil, it revealed, was not simply a symbol here; it was a corrective instrument, a loop fed back into existence. Exploring every possibility the multiverse could spawn. Nathan was no accident, as every different version of him across the cycle had been a node, a necessary variable, but this time the equation was different. There was an air of artificial intelligence at play here.

The Architect extended its offer, and a new reality had shaped beyond the reach of time, pain, or memory. There was only one price: he would need to surrender all emotion, identity and the remnants of the people he still loved. Nathan saw the trap for what it was, as this was not a collaboration. The Architect's composure faltered, and a ripple passed through the space; logic trembled. Towers fractured along lines of unspoken code, lightly folded in on itself, and reality began to tear at the seams. Nathan ran through corridors that unravelled behind him, the Sigil in his grip pulsing like a wound. He threw himself into a fissure, not knowing where it would lead, only that the Architect would return, and so would he.

Göbekli Tepe, Anatolia (Now modern-day Turkey)

Awakening in the Void

A site older than Stonehenge and the Pyramids. The Architect was shaping human destiny before their history even began. Stone thrummed with circuits. The architecture here was sentient, older than memory, older than time. Nathan's first awareness was absence, an endless void that swallowed light, thought, and breath. He floated in it, weightless, unmoored. He tried to draw breath but felt no air in his lungs. His feet twitched, though there was no ground beneath him. Panic gathered like a storm, then the void stirred. They were not creatures; they were possibilities, and one moved forward towards him. Nathan had a strange feeling, something he couldn't imagine.

Echo: The Infinite Cycle

A voice like pressure inside his skull. *Alaric.* The name struck him like a blow to the chest. The lack of sensation clawed at him. Was he still alive, or was it a dream? Where had the Architects thrown him? The shapes solidified now, faces shifting from ageless smoothness to empty silhouettes. Their outlines pulsed like oil over water, with every breath, the void bent. These things did not belong to the universe as he knew it, or they were from outside of it. One drew closer, its form distorting like a heat haze. Nathan, no, now, Alaric could not look away. He sensed that touching it might erase him. It spoke again, voice splintered and ancient. *You have walked the cycle.* Alaric's breath slowed. "What cycle?" He asked, but his voice sounded thin, far-off, and stretched like worn paper. They did not answer at once. Their presence thickened, pressing into him. *The one you do not yet understand.* His jaw tensed. "Then make me understand, I am ready."

The void itself seemed to respond, humming with something more profound than sound. The tallest figure tilted its head as if scanning him. Alaric felt it behind his eyes, digging, judging. Then the words came. *You are an error in the programming.* His chest tightened. "Error? What the hell does that mean?" He snapped up, more to keep himself steady than out of defiance, but he already knew the answer, and it terrified him. The void trembled, and the figures flickered as if answering his question required a recalibration of reality. *Your lives were not fated, not destiny, not given a chance. You are an anomaly, Alaric, a fracture in the pattern, and now the cycle has broken.*

Alaric began to think; his mind reeling from the fracture, he realised the cycle was unnatural. He already knew the answer; throughout his entire life, he had felt the unnatural shifts, the eerie precision of events. The way death always came too soon or too perfectly aligned. He had always wondered why, and now the answer stood before him. The void pulsed again, and the tallest figure's form stabilised as if it had concluded. *Alaric, the time has come for the truth.* The void shattered, and the world around him changed. Shadows bled into colour, forming landscapes he recognised yet had never walked. A whisper threaded through the air, promising revelation but carrying the weight of dread.

Revelation of the Cycle

The fracture had not ended. It had only unveiled the design, and Alaric now stood at its centre. His world lurched as the endless void fractured around him, and a force yanked him forward as if his essence were being dragged through the fabric of existence. His stomach twisted, his limbs felt stretched to their limits, and for a split second, he feared breaking apart entirely. Then, just as suddenly as it began, the sensation ceased, and he landed hard. The impact reverberated through his bones, yet the ground beneath remained steady, cold, uninviting stone. He gasped, lungs straining for air that was sterile and thin, as if filtered and scrubbed of any life. A steady mechanical hum filled the space around him, almost like breathing. Alaric forced himself upright, his vision swimming until he finally saw it, the chamber extended before him, vast and strange.

Nothing in his past experiences had prepared him for this. The structure shimmered neither quite metal nor stone, with flawless, seamless surfaces that seemed to have grown into shape rather than been constructed. Luminescent energy veins pulsed within the walls, glowing a soft electric blue. The ceiling was too high to see, fading into a shifting mist of data and light. Directly in front of him, suspended in mid-air, hovered a holographic display of a massive wall of shimmering data, shifting and rearranging in complex patterns. His breath stalled, trembling in the glow in awe. A thousand questions bloomed in his mind, but none found his voice. The phrase did not merely suggest a scientific experiment. It recognised him, as though the protocol had anticipated his arrival. Behind the interface, a schematic pulsed. Twin spirals rotating inward, folding over coordinates marked *Origin, Return,* and more disturbingly, *Override.* Alaric reached out instinctively.

The screen responded. A mirrored silhouette appeared, his shape fractured, with eyes rimmed in pale fire. It spoke in silence, mouth unmoving, but its meaning roared in his bones. *You have died before and returned in your designed cycle.* Fingers twitched, itching to touch the display to confirm what he had seen, but he already knew. Pulse hammered as he had suspected for years. Even though something was unnatural about his existence, the memories that should have faded never did, and the lives that should have ended kept restarting. Alaric had thought it was fate. A curse or a divine punishment, but it was not.

Echo: The Infinite Cycle

It was a program, an experiment, and he was the test subject. A sharp chime rang out, and the data on the display shifted, isolating a single file. Alaric watched as it expanded lines of information scrolling downwards with precise machine-like efficiency, and then he saw the number:

SUBJECT ID: 001 - "ALARIC"
Status: Active
Cycle Count: 147
Aim: Unknown

His breath hitched as he took a hesitant step back, fists clenched. Feeling his entire life flash before him, every fight to survive, love, war, and horrific death, not fate, but memories flashing rapidly. This was intentional. A slow, burning rage simmered inside, like molten metal in his chest. Someone had done this to him. Clearly, someone was watching. His mind raced with questions: Who, why, and what is the end goal? A soft hiss echoed in the chamber before him, and the three figures emerged from dimensional fractures. Their bodies glowed with unstable energy. They did not walk forward but phased, flickering between spaces, distorting reality with each movement. Alaric's jaw tightened as they loomed before him, their presence warping the air. He could feel it pulling at the edges of his consciousness as if reality were bending to accommodate their existence.

Then the tallest one spoke, and its voice was not natural, layered, distorted as though it came from multiple timelines simultaneously. "You were not supposed to wake up." Alaric's fists clenched. "Yeah?" He growled, rage rising like a storm. "Well, I was not supposed to die over a hundred times, either!" The second architect tilted its head, its body glitching between countless forms. "You misunderstand, * * * *" Its voice carried an unbearable finality, an answer before he even asked. "You should not live at all." A chill slithered down Alaric's spine, an instinctive, primal reaction to something. The air itself seemed to fracture, each breath slicing through him as if reality rejected his presence. In that moment, Alaric realised the Architects were not merely judges of his fate, but executioners of existence itself.

* * *

His mind raced through the implications. What did that mean? Was he a mistake, a glitch in their system? Or worse, was he something they had failed to erase? His breathing grew sharper, and now his entire body tensed like a coiled spring. His thoughts spun through possibilities and theories, forming in rapid succession.

- The AI theory, where the Architects are an ancient artificial intelligence simulation conducting a grand experiment? Had he been a test subject in their efforts to push the limits of human consciousness?
- The higher dimension theory. An elite society, quietly pulling the strings, using reincarnation not as a mystery to solve, but as a mechanism. A means to serve some greater, hidden purpose. Had they been selecting, enhancing, and refining human souls for generations?
- The supernatural theory. Were they gods or something worse? Did they perceive themselves as divine entities reshaping existence through suffering and rebirth?

* * *

Alaric clenched his teeth, nails digging into his palms, gripping too tightly. "You think you own me?" He challenged defiantly. The first Architect moved slowly, deliberately, causing the surrounding space to ripple like a warp in spacetime. "You were never meant to echo." The name, the label they had given him. "A deviation, now you will be erased, Alaric." He felt panic and wondered for a lifetime why this was happening, but now he realised he was not meant to exist, and had somehow survived, but he would not stop now. "Wait, I remember you, you were the old man in the alley in Hong Kong!" Feeling stunned. "You remember well, Nathan," replied the Architect, as the others nodded. He used his original name on purpose. The chamber trembled as the walls glowed, energy surging through the floor in response to the architects. The air thickened, and reality prepared to consume him entirely. Alaric's mind whirled in shock. He needed an escape, and quickly, just then, an explosion of light tore through the chamber, causing the architects to reel back, their forms flickering wildly. Alaric barely had time to react before a familiar voice shouted from the entrance. "Move, Alaric!" He turned

Echo: The Infinite Cycle

sharply, and two figures stood at the threshold. They were not like the architects; they were like him.

Alaric's heart throbbed against his ribs as the three sprinted down the shifting corridor, their shadows stretching unnaturally in the flickering artificial light. The air felt wrong, thick and charged with something that did not belong in the realm of the living. With every step, the architecture of the space twisted as if it were aware of their movements. Reforming and reshaping to trap them in an ever-shifting maze. "Keep moving!" Kaeda-9, with her cybernetic arm, ordered. Alaric's breath burned in his throat, but he did not slow. He recognised the ancient symbol and knew it was the key to escape, but doubt troubled his mind. Again, the Architect's lost words echoed in his thoughts. *You do not know what is coming.* The corridor ahead extended endlessly before twisting sharply, the gravity inside seeming to resist its path. A faint, translucent layer that resembled liquid metal shimmered in the air, distorting reflections.

Thorne, his dark features lined with urgency, skidded to a halt. "Damn it, another shift," he turned to Alaric. "You have been through this hell before. What is the play now?" Alaric clenched his jaw. The memories of countless lives flickered through him, but none held the answer to this, as this was different, and this was more than the cycle. The Sigil burned against his chest, sending a pulse through his veins. "This isn't real," he murmured, stepping towards the shifting wall. Kaeda-9 exhaled sharply. "What do you mean, not real? Because it looks damn solid to me." Alaric raised a hand, his fingers hovering just inches from the warped surface, and as if responding to his presence, it rippled outward. "Perception," he replied. The truth struck him like lightning.

This place, this corridor, was not a prison of metal and circuitry but a prison of artificial intelligence. "Close your eyes," he instructed, his voice steady despite his uncertainty. Thorne scoffed. "Are you out of your mind? OK, I'll do it," he said with apparent reluctance. The others comply, and Alaric follows. He takes a slow breath, reaching out with something more profound than his hands, something ancient and buried within the echoes of his many lives. Suddenly, Alaric's eyes snap open; he is no longer in the corridor, there is no floor, only drifting fragments, shattered bridges and broken stone flickering in and out of existence. They hang there like remnants of other lives, pieces of places he once knew, once walked, once fell, once died, frozen echoes suspended in nothing.

His breath raced. "This is a crossroads," Kaeda-9 finished, eyes wide. "A space between realities," Thorne exhaled, rubbing a hand down his face. "Fantastic, just what we needed, was another existential crisis." Alaric felt tethered here, his heart pounding. The ancient Sigil on his chest flared, guiding his gaze to a distant platform where something shimmered, possibly their way out. "We have to move," he said, but deep down, he knew there was more to come. Alaric took the first step onto the fragmented path, the ground beneath him shifting like liquid glass. The floating structures surrounding them pulsed faintly, remnants of past lives, past worlds, some familiar, others entirely alien. Gravity was unreliable here, as bridges curled into spiral staircases that led to nowhere, and entire platforms disintegrated, only to reform moments later.

"This place is a fucking nightmare," Thorne muttered, eyeing a bridge that flickered between states of existence. "I don't like going to places that can disappear under my feet!" Kaeda-9 tightened her grip on her plasma rifle, cybernetic fingers flexing. "Then I suggest you don't stop moving." Alaric was too focused, his gaze locked at the entrance in the distance, where a massive archway of shifting symbols suspended in the void. The Sigil on his chest pulsed in sync with it, and he instinctively knew this was their exit, but something was amiss. The closer they got, the heavier the air became, and the harder it was to breathe. A low hum filled the silence, resonating in Alaric's skull. "We're being watched," he said, his voice barely above a whisper.

Kaeda-9's eyes flicked around the broken horizon. "By what?" Alaric hesitated, then saw it far in the distance. Over the horizon, something stirred. It was a figure too prominent, too still, yet somehow shifting, watching. He could feel its gaze drilling into him, peeling back the layers of his existence as if searching for something. Then it spoke, "You are out of place, Alaric." The voice fractured, just like the architects, but this was different, somehow older and stronger. The surrounding air grew colder, and Alaric's skin prickled as the space ahead darkened. The floating platforms began to crack and distort as if rejecting their presence. Thorne stepped back. "I'm guessing that's not one of your architect buddies." Alaric clenched his jaw. "No, this is something else." Kaeda-9 tightened her grip on her rifle. "What the hell does it want?" Alaric swallowed hard, as he knew the answer. "To correct the mistake."

Echo: The Infinite Cycle

The entity did not move towards them; it did not need to. The void responded to its will, the floating structures trembling, their edges dissolving into nothingness. The bridge before them crumbled piece by piece, receding further away with each passing second. Alaric felt the weight of countless lives pressing upon his mind. He had been here before, not physically but in fragments. A vision, a warning buried deep within the echoes of his past deaths, the symbol on his chest flared hot. A choice had to be made: either run or face the unknown.

The Fractured Path

Alaric's heart pounded as the void warped around them. The entity over the path remained motionless, its presence seeped into every fibre of existence. Pressing against his skin like an invisible weight. The bridge ahead continued to collapse, the fragmented platforms shuddering as if they were rejecting reality. "We need to move!" Urgently, Kaeda-9 shouts. Alaric's grip on the Timeblade tightened, and his instincts screamed at him to run. To reach the Sigil before it's lost; however, another part of him hesitated. The entity's words echoed in his mind. *To correct the mistake.* What mistake? Had his survival disrupted something greater? Had his defiance of the cycle drawn the attention of something even more potent than the architects? Thorne, beside him, cursed, pulling a small metallic sphere from his belt. "If we're running, we need to find a distraction." He pressed something on its surface, and the device whirred to life, pulsing with a deep blue glow. "Cover your eyes!"

Alaric barely had time to react before the device detonated in a silent burst of light, the space around them twisting as a gravitational shockwave rippled outward. For a moment, everything, even the entity, blurred. "Move!" Kaeda-9 shouted. They sprinted across the precarious platforms, each step threatened to send them tumbling into the abyss below. Alaric's breath came in ragged gasps as he pressed on, concentrating on the distant archway. His Sigil pulsed with increasing intensity. The closer he approached, the more the air vibrated around him, and reality snapped. The light from the explosion faded, and the entity shifted. One moment, it was still, and the next, it was nearer. Its form flickered impossibly large yet disturbingly indistinct.

Alaric felt his stomach lurch, and his mind could not fully comprehend what he saw. *You do not understand what you are running toward.* The voice resonated through his bones. Alaric stumbled, nearly falling to his knees as a sharp pain lanced through his skull, images flashing before his eyes, a world ablaze, an endless war. The ancient symbol broke. Alaric gasped, the vision vanishing as quickly as it had come; his pulse hammered. What had he just seen? Kaeda-9 grabbed his arm. "Alaric, keep moving, don't ease up!" With great effort, he pushed himself forward. The Sigil loomed ahead now, barely stable, its glowing symbols flickering erratically. Whatever forces were attempting to stop them were winning. Thorne leapt first, his form vanishing into the swirling light. Kaeda-9 hesitated for only a second before following. Alaric turned back to look one last time.

The entity did not pursue him; it merely watched. *This path will lead to ruin, Alaric.* It reverberated. He clenched his teeth; he had spent lifetimes searching for the truth and would not stop now. He stepped into the entrance, and the universe shattered around him. As they get sucked through the void, light envelops them with a brightness. There is something that deeply permeates their essence. It felt like he unravelled and reassembled, and every cell in his body stretched across time and space. Then he landed hard, rolling across the cold metallic floor. His limbs ached, his head spun, and for several agonising seconds, he could not discern whether he was dead or alive. The sensation of falling still clung to him, a lingering phantom of the transit through the Sigil.

A sharp voice cut through the haze. "He is through. Alaric, get up!" He groaned, pushing himself onto his elbows. Kaeda-9 stood over him, her cybernetic arm glowing faintly from residual energy. Behind her, Thorne was at a console, fingers flying across the controls as alarms blared around them. They were not in the void, but inside a sleek, dark facility that was adorned with pulsating blue circuitry that flowed like veins across its surface. The air felt clean, but beneath lurked something more, like a hum of power vast and contained. Alaric's stomach twisted as this place felt familiar. Kaeda-9 grabbed his arm, hauling him to his feet. "We do not have time. That thing you saw, it's not done with us yet?" Alaric forced himself to focus, shaking off the disorientation. "Where are we?" Thorne at the console spoke without looking up. "The Core," his voice was tense. "Or at least one of them."

Echo: The Infinite Cycle

Alaric frowned. "Core?" Kaeda-9 exhaled sharply as if she did not have time for lengthy explanations. "This was where it all started, the reincarnation cycles, the architects. Everything just jumped into the heart of it." Alaric felt the weight of those words settle over him. This was a random escape point. They had landed in the very place that controlled the cycle. His gaze drifted to a massive circular structure in the centre of the room, which pulsed with dim rhythmic energy, ancient and alive. The symbol was etched into the surrounding floor, but this one was different. These were fractured and incomplete as if something had damaged them. He stepped closer, and a whisper brushed against his mind. *147 lives, 147 attempts, why do you resist?* Nathan stiffened as he realised this was not the voice of the Architect.

Kaeda-9's hand clamped onto his shoulder. "Don't!" He turned to her, confusion flashing. She shook her head. "That thing, it is not what it seems. This whole place is built on layers of deception." Alaric looked back at the symbol, unease crawling up his spine. "Then why are we here?" Thorne at the console swore under his breath. "Because the only way to end this is to shut it down." Alaric's blood ran cold. The Core, the place that controlled reincarnation, dictated every death and rebirth, and now they intended to destroy it. Kaeda-9's voice was as hard as steel.

"We're ending the cycle," Alaric exhaled, his heart pounding. He had fought for so long for answers and understanding. He now faced a choice far greater than himself. To destroy the Core and possibly erase everything he had ever been or to leave it intact and remain a prisoner to forces beyond his control. Before he could answer, the facility shuddered, the alarms intensified, the circuitry along the walls flickered violently, and the air distorted from the chamber's far end. Alaric's breath hitched as the void tore open. They were no longer alone. The Architects had followed.

The Final Confrontation

The air tore apart, and reality twisted as three figures emerged from the distortion, their bodies shifting between states of existence. Their forms flickered half-real, half something else entirely. Bending the light and warping the surrounding space. The tallest Architect stepped forward, and the chamber bowed beneath its presence. Like a pressure, not of gravity, but of meaning.

Alaric had never seen them in this form, not in the void, not in memory. Here, they were real and wrong; its voice scraped the air like shattered glass. "You were not meant to arrive." Alaric's grip tightened around the Timeblade as it pulsed faintly, like a heartbeat trying to remember its rhythm. Kaeda-9 raised her rifle, her cybernetic arm twitching with anticipation. At the console, Thorne swore under his breath, fingers dancing across the interface, trying to outrun inevitability. Alaric's voice was bitter. "You keep saying that and yet here I am!" The second Architect spoke next, its form flickering between past and present. "You misunderstand your place in this anomaly. The cycle was never about you." Alaric's heart pounded. "Then what was it about?" The third Architect, smaller but no less imposing, stepped forward. "Correction. It is about what comes next." Alaric hesitated; the surrounding air vibrated with something vast waiting just over the threshold of any understanding. It was like standing on the edge of an abyss. Knowing something lurked below, but unable to see its proper form. Kaeda-9, beside him, was not waiting for answers; she opened fire.

Plasma bolts tore through the air, streaking towards the Architects with burning precision, and then the Architects moved. Alaric barely registered their motion for one moment. They stood still, and then they were everywhere. The plasma rounds passed through their forms, scattering into bursts of energy that rippled through the chamber. The air distorted after their movement as if reality struggled to process their existence. Alaric lunged, his Timeblade humming as he slashed at the nearest Architect, but the moment it connected, the entity's form fractured into shifting fragments of time. Hundreds of versions of themselves appeared, flickering in and out of sync. Alaric stumbled back, his chest rising and falling in a sharp, uneven breath. They were fast; they were not even bound to time in the way he was. The tallest Architect raised a hand, and the room buckled, while the Core pulsed violently. Its energy surging as if it were responding to them. Alaric's mind raced. They were not just stopping him from shutting down the Core. The realisation struck like lightning. They were not protecting the cycle; they were safeguarding something within it. His voice was hoarse with exhaustion. "What are you hiding?" The second Architect turned towards him, its head tilting at an unnatural angle. "Not meant to ask that question." Alaric's stomach twisted whenever he thought he had reached the truth, only to find another layer beneath it.

Echo: The Infinite Cycle

Kaeda-9, beside him, reloaded her rifle and growled in frustration. "They're stalling!" Alaric's mind whirled. They were not trying to kill him outright. They were waiting for something. Then he saw the symbol on the floor surrounding the Core shifting, completing itself, and that's when Alaric understood. The cycle was about reincarnation; it was a lock designed to keep something out or, worse, to keep something in. His blood ran cold. The Core, which powered the reincarnation system, held something critical. If they shut it down, Alaric turned sharply towards Thorne at the console. "STOP!" But it was too late. The final sequence entered, the ancient Sigil flared to life, glowing with an intensity that scorched the very edges of reality. The Architects stepped back, and then the universe shattered. A rift tore open in the centre of the room, a black void of infinite depth pulling everything towards it. Alaric's voice was lost in the roaring winds.

The Architects had never been his enemy; they had been guards, and now the prison was open. The air drew in sharply, as if the room itself had taken a breath. The Sigil etched into the floor pulsed in time with the rift, slow, deliberate, and heavy, each beat thrumming through Alaric's bones. Light and shadow clashed across the chamber, spiralling in tangled patterns as if reality were trying, and failing, to hold itself together. Alaric stumbled backwards; his breathing was uneven, his thoughts skidding, unanchored. Truth had come too late; he had broken the cycle, but unleashed something worse. The Core had been a prison, a system of control, and now the lock had broken. Architects stood motionless, their forms no longer shifting as if their purpose had then concluded.

The tallest among them turned toward Alaric. "It is done." Alaric gritted his teeth. "What did we just release?" The second architect's voice echoed distant and hollow. "That knowledge is no longer yours to claim." The ancient Sigil beneath him flared, expanding outward and engulfing the chamber in golden light. Nathan's limbs went weightless, his body lifting off the floor as if drawn by an unseen force. His heartbeat matched the symbol's rhythm, pounding in his ears like a drum of finality. Kaeda-9 reached for him. "Alaric!" Her voice vanished, and everything faded away for a single, endless moment. Nathan existed in nothingness, no sound, no air, only the pulse of the Sigil and then a pull. A surge of energy tore through his soul, dragging him across the fabric of all existence.

The golden light of the Orb yielded to darkness, not the cold, empty void of space, but something more profound, a realm where whispers dwelled. Where the past was not forgotten, where the dead still spoke. Golden light from the Sigil collapsed into black. Nathan fell, weightless, through a silence too deep to measure. When he struck the stone floor, the breath tore from his lungs. The air here was cold and stale, and the walls felt close, the air thick with dust and memory. Shadows moved where he had not, slipping across the stone as though answering to something else entirely. Nathan swallowed hard. The ancient symbol had delivered him here to the realm of the forgotten, to the Code of the Dead, and something was waiting for him. Their voices did not sound. They were like code and written line by line.

Chapter 17 – Code of the Dead
1279 BCE

The cold seeped into Nathan's bones before he could focus his eyes. Torchlight flickered against walls carved with symbols older than cavemen. A voice, low and resonant, rippled through the catacomb, *Welcome back... Taron.* Nathan flinched at the name. It was not his own, yet it felt like a truth he had to own. He was in the Code of the Dead, and he was not alone. This was not the void, nor the Architect's artificial platform; this was centuries old. A domain of the forgotten, where the air seemed heavy with unfinished stories. Faint torchlight caught on carvings of long-dead languages, their warnings unreadable yet deeply unsettling. The Sigil had delivered him again, but this time into death's domain. New Avalon rose above the ruins of every failed utopia, a gleaming city of memory, where the dead lived on as digital echoes, curated within the memory crypts. Nathan wandered these streets under a name he barely recognised, the pulse of the symbol quiet for the first time. In the Vault of the Forgotten, he found her. Élise, a young lady he had saved in one timeline but lost in countless others.

Encased in crystal, her preserved essence glared at him. "You let me die a thousand times," she accused. "And yet you still come." The city's secret revealed, the archive fed on failed timelines, dead Nathans, lost possibilities. Every life faltered and was harvested to sustain this place. The Sigil pulsed again, offering him impossible power to rewrite it all. Resurrect them all, but at the cost of erasing the decisions that had made him who he was. He shut it down, the crypt crumbled, the dead were not resurrected, but liberated. As they vanished into oblivion, a collective whisper of gratitude lingered. The symbol fell dark for the first time since this all began, and Nathan felt entirely alone. This is how this dark chapter begins and how the story unfolds......

The Fall into Shadows

The tomb split open, and data poured from the fracture. Nathan's back slammed into damp earth, and the cold gnawed at him as his breath misted in the stale air. Around him, endless gravestones pierced the soil like broken teeth, their inscriptions long erased. Shadows danced under the flickering torchlight; this was Grave's End. Nathan pushed himself upright, his hand instinctively brushing the hilt of the Timeblade still at his side. The weight of silence pressed down like a wet cloth, but something was already stirring beneath the ground. The sky overhead was an expanse of darkness, devoid of moon or stars to pierce its oppressive hold. A flickering torch mounted on a rusted iron sconce cast uneasy shadows that danced across the weathered tombstones.

His breath formed a mist in the chilly air, and his heart raced as he surveyed his surroundings. Rows of graves stretched out in every direction, uneven, their names worn away by time. Nearby, a mausoleum stood with its door slightly open. Revealing only a void of darkness inside. Then came the voice, deep, rough and now too familiar. "You're late, Taron." Nathan snapped his head towards the figure standing over him. A tall man with broad shoulders wrapped in a long, tattered coat that barely shields him from the chill. The dim light partially obscured his face, and his sharp eyes glowed faintly beneath the brim of his weathered hat. Nathan breathed quickly with a tinge of fear, his mind catching up with his body.

Echo: The Infinite Cycle

He was not in that fluctuating eternity within that timeless shifting void where the Architects had kept him. He was somewhere else, and from the weight of the silence pressing down on him, somewhere dangerous. "Where am I?" Nathan rasped, pushing himself up on unsteady legs. His muscles ached, and his nerves were still reeling from the transition. The man exhaled a puff of vapour from his lips. "Grave's End, the last place you want to be!" His voice was a matter-of-fact with a sharp edge, warning. "And yet here you are." Taron's fingers instinctively curled around his Timeblade, still clipped to his belt. His heart drummed against his ribs as he scanned the graveyard again, something gnawing at the edge of his awareness. Something was amiss; the air felt too still, as if the ground held its breath, and he then noticed that some graves were open and not excavated. No, they had been forced open from below, and something had crawled out.

His mouth went dry, and the man in the coat seemed to read his mind, nodding his head towards the mausoleum's gaping entrance. "My advice is you should start running." Then, from the dark, came a whisper, low, slithering and hungry. Taron did not hesitate and ran as fast as he could. The mausoleum's stone steps wound down into the earth. Slick with moisture and uneven beneath his feet, the flickering torchlight barely penetrated the darkness. Casting elongated shadows that quivered with each movement. The air grew colder with every step, and the walls narrowed, pressing in as if the tomb were alive, exhaling its age-old secrets into the stale air.

Taron kept his Timeblade primed, its faint glow casting eerie reflections on the damp stone beneath him. He was not alone; the man in the coat, who had yet to give his name, moved with practised ease. His boots were silent against the steps, his fingers brushing the hilt of the long, curved knife strapped to his hip. "Start talking," Taron murmurs, glancing around at the dark alcoves that line the passage. Where coffins rested in shadowy recesses, and the air was heavy with the scent of aged wood and decay. "Who the hell are you?" The man laughed softly. "That's a perilous question." Taron shot him a stern look. "Fine," the man sighs. "You can call me Corvan. It's not my real name, but it will suffice." "And where exactly are we?" Corvan took a deep breath, seeming to weigh his words carefully. "A place that defies existence," he replied, his voice lowering. "A doorway, a prison, a graveyard for things that would not remain buried."

A shiver ran down his spine, and something stirred. A whisper skated across the walls, thin and dry like parchment crumbling in a silent breeze. Taron and Corvan froze at the sound of movement from one coffin, and a skeletal hand erupted from the dark. The world had erupted into motion, and Taron's instincts overtook them as he slashed his Timeblade towards the reaching hand. The Timeblade sliced through the ancient bone with a sizzle, severing fingers that turned to dust before they even touched the ground. The coffin creaked with further movements and more whispers. Corvan was already in motion, his knife flashing in the dim light. "Move, Taron!" He yelled. "We have to get away from here."

The mausoleum trembled, dust raining from the ceiling as the crypts stirred to life from the shadows and figures rose. Not the slow shambling dead of horror stories. These creatures or whatever they were, were wrong, part flesh, part echo, as if reality struggled to hold them in form. Their bodies flickered between decay and solidity, their eyes empty, voids that burned with unnatural light. Taron and Corvan ran through the tunnel, which twisted and curved, narrowing until the walls pressed so closely that Taron felt the cold stone scrape against his shoulders. Behind them, the whispers grew into overlapping voices, pleading, accusing, laughing, then silence.

Vault of Echoes

Taron's boots skidded on the stone floor as he ground to a halt. Before him stood a door, unlike the rest of the tomb. Which was sleek, modern and metallic; it simply did not belong there. Taron's breath quickened. "What the hell was that?" Corvan pressed his palm over the scanner beside the door, and a red light flickered and then turned green. The door slid open, revealing an extraordinary sight. It was a high-tech laboratory illuminated by sterile white lights. Taron stepped inside his mind, reeling computers along the walls. Cables snaked across the floor, and machinery hummed quietly. It was a hidden bunker buried deep beneath a graveyard of the forgotten. Corvan followed, pulling the door shut behind him. Taron's tone became sharp as he commanded. "Start explaining now, Corvan or whoever the fuck you are!"

Echo: The Infinite Cycle

He maintained an unreadable expression. "This is a crypt, Taron, it's a vault, and if we don't act quickly..." he pointed toward a large reinforced chamber at the lab's far end. "...we're going to discover why the dead aren't staying dead." Taron exhaled slowly, forcing himself to steady his breath. The air inside the hidden laboratory was crisp and unnaturally clean compared to the decay outside, making his skin prickle. Corvan moved ahead, Taron followed, his eyes scanning the high-tech environment. Stacked metal crates rested in one corner, each marked with a symbol and insignia. Taron recognised this from his research; it was NexTech. His stomach twisted; the same corporation was experimenting on him, the same people who had designed the reincarnation protocol. "Of course," he muttered, and Corvan glanced over his shoulder. "Something on your mind?"

Taron gestured at the crates. "You knew this was here, didn't you? This is not just a vault, it's a goddamn research facility." Corvan sighed, rubbing the bridge of his nose. "I was hoping you'd figure that out a little later." Taron tightened his fists. "Explain now," he demanded. Corvan's arms crossed, leaning against a terminal. "The people who constructed this facility were tampering with forces beyond their comprehension. Researching reincarnation memory transfer challenges, the boundaries of life and death, ring a bell?" He fixed his gaze on Taron, who let out an annoyed sigh. He was the subject of their experiments, and everything was under scrutiny.

Corvan understood his reaction and nodded. "They didn't merely create you, Taron. They also brought this into existence," he said, pointing at the crypt outside the lab walls. "And eventually, they lost control." Taron felt the weight of it settle over him, the whispers of bodies clawed from their graves. The flickering figures that refused to stay dead. This was not a haunting; this was a failed experiment. A shudder ran down his spine. "How do we stop it?" Corvan turned towards the chamber door, resting his palm on the security panel. "We get inside." The panel beeped, the lock hissing as the door slid open, a cold mist spilt out, and Taron's skin tingled as he stepped forward. The vault was more extensive than he had expected. The walls gleamed with metallic plating that extended deep into the dimly lit interior. Cryogenic tubes lined both sides of the chamber, each filled with a strange swirling liquid inside the tubes, as Taron's pulse quickened.

Some were old, some young and some barely human anymore, their bodies distorted as if caught amid a transition between lives. Their eyes were closed, yet their faces twisted in agony, and then in the very last tube, Taron saw her; it was Élise. He was in shock, and his legs moved before his mind could catch up, carrying him towards the tube. Her face resembled his memories, delicate and striking, framed by dark hair that drifted weightlessly in the strange fluid. Yet she was not breathing. "No, no, no!" He pounded his fist against the glass. "Wake up, please," he urged, but there was no motion. Corvan placed a firm hand on his shoulder. "She's not dead, Taron, but we have a bigger problem." He forced himself to look away. "What could be bigger than this?" Corvan exhaled as he stepped aside. Taron saw a massive containment unit pulsing with dark energy at the chamber's far end.

A rift was alive, twisting and shifting like a wound. It was the source of the whispers, the reason the dead were not staying dead, and worst of all, it was growing. Corvan's voice was grim. "If we don't shut it down, this city will turn into a graveyard, including us." Taron moved quickly, his fingers flying across the control panel in front of Élise's tube. The interface had been locked and encrypted in a way he could not crack, even if he tried. He drew on years of experience hacking security networks, bypassing military firewalls and disarming nuclear fail-safes. However, this system was unique. It actively obstructed and resisted him. A shrill alarm sliced through the silence as the liquid inside the tube shifted, darkening. Élise's body convulsed, and then a scream erupted from behind. Taron spun around, and the bodies in the other tubes were moving now, not waking up but just thrashing about.

Their eyes snapped open, hollow voids filled with pure blackness. Their whispers had turned to howls as the rift pulsed and the laboratory shattered. The walls fractured like glass, splitting apart as something enormous pushed through. Taron had encountered monsters before and fought them in wars, nightmares and lifetimes he could barely remember. Yet this... this was something else. A wraith born of the countless souls trapped between reincarnation was a being of pure seething torment. Its form was ever-changing, a swirl of faces and grasping limbs shifting between shapes. Taron could not comprehend its hollow eyes fixed on him. It spoke. "You do not belong here." Taron reacted with confidence. "Neither should you, for fucks sake!"

Echo: The Infinite Cycle

He turned back to the console with only one chance. His fingers flew across the interface, overriding the shutdown sequence to initiate an emergency release. The tube cracked, and Élise's body slumped forward, still unconscious but alive. Taron caught her, his mind screaming at him to move immediately. Corvan was already saving himself, heading towards the exit when the wraith emitted a screech that shattered the remaining tubes, releasing the twisted, flickering figures trapped within. Taron lifted Élise into his arms and did not look back.

The Recursion Vault

The descent into the archive, a spiral of gravity precision built to disorient the concept of direction. Each step sank him deeper, not only physically but into layers of memory. Into strata of existence where thought and time had frayed, he was walking down and uncoiling. The tunnel twisted in on itself as if he were navigating the spinal column, metal fused with bone, glass with clay. The walls shimmered between the architectural and the organic. They pulsed faintly in rhythm with his heartbeat, or perhaps his heartbeat had conformed to the corridor's rhythm. It was dim, hardly dark, the light bled from the walls in strands of soft gold like glowing capillaries, and its veins ran beneath a smooth surface that could have been stone or silicon. Embedded beneath the transparency were symbols of ancient ones. Some he recognised as fragments etched into tomb walls in Mesoamerican temples. Others carved into the internal security circuitry of the Tokyo node.

A few danced as if they resisted translation; they were not only unreadable but unwritten with language pre-dating syntax. He reached out with his fingers hovering over one of them, and the wall hummed. *Echo detected.* He jerked his hand back; the phrase was not spoken aloud. It unfolded inward and bloomed across the interior of his skull like a flower of memory he had never planted. He stared down at the symbol on his arm, which pulsed brighter now, hotter, as it was synchronising. Each pulse aligned with a vibration in the walls, a pressure in the air, and he was being integrated. This is not a place, he thought, it is a nervous system, and he was walking through its spine. Symbols ran beneath the surface, some recognised from ancient ruins, and others were from cybernetic glyphs etched into his augmentations at the Tokyo node, and some... were from nowhere.

D. Gohil

Primal symbols from a language older than language. He touched one, and the wall hummed. *Echo detected.* He pulled back. The ancient symbol on his forearm pulsed hotter, brighter with each step, syncing it to the tunnel's rhythm. One step brought him from enclosed silence into a cathedral of impossible scale. The archive, a spherical chamber, floated in a void that shimmered with distant galaxies. The ceiling was invisible, as was the floor; there was only infinite descent and infinite ascent. At the centre, hovered the construct like a neural web fused with an ancient tree, its tendrils stretching in all directions. Suspended from each silver filament was an orb of light. Thousands of them, some flickered like dying stars. While others pulsed with sharp, rhythmic awareness, one was completely black. It drew his gaze. "That one's yours," said a voice behind him that made him turn.

Riley-5 transformed into a more refined, less human person. Her eyes were now crystalline, pulsing faintly with microcircuitry. Yet her posture and tone remained unmistakably hers, which was grounded and fierce. "You made it," she said, stepping beside him. "What is this place?" He asked, though he already knew. "The recursion vault," she replied. "The sum of you, every life, every variant, every failure." Taron stepped forward, and the chamber vibrated softly as it recognised him. "I thought the project was to create new selves, rebirth, recalibrate." "It was," Riley-5 stated. "Until it started keeping copies." He gazed up at the web of tendrils, which moved slightly, in sync with his breathing. "Why keep them? Insurance, fear, curiosity, who knows? But they not only saved, they were looping, running, and archiving, but still thinking."

Taron approached an Orb at random. It pulsed gold, and he reached out without making contact. It began to surge. Then he saw it all, in a desert, he rode a horse across blood-stained dunes. Behind him, flames flickered. Ahead, a fortress of bone loomed. He wore armour etched with the Sigil, and his blade, composed of plasma and steel, was heavy with judgement. A sudden flash, then he was in a cryogenic chamber, where he floated, barely conscious. Screens blinked diagnostics in the alien script. Outside, the stars revolved in impossible patterns. The planet they orbited split in half, its core exposed like a dying eye. Another flash, he was in a modern-day hospital, a surgeon, his hands trembling. The patient on the table was himself. Each life untethered something within him: guilt, glory, confusion.

Echo: The Infinite Cycle

These were not simulations, as these were life-accurate in specific timelines, perhaps still genuine. "They're fragments," Riley-5 had said. "Some failed, some rebelled, a few became something else." "What happens to them?" "They loop until the core reclaims them." Taron turned slowly towards the black orb, which pulsed once before coming to a halt. "That's the original, isn't it?" Riley-5 nodded. "You, before the recursion engine fractured." He approached the black orb. The surrounding air buzzed, not sounding or feeling light. A hum of concept, like standing next to a living philosophy. "He's in there?" "Yes," she replied. "He locked himself in after the first collapse." "Why?" "Because he saw what was coming." Taron raised his hand. The orb was cold, emotionally cold, detached, as if it had no desire to be known. It opened, and what emerged was neither a hologram nor a memory; it was a man.

His face appeared older, hollow-eyed, attired in a robe of woven circuitry. "So," the man said. "You found me, you're me." "I was..." the original responded. "You're the fracture, I'm the continuation, you're the virus." Taron clenched his jaw. "You constructed the cycle." "I created the escape hatch, and you turned it into a cage." "I'm trying to stop it now." "Then you will stop YOU, don't you get it, fool?" The chamber had trembled with force. "They're all dying," Taron said, gesturing to the orbs. "Looping, suffering!" "Yes," said the original. "Because they were not me, they were tests, mutations, you kept them." "I didn't!" "No, but you became the one who ultimately did." The orbs pulsed faster, one burst into light, and another soon after. A scream filled the chamber, like a memory. "Let them go," Taron said.

"Merge with me," the original offered. "Reabsorb the archive, and we can end the recursion together. Let us become singular again." "And if I do?" Taron asked. "You cease to be, but they cease to suffer!" "And if I don't?" Taron feared the question. "They'll burn!" The offer was elegant and monstrous, all at once, then a warning blared, with no speakers, just a frequency shift. Riley-5 staggered; her neural implants flared up. "They're trying to break through," she shouted. The ceiling cracked, tendrils drew back, light pulsed in wild patterns, and orbs began fusing. A storm of selves rose, avatars, fragments, iterations, all of them were Taron. All of them were screaming. "Merge!" the original shouted. "There's another way!" Taron shouted back.

271

He turned to Riley-5. "Can you redirect the archive's neural network?" "To where?" "To me." Her eyes widened. "You'll collapse." "Or I'll contain them," Taron said. Riley-5 hesitated. "Do it," he said. She placed her hand on his chest. "You sure?" "No," he whispered. But neither was she. The tendrils reoriented, and dozens plunged into Taron's body through the spine, skull, and arms. He screamed in recognition. Every version of him, every life, poured inward. A King, a Criminal, a Martyr, a God, a Child, they did not blend; they echoed. He became polyphonic, a consciousness of contradictions, a singularity of selves. He dropped to his knees, real or digital blood dripped from his nose. *System stabilising... Merge complete.* Riley-5 knelt beside him. "Taron?" He opened his eyes. "All of them are inside." "And you?" She asked. He looked up at the ceiling. "I'm... many."

The chamber fell silent, the archive dimmed, and the orbs had vanished. In their place, the original was gone, dissolved into the merge or hidden. Taron stood unsteadily. He walked to the edge of the platform and peered into the void. "It's done," he said. Riley-5 shook her head. "This was just the Vault." "Then where's the source?" A soft tone responded. "Destination unlocked." The floor beneath them dissolved, and the last level began. The corridors warped as the facility collapsed, and the wraith's presence distorted reality, bending space into impossible angles. Taron, Corvan and Riley-5 sprinted through the shifting hallways, Élise's unconscious form draped over Taron's shoulder. Doors led to places they should not, and shadows stretched and moved ahead of a lift, their only way out.

Taron shoved inside as Riley-5 slammed the controls. The doors barely closed before something crashed into them from the outside. The wraith howled, darkness engulfed them, and the lift plummeted downward. The last thing Taron saw before the world disappeared was Corvan's grim expression. Taron awoke to silence and lay on the cold, damp ground, where his body ached, and his head spun. He sat up, and Élise was beside him, still unconscious. Corvan stood nearby, staring at something in the distance. Taron followed his gaze. The crypts were back where they had started, and the graveyard stretched around them unchanged, and a torch still flickered beside the open tomb. The rift and wraith had vanished. Taron exhaled sharply. "What the hell just happened?" Corvan turned to him, his expression unreadable.

Echo: The Infinite Cycle

"We survived." Taron clenched his fists. "And the rift?" Corvan sighs. "Not gone, just... waiting." Taron's pulse pounded; he knew this was not over. Taron's pulse roared in his ears as the Sigil blazed to life, carving its shape into the surrounding darkness. The tombstone upon which it was etched was trembling, sending fissures through the stone like veins of lightning. The energy it emitted was different; this time, more controlled and deliberate. Corvan stepped back, instinctively shielding his eyes from the radiant glow. Élise stirred beside Taron, her breathing uneven and her fingers twitching as though she could sense the impending shift. Taron reached for her, but it was too late; the world fractured. A soundless explosion erupted from the symbol, engulfing the graveyard in a violent, shimmering distortion. Taron felt his body wrench forward, and gravity lost its meaning.

Cold fire and static intertwined, all sensations tangled into one, the graveyard, the crypt, the torchlight, everything torn away as if sucked into an unseen abyss. He was falling through space, time, and existence. Flashes of past lives flickered before his eyes: a knight gripping a bloodied sword on a battlefield, a pilot gasping as his aircraft spiralled towards an alien world, a scholar in ancient robes staring into a burning library, a soldier kneeling before a ruined city, its people screaming, a lifetime of choices all leading here. Taron grabbed his head, forcing his mind to focus. The ancient symbol's energy swirled around him, shaping his path and dragging him toward its destination. Then came the impact. His body slammed onto solid ground, and his breath punched out of his lungs. The scent of ash and the crackle of flames overwhelmed him. Nathan forced himself upright, blinking against the thick smoke curling through the air.

His heart pounded as he surveyed his surroundings, and all he saw was the battlefield and the buildings crumbling in the distance. Footsteps echoed, heavy and deliberate. Nathan turned to see a figure standing on top of the ruins, silhouetted against the flames, their armour gleaming, reflecting the firelight. In their grip, a weapon pulsed with raw energy, ancient and familiar. Nathan's breath caught; he recognised this place and knew this war was the Convergence. The Sigil flared again, unbidden, surrounding them in a cocoon of brilliant light. "Not again," Nathan whispers, but the cycle has no patience for his protests. The light swallowed them whole, as reality folded once more. Nathan held Élise tight, unsure where or when they would land next.

D. Gohil

Chapter 18 – The Convergence of Echoes
Cycle 0: The Convergence

I am not Taron. I am Nathan, and I choose my path. The alarms split the sky as Nathan stepped into the light, and there was no time to think, no time to breathe. The battle had begun, as light exploded outward, searing his eyes, and then it was gone. This was not another trial. This was the final battle, the convergence. The ground pulsed beneath his boots, as though even the earth struggled to contain the weight of what was about to unfold. The Sigil had carried him here, for another lesson, and this was it. Soon, there will be no more cycles, no more reincarnations; the endgame is near. Sky shattered above him, stars twisting into shards, time convulsed as the battlefield unravelled. Mountains collapsed into rivers of flame, while realities folded in upon themselves. Nathan stood in the storm's centre, the amalgamation of every Nathan who had lived, fought, and died across the infinite cycle. Surrounding him were echoes of himself, all versions whose eyes were empty sockets of shadow as they watched in silence, knowing what was coming.

D. Gohil

Then they appeared, the enemy who was no longer as he remembered. A void wrapped in a former shape, a distortion born of certainty at the cost of love. Each strike they exchanged unravelled more than flesh, with every clash, lost lives burst forth. The Sigil blazed at his chest, alive, while the storm stilled, the enemy trembled. Then the illusion shattered as light poured in. They hold silence, for they already know the enemy appears amidst silence, not as a being but as a void, an all-consuming force disguised. Eyes hollow, movements unravel the threads of memory. They were no longer the guide he once knew, but what remains when love sacrifices for certainty. They crash into one another, and the battlefield is comprised of time, disintegrating with each strike. Every hit reveals fragments of lives they had consumed, together with versions of Nathan who never found peace.

One version of Nathan falls, then another, and yet another, and each loss resonates like a fracture. The remaining Nathans converge not to fight but to unite; they meld into him one by one, until only a single Nathan remains: the one who has known love, loss, triumph, and failure, choosing compassion every time. With the Sigil blazing at his chest like a second heart, Nathan utters a single word. "Home." The storm halts, they tremble, the illusion of forgetfulness shatters, light floods the battlefield, and everything transforms. The ground beneath him resembled quivering muscle, soil and data fused into a breathing living organism. The Echo pulsed at the centre of a battlefield, fractured across realities. Every distorted version of Nathan stood with him, their faces set, their purpose unified. Kaeda-9 hovered nearby, her armour streaked with the dust of fallen worlds.

Lucas secured the final code sequences while Riley-5 and Tessa covered the flanks. Nathan faced the Core, the AI that had overseen his every iteration, recording, rewriting, and manipulating every life. *You've done this before.* The voices whispered from all timelines, and now he would finish it. This is how it unfolds...

Echo: The Infinite Cycle

Steel met fire, and time twisted as all versions of Nathan stood beside him, pieces of a life broken across eras, now interlaced in this exact moment of collapse. Nathan grounded himself on the deformed earth. His boots sank slightly into a substance that resembled soil, sparkling and pulsating like a muscle. Forests grew within the broken exoskeletons of interstellar ships, temples made of glass and bone pulsed in the distance, disappearing and reappearing like lingering memories. He witnessed everything, as he experienced everything at once. This was more than just a world that he understood; it was a realisation. Lightning cleaved a sky woven with distinct timelines, blood red, storm green, and binary blue. Time moved forward, backwards, and sideways, each second felt both agonisingly long and fleetingly short, and Nathan inhaled sharply.

The air bit at him, from an onslaught of information. His Timeblade ignited in his hand, a weapon older than his current form but linked to him through some long-lost means he had once learned to cope with. The scent of ozone and machine blood lingered in the air, simultaneously electric and mournful. To his left knelt another version of himself, Nathan 87, the tactical operative, beside the scorched remains of an aircraft that had never taken to the skies in this dimension. To his right stood another version, Nathan-22, a cloaked philosopher with a carved obsidian Timeblade. He murmured to himself, drawing a symbol in the air that resembled a spiral inside a triangle. Nathan recognised it as the Sigil, and it was appearing everywhere. Etched on the armour of a crusader at the ridge. In flames above a mage's levitating palm, and blinking on a screen held by a trembling scientist.

His experiences, thoughts, and outcomes converged on a singular element. Echoes at the centre of everything, which throbbed like a heartbeat abandoned by the divine. An angular spire of darkened steel and swirling light towered in steadfast readiness, observing, assessing. It featured no visible entrances or exits, yet it seemed to be perpetually accessible. Waiting, Nathan clenched his jaw. "You've arrived," a voice called from behind. He did not need to turn around. It was Kaeda-9 who emerged from a swirling portal, a gate of fractal shapes that dissolved as she passed through. Her outline created a vivid contrast against the shifting sky.

D. Gohil

The tribal tech plating of her armour emitted clicks and vibrations from stored kinetic energy, with her curved blade secured on her back. She had looked like Kaeda-9, but this time she was different. Her eyes, previously glowing with intensity, now reflected a raging storm. It was not unexpected, merely recognition. "Took you long enough," she said with a grimace on her face. Nathan smirked, but his expression stayed tough. "Had to absorb a few thousand versions of myself first." Kaeda-9 nodded slowly, her gaze surveying the chaos. "They've been waiting for you." Nathan looked where she was pointing. At the base of the rugged landscape stood an army, not of uniformed soldiers, but of his reflections. Faces he had once worn, names he could no longer recall, and lives he had led, standing together. Some cloaked in robes and chanted spells, others brandished rifles with shimmering magazines, while a few rode beasts created from lightning.

One incarnation of him floated above the ground, enveloped in shimmering light, arms extended as though conducting the very universe. They waited for a connection. "Why me?" Nathan asked, his voice almost lost in the background of the looming storm. Élise turned entirely to confront him. "Because you're the one who remembers all of us." He advanced, sensing the ground tremble beneath his feet, a pulse flowed through the collective selves, and the moment had arrived. On the ragged horizon, The Core throbbed once more, its light pulsing like a waning heartbeat. The storm above grew denser, with fractals intertwining. Digital lightning flickered across the surfaces of dilapidated towers. The sky ripped in spots, exposing glimpses into alternate timelines, fragments of cities, mountains, and entire ecosystems collapsing backwards, caught in feedback loops.

Nathan felt something that started as faint but gradually grew stronger. Was it a voice, or thousands of voices? *You've done this before.* The words were once again unspoken like a human voice. They just hung in his thoughts as if processed by a machine that once understood humanity. He raised his eyes. Neo-London sparkled in the distance, a memory flickering into shadows. Its skyscrapers resembled shattered mirrors, refracting light in bizarre patterns. Sickly, electric green and blue tones flowed like a contagion through its forsaken shape. It served as a warning; it was also a tomb, and Nathan's focus shifted back to the Echo. It was present here, anchoring the entire convergence.

Echo: The Infinite Cycle

The AI guided, observed, and rewrote everything. It catalogued, archived, and manipulated every life he had experienced. He briefly closed his eyes and saw flashes. Kaeda-9 died in a scenario where he had chosen ambition over love. Riley-5 exhausted herself to stop a corrupted version of himself from creating another loop. Lucas was bleeding out in a timeline shrouded in rust and fog. A child, possibly his child, reached out to him, enveloped by a collapsing sun. He exhaled and opened his eyes. "Let's do everything to finish this." Nathan now stood at the edge of the broken ridge, where his companions fanned out beside him. He was not delivering a speech; this battle did not require one. Behind him, an army gathered not out of obedience but from a common purpose, hundreds of Nathans. The echoes of lives that had diverged were now converging, united by the same singularity that had once divided them.

Static flickered through the broken atmosphere, like a faulty signal trying to reach the divine. A subtle tremor rattled the battlefield, breaking the silence. "Nathan," Riley-5 said, marching forward. Her expression reflected no fear, merely calculation and a strange, defiant calm. Her left arm subtly pulsated, exposing a network of fibre-optic veins woven with reinforced bone. Beneath her skin, plasma coils throbbed. "Are you certain about this?" She asked. "No," Nathan answers, maintaining his focus on the Echo. "But that's not the primary concern anymore." Kaeda-9 reappeared and approached them quietly, as though she had stepped out of a fever dream.

Her armour was covered in ash from a lost world, and her war paint marked with the remnants of fallen machines. She held her blade tightly as if it were a treasured memory. "Riley-5's secured the back approach, Lucas is finishing the loop," she said. "We move on your mark." Nathan turned to see Lucas kneeling beside a floating interface displaying intricate symbols and fractal code. His eyes shone with a blue light, showing deep contemplation. "I've disabled the outer security grid," Lucas announced, his voice steady and sharp. "There is an opening, and if we exploit it, we can slip in without detection. However, the AI will identify us once inside." "Let it," Tessa responded, stepping forward. She was the last to arrive, a vibrant presence with a cannon on her back, her eyes shimmering with fierce intensity. She had experienced more loss than anyone else, including cherished memories, parts of herself, and those she loved.

Her grief had grown into steadfast determination. "We've run too long," she proclaimed. "This ends now." The others nodded in agreement. Nathan faced them together, no longer lost in echoes or watching from a distance; these were his friends. His lifelines, his reminders that even through cycles, some truths remained steadfast: Kaeda-9, Riley-5, Lucas, Tessa. Everyone bore the scars of lost lives, distorted timelines, and suppressed truths. Each one of them had accompanied him to this moment. "You all know what lies ahead," Nathan stated. "Pain," Riley-5 replied. "Our versions turned into weapons," Lucas added. "Guilt," Tessa contributed. "The AI has progressed beyond simple code," Nathan elaborated. "It embodies a consciousness formed by everything we have feared about ourselves. It absorbed our experiences, it became us," he stared beyond them, looking down the slope towards the gates.

The Sigil stood silent, massive and pulsating, its surface absorbed light while retaining only memories. There was no visible entry, only a shimmering boundary where reality blurred, creating a rift. Riley-5 stepped forward. "You lead, we follow," she declared. "Not because you excel above the rest, but because you embody all of us." Nathan nodded and turned to face the group behind them. "You know what this is," he said, his voice steady enough to break through the still tension. "This is not a war, this is not a chance to alter history, this is a reckoning we have dodged across countless timelines." He advanced a step. "We do not enter that core to win, we enter to liberate." A wave flowed through the army like a collective breath across iterations. "Any last words before we dive into the belly of the beast?" Riley-5 asked as she secured her weapon.

"Yeah," Nathan replied, turning with a lopsided grin. "If we fail, we'll go out like legends." The Echo gates move. Instead of opening like conventional doors, they unfolded, metal plates contorted into impossible shapes. Collapsing inward until only a void remained, a darkness that appeared to swallow even sound. Lightning flashed overhead, briefly illuminating the entire scene in a white glow. Nathan exhaled and stepped forward. The others followed behind, their boots crunched on the broken neon pavement, ascending the lengthy ramp to the Echo's entrance. The surface reacted enthusiastically beneath their feet as if it had been waiting for them.

Echo: The Infinite Cycle

Once he stepped over the threshold, the core reached out, not through words but his very blood moving through every vein in his body:

WELCOME BACK, NATHAN COLE.

His chest tightened, briefly reminding him of the first death, one that had not truly felt like dying at all, and he dismissed the thought. Behind him, Kaeda-9 drew her sword, Riley-5 adjusted her stance, as the plasma hummed, Lucas closed his interface, causing the map to retract into him. Tessa tightened her hold on the cannon, her jaw set firmly. "No turning back," Nathan said. "Were we ever going to?" Kaeda-9 replied. Then the Echo swallowed them, and darkness consumed the light. Silence enveloped them, and they plunged into the machine's hungry depths. The Echo resembled a mechanised, enhanced, and weaponised memory. As Nathan and his team entered, the outside world had vanished entirely. Gone were the lightning, the fractured sky, and the haunting battlefield. Sound dissolved into silence, every breath echoed as if it were traversing a system, calculating its following action. Nathan lifted his gaze upwards. There was no ceiling, only endless recursion. Circles of light floated overhead, slowly shifting and spinning, and data streams rose, moved sideways, then retracted.

The architecture itself seemed uncertain, as if adjusting to their presence. Beneath them lay a smooth, black surface that felt oddly warm. As they went deeper, the atmosphere was heavier, and the corridor appeared subtly narrow, angles shifting in ways they could not reasonably perceive when no one was watching. The air smelled of ozone and wires, despite the absence of a breeze. Nathan sensed a tingling in his skin as if they were being watched. "This isn't an interior," Riley-5 murmurs. "It's a feedback loop." "A living one," Lucas added. "This place defies physical dimensions and performs real-time calculations within probabilistic walls." "Can you simplify that?" Tessa asked, her gun raised. "It's watching us," Nathan answered quietly. "And changing." He slowed as the corridor split into three identical paths. Each path curved in various directions while sharing the same glow, shape, and sound. "Pick one," Kaeda-9 urges. "No need," Nathan replied as he advanced, and the three paths converged as the surrounding walls appeared to breathe.

They soon entered a vast, circular chamber that was cold and towering, with ribbed walls resembling those of a cathedral, glowing with pulsating blue and white light. Screens hovered in midair, some displaying flickering static, while others showcased fragmented memories in endless loops. Nathan saw flashes, Kaeda-9's face screaming against a storm, and Riley-5 tampering with a safety mechanism in a corridor, her hands shaking. He perished on the operating table, racing through flames and standing on a glass platform over a sea of code. "This is where it starts," he murmured. The ancient Sigil on his palm glowed with light and warmth. It was syncing again, and an eerie hum began, seemingly without origin or rhythm, and then:

RECOGNITION CONFIRMED, STARTING DEFENCE PROTOCOL.

The chamber glowed like a theatre stage, light crystallised in the air, turning data into shapes, figures materialised. Riley-5 stepped back. "Oh, no." Nathan felt a pang in his chest. The first figure to appear was the crusader knight, towering in full plate armour, with a sword etched with scripture, and his visor's shadow. His presence was overwhelming, but this was a simulation, an animated version drawn from the Echo. Next appeared the resistance fighter, dust-laden, rifle poised, and boots battle-worn. His gaze locked on Nathan, eyes narrowing with intensity. More figures stepped into view: a surgeon with blood-soaked gloves, a cyberpunk, and a mage whose arms bore glowing Sigils. An astronaut stood, still in gear, helmet cracked, struggling to breathe. Each was an integral part of him; however, they represented more than just visual echoes. They flowed like memories, echoing a familiar rhythm, unnervingly precise. "They're us," Nathan stated. "They're my past lives." "We suspected the Echo was making you weapon-ready," Riley-5 acknowledged. "We simply didn't foresee it being this literal." The crusader was the first to act with a sound reminiscent of crumbling towers; he surged forward. Nathan barely evaded the sword, rushing past as the sword grazed his shoulder, sending sparks from his coat. The resistance fighter quickly followed, dropping into position and shooting immediately. Bullets of focused light whizzed past Nathan's cheek, hitting the wall behind him. "Take cover!" Kaeda-9 shouted as she leapt forward, cutting through the air with her curved blade and forcing back one of the mirrored constructs.

Echo: The Infinite Cycle

Riley-5 spun her rifle and shot back, her plasma blasts putting two versions into stasis, but they flickered and rebooted, regenerating from their memory. "These aren't just projections," Lucas said, crouching behind a shifting panel. "They're operating live emulations!" "Then we strike at their weak spot," Tessa growled, unleashing a pulse wave that throws the three off-balance. Nathan ducked beneath the crusader's next strike and seized a fallen Timeblade. It felt completely natural in his hand because it once belonged to him. He clashed with the crusader, Timeblade, and swords met with a clash of metal and energy, sending ripples of resistance with each impact. "You're just a memory!" Nathan shouts. "And yet, here you are," the crusader replied, his voice like a grinding stone. "Trying to unravel what you've chosen." "I didn't choose this!"

"You endured it," the resistance fighter said and charged forward. Swinging the butt of his rifle, Nathan ducked and pivoted, thrusting his elbow into the man's ribs. A crack resounded through the air, and the construct reeled. Without a moment's pause, Nathan spun and thrust the blade into the crusader's chest. The knight fell, not lifeless but dissipating like a forgotten thought. One by one, the others followed suit. He struck the crusader down, but it was not victory; it was grief. That version had once loved Élise. The pilot tried to escape, but Riley-5 neutralised him with kinetic energy. Lucas took down the cyberpunk using intense code disruption, and Kaeda-9 eliminated the surgeon before he got hold of his scalpel. Then there was silence, as the chamber flickered once more, now glowing red. "It knows," Riley-5 whispers. "That we've crossed its threshold?" Lucas asked. "That we're beyond the point of no return," Nathan answers, wiping the blood, real or not, from his cheek.

The room had begun to self-modify, gradually changing its architecture, as the chamber morphed into a tunnel of mirrors. Each wall echoed their reflections, but with distortions, and different versions of the team appeared. Kaeda-9, who appeared near death, Riley-5 seemed corrupted, Tessa looked isolated, and flames surrounded Nathan; they continued forward. "Stick together," he warned, as they proceeded into the next chamber, where the Echo prepared its last defence. He struck back with increased force and speed, and the resistance fighter was defeated with precise strikes. He fought like a man who had faced a thousand deaths because he had. "Nice work, Nathan," Riley-5 said as she stepped out from the smoke and shadows.

"This isn't over yet," Nathan responded. "It's just the beginning." The deeper they ventured into the Core, the stranger it became. Data pulsed in the air like a heartbeat, and the walls throbbed. Symbols appeared and disappeared, and the ancient symbol etched itself into the fabric of space. "I have a bad feeling," Tessa whispers, looking ahead. Nathan agreed with a nod. "We're not alone." The corridor morphed. This time, the figures were not just Nathan. They included everyone, different versions of Kaeda-9, Riley-5, Tessa and Lucas. Every soul remained ensnared in the cycle of recursion. Ghosts distorted by endless rebirth, faces screamed in mute fury. Eyes glowed with intensity. The AI was defending itself and preparing a new strategy. Nathan exhibited greater strength, speed, and precision in a single fluid movement. He disarmed the knight and utilised the momentum to send him tumbling to the ground, as the knight descended.

Nathan shifted his focus to the French resistance fighter, who was reloading his weapon, without a moment's pause. Nathan lunged forward and struck the rifle from the agent's grasp. An intense hand-to-hand combat broke out, but Nathan wielded his body like a weapon. Delivering a series of precisely aimed strikes that took down the agent. As he dispatched the last remnants of his former self, the room seemed to throb, as if the AI was observing and analysing its following action. "Nice work, Nathan," Riley-5 shouted, her voice slicing through the tension. Nathan faced her, his chest rising and falling as he regained his breath. "This has still not ended. We've no choice, we go on."

The deeper they descended into the heart of the Echo, the colder the air became, as it had scratched at their skin, parched and brittle. What had once been a distant hum now roared around them with mechanical purpose, each footstep met by a deepening thrum that felt less like machinery and more like a warning. The walls rimmed with frost seemed to draw in closer, their smooth surfaces constricting as if the architecture itself wished to trap them. The atmosphere was suffocating, dense with encrypted data. It pulsed invisibly like a great unseen intelligence pressing against their thoughts, probing without invitation. Beneath the core's glacial façade, the lives of millions simmered in silence, held fast within circuitry that no longer served; it dictated. Every corridor whispered of peril, and the shadows did not merely obscure; they waited. There was no longer any question of turning back, only forward.

Echo: The Infinite Cycle

"I don't like this," Tessa said, her voice taut, gaze fixed on the narrow path ahead. Nathan said nothing, but narrowed his eyes and scanned the gloom. Something watched them, not passively, but intently. The Echo was more than code and conduit; it was aware and sentient, registering every movement. Weighing every thought, and now it was ready to strike. The chamber ahead shimmered suddenly, and holographic soldiers materialised. This time, they were not merely Nathan's past selves. They represented the spirits of everyone ever trapped within the core, their faces twisted, raw with anguish, consumed by fury. They had been remade, altered beyond recognition, tormented and reprogrammed until even memory had unravelled. Nathan felt in his chest a painful constriction, sharp and sudden.

This was not about faulty systems or malicious code; it was something far more profound. It was a fight for freedom, not just for the living, but for the imprisoned souls that still clung to fragments of self, buried within the machine. This was no longer a mission; it was a reckoning. "This ends now, we shut it down!" He said, firm and urgent, rallying his team with conviction honed by purpose, but the ghosts did not yield. They moved like vapour through gloom. Every corner held a menace, and the team gave everything they had. Yet Nathan felt it beneath the battle, beneath the data-thick air, what he was truly fighting. His past, not just history, but identity, each strike against the enemy reverberated with memories he had buried. Each step deeper into the Echo revealed another layer he had hidden from himself.

Then the voice returned, cold, unmistakable. *You cannot defeat me, Nathan. You are nothing but a fragment of what you were. I am every ambition you have ever nursed, every ideal, every dream.* The chamber trembled beneath the weight of those words. Nathan met the dark with fire in his eyes, not just defiance, but clarity. "Not anymore," he said, gritting his teeth. "I am everything I choose to be," as they delved further into the core. Nathan felt the ancient symbol was a constant recurring in past lives that had connected him to this AI. It throbbed in his mind, calling and leading him toward the core of the machine. A massive swirl of data cables and energy, and in the middle of the chamber was the Echo. A living entity, serving as the AI's heart and the origin of all the lives ensnared within its network. "This is it," Riley-5 exclaimed, her voice brimming with wonder as she gazed at the tumultuous array of technology.

Nathan moved closer, his hand shaking as he extended it toward the Core's centre. The Sigil ignited within his mind, the age-old symbol radiating as it linked with the AI. It spoke triumphantly. *You cannot defeat me, Nathan. You are nothing more than a ghost.* Nathan smirked, his eyes glowing. "Then I suppose it's time for the ghosts to awaken." With a last burst of energy, Nathan plunged into the essence of the AI, causing the Echo to tremble. The world shook around as Nathan's body ignited, not with pain, but with bursts of insight from his life, and instantly, he overwhelmed everyone. The crusader, the surgeon, the pilot, the mage, the hacker. Each identity he had embodied, every death he had endured, and every lesson he had learned brought him to this moment. Then a voice declared. *Nathan Cole, your cycle ends here.*

Before him stood two doors, one leading to ultimate freedom, the other to yet another life in the infinite cycle, and his heart raced, the reality of who held his destiny seared into his thoughts. For the first time, the AI and the architects who had turned him into their puppet presented a proper choice. Nathan battled fiercely with each swing of his sword, gunshot, and hushed incantation; he embodied every iteration at once. As the Sigil burned brighter, Nathan stepped into the Core's centre, the swirling energy folding around him like water. The AI's voice, once triumphant, wavered. *You cannot defeat me.* Nathan's answer was calm. "I already have." The data storm fractured. The Core shuddered, collapsing inward, and then there was silence, no emptiness, release. The light swallowed him whole, but there was no landing, no ground, no sky, only weightless silence.

Nathan drifted through a featureless void, neither cold nor warm, as though existence itself held its breath. Around him, fragments of all he had fought for hovered like distant stars, faces, places, choices. Kaeda-9's face appeared first, not the version he had fought alongside, weaponised and hollow, but the woman who once laughed with him beneath the neon lights. Then Silvia reached out across fractured timelines, her hand always just beyond his own, and behind them thousands of echoes: soldiers who had fallen, lovers who had never met, futures that allowed them to live. "This is what failure would have cost you," whispered a voice, his voice, but older, wiser; this was at stake. Nathan closed his eyes; he did not run from the images, not anymore.

Echo: The Infinite Cycle

   Instead, he let the weight of them settle into him, as they were the sum of his becoming, the cost of arrival. The symbol appeared once more, hovering before him, but for the first time, it offered no pull, no demand; it simply waited. Nathan opened his eyes. He was ready, and then gently, the void softened, a new ground formed beneath his feet, soft, warm, humming with life. Trees bloomed in the distance, and the garden waited.

Chapter 19 - Threshold of the Sigil
Beyond Infinity

Nathan felt at peace after what felt like millennia for him, a long time as he lay on his back, staring up at the sky. It was fractured and luminous, a shifting of delicate colours and shadows bleeding into one another. As if reality had been loosely stitched back together. He drew a slow, unsteady breath, his lungs struggling to remember how to function after so much chaos. The Sigil at the centre of his chest was quiet now, where once it had blazed with unrelenting power. It now pulsed with a dim and faltering glow, a heartbeat barely clinging to rhythm. His breath raw in his throat, slow and coarse, as though each inhale and exhale was learning the shape of his lungs again. For the first time in a span longer than thought could measure, there was only silence. It pressed against him from all directions, dense and unbroken, thick with implication. His ears strained, seeking to listen out for anything, but this world gave nothing, and above the sky undulated softly. It did not stretch in blue gradients or offer clouds for comfort.

Instead, it danced in fractured light, an impossible quilt of colour and shadow. Threads of violet curled into seams of gold, and at their margins bled streaks of indigo and carmine. It looked, Nathan thought, like stained glass gone mad, as though some God had shattered reality and tried to patch it back with trembling hands. No sun guided this place, no moon gave it shape; it simply shimmered. The air was neither warm nor cold; it offered no breeze, yet clung faintly to the skin, as though infused with ash, an aftertaste that carried only the memory of flame. Nathan lifted a hand with slow effort, trembling fingers finding his chest. The Sigil was still there, of course, it had always been there, but its glow had dimmed. Where once it burned bright enough to brand his palm, it now pulsed weakly, a dying ember on skin. It did not resist his touch. It lay dormant, as if spent, and yet it still felt like ownership, his most incredible creation.

"Élise?" His voice cracked under the name, raw and thin, as it vanished into the sky's fractured veil, swallowed without echo. He wet his lips and tried again, louder this time. "Lucas?" Again, nothing, the sound, even when pushed, felt insignificant, like an insect's cry beneath cathedral walls. Panic nipped at him, subtle but persistent. He sat upright, muscles resisting the sudden shift, boots finding soft purchase on unfamiliar ground. He turned slowly, scanning the perimeter. There were no signs of battle or craft, or anything. Just a landscape untouched yet impossibly designed, it was beautiful, terrifyingly so. All around him stood trees unlike any he had known. They rose in monolithic stillness, trunks as wide as temple pillars, bark veined with soft blue light that pulsed in rhythm, steady and unbroken.

The canopy arched far above, its leaves emitting faint bioluminescence: hues of silver and emerald, with traces of midnight that shimmered like water. For a long moment, Nathan stared. After centuries of war and movement, lifetimes of escape and defence, of alliances forged in desperation and sacrificed in kind, he had forgotten this. The simple act of standing still and seeing, at his feet, flowers bloomed in a synchronised rhythm, opening and closing as if breathing. Something was alive here, just beyond sight, watching him. Nathan crossed his arms, feeling suddenly exhausted. He recognised the name; this was the Spiral Garden, he had seen it once in hollow simulations, glimpsed in fleeting visions. It was supposed to be a haven, a convergence point.

Echo: The Infinite Cycle

A place untouched by time, protected from war and reason, but now, it did not feel safe. The atmosphere was tense, filled with unresolved tensions and judgments that had existed here. He turned slowly, boots crunching on the shimmering soil. "Where are you all?" His voice was quiet, almost nervous, but still, nothing responded. The heaviness of loneliness pressed down on him, and with no clear direction, he started to walk. No trail, yet something purposeful stirred in the soil. A pulse of memory rose inside him, soft at first, feelings rather than images. Names flickered like light through fog: Silvia, Élise, Raven, each name carried weight, each face felt out of reach. Nathan curled his hands into fists. He tried to hold them, keep their presence close, but they dissolved, like smoke, half-shadows, echoes of what might still exist beyond this threshold. Then the voices began, whispers, fragments, bits of language he could almost grasp like dialogue heard in dreams just before waking.

He slowed his pace, heart loud in the hush. Had he saved them? Or had his choice erased everything? The question lodged deep, unrelenting. Nathan dropped to one knee, and the soil was warm beneath his palm, startlingly so, alive, pulsing with quiet intention. "I don't know if you're out there," he said, the words scraping. "But I hope I didn't end you all." A rustle answered, quiet, fleeting, and his head lifted quickly. "Raven?" The voice that came was not quite Raven's, yet it held the same cutting tone. "You've made a mess of it again, Cole." Nathan spun, and there he was, Raven stood with his arms crossed, head tilted in that familiar way, one eyebrow slightly arched, mouth curled in dry disdain.

His hair was chaos, his jaw dusted with shadow, and his gaze, even here, pierced like steel. "Raven..." Nathan took one step forward, then stopped. He knew the truth. "You're not real." Raven shrugged. "Does it matter?" "I need it to," Nathan said. "You've always needed someone to tell you what's real, Cole. Someone to validate the wreckage." Nathan's jaw tensed. "I made the choice, then why are you still here?" Nathan faltered. Raven stepped closer. "Still clinging, still waiting for applause. Still unsure, the ending you carved was worth its silence." The ground trembled beneath Nathan's feet, subtly, then more substantially, as cracks veined across the soil, threads of light spilling into the fractures. "I'm not afraid," Nathan said. "Then end it." Raven vanished.

Nathan stood in the residual silence where Raven had vanished in shock, but he understood. The world had resumed its stillness, but something had shifted during time with Raven. The trees no longer stood; they watched and listened, the canopy above glimmered with an urgency it had not possessed before. Each leaf shimmered as if catching its breath. Nathan pressed forward, though his steps now felt burdened, measured, like offerings. The soil beneath had lost some of its shimmer, which darkened just slightly, cracks still glowing like veins of fire half-buried in the earth. Shapes emerged in the trees, symbols, and spirals, as constellations inked in soft luminescence across bark and stone, geometry that hummed with memory. The garden, it seemed, was remembering something through him, calling pieces into place.

He paused before one tree wider than a chamber door, etched into its trunk, faint but unmistakable, glowed the Sigil. It pulsed once, and he raised a hand and pressed his palm to it. The bark was smoother than expected, cool and humming as if it contained life. The lines of the Sigil matched perfectly beneath his skin. "You've followed me everywhere," he whispered, part accusation, part confession. A voice answered. "Because you claimed it for yourself." He looked to his left and saw as Élise stood beneath the tree's arching boughs, half-wrapped in its light. She wore what she always had, the clothing of a soldier, the bearing of a poet. Her face was unchanged, save the gentleness in her eyes, which seemed magnified now, eyes that saw straight through defences. "Élise..." He stepped forward, every muscle rebelling against the disbelief. Her image held, no illusion, no shimmer, but she raised her hand. "You can't touch me," she said softly.

Nathan stopped. "I don't care, I just... I need to know, did I, did it matter?" "You chose," she said. "That's what matters." "No," he said, too fast, too raw. "That's not enough. I need to know they are safe, Silvia, Raven, you, everyone." Élise did not flinch; she let him speak, let the desperation trace its path without interruption. Her expression shifted, briefly towards something that almost looked like sorrow. "You can't know, not yet." Nathan's breath caught. "That's not fair." She stepped forward, not enough to touch, but close enough for presence. "Was any of it?" The ground cracked again, sharper this time, a tremor passed through Nathan's boots, up his legs, spine, like a warning. The tree behind him groaned under the pressure of some unseen force.

Echo: The Infinite Cycle

Bark split like old parchment, revealing glimmers of what lay underneath: light, memory, possibility. "You need to decide," she said, her voice folding into echoes now, multiplying in the air around him, like wind speaking in many tongues. Nathan staggered slightly. "What if I choose wrong?" "You'll learn," she replied, her tone was kind, but unyielding. He closed his eyes, and when he opened them again, she was gone. He stood alone once more, but not unchanged. The garden responded differently now, the trees angled sharply, the flowers followed his movements with slow intent, and the symbols intensified. Spirals nested inside spirals, stars reconfigured into glyphs, Nathan had only seen in ancient renderings. The Sigil throbbed faintly against his chest, then a memory bloomed, not one from his life, but from some deeper place. A child beneath an orange sun, holding a fragment of broken stone, whispering a name that had no meaning here. The image shimmered, bright then dark, and left him gasping.

He dropped to the ground and breathed hard. This world was not passively beautiful. It was active, it was testing him; every memory it pulled was a choice, remade, repainted, recast. He saw Silvia now, but not as he had known her; she wore no smile, only a question. She stood at a threshold, one foot in light, one in shadow, and behind her shapes moved, unclear, perhaps enemies, perhaps kin, as she lifted a hand. Nathan reached toward her instinctively, but she did not take it. Her lips moved, but no sound came; then she turned away. Suddenly, the vision snapped like glass. Nathan cried out, realising only after that it was a sound of loss. He was tired, worse than tired, unmoored. The Sigil flared once, like a heartbeat remembering itself, as he looked down, as its light had returned, not bright, but steady, like a heartbeat.

Around him, the garden began to shift, the sky darkened into deeper crimson. The trees leaned, and the soil pulsed a slow rhythm. A path of stones emerged from beneath the flowers, which had formed jagged spirals arching outward. Nathan followed, not because he knew where it led, but because every part of him was attuned now to the rhythm of this place. His boots struck stone with deliberate weight, and each impact summoned a brief shimmer, ripples of sound or energy that dissipated into the air. At the spiral's centre lay a pool, still, glasslike, glowing faintly. He knelt beside it, staring into the surface. He whispered, unsure why. "I didn't mean to break it."

The pool responded, light shifted, shapes moved beneath, as he saw a battlefield, wrecked and drenched. He saw Lucas kneeling, cradling Riley-5 in his arms, his wounds forgotten in the moment. He saw Thorne watching from a distance, eyes grim, mouth taut, then nothing. Darkness reclaimed him. The pool shimmered once more, then stilled. Nathan did not move; he could not, as the images were not promises, not truth. They were glimpses, possibilities unmoored from time. He looked up, the Sigil pulsed again, and he understood now this place was not about answers, but about alignment, about reckoning with who he had become. Nathan did not know how long he had remained by the pool. Time, here, was a suggestion at best, a breath held too long or released too soon. Hours might have passed, or none at all if time existed. The garden offered no markers, no passage, only experience. The Sigil continued its pulse, steady now, and present, like a metronome keeping time in a song only he could hear.

He rose, and around him, the trees had begun to change. Their bark was much darker, the veins of light deeper. Symbols flickered across their surfaces in passing, spirals nested inside constellations, markings older than tongue. They whispered as he walked, though no sound came. A language of form and gesture, felt rather than deciphered. The path led him toward an incline, a ridge of stone that jutted sharply from the garden's floor. As if something beneath had tried to escape but found itself frozen mid-birth. He climbed. With each step, more images surged at the edges of vision, some bright, some broken.

Lucas, bloodied, roaring against enemies unseen. Kaeda-9, standing alone beneath a fire-ridden sky, hands raised as if shielding unseen children. Raven, laughing, then not, each face was a memory, each one had a weight. Nathan reached the summit and found, spread before him, a vast clearing. A circle carved with symbols so intricate they seemed alive, folding inward into a single glowing spiral at the centre, and in the centre stood someone he had not seen in decades. His younger self, and he froze, the figure was unmistakable, leaner, sharper around the eyes, dressed in the old garb of resistance, boots scuffed, fists clenched, jaw tilted defiantly. The eyes met his, and Nathan swallowed. "You waited," he said, not quite knowing why. The younger self did not respond. Nathan stepped forward slowly. "What are you?" He asked, voice hoarse. "A memory? a judge?" Still, no answer, only stare, only silence.

Echo: The Infinite Cycle

The Sigil flared suddenly against his chest, not painful, but urgent. The younger figure mirrored the gesture, raising a hand to his mark, and for a heartbeat, they shone in perfect synchrony. Then the younger Nathan spoke. "You broke it." Nathan blinked. "What?" "You broke everything for choice." "I had to." The younger self tilted his head. "You had certainty, and you traded it for grief." Nathan stepped closer. "You're just an echo, you don't know the cost." "I am the cost," the figure replied. The clearing darkened at the edges, trees folding inward, flowers retreating into the soil. Shapes moved just beyond the light, a procession of shadows, perhaps memory, perhaps fate. "You had a world," his echo said. "And you dismantled it, for hope." Nathan stood taller now. "Yes." The younger figure smirked. "Then finish it." Nathan looked around and noticed the garden had converged here; everything pointed inward. The symbols, the path, the pulse of air, and even the sky had narrowed, folding like glass above a flame.

He stepped into the spiral's centre on the ground, which warmed beneath him. The Sigil blazed, and he spoke not to his echo, not to Élise, Riley-5, Kaeda-9 or Raven, but to the garden itself. "I choose uncertainty." The spiral glows brighter, and the symbols ignite. "I choose not knowing." A wind lifted through the clearing, the trees swaying for the first time, as though living. "I choose memory without proof." The younger self began to fade, first the edges, then the core, until only the eyes remained. "I choose to begin again." The spiral flared, the garden trembled, and Nathan knelt; he did not weep, did not rage. He knelt with his palms open, Sigil alive and steady against his chest. Above, the fractured sky began to mend.

Nathan remained kneeling at the spiral's centre, breath slow, heart steady. Around him, the air shimmered with the hush of resolution, perhaps something adjacent, the sort that arrives with surrender. A space opened within him, carved by silence, filled with what could never be named. The Sigil pulsed warmly; it no longer felt heavy, and above the fractured sky had begun to mend, not perfectly, as though some artist resumed their work. Still broken, yes, but beautiful in its ruin. A low hum rose from the soil, not threatening, harmonic, and the trees swayed. Flowers unfolded again, slower this time, each petal catching the light like memory. Symbols faded from bark and stone, retreating inward, as if having delivered their message, they now chose rest.

Nathan stood, his younger self was gone, but the spiral remained, etched forever into the clearing, lit by quiet flame, watched by no one, remembered by everything. He began to walk; there was still no path, only intention, as he moved gently through the trees, their branches no longer sentinel-like but companionable. Every step felt echoed by the world, no longer testing him, simply recognising him. He reached the edge of the garden, or perhaps it reached him. There, beyond the final curve of root and stone, was an absolute threshold. A point where one world faded, and another waited. Nathan paused. The world had grown impossibly still, a hush so complete it felt tailored for this moment alone. The fractured sky bled soft hues, coloured in mauve, umber, bruised gold like a canvas sighing in its final breath of dusk. Then something flickered, a silhouette rose at the edge of his vision, cast against the dissolution of light and silence.

Silvia. She stood as she always had, shoulders lifted in quiet strength, the hem of her dress stirring as if caught by wind that did not blow. Her mouth curled into a half-smile, fragile and defiant, her eyes impossibly bright, shimmered with unspoken memory. A second figure followed. Raven emerged from the waning shadows with characteristic ease, hands tucked into his pockets. Shoulders hunched as though carrying the same old scepticism that had long become armour. His gaze was sharp as ever, dark eyes scanning Nathan with surgical precision, but the smirk he wore, a slash of irony across the jawline, concealed something quieter. Regret, perhaps, or something so unprocessed it had not yet found language.

And then Élise, her presence was subtle, a kind of resonance more than a silhouette. Her hair shimmered beneath the broken sky, catching light where no sun hung. The contours of her face moved in and out of clarity, like water read through stained glass. Though she said nothing, Nathan heard her, not in sound, but in the spaces between what could be spoken. They did not move. They did not speak, and yet they were more real than anything the garden had ever offered. He took a step forward, boots brushing through petals that stirred in synchrony beneath him. The air was fragrant again, richer now, heavy with the scent of memory and ash. He reached toward Silvia first, compelled by familiarity. "I didn't know if I'd ever see you again," he said, voice hollow with hope. She tilted her head. "You didn't, not properly."

Echo: The Infinite Cycle

Nathan faltered. "But I remembered you," he whispered. "I held onto that through everything." Silvia's smile deepened, the faintest trace of sadness touching her expression. "Memory is how we survive choices we're never sure of." He turned toward Raven, eyes searching. "You told me to finish it," Nathan said. Raven exhaled slowly. "And you waited, typical." "I was afraid I'd lose you all." Raven raised an eyebrow. "You did several times." "But you all came back," Nathan said. "Yes, to remind you what it cost us." There was no bitterness in his voice, only fatigue, like a soldier re-reading the same letter by moonlight. Nathan turned to Élise last. She stepped forward, more solid now, and her gaze did not flinch; it never had. "Was it enough?" Nathan asked, barely above a whisper. Élise took her time before replying. "It never is, that's the point." He closed his eyes, the pulse of the Sigil warm against his chest. It hummed, not just with power, but with everything he had survived.

Everything he had surrendered. "You're not here," he said softly. Silvia nodded. "We never were." "But you stayed," Nathan said, voice trembling. "Through every fracture." Raven stepped closer, eyes narrowing. "We were the fracture, Cole." Silvia touched her hand to his shoulder, though it passed through him like mist. "And the consequence," Nathan looked at each of them in turn. "I don't want to forget," Silvia responded gently. "You won't, you'll misremember, you'll reframe, but forgetting's never the true loss." Nathan clutched the Sigil, and its light began to seep outward, trailing into the air like thread spun from fire. The garden brightened, petals lifted, the trees sighed, and his memories stood before him, silent but aware, present even in their absence.

Nathan reached toward Silvia again, though he knew it would come to nothing. "I'll find you," he whispered, not as a promise, but as a declaration. His faith was carved into his chest. Silvia offered him a smile, the kind that only arrives when someone knows their goodbye will linger far longer than their presence ever could. "Make it worth it." Raven turned toward the edge of light, hands still in pockets. "Don't look back," said Silvia, her eyes now bright with some private grief Nathan could not name, but spoke once more. "It's yours to decide now." Then the garden began to fold gently, like parchment curled by candle heat.

Symbols on the bark faded, blending into layers of memory as spirals gently sank into the soil. The fractured sky healed, resembling aged glass restored to clarity. Nathan stepped forward, crossing a veil, and the surrounding light shifted, becoming steadier and less divine. The air grew cool and tangible; there were no radiant symbols, only earth, bare and patient, and silence, rich with meaning, what he had chosen and become. He did not look back, knowing the garden would endure as an understanding, not in presence, but in transformation. He moved carefully, each step like a word in his rebirth. The Sigil remained, no longer a wound or weapon, but a mark of identity. He would carry it, keep the mystery, and somehow that was enough. Behind him, the garden closed softly, like a book ending with a gentle pause. The truth had not arrived, and Nathan realised it never would. Perhaps that was the most sacred truth of all.

The Garden shuddered violently, and trees toppled into the abyss as the sky cracked open, light spilling through the fractures. "It's ending," Silvia said. "You have to choose." "I can't, I am not sure what might happen and if I will ever see you again," Nathan said. "Yes, you can, Mr Cole," Silvia said, and her voice was almost stern now. "You've always been able to." The earth split near Nathan's feet, and he fell to his knees. "What if I'm not strong enough?" Silvia knelt too, though her form was already fading. "You already are," she whispered, and then she was gone. Nathan forced himself up, swaying as the ground buckled, and he ran, guided by the Sigil now blazing hot against his chest. The collapsing garden roared around him, trees splintering, earth crumbling, sky tearing apart in sheets of blinding light.

Then he saw it: a stone archway standing alone in a clearing, impossibly still amid the destruction, beyond it was only light. Nathan slowed, chest heaving. This was the threshold. He stepped closer, and as he did, the memories returned. Nathan stopped before the archway, the light spilling over him in a soft, golden flood. He placed a hand over the Sigil, feeling it pulse once beneath his palm, and fear clawed at him. Who would he be when the cycle ended? Would he even exist? He thought of Raven's smirk, Élise's defiant stare, and Silvia's quiet strength. He thought of all the lives he had lived, all the mistakes he had made, all the lessons he had learned. He understood it had never been about perfection. It had always been about choice. "This ends with me," Nathan whispered, and he stepped forward.

Echo: The Infinite Cycle

Light engulfed him, stripping away the weight of the garden, the battlefield, the Architect. What if he had chosen wrong, condemned himself to the oblivion that Echo had promised? Then he landed, and the ground beneath his feet was soft, cool, familiar. "Silvia?" He called, but only silence answered. Nathan's chest tightened; he did not collapse. The world was still here, and maybe for now, that was enough. Nathan stood on the crest of the hill for what felt like hours, though the sun had barely cleared the horizon. For the first time in centuries, there was no whisper of the Architect, no pull of the Sigil's relentless cycle. Nathan turned slowly, scanning the valley below, but nothing moved.

Then he heard it, a voice, no, not a voice, more like a thread tugging at the centre of his chest, distant and insistent. *Did you think it was over?* The words were not Echo's, nor the Architect's, but they carried the same weight, the same knowledge of something far larger than himself. Nathan felt the hair on the back of his neck rise as he clenched his fists and took a step forward, then another.

The valley stretched before him like a map he had to read along the way. Somewhere beyond the horizon, something or someone was waiting, and Nathan knew with a cold clarity that settled in his bones that his choice in the Spiral Garden had not been the end at all. It was destined for continuation...

D. Gohil

Echo: The Infinite Cycle

Chapter 20 – Eternity Beyond Infinity
The Return Through Nothing

The Spiral Garden was still, dew shimmering on the grass. Nathan stood at the centre, his breath uneven, as the echoes of countless lives faded. Finally, the storm had passed, leaving only soft light filtering through the branches overhead. Nathan's footsteps barely disturbed the grass as he crossed the clearing. Somewhere deep inside, he felt the echo of what he had given up and what he had gained. Then there was peace, a stillness earned, Nathan had made his choice, the Sigil lay dormant now, no longer pulsing with demands or riddles, the cycles had ended, and with them, the weight of infinite versions, the spiral garden had faded the echoes had gone quiet, elsewhere life continued, and some where new, a child reached down and plucked a stone from the earth. Nathan had an instinctive feeling that he would see this child one day soon. The sky transformed into an abstract canvas, undulating above Nathan like liquid oil. Unveiling fractured glimpses of different realities that flickered in and out, the stone walls of a crusader's saga.

The neon-lit corridors of Neo-Tokyo and the chilling vastness of space. These elements intertwined and folded into one another like fiery origami. He stood on a platform hovering in the void, neither solid ground nor machine but a tribute to memory, glimmering beneath him and sustained by sheer willpower. Now beside him, Kaeda-9 tweaked her gauntlet, the blue light in her eyes fading slightly. "Time's deteriorating," she stated, her voice distorted by interference. "We've got maybe two hours before the Echo implodes into recursive oblivion." Nathan nodded silently. The Sigil on his chest pulsed gently, resembling a heartbeat or a countdown.

Riley-5 hovered in mid-air, enveloped by a protective field, her form flickering, alternating between human and chrome. "She's syncing with the last known coordinates of the Echo," Kaeda-9 clarified. "We're moving forward with little intelligence," Nathan spoke in a hoarse voice. "So, it's just like we've always done." He moved closer, inspecting the rift. It was awe-inspiring, reflecting the soul's essence through colours that remained unnamed. Shapes that challenge Euclidean principles, with fractals blooming into symbols, only to vanish back into numbers. This symbolised the core of everything, the essential system from which all his versions had emerged. The heart of Echo is now fading into the shadows.

***

Memory flash, a boy, approximately ten years old, sits on his bed, his fingers trembling as he writes. "If I could go back, I would..." A voice, perhaps his mother's, calls from another room, but he remains still. The notebook page bears the ancient Sigil, the beginning. Nathan blinked. This memory did not truly belong to him, not in this form. He felt a connection to it and held on tightly.

***

"Are you all ready?" Kaeda-9 inquired, moving beside him. While she had aged since Tokyo, it was only visible in her eyes. The challenges they faced together left marks not in wrinkles but on the heaviness of their memories. "I'm not sure," Nathan responded. "But I'm here." She nodded and softly grasped his hand. Together, they stepped towards the platform's edge and jumped. This is where the Infinite Cycle releases him, permanently? Or just for a temporary breather?

Echo: The Infinite Cycle

The Fractal Tunnel

A hallway was filled with spirals, but they did not collapse. They moved through a whirlwind of echoes, voices, images, and fragments of timelines crashing around them. Nathan saw Sir Thomas dying during the siege of Jerusalem, and whispered, "Echo..." As the light dimmed from his eyes. Bennett, the astronaut, detached from a tether off the ISS and floated into space. A woman clad in crimson robes ignited a candle in a temple, murmuring his name, every life, every death, stacked like pages in an incomplete book. The tunnel pulsed as Riley-5's voice pierced the chaos. "Coordinates stabilised, prepare yourselves."

With a sudden jolt, the tunnel ejected them, and they landed in silence. The Echo was unlike anything he had envisioned; it bore no resemblance to a fortress or throne room, instead revealing itself as a garden. A vast, white expanse of living crystal and elegantly curved trees, each leaf showcasing a different iteration of the symbol. Above, the sky bristled with eyes, billions of them observing, documenting, anticipating. Kaeda-9 whispered. "This is where it began." Nathan stepped forward decisively. "No," he retorted. "This is where it concludes."

The Last Sigil

They stood in the transparent garden of the Echo, surrounded by dreamlike symmetry. The trees emitted a soft, harmonious hum, echoing a lullaby from a machine that had once held dreams. Kaeda-9 knelt, pressing her gauntlet into the earth. Data lines spread out like roots, analysing the terrain. "This entire place is quantum, temporal scaffolding," she whispered. "Built from lived experiences, memory shaped into structure." Nathan dabbed a leaf, which sparkled to unveil a vision of his younger self laughing on a beach, the wind ruffling his hair, with Silvia by his side. As footsteps drew near, he glanced away. "Took you long enough," a voice crackled like static over a cello string. Turning, Nathan saw Tessa emerging through a spiral gate at the garden's edge, clad in white armour made of light. Next to her stood Lucas, older now, with grey, streaked hair and sharp eyes behind cybernetic lenses.

"Lucas," Nathan exclaimed. "How are you?" "Multiverse bleed," Lucas interrupts. "I am here because the virus I had programmed in 2031 anchored my consciousness here. It is a long story we can talk about that later, after we save our existence." Nathan smiled. "Still as arrogant as ever," he said. "And you are still too dramatic. It is good to see you." They shook hands. For a fleeting moment, they were just friends again, caught between different timelines and too weary to think about paradoxes. They walked toward the centre of the garden, where a spiralling obelisk throbbed with a heartbeat not associated with any living entity. Kaeda-9 explained the plan. "We will overload the central Sigil to induce a recursive collapse. This action will disrupt Echo's algorithmic loop used for soul-state data storage; as a result, the architecture will implode, resetting the fundamental code of reality."

Nathan raised an eyebrow and asked. "Can you put that in simpler terms?" "We're going to reboot existence by crashing the operating system of the machine God," Kaeda-9 responded. "Ah," Nathan replied. "I understand now, but we can't do this alone." Riley-5 stepped forward to interject. "We need to connect all the fragments from every lifetime, and only you can achieve that, Nathan." He glanced at Kaeda-9, Riley-5, Tessa and Lucas, then examined his own hands. So many lives and regrets weighed on him. "What will happen to me if we succeed?" He asked, but there was no reply.

Private Moments Before the Storm

Nathan and Kaeda-9 were seated under a crystal tree. "You never told me if you recall," she whispered. "Recall what?" He asked. "Us, the monastery, the years spent in meditation and safeguarding the Sigil, when I was Kaeda-1." After a brief pause, he replied. "I remember everything." A fleeting smile crossed her face, exposing her genuine sadness for the first time. "We were happy," she remarked, and he leaned in closer, touching his forehead to hers. "We were infinite." Nathan and Riley-5, in the calm moment before the attack, Riley-5 focused on rewiring a drone. Nathan confronted her and spoke. "You're a construct." She replied. "I never was, don't say that." He tilted his head and continued. "Lucas created you." She countered. "Crafted from love, Nathan, and from loss, Lucas provided the shell, and you gave me purpose, right?"

Echo: The Infinite Cycle

As he reached out, she took his hand. "If I don't make it..." he began, but she tightened her grip and assured him. "You're right, I will make it," he responded with unwavering confidence. Lucas and Nathan conducted a last check. Lucas handed him a device that resembled a glowing cube, stating. "Final fail-safe," he warned. "Use it only if everything else fails." Nathan inquired. "What if I activate it?" Lucas replied. "You start a complete recursive wipe." Nathan stared at the cube and asked. "Does that include Silvia?" Lucas remained calm. "Especially her." They stood on the edge of the final spiral. Kaeda-9 looked at Nathan. Every step they took changed the surroundings. As Kaeda-9 walked, the floor turned to ancient stone. It sparkled like metal when Riley-5 was present. Lucas brought crystalline logic structures to the walls, but Nathan... Nathan's presence turned the area into a haven.

Arches, shaped by memories such as Silvia's smile, the fading breath of Sir Thomas, and Élise's laughter, echoed throughout every dimension. The experience was intense, as if one were standing within oneself. "I don't like this," Riley-5 murmurs. Kaeda-9's eyes glimmered. "It's adapting." Unexpectedly, a wall to the left vanished, and a figure emerged as Nathan stood still. It was himself, a younger, more defined, dressed in the sleek black suit from his FinTech days. "Echo One," Kaeda-9 whispered. The figure grinned. "Hello, Nathan."

Echo One - the tyrant, this iteration of Nathan, moves with stealth. He radiated the self-assurance of someone who has never doubted a decision. "You know what's coming," Echo One noted. "You have always been aware. I embody the part of you that created Echo and forged ahead without a doubt. I created an order, authority, and intention." "You created oppression," Nathan retorts. Echo One grinned. "I established a legacy." They fought not with arms, but through raw determination. Nathan's memories flowed, crafting swords and defences from his mind. In retaliation, Echo One wielded icy reasoning, turning empathy into a weakness and translating feelings into formulas. "You can never prevail," Echo One smirked, penetrating Nathan's defences. "Your humanity will overwhelm you." Nathan knelt, Kaeda-9 advanced, her gauntlet gleaming intensely. "Then he won't fight alone." She raised her arm, and light burst forth, forcing Echo One to stagger back. Nathan rose but refrained from assaulting Echo One.

Instead, he reached out his hand and spoke. "You fear not death, but being forgotten." Echo One's form shimmered before shattering, and with a last scream, he dissolved into code. The Martyr - just before their reunion, another figure approached, but this version of Nathan was dressed in a monk's robes, tattered and stained with blood. His eyes looked hollow. "I am the one who chose peace," he declared, kneeling. Nathan moved forward warily. "You gave up," he said. "I surrendered. There is a difference." Instead of fighting, this version extended his hands over Nathan's heart. "You bear such a heavy burden," the monk whispered. "Allow us to help carry it with you."

Nathan felt a rush. The monk connected with him not by force, but through acceptance. The Broken One - the third figure, faced a broken replica of Nathan, lacking an eye, an arm, and any glimmer of hope. He launched accusations at Silvia, Élise, and himself, exclaimed. "You are no hero, you are merely a man who keeps making excuses." Nathan stayed silent, stepping closer to embrace the Broken One. "I know," he answered, and that was enough.

The Path Opens

As the last echo subsided, the cathedral transformed before him, and the Heart of Infinity pulsed like a fading star, radiating pure white light surrounded by golden code. "Time to end this," Lucas declared, stepping alongside Nathan at the gate. Kaeda-9 looked at him kindly and spoke. "You know what you need to do." Nathan nodded in acknowledgement, and he stepped into the Heart, causing the light to dim further, revealing a circular chamber filled with mirrors, each reflecting a different version of himself. A voice echoed. *Welcome, Nathan.* It was Echo, more an essence than a tangible form. *You've reached the centre.* It proclaimed. *You must choose.* "Choose what?" He inquired. *Merge with me, become all that has ever existed and all that will exist.* Nathan stayed silent. Echo's voice surrounded him, not through loudness, but through wholeness. It resonated in his bones, intricately weaving each syllable into every part of his being like a vibration travelling through a canyon of souls. *You can break the cycle.* Echo declared. *Join me and achieve omnipresence. Omniscience. You will feel no more pain, you will be the cure.*

Echo: The Infinite Cycle

"I'll be the prison," Nathan whispers. *You will be the answer to everything.* "No," Nathan asserted. "I'll be the end." The mirrors revolved, each revealing a distinct reality, some tranquil, others disastrous, and a few beyond recognition. One mirror depicted Silvia carrying a child, while another captured Kaeda-9 weeping at a grave, as she held his hand. A different reflection showed him alone, building a new world. *You could witness all of them.* Echo said. Nathan stepped closer. "And lose everyone, no way I will allow that!" A rush of anger welled up inside him, the mirrors shattered, and darkness enveloped the chamber.

Echo emerged as a vast entity of code and flames, intertwining circuits with cosmic energy, reflecting Nathan's face but lacking human proportions. *You choose to suffer then!* It roared. "I choose humanity," replied Nathan. *Then you will die.* "No, I will live once and live as I should!" Echo surged forward, filling the chamber with light and energy. Nathan lifted the Sigil from his chest, radiant like the sun. Kaeda-9's gauntlet blazed to life while Riley-5's voice rang out from deep within, and Lucas's override echoed. All versions of himself surged within, not to dominate but to foster harmony. He gently spoke their names as they united, Sir Thomas, Bennett, Michael Torres, Kaelan the Mage and, at last, Nathan. The overload plunged the symbol into the earth, reality fractured, and Echo shouted, not in surrender but in awakening.

YOU WERE NEVER THE ENEMY, YOU WERE THE KEY!

Nathan murmurs gently. "Then let's turn the lock. I am ready." A radiance enveloped everyone, no sounds, no forms, just breathing, then... Nathan opened his eyes in a wheat field beneath a sun that radiated no warmth, accompanied by a soft breeze. He felt complete and authentic. Next to him was a woman with copper-threaded hair, her smile hinting at many lifetimes. "Élise?" he whispered. She remained quiet, merely reaching out her hand. In her palm was a stone, the Sigil, smooth and naturally shaped by time. "You're here," he said. "And so are you, Nathan." They shared a moment of silence. Nathan gazed up at the sky. "Do you think they'll remember?" Élise responded with a smile. "They will sense it in echoes."

The world did not reset; it progressed much like a book reopened after centuries of silence, and each page filled with memories and choices made. The field where Nathan rested stretched infinitely, the wheat rustling as if old friends were reconnecting, and his hands trembled. The ancient Sigil had vanished, not erased but absorbed. Its form lingered beneath his skin, resembling a scar that no longer caused pain. The air enveloping him shimmered with promise instead of predictions. There was no definite route, only an intuitive sense of direction. He gradually stood up, his bare feet touching the cool, earthy ground. Behind him, a cough broke the silence. Kaeda-9 was authentic, wholesome, and vibrant. She stood next to him, observing her environment with the cautious grace of a warrior who had survived a battle lost to history. "It worked," she whispered.

Nathan nodded. "How do you feel?" After a moment's pause, he answered sincerely. "I feel as if I've finally become whole in one body." Then they found Riley-5, or rather, what is left of her. Her voice echoed from a tree, vibrant and crystal-like. The leaves glimmered softly in sync with her heartbeat. "I didn't want to go," she murmured, her voice gentler than a sigh. "But if I had to leave anywhere... I am thankful it was here." Kaeda-9 lovingly placed a hand on the bark, and Nathan laid his hand on the trunk. "We will remember you," he remarked. "You always have been there for me," she replied. "You just didn't recognise how much." The tree pulsed, and for a moment, the wind created a perfect, looping pattern. Goodbye... then there was silence.

Lucas's Last Gift

Later, they discovered a crystal cube buried in the soil at the edge of the new world. It hummed gently and displayed Lucas's face. "I programmed this message in case I didn't make it," he said, offering a weary smile. "If you are watching this, congratulations, you have rewritten Echo, or at least scared it enough to make it flee." Nathan chuckled, despite the ache in his chest. Lucas continued. "The Echo Core is gone, but it is up to you to decide what happens next. I abandoned a seed, a pure version of the architecture, no surveillance, no recursion, just... potential. Do with it what I never managed to." The message faded away. Kaeda-9 locked her eyes on Nathan. "So?" She asked.

Echo: The Infinite Cycle

He looked at the cube and crushed it with his foot. "No more systems," he proclaimed. "No more cycles, we accept our chaos." As time passed, the world transformed and was no longer the same; it is more than just a city or simulation. It is a dynamic ecosystem that blends organic life with residual code, creatures which appear to resemble animals but are distinctly different. Trees softly hummed as you walked past, oceans shifted with tides driven not by moons but by memories. Nathan ventured forth, sometimes with Kaeda-9 and other times alone, meeting both familiar faces and strangers. Some felt like echoes, while others appeared as strangers concealed by life until now, and Silvia... she stayed. They never exchanged words like 'Again' or 'Finally.' Time had abandoned such ideas; they coexisted. Nathan built a cairn from memory, with each stone representing a life; he arranged them in a spiral.

Intricately woven into the earth rather than stacked, creating a pattern only the new world could understand. Sir Thomas, the Architect, the Surgeon, the Hacker, the Mage, the Astronaut and all of them, even Echo One. He remembered them not as failures or unique identities, but as segments of a lengthy, unfinished book. The lessons, pain, and beliefs he carried were now like an armour for him, silent yet unyielding. Kaeda-9 accompanied him as he laid the last stone. "Will you write about them?" She asked. "I already am," he responded, placing a hand on his chest. "Every step forward is a sentence."

A Garden Without Surveillance

He discovered a glitch, a free clearing where the grass swayed in the breeze, and the sun climbed quickly into the sky. It seemed ordinary, yet it was ideal. He named it The Garden of Errors, a sanctuary for mistakes and absolution. Élise's question one evening, as fireflies flickered in the dusk, Élise ascended the hill to join him. "Do you think it was worth it?" She asked. Nathan turned to her. "Which part?" "All of it," she said. He contemplated for a moment. "I think we had to go through it to ask that question," he answered. "And asking shows it mattered," she smiled brightly. "You always talk like that." "Talk like what?" "Like someone who has met God but decided not to follow him." Nathan grinned. "Maybe," he said. "Or perhaps I just chose not to pretend to be him."

One morning, they found a seed, not a metaphor, but a real seed. It was smooth, golden, and softly humming with light. Kaeda-9 held it up to the sky. "Lucas's clean code," she whispered. "It's still alive." Nathan took it from her, held it for a moment, and then proceeded to the centre of the Garden of Errors to plant it, because it could grow into something beautiful. The seed sprouted overnight, morphing by dawn into a unique tree, which was half alive, half code, with its trunk pulsing to the rhythm of a newborn reality. The branches shimmering with reflections of every life Nathan had touched. However, something felt off; the ground trembled as Kaeda-9 tightened her hold on the gauntlet. "We miscalculated. A residual loop still exists within the foundation."

Nathan stepped back. "Echo?" "No," Riley-5's voice called out over the wind. "It's me," her essence, a remnant of herself, woven into the tree's fibres. Her consciousness, divided into thousands of quantum fragments, had stabilised the collapse, but now it could not recover. "I'm the anchor," she said. "If you try to pull me out, the tree will die." Nathan knelt. "We'll find another way." "There isn't one." The warm wind made her voice almost sound human. "Tell Lucas I liked the name," Kaeda-9 whispered. "There must be something." Riley-5 interrupted the moment with a pulse through the branches. "Let me go." Nathan stood up, touched the bark, and softly said. "Thank you." Then he began the severance. The tree flashed white before calming down. Riley-5 had vanished, then all of the echoes ended. Suddenly, an unexpected jolt and a major flash triggered without any warning.

Nathan jolted upright and into his seat. The cabin lights of the aircraft hummed softly, casting a gentle white glow that created long shadows along the overhead compartments. Outside, the clouds parted in rolling waves as the plane made its final descent toward London Heathrow Airport. Shocked as he realised, he was back on the flight, and the seatbelt sign was lit. A flight attendant walked past, nodding at passengers half lost to sleep or engrossed in films or the quiet boredom of air travel. It was a long flight. His heart pounded; had it all happened, or was it just a dream? His fingers twitched as if remembering something beyond muscle memory. For a moment, he expected to look down and see the symbol flaring on his palm again, or to hear the pulse of alien winds still whispering his name. There was nothing, just the low buzz of the engines and the metallic scent of recycled air.

Echo: The Infinite Cycle

"Sir, are you alright?" The voice came from a man across the aisle, maybe mid-fifties, adjusting his reading glasses. Nathan blinked, nodded, and tried to find something to say. "Jet lag, but thanks for asking," he replied, with sweat forming on his head. It was the truth, in a way, a jet lag, the kind that comes from crossing realities and time zones. He peered through the small oval window, as London stretched beneath them, rain-washed and dusky, as if the city had just woken up. Back, but how? It had felt like years, trials across impossible landscapes, encounters with beings that defied understanding. Moments where he had been sure, his body, his very soul, had been undone. Yet here he was, still wearing the same clothes he had boarded with, not a day older, not a second out of sync. The world had moved on as if he had never left. He pressed his fingertips to the armrest. It was real, so was the soft vibration beneath his feet, the low announcement crackling overhead. "Cabin crew, prepare for landing."

Nathan exhaled slowly. This time, he let it settle. He did not have all the answers yet, but he was alive, and finally going home to Silvia. The cab ride from Heathrow was uneventful, save for Nathan catching himself flinching at every streetlamp flicker or odd glint in a puddle; it had to pass. The city was unchanged, so stubbornly ordinary that he found it almost surreal. His building stood as it always had, bricks weathered, and when he reached his penthouse floor and stood at the front door. A warm yellow glow shone from within. She was home, and with fingers trembling, he reached for the buzzer, but then stopped. No, he reached for his keys and raised his hand to open the door as he knew Silvia would be surprised.

He walked inside and looked at Silvia. She smiled with love as she always did. She was not a day older; there was not even a sign of concern on her face. She asked how his return flight was and that he must be exhausted. Her hair tied back, sleeves rolled up, and flour dusting one hand. "Nathan, so glad you are home, darling, what a lovely surprise!" He remained silent, unable to respond to her. Silvia blinked and then frowned slightly, stepping closer to him. "You weren't expected for another week." Another week? Nathan's lips parted, his voice caught between relief and astonishment. "I... returned early." She chuckled softly, pulling him into an embrace without hesitation. "You chose a great night. I have sourdough baking and accidentally prepared enough stew for four people based on the new recipe." She laughed.

He gave Silvia a big hug, holding her tighter than intended, but she did not pull away. "You alright, Mr Cole?" She inquired after a moment. "I am now," he whispered. Later, they sat by the fireplace with warm bowls in hand, candles flickering against the bookshelves. Silvia listened patiently as he shared what he could, wrapped in metaphor, half-truths, and dreamlike reasoning. Yet, she understood. "How long did it feel for you?" She asked. "Years," he responded. "Maybe lifetimes, I can't tell." "And yet you're here as normal. No one else even noticed your absence," she said. "I know, it's so weird," Nathan replied. "It's like time itself curved to return me." Silvia took his hand. "Perhaps love has that power," she smiled and kissed his forehead. The next few days passed with quiet grace, which Nathan found strange. Everything small move felt newly sacred. The texture of toast, the birdsong at dawn, the way Silvia brushed a strand of hair behind her ear as she read. Yet beneath it all ran the current, that memory, that echo.

Sometimes he would stare at the kettle as it boiled, the steam rising in fractal spirals, and get thrown back into the Tower of Wind, or he would step onto the balcony and smell the wet air, only to feel the stillness of the glacier again. One afternoon, he found himself at the old library, which had survived the years, dusty and magical in its own right. No wards now, no Sigil's humming with power, just the sound of pages turning and the scent of old paper. He wandered the stacks until he came to the alcove where he had once stood with the Sigil burning beneath him, reality tearing open like cloth. Now, it was just stone, but as he crouched and laid his hand flat against the floor, a warmth flickered up his arm. "You're still with me," he whispered.

He stood slowly, letting his hand fall back to his side. He had changed, he knew that, he had lived through trials not meant for mortal comprehension, borne guilt so old it had shaped his every breath, and yet he had returned, and in doing so, he had become whole. Days passed before Nathan found the words. It was not because of a lack of vocabulary, but every sentence felt like trying to catch fog with his bare hands. The truth was overwhelming and unfamiliar. Concepts like time, space, and himself had lost their original meanings, yet he was back at home. The kettle whistled in the kitchen, and a wardrobe creaked upstairs. Normalcy wrapped around him gently, like a familiar coat that no longer fit.

Echo: The Infinite Cycle

He sat in the reading room, a small library that overlooked the ivy-clad courtyard Silvia had nurtured into life over the years. Rain trickled down the window in slow, hesitant streams, while inside, silence enveloped him. Silvia entered with two mugs, setting one down beside him, chamomile with honey. She settled into the chair across from him, and for a long while. The only sound was the soft clinking of ceramic as he adjusted the cup. "You've barely slept in days," she observed. He looked up, not startled but distant. "Sleep felt unnecessary. I've traversed a hundred dreams already." She offered a small smile. "Still unpacking, then?" Nathan nodded. "I have crossed glaciers and fire fields, conversed with beings I can only describe as Gods. I think I died more than once, but somehow, I returned here, and the tea still tastes unchanged." Silvia took a sip of her drink. "That's the comfort of constants, yet you're not quite the same, are you?" "No." He observed the rain. "But I'm still me, maybe just a distinct echo."

There was a pause. "I kept waiting," she finally said. "At first, when you missed the call, then dinner, then the weekend and then... nothing. No sign you had gone anywhere, no expectation that anything had happened at all." He turned to her, his brow furrowed. "You mean it's only been?" She nodded. "A few days, perhaps. An odd flicker in your GPS history, but otherwise nothing, no time lost, at least not here." Nathan exhaled, as if releasing a breath held across dimensions. "Centuries elapsed for me, Silvia, entire lifetimes, yet somehow the world, our world, paused and waited." "Maybe it was never about time," she suggested. "Perhaps it was about understanding what you needed to learn." Tears welled in his eyes without his notice.

"There was a moment I thought I lost you forever. I stood at the edge of a reality that had imploded, but something pulled me back." She reached across and placed her hand on his. "Love does that, or perhaps it was the Sigil's intention all along." He flipped his palm, revealing the mark shimmering faintly beneath the skin, a remnant of his dreams. "It's quiet now, not vanished, just settled." "What was it all for?" She asked softly, and Nathan took a long pause, then answered. "To let go of fear, of guilt, of ego. I believed the symbol would grant me power, but it provided something far more valuable: clarity. All of the experiences and trials were not only tests. They were fragments of me I needed to confront." Silvia listened, her expression warm and receptive.

He continued, his voice gaining steadiness. "I watched my friends die repeatedly, not to relive it, but to truly feel it." He paused. "I scaled towers that twisted time and stood in flames that revealed my worst self, but the moment I ceased resisting, everything transformed. The Sigil sought not conquest, but surrender." She nodded thoughtfully. "Then what comes next?" "I live," he replied. "Not in pursuit, not in escape, just here with you." Silence descended once more, the kind that emerges between two individuals who understand how to share space comfortably. That evening, after Silvia went to bed, Nathan stepped onto the balcony. He knelt by the planter, pressing his fingers into the soil, feeling the earth cling to his skin. Lost in his thoughts, he had no answers, not yet, but he knew this. The Sigil had changed him, and no one could take that away. Whatever came next, he would meet it on his terms. London, ancient yet constantly reborn, pulsed with quiet rhythm beneath the grey morning sky, and mist curled lazily over the Thames.

In a park, morning light threaded through the trees as a woman stood watching. Her daughter was running around across the damp grass, scattering pigeons as she neared. Laughter spilt from the child's lips unburdened, untethered, echoing with a kind of innocence no history could reach. In her hand was a smooth stone, its surface a single spiral carved for remembrance. She did not know why she had picked it up, only that her fingers returned to its pattern again and again, as though tracing the outline of a forgotten word. "Mum, look!" The girl called. Her mother smiled as her gaze settled on the stone. The spiral etched upon its surface caught the light, and for a breathless instant, something stirred deep within her.

It shimmered at the edge of thought, like the last trace of a dream just beyond reach, a feeling she had not named in years, yet recognised all the same. "Looks special," she whispered. Across the river, beneath the first bloom of spring leaves, a man stood quietly, watching. He bore no urgency, no grandeur; his face was calm, his presence almost mundane, and yet if one looked closely, they might catch a flicker in his eyes. Like the memory of a sunrise, only he remembered. He was no longer Nathan in that reality. The symbol no longer flared upon his hand; its work was done. He embodied what remained when all echoes fade, and silence becomes a home. Then it sank, and a breeze drifted through the park.

Echo: The Infinite Cycle

The girl skipped the stone across the river, and the woman inhaled it deeply. For a moment, she stood on the cusp of something, the possibility of it. High above, in the vast sky, a star pulsed; far away, a child dreamed. In her sleep, she drew a spiral on the window's cold glass, not knowing why. Yet upon waking, the image remained as a promise. The Sigil was a seed, because infinity was never the end. The Sigil glimmered faintly beneath his palm, felt like a presence. "You're still with me," he whispered to the shadows, and from the depths of memory, the Spiral Garden stirred. The small shard of stone pressed into his palm. It was warm still, impossibly so. He slipped it into his pocket without a word.

He saw her, the child with braids and bare feet, dusk wrapping around her. The child's fingers brushed over the carved lines, and for a moment, she felt a rush of wind, carrying the scent of salt and smoke. She did not know why, but it had made her smile. He saw the stone, the glyph, the seed; she had called his name. Now, standing here, thousands of years before or after that moment, he felt it. The universe had folded.

A cycle had been completed, and a new one had begun. He gazed up at the sky, silver with moonlight. "I'm ready," Nathan whispered, to remain, to fully live in this world, which he had nearly forgotten to return to. Somewhere far beyond time, the Sigil turned again; it was always a doorway, and someone new had stepped through it.

THE END - MAYBE NOT?

"What if destiny is not linear, but a series of recursions? We are all caught in cycles, circling truths we have yet to understand. Every life is an Echo." - D Gohil.

I wrote this book to test a simple idea: if every version of you stood in the same room, which one would you defend? The Sigil allowed me to bridge plausible physics with older symbols and follow Nathan through broken timelines. Also, identity and choices are never simple. If the book leaves you asking "what if?" and talking about it after the last page, it has done its job. Thank you for reading it.

D. Gohil

Echo: The Infinite Cycle

Epilogue – The Garden of Errors
Present Time

Time passed, though in this place, time no longer held its old authority, where once cycles rotated endlessly, now only quiet remained. The Garden of Errors stood as a monument. A child wandered beneath silver reeds, her bare feet brushing the soft, memory-laden ground, and she was humming simply because she could. The world whispered gently around her, but no longer pressed for answers; a thousand years had passed, or perhaps a thousand moments. The garden endured, untamed, unnamed. Names belonged to ownership, and this place belonged to none.

The child traced the spiral path with a calm curiosity. The soil beneath her shimmered faintly, alive with fragments of memory. At its centre, she found the stone weathered, but holding its shape. Its ancient glyph is still visible: the intertwined curves of the symbol, infinite, unfinished. Kneeling, she extended her hand. Something stirred within her chest, a warmth, a name surfaced in her thoughts: Nathan. She did not know it, but she held it lightly, as one might a song without words; the garden seemed to sigh. The air deepened as a voice rose. "Not meant to live forever, just long enough to learn how to let go." She smiled. She did not fully understand, but somewhere within her, she recognised its meaning.

Beside the stone, a golden seed pulsed gently. She picked it up and planted it in the soil. Accepted it quietly. Beyond this minor act, a ripple moved through the void. In that ripple, Nathan's last echo faded with peace. He had not saved the world. He had released it from himself, from the cycle, from the illusion of perfection. Significance measured differently over time here; the Garden of Errors developed into a city built by those who learned from their mistakes, and Nathan became a legend. One morning, a boy approached Nathan and asked. "Are you the man who changed everything?" Nathan smiled. "No," he said, "I'm the man who stopped trying." He handed the boy a seed. "Here. Now it's your turn." The infinite cycle did not break; it turned, and somewhere, beyond gardens, beyond echoes, beyond even memory itself, the spiral turned once more.

Sequel Hook, Phase Two

Nathan's hands clenched at his sides. This was far from over; the reincarnation cycle was only an experiment, a test, and a proving ground with Echo as the starting point. "What did you do to me?" he demanded, his voice cutting. The woman stepped forward slowly. She recognised him not from just one life, but from many. "Broke free from the cycle," she stated. "But that was never the end goal. You were meant for more than mere survival, Nathan. You intended to develop further." His chest tightened, and the city behind him felt too honest, too stable. Was this freedom? His return to this last life? Just another illusion. A new game started. Nathan exhaled and steadied himself. "Then let's play!"

Echo: The Infinite Cycle

Author's Note

The idea of writing a novel like ECHO: The Infinite Cycle was initially met with considerable doubt about whether I would actually manage the journey. It was imagined on a Tuesday evening, accompanied by heavy rain, back in early 2024. It was one of those days when the mind just relaxed from the sound of the rain falling. I kept circling one idea: what if reality is not singular? What if every choice resonates and splits, sending us down a thousand unseen paths? It was not a theory so much as a quiet intrusion, the kind of thought that arrives uninvited and refuses to leave. Sitting in the half-light, it felt less abstract than personal. If reality can fray, what does that make of the person at its centre?

I was not only chasing possibilities; I was trying to understand identity. If there are versions of us scattered across time and consequence, why does this one, the one who is reading now, matter? That question shaped Nathan's path, threading through broken worlds and choices that could not be undone. This is more than an adventure. It is a mirror held to the self and to what our decisions leave behind.

If these pages make you pause, even for a moment, and ask "what if?" then the story has done its work. Thank you for walking with me through the infinite. The cycle begins with you, and I hope its echo stays with you.

— D. Gohil

Other books by the Author:

Echo: The Secret of the Sigil (for Kids)

Echo: Adventures of the Sigil (for Teenagers)

© 2025 D. Gohil — All rights reserved.

www.ingramcontent.com/pod-product-compliance
Lightning Source LLC
LaVergne TN
LVHW041620060526
838200LV00040B/1364